Psychic Surveys: Book Three

44 Gilmore Street

EVE: A CHRISTMAS
GHOST STORY
(PSYCHIC SURVEYS
PREQUEL)

PSYCHIC SURVEYS
BOOK ONE:
THE HAUNTING OF
HIGHDOWN HALL

PSYCHIC SURVEYS
BOOK TWO:
RISE TO ME

PSYCHIC SURVEYS
BOOK THREE:
44 GILMORE STREET

PSYCHIC SURVEYS
BOOK FOUR:
OLD CROSS COTTAGE

PSYCHIC SURVEYS
BOOK FIVE:
DESCENSION

PSYCHIC SURVEYS
BOOK SIX:
LEGION

PSYCHIC SURVEYS
BOOK SEVEN:
RISE TO ME

PSYCHIC SURVEYS
BOOK EIGHT:
THE WEIGHT OF THE
SOUL

BLAKEMORT
(A PSYCHIC SURVEYS
COMPANION NOVEL
BOOK ONE)

THIRTEEN
(A PSYCHIC SURVEYS
COMPANION NOVEL
BOOK TWO)

ROSAMUND
(A PSYCHIC SURVEYS
COMPANION NOVEL
BOOK THREE)

THIS HAUNTED WORLD
BOOK ONE:
THE VENETIAN

THIS HAUNTED WORLD
BOOK TWO:
THE ELEVENTH FLOOR

THIS HAUNTED WORLD
BOOK THREE:
HIGHGATE

THE JESSAMINE SERIES
BOOK ONE
JESSAMINE

THE JESSAMINE SERIES
BOOK TWO
COMRAICH

REACH FOR THE DEAD
BOOK ONE:
MANDY

REACH FOR THE DEAD
BOOK TWO:
CADES HOME FARM

CARFAX HOUSE:
A CHRISTMAS GHOST STORY

Psychic Surveys: Book Three

44 Gilmore Street

Some things are never over…

SHANI STRUTHERS

Authors Reach
www.authorsreach.co.uk

ISBN: 978-1-9999137-8-6

For Rob –
I couldn't do this without you.

Acknowledgements

Once again thanks to my trusty band of beta readers, who pick up on so much that I can't see and make me change it! You know who you are but I'm going to name you anyway, Rob, Louisa, Alicen and Lesley, I couldn't do this without any of you either. Thanks also to Jeff Gardiner, for the first edit, Veronica McGivney for the second edit, grammar is not my strong point, but I'm learning all the time, and Gina 'Genius' Dickerson for yet another amazing cover! You really are one of the best in the business! Thanks also to the readers who keep me going with chat on Facebook and Twitter and who leave such lovely reviews on Amazon – I appreciate it very much.

Prologue

"IT'S done. It's over."

"Yeah, yeah, I know it is."

"Then don't look like that, Ruby. You should be happy."

"I *am* happy, Cash. Honest." She thought about his words. "Hang on. Look like what? What do you mean? What's wrong with the way I look?"

Cash laughed. "You look beautiful. You always do. Just… try and relax."

Turning away, he murmured something about it having been one heck of a day and that he was knackered. Within seconds he was snoring.

Ruby turned over, switched off the bedside lamp, and lay in the darkness. She could feel movement at the foot of her bed: Jed, turning several circles before settling himself comfortably too.

She tried to smile but couldn't. The dark, never a worry before, unnerved her, ever since… ever since…

Stop, Ruby. Don't think about it.

And remember Cash's words. *'It's done. It's over.'*

The entity that had been a part of her life for so long, her mother's and her grandmother's too, was gone. They'd finally rid themselves of it. Except… it didn't feel like that. It still felt close. Not just close, but in her. Actually *in* her.

'Don't feed it,' Gran had warned. 'Starve the bad wolf.' Or take your mind off it, which work did at least. But sometimes there was no escape, like now for instance, when those around you were deep in slumber – leaving you, for all intents and purposes, alone. *Abandoning* you.

She studied the shape of Cash beside her. How did he do that? Fall asleep so quickly. It's as though he didn't have a care in the world, whereas she was weighed down with them.

Ruby, lighten up, for God's sake!

For *her* sake would be more apt. After what had happened, the victory of it, she should be euphoric, swinging from the chandeliers, not walking, but positively skipping along pavements, full of enthusiasm for a life that could be lived more freely. If only that were so.

The darkness closed in on her. With one hand she reached for her eye mask and positioned it. It grew darker still, intense – a lonely kingdom where no light dared to encroach. It seemed familiar, this kingdom. As if it welcomed her. As if she belonged. And, in the hidden depths of her, something stirred, and welcomed it too.

Her breath began to quicken.

Work, she'd think about work and what the next day had in store for her. It'd be busy, no doubt about it, and she had to find sleep: oblivion – *blissful* oblivion.

She screwed her eyes shut, and willed it to come.

Please, please, please…

And it did. Slowly. Teasingly.

Falling back as though through layers and layers of gossamer, her breathing grew more regular as the body went into temporary shutdown.

But the mind, oh the mind… Still her thoughts plagued

her.

'It's done. It's over.'
But was it? Was it really?
Some things are never over.

Chapter One

Present day

"OKAY, if you won't take a week, how about a long weekend? You need a holiday."

"I *don't* need a holiday."

"*Everyone* needs a holiday at some point."

Ruby sighed. Theo meant well but this really wasn't the time to take a break of any kind. Psychic Surveys, the high street consultancy she ran in Lewes, specialising in spiritual domestic clearance, was at the stage where she was thinking about hiring an extra freelance team member. Case after case came in, as though the afterworld had gone on strike, refusing to let any more souls cross the great divide. A nonsensical concept, but that's what it felt like. Heading off for a few days was not on the cards.

The two of them were sitting in Ruby's attic office, with spring sunshine filtering through the lead window and lighting up surroundings that had a tendency towards gloom. Even the dust motes dancing in the air held a certain charm. It was Monday morning, after nine and Theo had popped in to get the lowdown on new cases that Ruby had been spent all weekend fielding. When it came to the nine to five rule, the spirits didn't give a damn.

Like Ruby had done earlier, Theo sighed – very long and very low.

"Darling," she said, leaning across the desk to take Ruby's hands in her own, "after what you've just gone through, a break is essential. I'm worried. You're in danger of becoming a workaholic."

"What I went through – what *we* went through – was a while ago now."

"But there are dark circles around your eyes. You look… tired."

"I'm fine. It's just… you know how busy it's been lately."

"I do, I do," Theo conceded.

There was also Cash, her boyfriend; he took up a lot of her time too. Theo, renowned for her ability to 'catch' thoughts on occasion, caught that one.

"I'm sure he does, sweetheart," she remarked. "Ah, the first bloom of love, I remember it well." Referring to her husband, Reggie, who'd long since departed this world, she added, "I still miss him, you know?"

Ruby didn't doubt it. Theo was always jolly, relentlessly so at times, but sometimes she had a wistful look about her, the slightest air of melancholy. Ruby couldn't catch thoughts, not like Theo or Ness, the third member of the Psychic Surveys quartet, who also had the ability, but it was at those moments she surmised that Reggie was on her mind.

"And you'd be right," Theo admitted. "Spot-on."

This was turning into one of those wistful moments.

Releasing Ruby, Theo clapped her hands together, which broke the spell.

"Right, this holiday—"

"Theo, let's just sort out these new cases. They're mostly local but there's one in the Lyme Regis area, linked to a period cottage, dating back to the seventeenth century and recently purchased to let. It's got ghosts galore apparently. The new owners, Rachel and Mark, claim to have seen at least several different apparitions. They're not bothered by them, funnily enough, but they think prospective tenants will be."

"Lyme Regis? Now, why don't you and Cash carry out the first survey on that one? You could combine it with a—"

"Yeah, yeah, I know, a holiday."

"Indeed," Theo replied, looking nothing if not smug.

Cash was not the fourth member of the team. He was a freelance IT specialist with enough work of his own. Corinna was the fourth member. Not a psychic but a sensitive, in her early twenties and keen to hone her skills. Although she worked in a pub, she'd been doing increased hours for Ruby lately. They all had – despite Theo having turned seventy and Ness coming up to fifty-six. Ruby worked at the business full-time and then some. But workaholic or not, as she'd just been accused, she loved her job. There was nothing more satisfying than helping a spirit that was grounded. Dealing with the *non*-spiritual, however, that which had *never* been human, was another matter – one she didn't want to think about. Not after last year.

"But you *are* thinking about it, aren't you?"

"Theo—"

"I'm not contradicting you, I'm just saying."

The door burst open and Cash bustled in, his arms full of something.

"Babe! Guess what I've got here?"

Ruby grew even more fractious; she could see well enough.

"Holiday brochures," Cash continued enthusiastically. "I've just picked them up. I've got the Caribbean, the Far East, America, the lot. I have to say, if it were up to me, we'd be heading to Barbados pronto. Mauritius looks good too, though. The beaches go on for miles and miles and they're so white."

"Are you two ganging up on me?"

Some of Cash's enthusiasm waned. "Sorry? I'm not with you."

"Theo's been saying I need a holiday and now you. Have you two been scheming behind my back, concocting this between you?"

He seemed genuinely taken aback. "I swear I haven't."

"So how did you know?"

"Know what?"

"That we were talking about holidays!"

His familiar grin returned. "Ah, well, that would be the psychic in me."

Ruby couldn't help but smile too. Cash was *not* psychic but he was intuitive, becoming more and more so over the months she'd been with him. He always said hanging around with psychics was the reason why and maybe he had a point. Either that or it really was coincidence.

"Look, Cash, I'd love to go on holiday with you," – it would be their first – "but we're really busy so there's absolutely no way—"

There was another interruption. The door to her office opened and a face peered round it. All three of them stared in surprise. This was the attic. People didn't just walk in off the street. Usually they phoned first or made an appointment. More usually, Ruby and the team went to visit clients – or rather the four walls the clients deemed 'haunted'. The attic was simply too small to hold consultations with the general public.

Everyone continued to stare, as though engaged in a contest.

Finally, Ruby spoke. "Erm… hello, can I help you?"

"Psychic Surveys?" the girl responded. She was young, not far out of her teens, around twenty-one or twenty-two, with brown hair – a mousy shade not dissimilar to Ruby's – and timid blue eyes.

"Yes, this is Psychic Surveys."

Relief flooded her features. "Oh good. I mean, I know it is, I checked I had the right address before I came here. Then I met one of the men in the offices below. He was really nice, he opened the door, said for me to go on up, that you wouldn't mind. I hope you don't, mind that is. It is okay, isn't it?"

The girl was rambling. What could she say? *'No, it's not okay, come back when you've made an appointment?'* That would seem churlish.

Ruby stood up and gestured towards a second, smaller desk. *Her* desk – purchased from Ardingly Antiques Fair and massive with an inlaid green leather top – was where she, and she alone, sat. It might be massive but it was cluttered too, with all sorts of files, books and random pieces of paper as well as her computer, keyboard, printer and phone. The other desk was where team meetings were held – it was here she invited the mystery guest to sit, whilst offering her the obligatory cup of tea.

"I don't drink tea. A cup of coffee, though, that'd be

cool. I take it with lots of milk and two sugars. My name's Elisha Grey, but call me Ellie, everyone does. And you're Ruby Davis, aren't you?"

Ruby confirmed that she was and introduced the others as Cash Wilkins and Theo Lawson. They shuffled over to the meeting table and Ruby included them in the drinks round. When all four had their respective mugs, Ruby asked Ellie the purpose of her visit. Immediately, Ellie started scratching at her arm.

"It's… well… I've got a bit of a problem."

"A problem of a spiritual nature?" queried Theo.

"I don't know what you'd call it, to be honest."

"Are you being haunted? By a ghost, I mean."

It was Cash who'd asked that, cutting to the chase as usual. Ruby didn't call grounded spirits 'ghosts' but as most of the world did, she supposed it did no harm to use the layman's term every now and then. Again, Ellie looked embarrassed. People often did when talking about psychic matters; either that or manically excited as though the real world was not quite thrilling enough for them, wanting to spice it up with a dose of the supernatural. Ruby and her team called those types of people the 'wannabes' – they *wanted* to be haunted. Generally, though, it was easy to tell the difference between those who were and those who weren't. There was no disguising genuine fear. With Ellie, however, it *wasn't* easy. Ruby glanced at Theo. She was having trouble deciding too.

"Are you being haunted?" Ruby repeated Cash's words.

Ellie took another sip of coffee.

"I think I'm tuning into a past life."

"A past life?" Ruby hadn't expected that. "You mean reincarnation?"

"Yes, that's it, reincarnation. I… I was told something, a short while back and, well, it's like it's set something off in me."

"Oh?" prompted Theo.

"It's like a door's been opened in my mind, a door that's always been there but was shut tight, until now." Ellie hung her head, her brown hair falling forward. "Do you know what I mean? Am I making sense?"

Ruby's eyes travelled to where the girl was scratching, the skin was red, sore-looking: eczema perhaps.

Theo had noticed too. "Tell us more," she said, her smile indulgent.

Ellie looked grateful that the older woman was interested. "I've started dreaming." She tutted – seemingly annoyed at such a trite statement. "We all dream, I know that, but these dreams are different, they're like, really vivid. Familiar too, that's what gets me about them. It's hard to explain."

"You're doing well, go on." Again, it was Theo gently cajoling her.

"Lately, in the last month or so, I've been getting… I don't know what you'd call them, waking dreams I suppose, not even that, flashbacks or… snapshots. Yeah that's it, snapshots describes them better. There's always a woman in them, me I presume. I'm standing in a kitchen. There are dishes in the sink and the weather's miserable with grey skies and rain. It's always dark too. Not pitch black, I don't mean that. It's like one of those energy-saving bulbs has been switched on but never quite gets to full brightness. There's a smell in the kitchen too, damp or mould or something. The smell settles deep inside you, it makes you feel unclean, contaminated even. These snapshots are as vivid as the dreams."

Ellie kept shaking her head whilst recounting as if perplexed by the whole dream/snapshot scenario. She wasn't the only one. So was Ruby.

"It does sounds interesting," she conceded, "but we don't really deal with reincarnation cases, if that's what this is. We deal with grounded spirits, with the business of moving them to the light."

"The light?"

"It's what we call home, where your soul goes once you've passed."

"How do you know we're supposed to go there?"

Ruby had been asked this question countless times. "Because sometimes we can see the light too, albeit in the distance, and when a spirit walks towards it, the cares they've accrued during the life they've just lived, fade. There's only relief on their faces, and joy. That can't be wrong, can it?"

Theo joined in. "If you want a more technical explanation, spirit is energy and the bodies we walk around in are merely a receptacle for that energy. The light is the source of all universal energy; it's all-powerful, we come from it, and we go back to it. In simple terms, we're spirits on a human journey; we have the freedom to make decisions, to explore, to follow certain paths and to find out what holds value and what doesn't. It's a learning process. And when that journey comes to an end, we continue onwards."

"Except some spirits don't get that?" enquired Ellie.

"A *lot* of spirits don't get that."

"Cash!" Ruby admonished.

"Well, they don't. That's why you're so busy!"

Ruby shot him a warning look. Some things needed much more careful explanation than he was sometimes prepared to give. "Spirits can remain grounded that's true. A fear of the unknown is a very human fear and it can easily become ingrained. Our line of work involves communicating with the spirit to show that there isn't anything to be afraid of, certainly not the fire and brimstone of ancient teaching. In the light, love and understanding await."

"Even for serial killers?"

"Even for them. But I don't think they get away with it, that's not what I mean. I'm certain there's rehabilitation on the other side. A spirit needs to know what harm he or she has caused. They need to realise the consequences of their actions; feel what emotions they've invoked in others, whether that be terror, despair or horror, and experience it too, every last bit of it in order to understand, to feel remorse and to evolve."

Theo nodded in agreement. "It's a case of learn from the past, then let it go. In the spirit world, dear girl, the only way is up."

Ellie had finished her coffee and was sitting back in her chair.

"Sorry," apologised Ruby. "What we're saying, it's complicated."

"I've got the gist of it. It's what you're *not* saying that concerns me."

"What we're not saying?" Ruby was confused. What did she mean?

Ellie leaned forward, looking earnest. "You're talking as if we never come back. That when we die, that's it; we move to another dimension."

"If fear doesn't ground us," Cash pointed out.

"If fear doesn't ground us," Ellie echoed. "But I don't agree. Ever since this happened, I've been finding out all about reincarnation. I never realised there were so many books on it, a load on the 'net too. There are countless people who swear they've lived before, case after case that's been documented. Yeah, I get it, we die, we go somewhere for a while, a resting place maybe, but a lot of us come back and it's here we come back to."

As it seemed everyone was waiting for her to speak, Ruby obliged. "We're not in the business of dealing with reincarnation, Ellie," she reiterated. "I really think you'd be better off contacting someone who specialises in that field."

"Can you recommend anyone?"

"Erm... no, I can't. Theo, what about you?"

Theo shook her head. "But our colleague Ness might know someone, we can ask her. And if she does, you can trust her word, she doesn't suffer fools gladly. There are a lot of charlatans out there, people you want to avoid."

And didn't they know it – they'd even been called charlatans themselves. Thank goodness it was only occasionally, though. In their line of business, customer satisfaction was everything.

Despite the offer to find relevant contacts, Ellie seemed dissatisfied. "I haven't told you what my friend said to me. Aren't you interested?"

Theo's voice was wary. "Does this friend have psychic abilities?"

"It looks like it. And when I say friend, I mean friend of a friend. I don't really know her. It happened we were all out for a drink one evening, that's when I was told what she could do. By taking hold of your hand, this woman,

Katharine, can tune into your past life. She gets images in her mind; sometimes they're strong, sometimes not. With me they were strong."

How convenient.

Theo cottoned on to Ruby's cynicism – her look told Ruby she needed to be more open-minded.

"So what images did she see?" Ruby asked, bowing to Theo's wish.

"She saw the sink with the dishes in it, the one I've been seeing in dreams. She heard music too, playing in the background. She said the music comforted me. She couldn't quite get a handle on the exact song but she thought it was something old, Elvis perhaps or The Beatles."

"That dates it then, doesn't it?" said Cash. "To the fifties or sixties."

Theo shrugged her shoulders. "Not necessarily, Cash. People still listen to Elvis and The Beatles nowadays, plenty of people. Your mother for one."

"True," Cash agreed.

"If we're trying to date this past life, perhaps clothes might give us more of an insight," Theo suggested kindly. "Could she see what you were wearing?"

Ellie leaned her head to one side. She was pretty, Ruby realised, surprised it had taken her this long to notice. "She did mention clothes, but they were plain, nothing out of the ordinary, a blouse and a skirt."

"No beehive hair or platform shoes?" suggested Cash.

Ellie smiled shyly at him. "No."

"More's the pity," Theo commented.

"It's what I was feeling she was most concerned with – Katharine, I mean. She said I was really upset, but not only that, frightened and angry too. She said I felt *crushed* by my emotions."

"Did she have any idea why you felt that way?"

"No, sorry… it's Theo, isn't it? I like your pink hair by the way, it's cool." Theo smiled her thanks – her choice of hair colour was certainly more interesting than the grey it should be. "No, she didn't. She dropped my hand after that, tried to make light of it, said whatever had happened, it was over and not to worry, to be glad that it was. And to be honest I didn't worry about it. I thought what she'd said was interesting but nothing more than that. I got on with my night out, made the most of it. But then the dreams started, the snapshots and… well, you know the rest."

Despite the further information, Ruby stood firm. She explained once again to Ellie, the stranger who'd come calling, that hers was a 'problem' she was best off taking elsewhere. Whilst she did, she refused to look at Theo or Cash. She didn't like turning away those who asked for help any more than they did, but the girl didn't look distressed, merely curious – until now. Now a shadow darkened her face.

"Your reputation's good, really good. Please help me."

Ruby was curious. "How do you know that?"

"I've seen your website."

"The testimonials you mean?"

Ellie nodded.

Cash had designed their website as modern, fresh and welcoming, emphasising the *normal* in paranormal. Clients were usually happy to be quoted as long as only their first name and town appeared. *Psychic Surveys have made such a difference to our lives, my daughter can sleep in her room again, which means we all sleep!'* and *'I was suffering from constant headaches in my new house, depression too. After Psychic Surveys performed a spiritual cleansing I feel much better'* were typical of the comments included. Despite their website, however, and their high street presence, the usual route people came to them was via private referral.

"Do you know anybody we've had dealings with?" Ruby asked.

"No, I don't."

So you believe everything you read. She thought it but didn't say it. It was just lucky in this case that what she'd read was true. Still, it indicated gullibility on Ellie's part and strengthened Ruby's resolve. "We can't help you."

Not just troubled, Ellie was shell-shocked by her blatant refusal.

"But… those feelings, the despair, the horror, the fear, it's like they're getting stronger with each flashback, they're beginning to frighten me too."

"As I said, someone who specialises in—"

"You're a specialist!"

"I am but not in regression."

Ellie started gnawing at her lip. "It's just… I think something happened to me, something awful."

Still Ruby tried to reason with her. "If so, it was in a past life. You're not in any danger now."

"I don't think that's true. I don't know why, but I'm really uneasy. Whatever happened, whoever did it, they weren't brought to justice."

Ruby couldn't believe it. "How can you possibly know that?"

Ellie floundered but not for long. "Call it instinct. Something that you obviously draw on too."

"Ellie—" But before Ruby could continue Theo held up a hand, all trace of amusement on her face was gone.

"Ruby, perhaps we ought to have a discussion about this case in private. Granted it's unusual, but we've never shied away from the unusual."

"Theo, we haven't got time to get sidetracked, to deal with… with…"

"An unsolved crime?" Cash offered.

Damn it, he was right – an unsolved crime, if indeed that's what this was and not simply delusion brought about by the power of suggestion. There was every chance Ellie was a highly imaginative girl; that a seed had been planted in her head and from it an entire lifetime had grown.

Deciding she'd had enough for one morning, Ruby sat up straight and did her utmost to adopt an air of authority – a '*glamour*' as Theo called it – an old psychic trick that made you look more formidable than you perhaps felt. "If we're talking about an unsolved crime you'd be better off seeking help from the police as well as a past life regressionist. We deal with 'hauntings' for want of a better word, domestic—"

"Spiritual clearance. Yeah I know. Which is exactly why I've come to you."

If the girl interrupted her again, she'd scream. More so because Theo and Cash seemed annoyingly impressed by how determined Ellie was.

"Look—"

"No, *you* look," said Ellie, and, for someone whose exterior was timorous, the fire in her voice was startling. "I don't want to appear rude, I swear I don't, but if it's hauntings you deal with, then I do qualify for help."

"I still don't understand why."

"Because in answer to your original question, yes, I *am* being haunted."

"By who?" Ruby asked.

"By me. I'm being haunted by myself."

Chapter Two

GET the fuck out!

Hearing Ness groan, Ruby had to suppress a smile – the poor woman looked physically pained. How many times had they been told to 'fuck off' by the spirits? More than she cared to remember.

The new owner of 44 Gilmore Street, a terraced house near Brighton Station, had first called her on the phone to discuss what she described as a 'negative presence' in her home.

"I've been watching *Afterlife* on catch-up, you know that TV series about that psychic woman. That's what gave me the idea to call you. It's also got that man in it from *The Walking Dead*. Ooh, I love him, what's his name?"

Thankfully Ruby didn't have to rack her brain as to his identity as the woman – Samantha Gordon – suddenly remembered.

"Andrew Lincoln, that's it! Oh God, he's gorgeous."

Although Ruby agreed, she nonetheless brought the conversation back to business; it was the middle of the day and she had other things to do.

"A negative presence you say?"

"What? Oh yeah, yeah, seriously, it gets really spooky in here at times, and I keep thinking I can see him, out of the corner of my eye. It feels like he's glaring at me, you know.

My daughter, she feels really uneasy too, as if he's glaring at her. It's like he's always there, in the shadows."

"How do you know it's a 'he'?"

"It's the bloke who used to live here before, I reckon, an old bloke. The place was a right mess when we bought it, you should have seen it. Hadn't been decorated since the beginning of time. That's why we got it cheap at auction. Not that anything ever is cheap in Brighton. The cost of property and the cost of parking... they'll be charging us for breathing fresh air next. My husband, he's always saying that."

"Mrs Gordon," said Ruby, again trying to focus their conversation, "would you like Psychic Surveys to carry out an initial survey of your house?"

"Yes please; well that's why I'm ringing, isn't it?"

Ruby was beginning to wonder. "You've seen our website, you're aware of our charges?"

"I have and I am," Samantha confirmed. "I'm very open to these things, you know, the spirit world and all that. I've told you I watch *Afterlife* and I truly believe that that poor woman goes through hell because of what she can see." There was a slight pause. "Is it hard for you too?"

Ah, the tales I could tell... But this wasn't the time.

"It's what you make of it. You can choose to find it hard or you can channel your gift towards something useful. I prefer the latter, helping the grounded to move on, which in turn helps the living. It's far more constructive. Now, I could fit you in this coming Tuesday if you'd like. 10 a.m.?"

"That'd be perfect," Mrs Gordon replied happily enough.

And now it was Tuesday. It was well past 10 a.m. and

the spirit – certainly that of a man as Samantha had guessed – was swearing at them, the venom in his voice all too obvious. Thankfully, Samantha wasn't here. After an hour of nothing happening, she'd seemingly got bored and excused herself to go and meet a friend for coffee at Divalls Diner, just around the corner.

"I won't be gone long," she'd said, "but it'll give you a chance to, you know, crack on with things. Call me if anything happens, you've got my mobile number."

The second hour was quiet too; little wonder Samantha had got bored. Ruby had called Ness in to help on this occasion. Usually, when carrying out an initial survey, she went alone or took another member of the team with her. They'd make a connection, find out what was grounding the spirit, and assure them it was 'safe' to move on, encouraging them to leave, to go home. More often, it took a visit or two to persuade them – the part of their soul that held onto its 'humanity' could be territorial. This spirit certainly was. As soon as the second hour was up, he'd kicked off. Big time.

You slut!

There he went again. His voice – only audible to the clairvoyant – was low, gravelly, as if in life he'd been a chainsmoker. Certainly, as soon as she'd entered the house she could smell cigarette smoke and so could Ness, despite the Gordons being non-smokers. There was nothing necessarily paranormal about that, though. If whoever had lived here before had been a heavy smoker, the smell would linger in the atmosphere for a long time, even if the walls had been given a lick of paint. No longer 'a right mess' as Samantha put it, the house was light and bright with each room a different colour, although all were tastefully neutral in shade – a good choice, thought Ruby, as anything darker would make the place feel claustrophobic. Apparently, the Gordons had had to rip out carpets, curtains, basically everything that wasn't nailed down.

'Mind you,' Samantha had said, 'we removed quite a few things that were nailed down too. You know the saying, leave no stone unturned.' If only they'd left *something* of him, though, something that would enable them to connect further; to get an idea of why he was being so belligerent. Handling objects wasn't always necessary but sometimes they provided a useful insight into their owner's life. The practice was called psychometry and in a case such as this, every little helped.

Ignoring the copious amount of profanities spewing from the spirit, Ruby tuned in again; tried to capture the essence of the man. She knew Ness was doing the same. The information they had was that the previous occupant of 44 Gilmore Street had lived there for over forty-five years. He wasn't married, seemed to have no children, and kept himself to himself. As yet they had no idea what his occupation had been, but he'd died in his early eighties, alone at home, a heart attack the cause. It had been several days before he'd been 'discovered', neighbours noticing that the curtains to his living room remained closed. This wasn't wholly unusual, but he did open them on occasion. Growing suspicious, they had called the police. The stink that hit them upon entry told them all they needed to know.

It appeared to Ruby that the man had lived a sad life; a lonely one. Or maybe she was doing him a disservice. Maybe he had been happy on his own? Some people were. But happiness was not the feeling rolling off him right now; his emotions were black – there was anger, hatred, and confusion. Ultimately, however, there was fear – just *what* was he afraid of?

"Ben," (that had been his name, Benjamin Hamilton), "we're not here to antagonise you, we're here to help. You've passed. You're in the realm of spirit now, no longer connected to your physical body. Perhaps that's why you're confused. If your passing was sudden or unexpected—"

Get out!

"Tiresome soul, isn't he?" Ness muttered. Being called all the names under the sun was truly beginning to grate.

Taking a deep breath, Ruby tried again. They were in the kitchen, where his presence was strongest. She was surprised about that, because he'd died in the living room, sitting in his chair in front of a blaring TV, flies gathering around him attracted by the aroma of decay. Perhaps he wandered round the house. Some spirits did, whilst others remained tethered to the exact spot where they'd met their end – there seemed to be no hard and fast rules, no black and white. As they'd been in life, each spirit was unique.

"Ben, you need to let go of this realm, there's nothing more for you here. Can you see the light? If you can, go towards it. You'll find peace there. You'll be welcomed. The light is home, Ben."

You know shit!

Ruby flinched. The voice – *his* voice was right by her ear. Previously there'd been distance between them. She hadn't expected him to come this close, hadn't felt a sense of him rushing towards her. If only she could see him, get an impression of what he looked like. She'd have to dig around, see if she could find a photo. There must be one. Maybe the press had used one when reporting his death. A photo would help to demystify him, whereas a disembodied voice was often unsettling; she was human and could admit that. Seeing the whole package would be better. Manifestation, however, didn't seem to be on the cards. She got the impression Ben didn't want to show himself. He wanted to hide, or maybe he was toying with them. That was something else the spirits did – thinking they had the upper hand and exploiting that position. More often than not, though, it was a protection mechanism. They *wanted* to stay, or thought they did, and so would do anything in their power to scare away those who could sense them. But if they stayed they'd grow more frustrated by their limitations; become more destructive. It was then that interaction with the living could prove fatal. Fear could kill a person. She knew that. Failure wasn't an option.

Ness was picking up on her thoughts. "Ruby, don't be so hard on yourself. If we make no headway today, we come back again."

The words were barely out of Ness's mouth, when a roar sounded in Ruby's ear, setting every nerve ending she possessed on edge. Ruby looked at Ness and saw alarm on her face – she'd heard it too. Between them, they started to ramp up protection levels to maximum. Before making a psychic connection, it was imperative to surround yourself in white light, drawn straight from the universal source, visualising it as an impenetrable shield. Ruby also wore a tourmaline necklace, an heirloom from her great-grandmother, and one of the strongest protection stones. Ness, preferring snowflake obsidian, had a huge chunk of it on her finger. Black tourmaline spray was another 'Ness staple', used to cleanse the atmosphere, to form another line of defence. They'd doused the house with it on their initial walk-through – the smell both comforting and clean.

"Ben, let me reiterate, we are here to help you, please allow us to do that. We're not afraid of you. Don't be afraid of us. We mean you no harm."

The atmosphere, already oppressive, became even more so. Her words were angering Ben – a common enough reaction; spirits often became defensive initially. Patience and perseverance were imperative, as well as refusing to take any abuse from them, whether verbal or physical (although thankfully it was rarely physical). The amount of energy required on a spirit's behalf to become physical, to interact, was just too immense.

Not that that stopped Ben.

The blow to her stomach caused Ruby to double over. As she did, the breath left her mouth in a whoosh. In an instant Ness was by her side. Jed – a black Labrador that had attached himself to Ruby over a year before, a *dead* black Labrador – materialised and started fussing over her too.

"Jed, Jed, I'm okay. Ness, I'm fine."

Despite her protests, Ness looked furious. "You are *not* fine!" She whirled round, faced what they could not see. "Ben, I'm warning you, we won't stand for this!"

"Ness, I don't think that's going to—"

But Ness wasn't listening.

"You don't belong here, not anymore. This house belongs to others now. You can see the light. I know you can. We can *all* see the light, no matter how much we pretend otherwise. It's there and it's waiting. Go towards it, rest in peace and give the new occupants of Gilmore

Street a break too."

The spirit was getting ready to attack again; Ruby could sense it well enough this time. She braced herself but Ness stood in front of her, quickly retrieving the tourmaline spray she kept in her jacket pocket and spraying it in short, sharp bursts. Jed too shielded her – her allies, her friends, putting themselves on the front line, as they'd done so many times before. Such bravery lent her courage. She drew herself up, adopted what she hoped was a formidable stance and echoed the sternness of Ness.

"You've no reason to attack me, Ben. Please don't do it. Your time here has come to an end. You simply cannot stay any longer."

His scream even made the dog shudder. There was the flick of a switch. She tried to place it. Was it the kettle? The radio also burst into life as he directed his energy towards implements that could be easily manipulated. Plates stacked neatly on the draining board started to vibrate. It was bright outside – a crisp March morning, but the light seemed to want to find an escape. The room grew darker. Had clouds suddenly covered the sun?

The kettle started boiling, the sound of water bubbling rapidly usually an innocuous one, but not this time – there was a threat behind it, a serious one. Something was going to come hurtling their way soon.

"We have to get out, come back with Theo and Corinna in tow."

Although Ruby hated to admit defeat, Ness's suggestion was a sound one – there was safety in numbers: the four of them stronger than two.

Jed barked.

All right, the five of us!

26

Had she not been preoccupied with what was going on, the dog's insistence would have made her smile. Imminent danger, however, had wiped out humour. Just before she turned towards the door, a cup from the draining board was seized upon and lifted upwards to hover in mid-air.

"Go, go, go!" shouted Ness, clearly as fed-up as she was at being forced out, but not willing to chance a face full of crockery. When she reached for the handle, the door suddenly shut, as though with an almighty push Ben had shoved it back in its doorframe. The radio grew louder, vying for attention with the rattling plates. The kettle continued to boil.

Ness took charge. "Hunker down, protect your head."

There was nothing more they could do. Ben's fury was too great to reason with. As she obeyed, Jed doing his best to shield not just her, but Ness too, Ruby heard another door slam – at the front of the house this time.

"Yoo-hoo, it's only me. Where are you, in the kitchen?"

It was Samantha, back from coffee and sounding bright and breezy. "Hello," she called again. "I'm coming in, is that okay?"

Ruby held her breath as the door opened before she could warn Samantha to stay where she was. The moment she entered, however, the kettle stopped boiling, the radio switched off and the mug crashed back down to join the plates, somehow remaining intact. All was normal. Or as normal as it could be in a house haunted by an extremely pissed-off spirit. Even the atmosphere was lighter as if he'd retreated, the sun's rays shining fully through the windows. Perhaps he had slunk back into the shadows, but he wasn't gone completely, she knew that – she could still feel his presence, albeit in a more distant sense, his lingering anger too at his 'performance' having been interrupted.

With almost indecent haste, Ruby scrambled to her feet. "Samantha!" She hoped her voice held no trace of alarm. "Good to see you!"

Beside her, Ness was also standing; her forced smile something of a rictus grin.

"Everything all right?" Samantha asked, frowning slightly at such enthusiasm. "Anything happen whilst I was away? Did you make contact?"

You could say that.

Ness glanced at Ruby, clearly catching her thought.

Striding over to the kettle, Samantha offered to make them a cup of tea. When she got there she was surprised to find the water in it was hot already.

"Oh, have you just had one?"

Keen to assure her they'd not been shirking their duties, Ruby asked her to sit. She explained what had happened, dressing it in plain terms. This was Samantha's family home – their *new* family home – and the last thing she wanted was to scare her out of it. It was imperative they stay and inject it with fresh energy. Besides, she had a sneaking suspicion that what Samantha had experienced was tame compared to what had just taken place. She asked her client for more details and was proven right.

"Well, it's really what I've told you already," said Samantha, tucking a few stands of blonde hair behind her ear, "I haven't seen anything; it's more 'felt', you know? And yeah, a lot of the time it's in the kitchen, eyes boring into my back, that sort of thing, and feelings – bad feelings, mainly aimed at me."

"Not your husband or children?" asked Ness. Children were usually highly sensitive to the paranormal so Ruby listened to the answer with interest.

"Well… as I've said before, maybe my daughter. But no one likes it in the kitchen much. I mean, we don't eat in here or anything. We used to, when we first moved in, but then the arguments started and mealtimes became something to endure rather than enjoy. Pretty soon, the kids started refusing to eat anything at all. As a family we get on, so this behaviour was unusual. We've started eating in front of the telly instead. It's not ideal, but at least the bickering isn't as bad."

As Samantha spoke, Ruby nodded. A spiritual presence could affect a person in a number of ways, argumentative behaviour and loss of appetite being two of them. Ways in which she herself had reacted when being haunted. But that haunting was over and this was about Samantha, not her.

"So it's you that's the sensitive one?" she queried.

"I suppose." Samantha actually looked quite proud as she said it. There were some people who didn't mind being 'different'. Even so, it wasn't a false pride and she was no 'wannabe'. Putting her mug down, which she'd been sipping from, the same one that had hovered in mid-air a short while before, she added, "I get the feeling he doesn't like women."

"I think you're right," Ness replied. "What we need to do is find out why."

"Do you know anything else about Benjamin Hamilton," asked Ruby, "other than what you've told me?"

Samantha shook her head. "Sorry, no. The neighbours might, though."

"Good point, and he must have had family."

"Not necessarily," observed Ness, a shadow darkening her features.

Ruby conceded. "He was old, a lot of his family could well have died off." Solely addressing Samantha, she continued, "There *is* a spiritual presence in your home and one that's not particularly keen to leave. I'd like to come back with the rest of the Psychic Surveys team if that's okay, and carry out a thorough spiritual cleansing, using purely holistic methods of course."

"I've read about that on the website, but remind me again what's involved."

"Aside from psychic connection, we use smudge sticks, which are herb bundles, made up of white sage primarily, to cleanse dark corners; bells to break down negative frequency, and we also promote the use of crystals in the home, tourmaline, obsidian and pink quartz for example, which repel negative energies, discourage them in other words." As Ruby explained, one hand went up to caress her tourmaline necklace, a 'comfort blanket' as she often thought of it. "The more crystals you have around the house the better – we can provide some but they're relatively inexpensive to buy. I can point you in the direction of shops that sell them. We'll also arm ourselves with more information about Ben. If we can understand him, we can empathise and hopefully encourage him onwards. You can help us with this, Samantha, if you don't mind. We'll dig deep officially, but are you happy to talk to your neighbours about him? We could go knocking on their doors, but two psychics visiting out of the blue might not be appreciated."

Samantha assured Ruby that she would.

"That's great. In the meantime, you and your family are

staying put?"

"Of course! We've scrimped and scraped to buy this house, put every penny we've ever earned into it. He's had it for long enough, the selfish beggar. It's our turn now."

Ruby only hoped Benjamin would see it that way too – in time.

Chapter Three

AFTER saying goodbye to Samantha, Ruby and Ness stood outside on the pavement. 44 Gilmore Street looked innocent enough, but then most exteriors were benign. It was what was on the inside that mattered.

Ness kept checking that Ruby was okay – that blow to the stomach had had quite a bit of weight behind it, despite being spirit-delivered. Certainly, it had shaken her up, but she didn't want to dwell on it and assured Ness she was fine. Ness was still furious about it, though, she could tell. Her eyes had a glint to them she'd never seen before. Only slightly appeased, her colleague turned her attention from Ruby to stare at the house's exterior. Number 44 was magnolia in colour, but its rendered front was ingrained with years of grime. No doubt the Gordons would get round to rectifying that soon too. Whilst Ness stood in contemplation, Ruby checked her mobile phone for messages. Cash had texted asking if she wanted to meet for lunch. She replied saying she couldn't but that she'd see him that night. He spent most evenings at her flat, anyway, when they weren't out with friends, most of whom, after more than a year together, had blurred into 'mutual' territory, including Cash's brother, Presley, who'd been seeing Corinna for a good few months.

Thinking of Corinna, there was also a text from her,

checking in for the day, and one from Theo, the wording very similar. There was a special bond between the oldest member of her team and the youngest, which reminded Ruby of a mother/daughter relationship, but she was surprised to find it extended to echoing each other in texts. Smiling at this, she was about to switch her phone off when another text came bouncing through from Ellie.

Hi, I hope you don't mind me texting, I was just wondering if you had any more thoughts about my case, Ellie x

Ruby couldn't believe it. How the heck had Ellie got hold of her mobile phone number? She hadn't given it to her. As for the kiss at the end, it was far too familiar for her liking. She wondered how to answer; *why* she had to answer. She'd made herself plain. Reincarnation was not their area of expertise, end of conversation as far as she was concerned.

Ness must have noticed the frown on her face.

"What's the matter?"

"Nothing, it's just…"

"Just what?"

They started to walk to the train station, Ness falling into step beside her. Normally Ruby drove everywhere but considering how much it cost to park centrally, the train was the more sensible option. Grabbing a coffee for each of them from a stand on the concourse, Ruby enlightened her as to 'just what' was on her mind once they were onboard.

The journey was only fifteen minutes and, by the time they'd disembarked, Ness wore a matching frown.

Walking back up the hill that led to the high street, the older woman admitted she actually found Ellie's case interesting. She thought exploring it might add a string to their bow, so to speak.

"We're busy enough, Ness."

"I realise that, but the paranormal world, what's in it, how it operates, is vast. Anything that increases our understanding is a good thing."

Ruby could feel irritation rise in her again. Her level of understanding of all things paranormal, whilst perhaps more developed than in those that were non-psychic, could certainly be improved upon. But on the other hand she knew more than she ever wanted to. What the last year had been taken up with – dealing with something spawned of the human imagination, but with no human attributes whatsoever – had 'increased' her knowledge in a way she could have done without. Perhaps Theo was right: she was still recovering from the ordeal. And little wonder. Whatever it was – a thought form made manifest, an entity, or a demon – had haunted Ruby for most of her life. And not just her, but her mother too, who, together with her lover, Saul, had conjured it in the first place, the pair of them coaxing it forwards from the very lowest of planes. Jessica had suffered a nervous breakdown because of it, had hidden within herself for so many years, becoming at times unreachable. It was Ruby's grandmother, Sarah, who'd looked after them both, her devotion tireless. Having faced the entity, Jessica was in recovery too but it was a process that couldn't be rushed.

They had reached Ruby's office. Outside, the street was bustling, by Lewes standards at least. People were either shopping in the many bespoke shops that the county town specialised in, intent on emptying their purses, or heading out to grab a late lunch from one of several delis and cafés nearby. Ruby had been hungry too but thinking of the past curbed her appetite.

"What's on the agenda for the rest of today?" Ness asked.

"I'm going over to a house in the Malling area to do an initial survey. They're complaining of nasty smells in the spare bedroom."

"Nasty smells? And they think that's a psychic matter, do they?"

"It could be, if someone's buried beneath the floorboards."

Ness grimaced at the prospect. "So you'll finalise a date with Samantha?"

"Yeah, once I've checked my diary and the sooner the better I think. And you're okay for tomorrow's survey are you, that house in East Preston?"

"Of course, your second visit and my first."

"Corinna's going to join us on that one. I sensed it's an elderly woman that's still in residence, quite benign, very pleasant, in fact, just... stubborn."

"Stubborn? That's one way of putting it. Do you want me to come with you to Malling?"

"You've got work of your own, haven't you?"

Ness not only worked for Psychic Surveys, she also specialised in balancing chakras, centres of activity in the body that relate to health, both of a mental and physical nature. She had a long list of clients that sought her out on a regular basis, but thankfully she always put matters of spiritual domestic clearance first. If there was trouble at Psychic Surveys, she was there, her loyalty – her *priority* – unquestionable. Ness had also worked for Sussex Police as a medium in the past, and Brighton Council too: it was amazing the number of houses that tenants insisted were haunted. According to a recent YouGov poll, 39% of UK citizens believed that to be the case. According to Psychic Surveys, a fair few percent were right, taking into account the private sector too. Nowadays, Ness's work was mainly with Psychic Surveys. 'It's an easier life I prefer now,' she had said to Ruby once by way of explanation. 'It's not as if I'm getting any younger.' Ness never talked about when she was with Sussex Police, despite Ruby having probed a couple of times. Ruby wasn't sure if that was because of reasons of confidentiality or something deeper. Either way, she was surprised to find that Ness considered her work with Psychic Surveys contributed to an 'easier' life by comparison.

"Oh, it does," said Ness, catching the thoughts that were blazing a trail through Ruby's mind, "with the possible exception of last year of course."

Ness smiled as she said it, trying to make light of 'last year', to remove the seriousness from it, which Ruby was grateful for. It helped. Her earlier irritation fizzled out. Instead she recalled one of Theo's favourite sayings: 'Angels fly because they take themselves lightly.' It was a good adage to keep in mind, a sound ethos to follow. And most Psychic Surveys cases *were* pretty standard to be fair, with very little drama involved at all.

Ness looked at her watch. "You're right, I have got clients to see, but if you need me, Ruby, I'm on the end of the phone."

"Thanks, Ness."

"As for Ellie, I know you're reluctant but, as Theo guessed, I do know a woman who specialises in past life regression. She's rather brilliant at it."

Despite herself, Ruby was curious. "Has she ever tested her skills on you?"

Ness's smile faded. "Actually, yes, she has. I was psychic in a past life too, apparently. A rather unfortunate time to be psychic, the seventeenth century." As she said it, she glanced pointedly to the right, towards Lewes Town Hall. Formerly The Star Inn, from 1555 to 1557, ten people were imprisoned in the cellars there whilst waiting to be burned at the stake, not for their paranormal powers but for their religious beliefs – it didn't do to admit to being anything other than Catholic during the reign of Queen Mary. When the time came, they were dragged outside to a jeering crowd and set fire to. Ruby could barely imagine a worse way to go. A memorial to them was finally erected in 1901, on Cliffe Hill. Although it had been constructed at some distance away, the obelisk was deliberately visible from the spot on which the martyrs had been killed, a reminder of intolerance should anyone bother to look. Their deaths were also marked on Bonfire Night for which Lewes was famous; a burning cross lit for each of them and carried through the town.

Remembering this, Ruby was stunned. "You were burnt at the stake too?"

There was a strange look in Ness's eyes, as though she'd become disconnected, but she rapidly recovered. "No, of course not, I'm just kidding. Besides, witches weren't burnt in England, only heretics were. They were hanged instead." She reverted back to their earlier conversation. "Now, if you change your mind about the regression and you want my friend's number, let me know. She's called Ailsa Isaacs. I'm sure she'll be pleased to help out."

As Ness walked away, her figure clad in dark clothing and so slight, so fragile, Ruby was still trying to come to terms with the 'joke' her colleague had made. Considering the history of their town it was insensitive, and Ness *wasn't* an insensitive person. She was equally aware of the residue of terror, shock and pain that lingered a few feet down the road, and had indeed remarked on it several times. Such feelings took time to dissipate, although thankfully it was *just* the feelings that remained, and not the poor, tortured spirits themselves, endlessly reliving their plight. Just kidding? Ruby didn't think so. She shook her head. It was even more reason not to get involved with Ellie, or Ailsa for that matter. The past should stay exactly that.

Chapter Four

SITTING in Ness's living room – the first time she'd ever been there surprisingly enough, despite having known her for nearly four years – Ruby could hardly believe it. How had she got roped into this? If Cash were here, she'd direct one of her hard 'Paddington' stares in his general direction. It was him she held responsible for changing her mind. It was Thursday, and ever since Monday evening he'd been trying to persuade her to take Ellie's case on. Last night the excuse of being 'too tired to discuss it' had started to wear thin. She'd felt obliged to listen to him at least.

"Don't get me wrong, spirits and the paranormal world, it's fascinating stuff, but reincarnation, that's a whole new bag. The very thought that we return here, to this world, time and time again is incredible. Why is it do you think? What's the lure? Is the beer really that good? The pizza?"

Trust Cash to relate everything to food – he was obsessed with his stomach and the process of filling it.

"*This* pizza's good," she said in reply, her mouth full. *He'd* made it, right from scratch, the base and everything. His obsession had a flip side at least.

Warming to his subject, his dark eyes had grown serious. "Do you think we return because we want to or because we have to? Do we get a choice?"

She put her knife and fork down. "Cash, I really do find

it sweet the way you think I'm some kind of authority on this subject, but I'm not. I've got as many questions about reincarnation as you have."

"I know, I know, but come on, you've got a better idea than most." The skin around his eyes crinkled as he smiled at her.

"I haven't."

"You have."

"Cash!" As much as she loved him, he could be exasperating at times. "Look, for what it's worth, and I'm guessing just as much as you are here, we don't *have* to return; we *choose* to return. Perhaps it's because we feel we haven't quite developed enough to enter a higher plane; perhaps it's as you say, because we love it in this realm and we want to enjoy it—"

"Or endure it."

"Or endure it some more. We could return due to unfinished business—"

"Ah, unfinished business. That's what Ellie's on about."

"Pardon?"

"That whole unsolved crime angle. She's got a feeling something bad happened to her in a past life, perhaps she was murdered, buried in the cellar or something and her body never found. She wants vengeance, justice to be done, so she's started to remember things, stuff that will lead her back to her killer. He might have reincarnated too, and she's chasing him through time and space. *That's* her purpose for returning and you can help fulfil it."

Ruby grew tired just listening to him. She leant back in her chair and closed her eyes as she sighed. Cash was immediately all concern.

'Ruby, what is it?"

Perhaps Theo was right, she did need a holiday. She felt drained, exhausted, wanted to continue keeping her eyes closed; to sleep. What should she do? Be honest and say that was the reason she didn't feel like taking it on, because she was so knackered? She decided to go for it.

"Cash, aside from this bloody pizza, I've got enough on my plate at the moment. I honestly don't think I've got the energy to devote to this one."

"Then sit on the sidelines, observe. Let that woman Ness knows do all the work."

"But why?"

His insistence really was mystifying her. Perhaps he was mystifying himself. He wrinkled his nose and shrugged. "Because this case is *different*, that's why. Because... she seemed as if she really wanted your help, no it was more than that, as if she *needed* it. And that's what you do, Ruby, you help people, dead or alive. That's what you're good at."

She started clearing their plates; he had virtually finished anyway. "And because of that I'm supposed to help *everyone* who looks at me like the cat from *Shrek*?"

"The cat from *Shrek*?"

"Yeah, the one who turns on the big sad eyes whenever it suits him?"

Cash got up too, took their wine glasses to the sink, and emptied the dregs. "Okay, forget I said anything. If you're not interested, you're not interested."

"It's not that I'm not interested."

"You could have fooled me."

"It's because I'm tired, Cash!"

"Then let's book a bloody holiday!"

"No... I." She sighed, heavily this time. "I suppose I

could pass on Ailsa's details."

"You could."

"It wouldn't do any harm, would it?"

"None that I can see."

Coming up behind her, he put his arms around her waist. She leant back into him, relished how solid he felt, the familiarity of him. She'd never been with a man as long as she'd been with Cash. In the past, boyfriends had tired very quickly with her 'otherworldly' dealings. The fact that Cash was fascinated by it was a bonus, but perhaps too much of one at times.

She turned to face him. As she did, he lifted her chin and planted a kiss on her lips.

Breaking away, he murmured, "Don't you ever wonder if you've been here before? Who you could have been?"

She thought again about what Ness had said.

"No."

* * *

It wasn't fair to blame Cash – Ellie's big sad eyes had got to her as well.

"It'd be cool to meet Ailsa," Ellie had said when Ruby called her back, "for her to be the one to regress me, but it's Psychic Surveys I came to about my case, and I'd really like it if Psychic Surveys could oversee it at least."

"Because of our reputation?"

"Well, yeah, like I said, it's good."

Ruby had to admit to a grudging admiration for how determined Ellie was. She reminded her of herself. Determination was a necessary ingredient to make a business like Psychic Surveys succeed. It was no mean feat to get the paranormal to be taken seriously by the general public, not to be laughed at, or to be ridiculed or indeed feared. And in the end, she supposed that was another reason why she'd allowed herself to be roped in – their *similarity* – why she was sitting here with a notepad on her lap, her pen at the ready.

Ness's sitting room was a decent size given she lived in a tiny terraced house. It wasn't dissimilar to the one in Gilmore Street, although its classic red brick Victorian exterior was a little easier on the eye. As curious as she was about Ellie, Ruby was even more curious about being admitted into Ness's inner sanctum. She couldn't believe it when Ness had suggested her house as a venue. She preferred to keep her private life just that – private. Of the team, Theo knew her the best; their friendship went back to the late nineties. But if *she* was aware of anything significant in Ness's past – anything responsible for her enduring sombreness – she wasn't saying. And why should she? Ruby respected that decision. Even so, looking around someone's home was like looking at *them*. It reflected who they were, their tastes and personality. Ness's, however, was minimalist. There were barely any knick-knacks or photographs, no mirrors either, just one in the hallway. Disappointingly, there were no clues to the deeper person at all.

Ailsa, a short but imposing woman, dressed in natural shades of cream and brown, had an obvious penchant for owls. She had owls of the metallic variety hanging from her earlobes, and one attached to a chain around her neck. Catching Ruby looking at them, she informed her they were her spirit 'power animal' – a Shamanic term for a spirit guide.

"I've got a dog," Ruby replied, referring to Jed.

"I know."

How she knew was another mystery, it wasn't as if Jed was in the room. He was off playing in some sun-dappled meadow somewhere, or so Ruby liked to think. She didn't sense a psychic connection with the woman – there was no meeting of minds, not on her side anyway. Whatever the case, as Theo had said, Ness wouldn't recommend someone who wasn't the real deal.

"Let's get started, shall we?" Like Ness, Ailsa had an air of authority about her; a confidence in what she was doing. A *belief.* Ruby wondered if she thought the same about her, or whether it was something that came with age.

She caught Ailsa looking at her, one eyebrow raised. Ruby winced. Perhaps it was insensitive to think confidence only came with age.

"Ness, Ruby, are you happy to stay in the room?"

"If the client doesn't mind," answered Ness.

Ellie glanced nervously at Ruby. "Please stay."

Ailsa again took charge. "Ellie, if we're going to be successful, it's vitally important you feel relaxed whilst I regress you. If it suits you to have other people in the room that's fine, I don't mind a jot, but you must be sure."

"I'm sure." She suddenly looked much younger than her years, little more than a teenager. Instead of being irritated with her, Ruby felt a pang of sympathy. When they'd talked on the phone prior to this appointment, Ellie had informed her she'd had another insight into her 'past'.

"There was blood," she'd said.

"Your blood?" queried Ruby.

"I think so, who else would it belong to?"

"Was there anyone else in the room with you?"

Ellie had faltered. "There was, but I can't see who it is,

not yet."

"Dreams are strange, we all know that," countered Ruby.

"So are snapshots. That's what this was."

Ailsa, who had had the case explained to her, including this event, saw no need to quiz the client further. She preferred to 'learn' on the job.

The curtains had been pulled together, although not fully. A thin sliver of light was allowed in, lending the atmosphere an almost ethereal touch.

"Lie back on the couch, Ellie," Ailsa instructed. "Place the pillow under your head, close your eyes and make yourself comfortable." She had previously removed her shoes, revealing pale grey socks with a hole in the toe of one.

"You and I need to connect," she continued, "and we do that by breathing together, in for five seconds, and out for five seconds. That's it, that's correct. And again."

Ruby found herself joining in the breathing exercise, which was repeated several times.

"Good, good, that's wonderful," praised Ailsa, her voice low, monotone even, as relaxing as the breathing itself. "Now we're going to count backwards from ten to one, and with each number you'll be going deeper into yourself, down, down, and further down." The word 'down' was emphasised each time it was uttered. "Ten and down, nine and down, eight and down – good, good, that's right, going down, deeper and deeper down, seven and down..."

In the dimness of the room, Ruby felt herself growing drowsy too. Sensing this, Ness gently nudged her, a reminder to stay alert.

When they reached 'one', Ailsa started talking about a

passageway and asked Ellie to describe it.

"Erm… the wallpaper it's got flowers on it but it's not pretty. It's brown as if it's stained with nicotine or something. There are floorboards beneath my feet and some sort of runner. It's dark and dingy too. Above there's a light, a bare bulb, it's swaying slightly, as if it's caught in a breeze."

"Good, good," Ailsa was nothing if not encouraging. "Don't be afraid. Walk down that passageway, right to the end, that's it. Notice how it slopes down. At the end of the passageway is a lift. The doors are open, step inside. On the right is a panel. Can you see it?"

"Yes," Ellie responded, her voice distinctly drowsy.

"How many numbers are on it?"

"Six."

Ailsa looked impressed. "Six? That's good. Which number appeals to you the most?"

There was silence for a moment, Ellie clearly thinking about it.

"Take your time, there's no rush; ask for guidance if you like, from your higher power. Six is the number of lives you've lived before. Which one is it that you want to know more about?"

At last Ellie answered. "Six."

"Six," Ailsa repeated, "the life just before this one. Let's go back there, shall we? Press the button with six on it and watch as the lift doors close and we descend, down through the floors, down, down, further down until we reach floor six, the lift lowering gently, taking you to where you want to be."

Ruby blinked; it really was hard to keep your eyes open, Ailsa's voice was so soporific. She'd love nothing more than to curl up on the sofa too and fall into a deep sleep – a dreamless sleep that is.

"You're on floor six," Ailsa told Ellie, "the lift doors are opening, step out."

The last two words were a command. Ruby's interest perked up, what was going to unfold? Even Ness seemed to be on tenterhooks.

On the sofa, there was silence.

"Is it day or night?" Ailsa asked her.

"It's… day, but it's not bright."

"Is it cloudy outside?"

"It must be."

"Is there a window nearby?"

"Yes."

"Look out of the window. What's the weather like?"

"I… don't know. I think it's cloudy. Yes it is. It's cloudy. Raining too."

"Good, well done, that's good. Look at your feet, do you have shoes on?"

"Erm… yes."

"What type of shoes?"

"They're flat, nothing special."

"Look at your clothes, what are you wearing?"

"A skirt, knee-length."

"You're a woman. Do you have a blouse on too?"

"Yes, it's light blue I think, made of nylon or something. It feels scratchy." As if to prove her point, Ellie started rubbing at the inside of her arm – she definitely had a patch of eczema there.

"Hold your hand out."

"Okay."

"What colour are you?"

"Colour?"

"Your skin."

There was a slight pause. "I'm pale."

"On your left hand, is there a ring?"

"I… Yes."

"What type of ring?"

"It's gold, a wedding ring I think."

Ailsa nodded. "Do you know how old you are?"

"Young. I'm young."

"Do you know your name?"

"I don't have a name."

Ailsa frowned, puzzled by this response. "We can find out your name later. What I want you to do now is to describe the room you're in, the wallpaper, the light fittings, what's in it, just like you did in the passageway. Tell me also how you're feeling as you look around."

"How I'm feeling?"

"That's correct. It's your emotions I want you to concentrate on, they'll paint a picture, help you to see."

"Okay," repeated Ellie, swallowing noticeably. "I'll try."

Chapter Five

"I'M in a room, a kitchen. There's a sink over by the window, it's got plates, and mugs in it, lots of them, slick with grease and piled high. I don't want to do the washing up. It's all I ever do. All I'm good for. I hate this kitchen. I hate it!"

"Look around, tell me what you see. What else is in the room?"

"What else? Erm… there's a clock on the wall, the sound of it ticking seems so lonely somehow. It's like a ritual, the meticulous counting down of the hours. There've been too many hours spent here, too many minutes, too many seconds – an eternity. There's an oven, not a modern one, nice and shiny, it looks old; the white enamel on it is chipped, revealing layers of black underneath. It seems relevant, as if everything – *everyone* – is black underneath. Appearances can be deceptive."

"We need more detail. The floor, what's it like?"

"It's sticky, linoleum. I've just washed it, but it never comes clean. The pattern reminds me of crazy paving, all sharp and jagged, it's hard on the eye. It's mostly cream but there's brown in it too and dull flecks of orange. The units are wood, but it's not oak or anything. It's old-fashioned, the whole room is. I don't want old-fashioned. I want light and bright. He knows that but he doesn't care. I hate thinking of him. When I do, my stomach hurts."

"So, it's a man you're frightened of? Why does thinking of him make you feel that way?"

"It just does – every time I see him my skin crawls and I want to be sick. It never used to be that way. My breath would catch in my throat at the thought of being with him. But it's different now. He's different. But then… *I'm* different too. I'm not me anymore. I don't know who I am."

"But you have a name?"

"A name? Of course I have a name! I… I don't know what it is, though. But I do have one; everyone has a name. Why can't I remember it? Is there something wrong with me? He thinks there is. He's always saying it. 'You're lazy, you're selfish and you're a bitch.' He shouts those words at me over and over again. But I'm not lazy, I'm not selfish, I'm not, I'm not, I'm not!"

"Calm down and remember to breathe, in for a count of five, out for a count of five. I'll breathe with you."

"Your voice, it's gentle, it reminds me of Mum. I miss her so much. Breathe in, breathe out, yes I'll do that. That's it, that's better. I feel calmer now."

"You're doing well, really well. Is there a table in the kitchen?"

"There is, a small table, only room for two. There's a fridge and cupboards. All the cupboards are closed."

"Go to one of the cupboards and open it. What's inside?"

"Tins, quite a few of them – spaghetti hoops, baked beans, soup as well. There are Oxo cubes, and a jar of instant coffee. Cheap food, basic, but we can't afford any better. I hate cooking too. I'm no good at it, was never taught, you see. Mum did everything for me. How can you learn if you've never been taught? He calls my cooking 'pigswill'; throws it at the wall sometimes or at me. He's good at throwing things, particularly his fists. He loves to get heavy with them. Wait! I can hear a sound, a song playing."

"A song? Can you make it out?"

"It's a man singing, his voice is deep and low, one word keeps repeating – 'green', that's all I can make out. The song, it makes me feel… wistful."

"Are there any other sounds around you?"

"Yes, the kettle on the stove – the water's boiling. He'll be expecting a cup of tea. He drinks so much tea, cup after cup. I'm always making it. I used to like a cup of tea but not now, now I hate it; hate the way he clicks his fingers when he wants a cuppa too; doesn't even ask anymore, he just does that. I wish he'd drown in it. I wish he'd take a mouthful and choke, fall to the floor and die. I wish he'd leave me alone. That I'd never met him."

"Is this man your husband?"

"He… he thinks he's God. And in this house he is. But I don't believe in religion, I don't believe in God. It's evil that exists, that I live with."

"You think he's evil? Truly evil?"

"He keeps me here. I never go out. This hovel of a kitchen, I'm chained to it, like a slave. He despises me, but why? I don't know why. He loved me once and I loved him. You can't fake love. That look in his eyes, it was genuine at one time, I know it was. I'm not that much of an idiot. What have I done to turn love bad? I can't work it out. I try but I just can't!"

"Would you like me to bring you back?"

"Bring me back? What are you talking about? You can't bring me back. He won't let you. He'd kill me first. I wouldn't even make it to the front door. And he *will* kill me. That's one thing I'll say for him, he's good for his word. He'll tear me apart if I try to leave. He's told me that; he's said so."

"I think we'd better bring you back. Listen to my voice and do as I say. Turn around, slowly, until you see the elevator. Walk over to it, step in, do it now. We're going to come back, up to the surface, all the way up. Can you hear me? Show me you can. Nod your head or something. Ellie…"

"Ellie? Who's she? I don't know an Ellie. And elevator doors, what are you talking about? This is a house not a hotel. Hang on, what's that? Metal doors! I don't believe it. It's an elevator, where the kitchen door should be – the door that leads to the hallway, to the living room, his room, his *lair*."

"Walk towards the lift and get inside. I can keep you safe inside."

"There's no safety, not inside, not anywhere."

"There is, walk towards the lift."

"I'll… I'll try. And you can keep me safe? You're sure? You sound really confident. I like that in a person. I've never been confident. I've only ever felt special once, on my wedding day. The irony of it. I don't know how I'm going to move my feet. They're heavy all of a sudden, weighted, like I'm wading through quicksand. It feels strange, as though it's not just him that doesn't want me to leave, it's the house too. Together they're strong, all powerful."

"Get in the lift, now."

"I will. I am. I can do this. I can leave. The lift isn't far. I can make it. I'm getting close, so close. If I stretch out my hand, I'll be able to touch the doors. Just a few more steps and I'll be inside. Just a few more… I can hear footsteps. They're not mine. They can't be, I'm no longer moving. It's getting dark in here and the air's turned cold, so cold, but I'm sweating, I'm clammy. My breath – I can't breathe. I can't do anything except stand here and wait for evil to find me. Again."

"Ellie, I'm going to snap my fingers and you'll come to."

"If only it were that easy."

"Ellie, listen to me."

"Nothing's ever that easy."

"Ellie, focus on my voice."

"The lift's gone, the doorway's back, framed in black, everything's black. But there's something blacker in it. Him. A slug of a man, that's what he is. Not lean anymore, but big and heavy, shuffling towards me. He doesn't have to hurry. He can take his time. Prolong the agony. After all, there's nowhere I can go, no place to run. I'm scared. I can't move. I'm trapped."

"You're *not* trapped—"

"I am. I'm trapped. And his face… Oh God, the look on his face!"

Chapter Six

"SIT up, nice and easy and breathe through your mouth. Don't rush, slowly, slowly. Good, very good, you're doing well." To Ruby Ailsa said, "Fetch her a glass of water please, tepid not cold, we don't want to shock the system."

Any more than you have already, thought Ruby, as she hurried into Ness's kitchen to get the glass. Selecting a tumbler from one of several sitting on a round tray, she filled it to the brim, contemplating whilst she did, what had just happened. The first time she'd ever sat in on a regression, she hadn't expected it to be quite so dramatic. Not everything Ellie had said had been coherent but her terror was palpable enough, especially at the end, when she'd felt so trapped, so vulnerable. She'd done what a spider would do – curled up into a tiny ball and tried to make herself invisible.

Not wanting to miss out on any of the subsequent conversation, Ruby swiftly returned to the living room to find all was calm. Ness hadn't moved from her chair, wary of interfering, but Ellie was sitting up now, her body hunched slightly, her head cupped in her hands. Ailsa was beside her. Ellie took the proffered glass gratefully, Ailsa instructing her to resist the temptation to gulp it.

"Let the water cleanse you, both inside and out."

Ellie did as instructed. She looked pale and her blue eyes

glittered slightly. Draining the contents, she wiped her mouth with the back of her hand.

'Wow! That was a ride," she said.

Ruby smiled, the girl had a sense of humour at least.

"Can you remember most of it?" asked Ailsa, also looking relieved.

"A fair bit, yeah, it's… very similar to what I've seen already. I'm scared of someone, someone I live with I think, I definitely get a sense we share the same house. A man. It must be my husband."

"It could be." It was Ness, deciding the time was right to come closer too. "You were wearing a wedding ring, so we know you were married."

"And this man – my husband – he keeps me prisoner."

"You're locked up?" Ruby enquired.

"Yes, no, I… sometimes it feels like it. The word that comes to mind, it's a strange one, I feel *entombed*." She shook her head. "It sounds awful, doesn't it? I'm entombed but at the same time I'm able to move about freely, within the house that I'm in anyway." A violent shudder coursed through her. "What the hell did that man do to me?"

Ailsa reached over and patted Ellie's knee. "Whatever he did, it's important to remember it's over. It's the past we're recalling, not the present."

"But it doesn't feel over," Ellie protested. "That's just it. Those emotions, they're still such a part of me." She looked at Ruby, "I'm still scared."

"Then perhaps it's best not to delve anymore," Ness suggested, a rare gentleness in her voice. "The past is the past. Yes, it shapes the way we are; all our experiences do, the good and the bad, but we have to move on, in this life and the next. Perhaps what you learn from this is to let go."

"Let go? I can't. What if he's still alive?"

"The man you feel threatened by?" Ailsa was aghast at the notion. "Did you manage to glean an idea of the era you were in?"

"No, I couldn't tell."

"But you were in a kitchen, one with a stove, a sink, a kettle, so it's a fairly modern era. And that's fine, that's nothing out of the ordinary, a past life can be surprisingly recent. How old are you, Ellie, twenty-one, twenty-two?"

"Twenty-two," she confirmed.

"You mentioned a kettle boiling," Ailsa continued, "can you tell me what the kettle looked like?"

Ruby listened, intrigued to see where this was going.

Ellie chewed on her lip as she tried to concentrate. "It's not an old, old kettle, like the ones you see in museums, those black ones, made of cast iron, I mean. It's more modern than that, silver in colour, shiny, aluminium I presume. It had a black handle across the top."

Ailsa nodded. "And the stove, can you tell us more about that?"

"The stove? Why?"

"Like emotions," Ailsa explained, "details help flesh out past memories too."

"Erm… it's basic, four rings, although it could well be three. It's strange, what I recalled, it wasn't always clear. It was hazy at times, as if some sort of shadow is lying across my vision."

"That's normal," Ailsa assured her. "It might be you in essence, but in a way you're looking through someone else's eyes."

"Yeah, that makes sense." Trying to recall further

details, Ellie continued, "There was a water heater too, just above the sink and that I have seen in museums, in Amberley Museum, in fact, near Arundel, do you know it? It's full of old stuff. My dad loves it there; it used to be a favourite day out for my family and me when I was a kid. The water heater's got two taps, one is a sort of spout tap, long and thin, you can move it back and forth."

"I know the kind you mean," said Ness, "they were very popular in the 1950s and 1960s. Some houses still have them."

"So it could be that era we're talking about?"

Ellie shrugged her shoulders. "It could be."

"Perhaps googling images of kitchens in the fifties and sixties might help," Ruby suggested. "You can see how 'familiar' they seem."

"Sounds like a good idea," Ellie agreed.

"But," continued Ruby briskly, "I think Ness is right. I know you're okay now, but you seemed to be genuinely distressed during the regression, particularly towards the end. It might be better to leave well alone. No, hang on, listen to me. I'm not denying your fear is real; a crime against you may well have been committed, but karma has a way of putting things right – eventually – even if we're not able to. If the perpetrator is still alive, which is highly unlikely, and you manage to find out his identity, it would be the police you file this matter with, not us." Ruby looked at Ailsa, "Maybe Ailsa's willing to carry out more regressions with you if that's really the route you want to go down, but as far as Psychic Surveys is concerned, we've come to the end of the road."

Ellie became agitated again, nails scratching at her arm.

"I don't agree," she said. "You *can* help me."

"I honestly don't see how."

"You can help me to understand."

"*I* can help you to understand," Ailsa interrupted them. "I'm willing to carry on with more regressions, Ellie, if that's what you want." She paused briefly, "Although if we do, we have to tread carefully, very carefully."

Ellie continued to look at Ruby, almost ignoring Ailsa. "My spirit can't rest."

"But you're alive," insisted Ruby.

"But a spirit's a spirit, isn't it? It doesn't matter about the body."

"That's not the point—"

"It *is* the point!" Aware of her outburst, Ellie looked at her feet, her cheeks reddening. "Money's not an issue," she said quietly. "I'll get a job, in a bar, a restaurant, anything. I've been… down on my luck lately. A bit depressed. Home life's been difficult. I'll raise it somehow."

"It's not about the money," Ruby assured her.

And it wasn't. There were plenty of jobs they were paid a pittance for, a sliding scale according to individual circumstance coming into play. No, it was about time and energy; being outside her comfort zone. There seemed very little professional point to any of it, except satisfying a client's curiosity.

Ness turned to Ruby, caught her eye; more than that, caught her *thoughts.* "On the contrary, Ruby, I think there *is* a point to it, granted not one that's clear at the moment, but perhaps it'll become clear in the fullness of time. On behalf of Psychic Surveys, I'm willing to take on Ellie's case."

"Ness—"

"Would you allow me to do that?"

Ruby's eyes widened and she had to strive to keep her mouth closed. It wasn't just a question, it was a challenge. She couldn't believe it! Ness had put her in an awkward situation – publicly. If she felt so strongly about this case, she should have discussed it privately, not put her on the spot.

"Ruby?" Ness persisted.

Ruby stood up, an abrupt gesture she knew. "If it's a Psychic Surveys case, we'll *all* be involved, Ness. Regarding another meeting, I'll be in touch."

And with that, she left the room.

* * *

This was more like it. This was definitely more like it. There was a lot to be said for bog standard cases, the kind you could deal with in an afternoon, that didn't go on and on. Ruby and Corinna were at the house in the Malling area of Lewes, the house whose owners had complained of 'nasty' smells. She'd done an initial survey earlier in the week and, after tuning in, had connected with a spiritual presence, although she couldn't work out just who it was, hence returning with Corinna in tow, to see if two heads were better than one. In cases such as this, where the spirit detected was deemed benign enough, they didn't tend to turn up 'en masse' for fear of overwhelming the living *and* the dead. Besides which, Ness had another case to attend to, which she'd gone to with Theo. And after what had happened with her this morning, Ruby was glad.

Corinna, being the 'sensitive' she was, was certainly sensitive to the mood Ruby was in, and before entering the Malling house, asked her what the matter was.

"It's nothing, honestly, I'm fine."

Sadly, she'd fooled no one.

"Look, you might as well tell me," Corinna insisted. "Not just because we're friends, but because you know as well as I do that we need to go into a cleansing in a positive frame of mind. We don't take anger in with us."

Corinna's words hit their mark. Why did it annoy her so much that everyone was gunning to get involved with Ellie's case except her? Why couldn't they see her point: that they were busy enough and didn't need to diversify? Despite resisting a holiday, right now, lying on a beach somewhere with Cash, far, far away, surrounded by blue sky, golden sands and azure sea, seemed irresistible – as long as no one from the spirit world decided to holiday alongside them – a thought that made her smile. Almost.

"Ruby, I'm not going in until you've told me what's wrong."

Corinna was right – negativity in her might provoke negativity in the grounded spirit, and who knew where that would lead?

Quickly she explained what had happened during the regression with Ellie, growing heated again when she talked about how Ness, rather than talk to her in private, had publicly overridden her decision.

"It's not that I mind, not really. She can take Ellie on as a private case if she wants to, but she doesn't; she wants to take it on as a Psychic Surveys case. I'd already said no, that we'd taken it as far as it can go, but she completely ignored me. Anyone would think it was her business, not mine!"

Corinna did indeed look perplexed. Her green eyes, usually so bright, looked a shade or two darker, and she was chewing the inside of her lip. Whilst she contemplated, Ruby admired once again her friend's Titian-coloured Pre-Raphaelite head of hair, now the longest she'd ever seen it, almost halfway down her back. She really did have hair to die for.

At last Corinna spoke. "You say you've taken it as far as it can go, but what if you haven't? It seems to me there's a lot more to discover. And as you said, she's happy to raise money for the fees."

"Why does everyone thinks it's about the money? It isn't!" Ruby burst out, before pausing slightly. "Anyway, she's unemployed, we can't charge her."

"That's up to you but you don't charge much as it is. I'm seriously thinking we might have to register as a charity at this rate."

Now Ruby did smile. "Psychic Surveys as a charity! Can you imagine?"

Corinna smiled too. "I can actually. If people so much as heard a bump in the night, they'd be on the phone. We'd be swamped, more than we are already." Serious again, she continued, "I hate to say this and I don't want to make you even more angry, but I think Ellie's case *is* an interesting one, Ness might have taken the reins, but you're the one the client wants to spearhead it, so why not give it a go?"

Ruby was dismayed. "Corinna, I thought you'd be on my side at least."

"It's not about taking sides. Just see where it leads you. You never know, you might unearth a killer."

"Unearth? That's an unfortunate analogy; he might well be six foot under. And if he is, it's a cold case, even the police won't be interested."

"Or he might be alive and kicking. In which case, the police will be *very* interested and you'll be a hero."

"I don't want to be a hero."

"I know you don't, but you will be to all those who've suffered at his hands."

"*If* there have been any others who've suffered."

"Which is something you're never going to know, not unless you continue with the case. Ruby, I know you well, or I like to think I do. I know what a strong sense of right and wrong you have. I don't think you'll be able to walk away from this case no matter how much you protest."

She was right. The man Ellie was complaining of sounded like a bad lot. What if he had hurt others in his lifetime, not just her? It was a slim possibility but as long as it existed, could she ignore it?

"I've got a feeling about this case, that's all."

"A bad feeling?" Corinna probed.

"There's something not quite right with it. Also, Ellie comes across as Little Miss Victim, but I don't know. She's got steel running through her, that one."

"Is that such a bad thing?" Corinna did indeed look confused.

"No, it's a good thing. I know it is." Again, Ruby tried to explain her unease. "She got hold of my mobile number even though I didn't give it to her."

"Ruby, she came to your office, didn't she? You have business cards. Maybe she saw one and helped herself."

Ruby rolled her eyes; of course! Why hadn't she thought of that? She was more tired than she realised. "She just seems so intent on it being *me* who helps her."

"And you know why that is?"

"Why?"

"Because you're good, Ruby. Your reputation goes before you."

Which Ellie herself had pointed out, but still that feeling of danger – *personal* danger – wouldn't dissipate. Ellie's case was going to prove trying, and not just for her, for all of them. Right now, though, she needed to focus on the Malling house; on the job at hand.

Chapter Seven

"GOODNESS, that smell!"

Ruby and Corinna were standing in the spare bedroom of the home belonging to a young career couple – Alicen and Andy Haire – a lawyer and an accountant respectively. The smell was even stronger today, quite eye-watering, in fact. Ruby tried to explain why.

"If a psychic has made a connection with the spirit in the house, it can unsettle the spirit further, initially that is." The Gordons' house was a case in point. Although thankfully when she'd done a follow-on call to check with Samantha that Ben hadn't become more 'unsettled' since their visit, Samantha had reported back that he was neither less nor more so than before. "Activity can intensify but it's usually very brief," she continued. "A spirit is grounded because it's confused. Once we've communicated with them, explained their situation, they're usually eager enough to leave."

"It's that easy, is it?" asked Alicen.

"You'd be surprised at how straightforward it can be." The less straightforward times they didn't need to know about.

"So," Andy joined in, "it's all about getting the grounded to see the light? In a literal sense as well as metaphoric." Tall and lean with an open countenance, he seemed genuinely fascinated.

"In a nutshell, that's exactly it," Ruby replied.

"It does sound a bit New Age, though," he said.

"A bit space age actually," Alicen declared.

"I know it does." It was something Ruby always worried about, that whole 'New Age' thing. "But the fact of the matter is, it's ancient practice that we draw on, and it's proved itself over and over again." She only just stopped herself from adding 'honestly' to the end of that sentence.

Andy smiled, seemingly content with that reply. In contrast, Alicen, quite a bit shorter than her husband with perfectly teased honey-blonde hair, merely looked bemused. "All I'm worried about is the smell and whether you can get rid of it or not. It's embarrassing when guests come to stay. Oh, and another thing, and this is fairly recent, but when I've woken up at night and gone to get some water or something, I've heard scratching too, really faint but it's coming from inside this room. It's beginning to freak me out."

Beginning? Ruby was impressed. These people were hard-core.

Ruby had already checked the history of the house – built in the Victorian era, there was nothing on record that anything untoward had ever taken place within it. That was not to say it hadn't, of course. So much remained private. She'd also checked whether the Haires had contacted maintenance men before Psychic Surveys, plumbers for example; blocked pipes could be responsible.

"We've done all that," Alicen assured her, "had a few of the floorboards up, the works, but it's not just the smell to be honest, or the scratching. There's a feeling in here. Not evil exactly, I wouldn't say that, but it's different from the feeling in the rest of the house. Our recent guest sensed it too; she ended up leaving the room in the middle of the night and went downstairs to sleep on the sofa."

"Mrs Haire," Ruby tried to explain, "because a spirit is grounded doesn't make them evil. It's like I've just said, they're confused and frightened, unsure of what's happened to them. That's *often* the case, especially if their passing was quick or unexpected. Evil's the last thing they tend to be."

"Oh, come on, come on," Andy argued, "there's got to be a few evil spirits hanging around, a lot of them I should imagine, intent on terrifying the life out of those of us still lucky enough to be alive."

"Not in my experience," Ruby countered. Keen to discourage this line of questioning, she returned to the subject of their spare room.

Immediately, Andy's manner changed to one of brisk efficiency. "Yes, yes, you'd best get on with it, time is money."

Spoken like a true accountant, thought Ruby, suppressing a smile.

The pair left her and Corinna to it, returning downstairs to the kitchen to wait. Ruby was thankful. Some clients insisted on sitting in on proceedings and she had quite a job to dissuade them – the process of connecting with a spirit was even harder when you felt like a performing monkey.

Hearing Corinna complain of the smell too, Ruby placed her bag of cleansing paraphernalia on the bed, opened it and retrieved two smudge sticks. She handed one to Corinna, lit them both and they started cleansing the corners of the room as well as dark spaces such as the interior of the built-in wardrobe – empty apart from some forlorn-looking hangers – and underneath the bed.

"Smells a bit better now, doesn't it?" she said to Corinna, referring to the heady sage scent of the herb bundles.

Corinna wasn't so quick to agree.

In a while they would open the window, offering a physical exit for the spirit that inhabited this room. Sometimes the spirit seemed to need a gesture such as this; sometimes they didn't, walking in the general direction of the walls instead and disappearing right through them.

After cleansing with the smudge sticks, Ruby placed several lumps of amethyst around the room. This was not a 'threatening' spirit and so she saw no need to get heavy with obsidian or tourmaline, stones which were good at absorbing negative energy. With its soft purple facets, the stone was ideal for promoting a calm and peaceful atmosphere.

Finally, after wrapping themselves in white light, Ruby and Corinna stood side by side in the centre of the room and tried to connect. After a few moments, Corinna turned to her.

"It's odd. There *is* something here. I just don't know what it is."

Ruby felt an ice-cold trickle of fear. "What do you mean, what *it* is?"

Had she underestimated this job, been fooled even?

Corinna could sense her unease. Immediately, she placed a hand on Ruby's arm. "No, no, I don't mean it's non-human, nothing like that. Although… it's not human, is it, not exactly?"

"What is it then?" Ruby replied, not completely

appeased.

Corinna nodded towards the far corner of the room. "There's something about that spot there, something under the floorboards even."

"They've had the floorboards up."

"Every single floorboard?"

That she couldn't vouch for. Trying to work it out, Ruby heard movement to the side of her, a soft movement, barely detectable. As something brushed past her, she flinched, felt every one of the hairs on her arms stand up. When she saw what had touched her, however, she laughed in relief.

"Jed! What are you doing here?"

But the black Labrador wasn't listening, he'd gone straight to the spot that Corinna had identified and was busy sniffing around. The sight of his tail wagging was also welcome; Jed was very excited about whatever 'it' was.

Ruby drew closer.

"What's Jed doing?" Corinna asked, following close behind.

"Sniffing by the looks of it and wagging his tail."

"He's not worried then?"

"He's not worried at all."

And, because he wasn't, she relaxed.

Not content with sniffing, Jed began digging instead with his front paws scraping back and forth. Bending down beside him, Ruby wondered what to do. There was no carpet on the floor, but the floorboards were nailed down. They had also been lovingly sanded and varnished. Just how receptive would the Haires be to a bit of vandalism in the name of spiritualism?

Sinking to her knees, she started feeling around the area

that Jed was pawing. The wood – oak it looked like – was warm to the touch.

"Wait," said Corinna, placing a restraining hand on Ruby's shoulder. "Seriously, I've got a feeling we just need to wait."

Not one to dismiss Corinna's 'feelings', Ruby stood up and they retreated to the bed, perching on the end of it.

"Can you see Jed at all?" Ruby asked Corinna.

Corinna shook her head, "I wish. It's frustrating only being able to sense things rather than see them"

"Have you truly never seen anything?"

"I've caught glimpses, but I've never seen the way that you, Theo and Ness can see."

"That's not such a bad thing."

Corinna paused for a moment. "No, I know it isn't."

The minutes passed and, although the silence was companionable, Ruby could feel the first stirrings of impatience. Jed was sitting now, staring at the floorboards, his head tilted to one side in a puzzled manner – an angle not dissimilar to hers and Corinna's. She tapped the fingers of one hand against the other. Corinna obviously noticed.

"We need to wait, Ruby. I honestly think that's the best thing to do."

Making an effort to sit still again, Ruby started looking around the room; at the feature wall painted a dark shade of grey; at the minimal but clearly expensive furniture: a chest of drawers with a vase placed artfully on top, a small wardrobe and pale blinds at the window in a coarse linen material. Although it was a spare room, she had a vision it wouldn't be that for much longer. It would have a change of décor soon – yellow paint with cheerful murals on the wall, and a crib with a mobile hanging over it. It was rare she had such a moment of 'foresight'; that wasn't her gift, but whether Alicen was pregnant or not, she soon would be. The room would be spare no longer.

Jed slumped, started whining, his patience wearing thin too.

Ruby made a decision. "We need to get Alicen and Andy back in here and ask about the previous owners."

Corinna agreed. "Yeah, you're right, we can't wait forever."

A few minutes later all four were back in the room, Jed still in the corner, occasionally nudging the floorboards with his nose. Although she knew nobody could see him but herself, Ruby pointed to where he was and asked the Haires if that area had been checked too.

"It was all checked," Alicen said, looking at Andy for confirmation.

"It was," agreed Andy. "Or at least I asked them to check everywhere."

"The plumbers?" Ruby queried.

Andy nodded.

"Were you in the room when they were checking?"

Again, Alicen and Andy looked at each other. "Erm, no… but I hardly think they skimped. We only use reputable firms you know."

Nonetheless, Ruby had a feeling they'd done exactly that – skimped. "There's something about that particular spot."

Alicen's hands immediately flew upwards. "Oh my God, there's a body under my floorboards!"

"Not a human one," Ruby rushed to assure her. "But… maybe an animal."

"An animal?" queried Andy. "What kind of animal, a cat, a dog?"

"We're not sure yet," admitted Ruby.

Andy walked over to the corner and – unknowingly – stood right beside Jed, so much so the dog had to shift.

"There can't be an animal under the floorboards," he decided.

"Why not?" asked Alicen.

"Because as the body decomposed, it would… leak."

"Ugh." The colour certainly leaked from Alicen's face.

"He's right," Ruby admitted. "But even so, there *is* something under there." She asked the Haires if they'd ever had a pet.

"No! Whatever it is, it's got nothing to do with us!"

"I wasn't implying…" She stopped. "What about the previous owners, did you know them at all?"

"Not exactly, but they were perfectly lovely during the exchange. They're an old couple, the Milligans, Alex and Wendy. The poor things couldn't manage the stairs anymore. They never talked to us about having an animal, though. They never mentioned this room either, or the smell."

"Do you have a contact number for them?"

Alicen frowned. "Yes, yes, we do. Are you suggesting we call them?"

"Or I can," offered Ruby, "but it might be better coming from you."

Alicen seemed unsure. "What should I ask them?"

"Ask them about an animal they *used* to have."

* * *

In the kitchen, Ruby and Corinna downed a cup of coffee whilst Alicen made the call. She returned a short while later, a look of complete astonishment on her face, poured a cup of coffee too, and sat down.

"You're right, the Milligans did used to have an animal; not a dog, though, or a cat. It was a rabbit, would you believe, a house rabbit! I never realised you could look after rabbits indoors but they enlightened me on that score; he was perfectly house-trained. The way she talked about Arthur, that was his name by the way, you'd have thought it was a beloved child."

A *rabbit*? She hadn't expected that.

Alicen continued relating what she'd been told. "Like I said, he was like a child to them. They doted on him, but something happened. They weren't here at the time; they'd gone for a long weekend to visit the D-Day landing beaches in Normandy. Mr Milligan's a war veteran you see and there was some sort of trip organised. They asked their niece to look after Arthur whilst they were away. When they got back he was gone. The niece was distraught, said she took him into the garden for some fresh air and he disappeared; a fox must have got him. She wasn't supposed to take him into the garden, not without his special lead on. Poor Mrs Milligan, she got quite choked up talking about it. The second bedroom was his room." Again, she seemed incredulous. "A rabbit with his own room! How spoilt."

As Alicen was speaking, Ruby looked at Corinna. Was the rabbit responsible for the smell and the scratching – his way of letting them know that a fox hadn't run off with him, and that he'd met a different fate entirely?

Jed, is it Arthur that's here?

Jed leapt to his feet and started wagging his tale enthusiastically. Taking her by surprise, he sprinted past her and out of the room.

"Erm, do you mind if I pop into the living room?" Ruby asked, realising he wanted her to follow him.

"If you want," Andy replied, shrugging.

In the end they all went into the living room. Jed was barking enthusiastically at a silver-framed picture of two cartoon rabbits embracing.

Noticing Ruby looking at it, Alicen explained, "That's one of our wedding presents, we're the Haires you see, so it's kind of apt." Understanding dawned. "The smell, the scratching, it's the rabbit, isn't it? And we're the Haires. What a coincidence!"

Andy appeared thunderstruck too. "You couldn't make it up!" he said.

Ruby's mind was calculating what to do.

"We need to look under the floorboards," she decided.

"You mean take them up again?" asked Andy.

"That's right."

"Like I said, there's no way something's buried beneath those floorboards, we'd have known about it if there was." He shook his head as though exasperated. "And besides, we're only talking about a rabbit here."

A staunch vegetarian, Corinna was also an avid Animal Rights supporter. Ruby guessed she'd have something to say about that, and she was right.

"It doesn't matter if the spirit grounded is that of a person or an animal, they're of equal importance."

"Really? Is that what you believe?"

"Yes I do."

Andy didn't seem convinced. "I never realised animal spirits lingered."

Ruby stepped in. "Normally they don't, not in my

experience anyway." In her experience she'd only ever dealt with Jed. "Animals normally have no trouble passing into the light, but every now and again…" She paused, did her utmost to emulate the authority of Theo, Ness and even Ailsa, to show she knew what she was talking about. "Every now and again, one gets stuck. But it's not a problem. We're, erm… we're used to dealing with the unusual."

"Even so," Andy stated, "there's no way I'm taking up my floorboards. Can't you use your powers to see what's under there?"

Her powers? He was making her sound like a character from a Marvel comic. Well, she'd give it a go. After another hour, however, Ruby, Corinna, and even Jed had to admit defeat. She still had no clue as to what was under the floorboards. She was almost thankful the smell was growing stronger. At least it proved to the Haires, who were both holding scarves over their noses by this stage, that they weren't entirely mad, not if the non-psychics in the room were being affected too. What was that smell, Ruby wondered, what did it remind her of? It was familiar, so familiar. She closed her eyes and focused on that instead; let familiarity be the thing to guide her.

Come on, Ruby, think. What is that smell?

A memory of waking up in her room came to mind, one dark winter's night, and the thing that had haunted her – the entity – in the flat with her, glaring at her from his hiding place in the shadows, like the spirit in Gilmore Street glared at Samantha. She remembered how she'd scanned the room for it, had tiptoed out of bed, crept to the door, and then, panic overtaking her, yanked it open, belted down the hallway and burst into the night, desperate to escape her 'stalker'. The smell was fear. Of course it was. Whatever had happened to Arthur, it hadn't been pleasant.

Ruby came to a decision.

"Alicen, where did the Milligans relocate?"

"Not far, a retirement village in Ditchling."

"Is it possible you could phone them again, get them round?"

"Get them round?"

"Or I can go and pick them up. Ditchling isn't far."

"I… well, I can see what they say I suppose? They might be willing."

"It won't do any harm to ask."

"But should I explain why exactly – that we're being haunted, by their pet rabbit of all things?"

"You didn't mention that last time you were on the phone then?" Ruby couldn't help but tease.

"No." Alicen looked slightly aghast at the thought. "I rang up on the pretence of some issue about the pipes. I also said I was thinking about getting a dog – I'm not by the way – but I figured it would pave the way to asking them if they'd ever had any animals whilst they were living here."

"Good thinking," praised Andy.

Ruby agreed. "But tell them the whole story this time. We need them here."

* * *

By the time the Milligans arrived, Ruby had to admit this was far from a standard case. When she eventually got home tonight, a bath and bed would be all she'd be good for. She wouldn't even have the energy to see Cash.

According to Alicen, once she'd explained to the

Milligans the scenario going on in their former house, they'd needed no further cajoling. In fact, Mrs Milligan let on that she half suspected that had been the reason behind the first phone call. When she entered the house – a tiny woman, birdlike in stature – her eyes, a bright shade of blue despite her years, were fierce.

"I knew it," she said. "I knew a fox hadn't got him! It was our niece, Tasha, the one who looked after him. She did something to him, didn't she? She's gone off the rails that one, a lost cause. We should never have gone to Normandy and left Arthur with her." Abruptly, all fierceness left her and she just looked sad, terribly sad. "Poor Arthur, he came a cropper, didn't he?"

Her husband was behind her and he too seemed full of woe, his eyes pale compared to his wife's, and glistening with un-shed tears. Staring at him, at them both, Ruby was touched, extraordinarily touched. Their love for Arthur – and never mind that he was *only* a rabbit – was plain to see.

In the bedroom, Mr and Mrs Milligan sat on the bed, in the exact same spots that she and Corinna had occupied earlier, to catch their breath.

"This is Arthur's room," Mrs Milligan said, looking round, "we had a little bed made up special for him. He was toilet-trained, you know," she added proudly. "Never messed anywhere he wasn't supposed to. Free rein of the house too, but not the garden; we never let him out unsupervised."

All the while Mrs Milligan was speaking Mr Milligan nodded in agreement.

"Do you know what could have happened to him?" asked Ruby tentatively.

Mrs Milligan shook her head. "But I can tell you the

problem with Tasha. It was drugs. We don't have anything to do with her now. She was smoking that puff even at sixteen, that's how old she was when we agreed she could look after Arthur. It does strange things to you that puff, it warps the mind."

Ruby couldn't help but agree. Drugs opened up doorways in your psyche that were sometimes – *oftentimes* – better staying closed. They made you act in ways you perhaps normally wouldn't. With that in mind she tried to tune in again, even whilst smiling benignly at the Milligans. A flash of temper, she sensed that. Sensed also that the rabbit *had* messed in the house, perhaps due to separation anxiety; he'd messed repeatedly. A foot came out and kicked, not once but two or three times – an attempt to chastise him, but a bit of an extreme attempt. Terrified, the rabbit kept messing. Another blow, the girl not just angry but fed-up too, the blows turning fatal. Temper swiftly dissipating as horror surfaced instead. Sorrow and panic too. Ruby understood that Tasha wasn't a bad girl. Not really, despite her actions. But a girl with problems, she was that all right – hence the drug use, which was a Band-Aid rather than a cure. A vicious circle that turned her vicious. Occasionally.

She broke the connection. She'd seen enough.

"Were you having building work done when you went away?" she asked.

"Nothing much, just some home improvements," Mr Milligan answered. "Tasha was taking care of that too, you know, letting the builders in, making them tea, supervising, that sort of thing."

"This room was also being 'improved'?"

Mr Milligan confirmed it was. "A few wonky

77

floorboards needed fixing. We didn't want the builders to do that until we'd got back, didn't want to upset Arthur's routine further, but they didn't listen, builders don't do they? They went ahead anyway." She paused. "Why do you ask?"

"I…" Ruby faltered. She really didn't want to upset this couple. She looked at Jed, he was staring at her, in his own way urging her on. He was right; they had to know. "We think – that is my colleague, Corinna and I – that he's still in this room. He's not buried here, not as such, but something of his is. A special toy perhaps? A blanket? Something that perhaps had blood on it. Evidence in other words." She pointed to the area Corinna had previously identified. "If the floorboards were up, well, Tasha knew they had to go back down."

"A special toy?" Mrs Milligan turned to her husband. "He had so many of them, didn't he?"

"He did, he loved them all. I never noticed if any were missing."

"Me neither. Only his lead was gone."

His lead? That was probably under there too, to corroborate Tasha's story of Arthur having been attacked by a fox.

"And that spot you just picked out," Mrs Milligan continued, "that's where his bed was, it's where the sun streams in through the window. He liked nothing better than to bask in it. Lazy little tyke he was at times, wasn't he?"

Before Ruby could say another word, Mrs Milligan burst into tears. With a swiftness belying his years, Mr Milligan put his arm around her and hugged her close.

Andy, who'd been standing silently in the room with

Alicen, looked visibly moved by this display of emotion but nonetheless muttered, "The thing is, I really don't want my floorboards taken up."

"It's okay," Ruby assured him, "you may not have to. Now that Mr and Mrs Milligan are here, perhaps they can break Arthur's attachment to that corner – the good and the bad memories associated with it – and coax him forwards. Turning her attention back to them, she continued. "I know this sounds silly, but can you speak to Arthur and tell him you're here, that you know what happened? Let him know he's safe; that he can go home, to his real home, on the other side."

Mr and Mrs Milligan just stared at her. Slightly nervous, Ruby held her breath. Then Mrs Milligan spoke. "It doesn't sound silly at all, dear."

They did as she asked, their voices soft and cajoling, but not only that, full of love. Everyone in the room, without exception, felt not just their pain, but also the intensity of their feelings towards such a small animal, and their relief too, at finally finding out his fate, no matter how hard it was to take.

Ruby and Corinna had gone to join Andy and Alicen, who were rapt. Jed stayed where he was, occasionally turning full circles in excitement.

"You're doing well," encouraged Ruby, "really well. He'll be here soon."

The smell that had been in the room began to fade. A scratch or two was heard then also ceased. The room brightened, despite the dying day. As it did, Ruby focused on the grounded spirit and willed him to tune in too; to materialise. At long last a shape appeared, larger than she expected, with soft grey fur, floppy ears and almond-shaped sparkling eyes. Jed barked and circled twice more. If only the others in the room could see what she could – the shade of Arthur. She'd love it if they could. Even so, all sensed a change in atmosphere and smiles lit faces one-by-one.

"He's here, isn't he?" asked Mrs Milligan.

"He is," confirmed Ruby, "he's making his way towards you. But he won't stay long, don't ask him to. Let him go. Give him his freedom."

More tears coursed down the old woman's face as she bent forwards and whispered words that only she, her husband, and Arthur could hear. Eventually, the rabbit continued onwards, walking right through the pair and disappearing entirely, Jed following on behind, intent on a playmate perhaps, someone to frolic with in those sun-dappled fields of his.

Afterwards, Mrs Milligan asked if Ruby thought she was the silly one.

Ruby was nonplussed. "No, why?"

"Because we loved Arthur so much."

It was Corinna who answered. "You know what I think? Loving something so small makes us bigger and it makes them bigger too."

"It doesn't seem trivial to you then?" Mrs Milligan quizzed Corinna further. "Moving on the spirit of an animal instead of a human?"

"There's nothing trivial about it. Not as far as I'm concerned, and I know Ruby feels the same. It was a privilege to help Arthur. And hopefully to help you find peace as well. You're good people."

Andy was decidedly misty-eyed, as for Alicen, she was crying along with the Milligans. In a sudden change of heart, Andy offered to take the floorboards up after all. "You might want those things of his."

Mr Milligan laid a hand of his arm. "No we don't, son, not if they've got his blood on them. You get rid of them if you want to. Meanwhile, we're going to stick with memories of happier times." Smiling at his wife, he added, "And we've got plenty of happy times with Arthur to remember, haven't we?"

"We have," she answered, "including today." She hesitated. "But… do you have any idea of where his body might be?"

Ruby nodded. "I think Tasha's story that a fox might have got him is partly true." But it was after the event – his body left out as bait almost.

Mrs Milligan didn't question her further.

After another cup of coffee – all of them needing a little bit of time to 'come down' from the experience – everyone said their goodbyes and Ruby and Corinna walked back to Ruby's old Ford.

"Time for a quick drink before we head for home?"

"Not tonight, Corinna, but soon, definitely."

Later, ensconced in her own home, she glanced at her phone. There were several messages and missed phone calls. But whoever wanted her and on whatever business, they'd have to wait. She'd dash off a quick text to Cash, then go to bed. Despite their success with Arthur, she was beat.

Chapter Eight

SITTING at the breakfast table in her kitchen the next morning, Ruby smiled as Jed sloped in through the door. Whereas she felt refreshed after a good night's sleep, he looked knackered.

"What's the matter, Jed, too much bunny chasing?" she asked, wishing for the umpteenth time she could reach out and stroke him as you could a living dog. She imagined how soft his fur would be, the warmth of his skin. Unfortunately, if she tried, her hand would go straight through him.

In answer, Jed slumped at her feet. Ruby reached down anyway.

"Thanks for your help yesterday, it was good to have you on board."

There was a slight wag of the tail before he drifted off, twitching occasionally at the imaginary bunny in his sleep she presumed.

The phone rang. *Who's it now?* No amount of psychic ability enlightened her. Already she'd had a productive morning answering texts and making various appointments, including one with a neighbour of Samantha Gordon's – a woman called Delia who'd known Ben or at the very least known *of* him. She'd agreed to talk to them, tell them what she knew about his disposition, hopefully providing them with vital clues on how to deal with such a fractious spirit. Reaching for the phone, she noticed the caller ID – it was Ness. She took a deep breath before answering.

"Hi, Ness, how are you?"

"I'm fine, thanks, and you?"

"I'm good."

"Glad to hear it."

The formal tone in Ruby's voice was echoed in Ness's – if she was feeling awkward so was her team member.

"I've just made an appointment with Samantha—"

"Ailsa and I have arranged for another regression with Ellie—"

They both cut to the chase, speaking at the same time. When Ness's words sank in, Ruby could hardly believe it.

"*You've* made another appointment with Ellie?"

Ness was unrepentant. "I did because it was me Ailsa rang with times when she was free. I tried to ring you but you weren't answering your phone, so I took the bull by the horns, went ahead and booked Ellie in. I'm letting you know what I've done at the first available opportunity."

It was a fair comment. She *had* been unavailable since the Malling job yesterday. Even so, what was to stop Ness from leaving a message?

"When is this appointment?" God, her voice sounded tight.

"It's this afternoon, at 3 o' clock. If you can't make it—"

"I *can* make it." Whatever else was in the diary could wait. "As I was trying to say earlier, I had a phone call from Samantha Gordon. Apparently we can talk to one of the neighbours who knew Ben. I've got an appointment for this morning. However, if *you're* busy…"

"I'm not," was Ness's immediate reply. "What time is

it?"

"It's in an hour."

"I'll see you at Samantha's."

* * *

On her way to Gilmore Street, driving this time, despite the parking issues, Ruby decided it was time she got a grip. She was working with Ness all day; the atmosphere that had erupted between them couldn't continue, it would wear them both down very quickly, and to be honest, Ruby felt worn down enough already. As she drove along the A27 past Sussex University and the football stadium, she wondered why she'd allowed herself to become so agitated. Overcoming the 'demon' that had plagued her family for so long should have brought with it a sense of relief, but the reverse was true. She still felt drained all of the time. And she was tetchier than before, much quicker to fly off the handle. She was more light-hearted when the 'demon' *had* been in her life – the logic of which escaped her.

Parking as close to Samantha's as possible, which wasn't close, but several streets away, she fed the meter and hurried along. The fight was over – with the darkness and with Ness. She mustn't let either continue. By the time she spotted Ness, she'd managed to cast off any lingering ill feeling and had a smile firmly plastered on her face. Ness, who had clearly been expecting her to storm around the corner, looked almost comically surprised. The fact that she did genuinely amused Ruby, she bit on her lip to stop herself from laughing and then thought 'what the hell' – and laughed anyway.

Relief quickly replaced surprise on Ness's face. "You're not angry with me?" she asked.

"I... no. Of course not."

Ness wasn't convinced. "Look, I'm sorry if you thought I was going over your head, I did try to call yesterday to discuss the appointment with Ailsa."

"I know you did, twice. Corinna and I were caught up on a case and by the time it ended I was so tired, I didn't even bother to check my messages. Besides, there's no going above me, we... work together." Which was another thing she needed to keep in mind. "I'm the boss of no one."

"Kind of you to say so, Ruby, however, it is your business and I do realise that. I'm also sorry if you think I'm forcing the issue of Ellie—"

"It's an interesting case, let's see where it leads, but..." and she wanted to be clear about this, "it really might not be something Psychic Surveys can take further. At the moment, I don't see us diversifying too much."

"As you say, let's see where it leads."

"Fine," Ruby replied, bristling again at the slight dismissal in Ness's voice. "First things first, let's go and see Delia. Samantha said she'd show the way."

At the mention of her name, Samantha Gordon materialised. Opening the door of number 44, she walked to where they were standing.

"You're bang on time, good. Best not to keep Delia waiting."

Before they could respond, Samantha crossed to the opposite side of the road, stopping at number 67, cream-coloured with no evidence of grime at all. It was as though the occupants could hear people approaching in this street as Delia too appeared at the door before they had a chance to knock. "Come in," she greeted enthusiastically, "come away in."

She had a Scottish accent, very subtle, subdued perhaps by years of living in the south. A small woman with a cloud of white hair, she ushered them down the hallway into her living room – not modernised, but more like Ruby imagined number 44 used to be, although much cleaner and floral.

"I'll fetch some tea," Delia said, winking at them.

Hurrying from the room, she returned a few minutes later with a tray. As she poured the contents of the teapot into fine bone china cups – also floral – she wasted no time in getting to the heart of the matter.

"Ben, he was a one, wasn't he?"

That's what they were here to find out.

Settling herself into a chair, the arms either side well worn by elbows and hands, Delia continued talking. "Kept himself to himself he did; don't know what he did for a job, I think it was something to do with the railways, but he was retired by the time I moved here, which was nearly eighteen years ago, would you believe? Used to see him pop out to the shops and come back clutching a wee bag with some bits and bobs in it. Always used to say hello to him. I'm from a wee village you see, a few miles outside of Inverness, I was brought up that way, to treat neighbours as friends."

"Did he say hello back?" Ness asked.

"Aye," replied Delia, "after a fashion. It wasn't so much hello as a grunt." She laughed heartily, clearly enjoying her own joke.

"What did he look like?" asked Ruby. She had done

some digging concerning him but had found very little. There'd been a mention of his demise in the local newspaper, The *South Coast Times*, but no photograph. She'd also sourced his birth certificate from the national archives online but again the information given was scant. He'd been a Brighton man through and through, had lived and died there, been cremated but with no plaque or headstone up at the cemetery *in memoriam* – something else Ruby had checked, along with a possible Facebook profile: after all you never knew your luck. She barely used her Facebook account, but she realised what a lifeline it could be to some people, how it connected them with the world beyond their windows. Sadly, Ben seemed to have eschewed it too. They needed an insight into the personality of the man and that's where Delia came in. Opening her notebook, she started to take notes as the old woman spoke.

Benjamin Hamilton, in his latter years anyway, was not of spectacular height, rather he walked with a bit of a stoop, dressed in dark clothing – 'drab' Delia described it as – had a sparse head of grey hair and eyes that might have been brown but which had faded considerably. He was also a loner.

"Never saw anyone visit him," Delia imparted. "Such a shame. So many forget the elderly."

Looking at the myriad-framed photographs of young men and women on Delia's mantelpiece – some clutching babies in their arms, others standing together in clusters – Ruby only hoped they didn't forget their mother or grandmother or whoever Delia was to them. She got the feeling they were a close-knit bunch, though. Certainly, the atmosphere in Delia's home was a contented one.

"Did *you* visit him?" Ruby asked.

"Aye, I'd knock on his door, take a wee slice of fruit cake over and ask him if he was all right." She shook her head at the memory. "He always took it, never refused, thanked me too, but never invited me in. Never even really looked at me, he always looked away. You know something? I think he may have had that condition that's been in the news a lot lately."

"Autism?"

"Yes, but there's another word for it."

"Asperger's?" Ness offered.

"That's it! That's the one. He did eventually start to talk to me; he couldn't not with me stood on his doorstep, but he always appeared embarrassed; used to do that shuffling thing with his feet, do you know what I mean? Nonetheless, we managed to exchange pleasantries."

"Pleasantries?" queried Ness, obviously remembering his less than pleasant attitude towards them. "He never seemed, erm… disgruntled?"

"No, he kept himself to himself for certain, but he was never rude, not Ben. I'd say he was more… shy."

"Shy?" burst out Samantha, who up until now had been listening intently. "He's not shy! It's as if he's looking at me, all the time." She held up a finger and thumb, just a fraction apart. "Sometimes, it's as if he's standing this close to me, drinking in every bit of me, and I mean *every* bit."

Delia's hand came up to her throat as she inhaled deeply. "Dear, oh dear, you make him sound quite menacing."

"He is," Samantha nodded, caught up in the drama of it all. "He doesn't want us there, that's for sure, he wants the house back for himself."

Something Ruby and Ness could confirm.

"Sam's explained the whole story to me," Delia said, now looking at Ruby and Ness, "that she thinks it's Ben haunting their house, that you're psychics trying to move him on." She leaned forward, "I could tell you a few haunted house stories if you like, from my time up in Scotland. Och, now there's a mysterious place, Scotland. Have you ever been? They're a fey bunch the Scots, although to be honest, my mother used to say I haven't got a fey bone in my body." Again, she laughed, clutching at her belly as she did so.

Ruby smiled too. "It was kind of you to visit Ben regularly, Delia. It sounds to me as if he was lonely."

With some effort, Delia stopped laughing and wiped at her eyes instead. "Lonely? I used to think that too. One day I decided to come right out and ask him."

"If he was lonely you mean?" Ruby admired her no nonsense approach.

"That's right. Well, there's no point in beating about the bush is there? I'd invited him over to mine for a wee spot of lunch a couple of times but he never accepted the invite. Being as he wouldn't let me in his house, I thought I'd entice him over but no such luck. One day he asked me why I kept coming over – not unkindly, he seemed more puzzled by it than anything."

"Perhaps he wasn't used to people bothering with him," suggested Ness.

"It could be, it could well be. Anyhoo, I answered his question with one of my own. I said 'you're lonely, aren't you? I hate to see a person lonely.' It was a candid moment between us, an honest moment, real you know? Getting down to brass tacks."

Ruby did know what she meant. "What was his response?"

"He denied it," she smiled, gave a shrug of her shoulders. "He actually looked at me, a rarity for him, and said, 'I'm not lonely anymore', which I thought was sweet. I used to think sometimes I was being a nuisance but perhaps not, perhaps he enjoyed my wee visits."

Possibly. Even so, by and large, Benjamin Hamilton seemed happy with his own company, but if he was in life, he wasn't in spirit. He'd attacked Ruby physically, an occurrence that was rare as it involved a huge amount of energy. What had angered him towards the end – had grounded him?

"Delia," Ruby asked, "when was the last time you saw Ben alive?"

The old woman's mood turned solemn. "I feel so guilty, you know?"

"What about?"

"That he lay dead in that house for almost a week before I cottoned on, before any of us did." Remembering that the new owner of the house was in residence, Delia lifted her head and issued a swift apology. "I'm sorry, wee dear, you don't need reminding."

Samantha waved her hand in the air. "People die, it's inevitable. We're not worried that he died in the house, we're worried he's still there!"

"Aye, aye, of course you are." Turning to look at Ruby, Delia answered her question. "The last time I saw him was about two weeks before. I hadn't been feeling too well, I'd had a cold and my arthritis was playing me up a treat, but I hobbled over and asked him if he was keeping well."

"How did he seem?" Ness too was eager to find out.

"Tired. To be honest, I had a feeling in my bones he wasn't going to last much longer. Although as you do with these feelings, you tend to dismiss them, don't you. You think you're being silly."

"He… didn't seem angry?' Ness probed.

Delia was perplexed. "No, he wasn't an angry man, I've told you."

"He never swore at you?"

"No, he did not! And I wouldnae have stood for it if he did!"

Ness leaned back, a frown on her face. "He was a nice man, as you say."

"He was. He was nice enough."

Despite his spirit lingering, Delia clearly didn't approve of talking ill of the dead. But the man behind the mask, who was he? Had he indeed suffered from a condition such as Asperger's? If he had it would explain the averted gaze, the refused invitations to mingle. Ruby wasn't an expert on the condition, but she was well aware that symptoms included difficulty in interacting and communicating with others, which could lead to immense inner frustration and a build-up of anger; anger he hid from Delia but which he certainly wasn't bothering to hide from them. On the other hand, his disposition could have nothing to do with Asperger's. It could just be the simple fact that behind closed doors people were different. Polite on the surface, amenable even, there was often no telling what simmered beneath. Ben was a loner, that much they knew. Also that he harboured hatred as well as anger. What they had to do was find out why and, the way it was looking, perhaps only Ben himself could tell them that.

Chapter Nine

"ELLIE, you know the procedure: you need to lie down, close your eyes and breathe with me, in for a count of five, out for a count of five…"

After the meeting with Delia, Ruby and Ness had made an appointment to go back to 44 Gilmore Street on Monday, when the other members of the team would be accompanying them, and Jed too, hopefully. They had then returned to their respective cars and driven back to Lewes, to Ness's house, where they were meeting Ellie and Ailsa. On the way over, Ruby wondered if it was worth mentioning to Ness that any future regressions with Ellie – *if* there were future regressions – would be better off taking place on more neutral ground; neutral to her and Ness at least. Perhaps at Ailsa's home or even Ellie's? At Ellie's would be more logical. At the moment and despite the truce with Ness, the bias seemed to weigh in her favour. In her own house, Ness called the shots.

Once back in the house, she and Ness resumed their former positions, sitting side by side. The curtains were partially closed and Ailsa's voice was mellow and comforting. Again, Ruby had to fight to keep her eyes open, to focus.

Ailsa wanted to take Ellie back to a 'happier' memory of the life that was 'haunting' her.

"You think the man you're having problems with is your husband, and certainly we know you're married to someone because of the gold band on your finger. Well," she reasoned, "if you married the man, hopefully you weren't coerced into it. At one point, perhaps you weren't frightened of him. That's something we can try and find out. Choose the same number on the keypad as last time – six – and return to that life, but to something good in it. It could be the first time you met your husband-to-be, your wedding day, your honeymoon perhaps."

When Ailsa suggested this route, Ruby knew the expression on her face was one of bemusement. Ness, however, simply nodded in agreement. She clearly thought a return to 'happier times' was a good idea too.

Ailsa's monotone continued. Allowing herself the luxury of closing her eyes, Ruby stilled her mind. If she couldn't beat them, she'd join them, and listen to what it was Ellie had to say.

* * *

"We're standing outside a building, not too far from the sea. I can hear seagulls circling overhead, the noise they're making is deafening."

"Describe the building."

"Erm… it's an imposing sort of building – red brick with stone windows. It looks… official, I suppose. Oh, there's a couple coming out; they seem so happy. She's younger than him, pretty. He looks like he could be somebody; he's got that older, distinguished look about him. A crowd gathers round them. There's confetti on the floor. People are laughing."

"Could it be a registry office?"

"A registry office, yes, of course it is. And it's our turn next. We're going to be married! I'm happy too, excited. I admit, when he first suggested a registry office I wasn't keen. I wanted a church wedding, you know – the white dress, my hair done, my make-up, the works. I wanted the fuss. But he refused outright; he's not a church-going man. I tried to persuade him but it was no use. You can't persuade a man like him, once he's made his mind up, that's it. I like that about him, though – his strength of mind; his strength overall. He's a big man, tall and broad. He makes me feel feminine. Do you know what my favourite book is?"

"I'd love to know, tell me."

"*Wuthering Heights.*"

"By Emily Brontë?"

"That's it! That's the one! As soon as I saw him he reminded me of that man in it, how I imagined him to be, dark and brooding. Do you know who I mean?"

"I do, Heathcliff, the hero of the book. But what's *his* name? Your husband?"

"I… I can't remember, not yet. Why can't I remember? Everything's so dark."

"It's not dark, it's your wedding day, a bright day, a happy day. Tell us more about the man you're marrying."

"Okay… I can see again, I can feel. There are so many different emotions in me and they're all fighting for attention. With him it's like I'm the chosen one, you know? He chose me. He wants to spend the rest of his life with me, this strong and brooding man. It *is* a happy day, but you're wrong about something, it's *not* bright; the sun isn't shining, it's raining. I wish it wasn't. I don't like the rain, what bride does? He got annoyed when I mentioned the weather, told me to stop moaning, to be satisfied. And he's right. What am I thinking of, complaining? I'm happy, so happy."

"Look down, what are you wearing?"

"I'm wearing… everything's so hazy. I get so far and then it's like… I don't know – my mind closes in on itself. It collapses."

"Try to focus, to concentrate."

"I am trying, honestly I am. My dress – it's white I think. No… it's not white: it's cream. I'm not, well… it would be wrong for me to wear white. The dress is short, not too short, though. He doesn't like me to show too much leg but it's nice enough, just above the knee. I've got flats on. I wanted to wear heels, but he doesn't like them either. He wants a respectable wife, not a whore. I don't think heels make you look like a whore but I don't want to upset him further."

"There's a lot your husband doesn't like, isn't there?"

"But he likes me – he loves me. And I love him."

"Who else is at the wedding? Can you see?"

"It's not like the other wedding. It's just us. Oh, hang on. Wait. There are two other people, but I don't know them. They're witnesses, but they're not friends. I… it's so hard to remember, I think they're passers-by, we've asked them if they'd stand in, or rather he's asked them. They look a bit uncomfortable actually, a bit disinterested. Again, it's a shame but I don't say anything, not this time. When the ceremony's over, there's no one waiting to throw confetti, not like the last couple. There's no one to cheer. We just leave the building and walk through the town, towards home – our home. We're renting a house, I haven't seen it yet; it's a surprise. But he said it's a nice house. It's a nice town too. I've not been here before. I think I'm going to like being by the sea. The sound of the seagulls above, it's really starting to irritate him. He wishes they'd shut up."

"Aren't your parents there? His parents?"

"No, no parents. I've never met any of his family. He says I wouldn't like them. To be honest, I don't think he likes them either."

"What's the matter? You don't seem happy now."

"No… I… I'm fine, I… I just wish my parents could have come. I'm their only child, they've always doted on me, but they don't like him, they think he's trouble. Their opinion's unfair. They've only met him the once, hardly even spoke to him. They don't like his job. He's worked the fairgrounds up until now. He's travelled up and down the country doing that. Even been over to Europe. Can you imagine? I want to go to Europe one day. My parents, they said they wanted someone better for me, I think they meant someone who'd been to university. That's their definition of 'better'. But you can't help who you fall in love with, can you? Oh, I remember now! The fairground's where I met him, he was on one of the stalls. He swept me off my feet that night, singled me out, ignored the girl I was with, she's taller than me and a looker, with masses of blonde hair. He ignored her, even though she tried to get his attention. And that made me like him even more. I went back the next night. He said he knew I would. He kissed me, said he wanted me, said he'd never wanted a girl as much. And I wanted him. I *ached* for him. My parents tried to stop me from seeing him. Threatened to lock me in my room. Can you believe that? But you can't stop a stone from rolling, that's what he says – we're two rolling stones. So we've come away, to this town, this house. It's a new start for me as well."

"It's a seaside town you live in? Do you know where?"

"There's a pier and he's going to try and get work on it. That'll be fun, my husband working on the pier. I'll go and visit him every day. He said he's looking forward to that and to getting home every night, to having his tea waiting for him. I'm not a good cook, but I'll learn, of course I will. Lots of magazines have recipes in them, don't they? It can't be that hard."

"Which magazines? What are they called?"

"I… erm… I don't know. I can't remember. 'Good' something? It's the fashion magazines I like really, but I've no time for them now, I've got a husband to look after. I'm going to become a good cook, because that's the way to a man's heart, through his stomach. My mum used to say that."

"Your husband's name, you must know it."

"I… of course I do. It's…"

"What's the matter? Why are you hesitating?"

"My husband… those words. They sound strange."

"Strange? How?"

"Wrong."

"But you've just got married, you've just said so."

"But it's wrong! Why is it wrong?"

"You did get married, didn't you? You went through with the ceremony?"

"Yes, yes! Of course we did. I'm a respectable married woman. I've got the ring on my finger to prove it. I don't know why it's wrong. I get mixed up at times. I get so confused."

"Okay, don't worry, don't get agitated. Breathe with me

97

again. Good. What did you do after the wedding? Did you go somewhere to eat?"

"Eat? At a restaurant you mean? I'd like to have done. It would have been nice. But we've only got enough to tide us over until he gets another job. So no, there's no meal out, there's no honeymoon, there's only us, walking through rain-drenched streets, past shops with their lights on, even though it's the middle of the day. The glow from within should match mine, but it's a cold light that falls onto the pavement, a pale, sickly yellow. I'm shivering. I'm hoping he'll put his arm around me but he doesn't. He's got his hands in his pockets instead, his head is down; he wants to get home. He's eager to show it off I think. My clothes, the stuff that I brought with me, he's taken it there. Said my dresses are hung up in the wardrobe already. I wish I could have brought my records with me. I love music. Love Elvis. Have you heard him? They call him the King of Rock and Roll and I agree. There's no one to match him. But I could only bring what I could carry. It's funny…"

"What is, what's funny?"

"I miss my records as much as my mum and dad. I really did have quite a collection. We've stopped. We're no longer walking through the streets. There are no more shops, there's no light either, there's only rain and it's soaking us to the bone. He's pointing. This is it, the house he's rented. It's… small, much smaller than my parents' house. He'd acted like it was special. That's why I wasn't allowed to come here with him when he dropped our cases off. But it's *not* special. Even from the outside I can tell how dirty it is. The house looks… unkempt. Oh no, he's seen it."

"Seen what? Tell us what he's seen."

"My expression. Quickly I smile again but too late. He's noticed. He's angry. I can tell. But I am too. I'm so angry with myself. I'm spoilt that's what I am. It's not his fault he can't afford a better place for us to live. When he gets a job, it'll be different. But for now, this is good; this is fine. I turn to him and try to say how excited I am. But he turns away. Puts the key in the door. Unlocks it. The hallway is so dark. And there's a smell, it hits you straightaway, the smell of dirt and neglect. I'm still smiling; I'm forcing myself to. We can clean it. *I* can clean it. It's going to be a little palace by the time I'm done. We go inside and he shuts the door. And that's… that's when it happens."

"When what happens? Don't hesitate. You can tell us."

"When it all turns to shit."

Chapter Ten

CASH was beside himself.

"A rabbit? You're serious? You've moved on a rabbit?"

"Yes, Cash, a rabbit, an animal spirit. He'd erm… well – he'd met a murky end. His poor little soul was grounded."

Cash burst into hysterics. "A rabbit? A bunny?" She could swear there were tears pouring down his face. "Psychic Surveys are now in the business of moving on grounded bunnies! That's priceless!"

Even Jed – who normally adored Cash, who took the opportunity to curl up by his feet whenever he was around – was shooting daggers at him.

Echoing Corinna, Ruby started lecturing him on how animal spirits were as valid as human. Heck, even more so. Their souls tended to be a lot purer. But it was no use, he wasn't listening, he was too busy laughing.

Drumming her fingers on the table and making a show of sighing heavily, she looked forward to the others turning up, even Ness.

Now, now, Ruby, she quickly admonished, *of course, Ness!*

Cash was still at it when the other members of the Psychic Surveys team bustled into the office, Jed jumping up to greet every one of them.

"Hello, boy, it's good to see you too." Theo returned his

enthusiasm. Of all her team she could sense him the most clearly, even if she couldn't always see him. Only Ruby's mother, Jessica, seemed to be able to see him with no problem – her psychic connection almost as strong as Ruby's.

Straightening up, Theo turned to Cash. "What's so funny?"

"Funny?" Cash managed. "The bunny…" he said before dissolving into laughter all over again.

As they congregated round the meeting table, Corinna shot him a look too.

"Leave him, he'll calm down soon," Ruby told her. "Tiny minds and all that."

"Haire today, gone tomorrow. That was their surname, wasn't it? The people haunted by the bunny. Haire. Oh come on, it's golden, Ruby, golden."

It took a full five minutes for him to collect himself.

"Right," said Ruby, "now you've finished, can we continue as normal?"

"Normal?" There were still tears on his cheeks. "We can try."

Ruby kicked him under the table lest he start all over again.

She cleared her throat in what she hoped was a suitably authoritative manner. "First of all, thanks for coming in on a Saturday morning. We need to be at Gilmore Street first thing on Monday so obviously we've got to get you guys," and here Ruby nodded specifically towards Theo and Corinna, "up to speed before then. First though, let's do a quick recap on what else has been happening this week. The old woman in East Preston, the one Ness and I went to visit, that all went smoothly. She was stubborn, as we'd gathered, but there were no fireworks or anything. We had a bit of a chat with her and off she went. She was a bit set in her ways, that's all, a bit too fond of her usual routine. There was also the Malling case, the one Cash finds so hilarious, where Corinna and I moved on the spirit of a rabbit."

Theo burst out laughing now. "Sorry," she said, just as quickly holding up a conciliatory hand. "Corinna's told me all about it. It's a great case. My grandchildren are going to love it when I tell them." Her entire body was shuddering with mirth and even Ness seemed amused. Corinna glanced wearily at Ruby.

"Carrying on," said Ruby pointedly, "Ness and I have also been embroiled in this regression case but more about that later. Theo and Corinna, you've had some cases to deal with too, how did they go?"

"Pretty standard," Theo's words were punctuated with bursts of laughter. She and Cash really were incorrigible. "I've typed up the reports and emailed them to you for filing. Two were non-starters. One, the house in Hove, had negative energy but it was residual, the spirit had long gone, but whoa, what a tortured life he'd led." She lowered her voice in a conspiratorial manner. "Drugs," she added, "and an overreliance on the vodka too." Returning to her normal pitch, she continued, "We gave the house a psychic sweep, advised on oils and crystals, and then went on our merry way. I've told the man who lives there now, Toby, to get back in touch with us if problems persist, but they won't of course, not now we've been in. No, I'm afraid the star case went to you this week, Ruby. Oh, how I wish you'd given me a call on that one."

"And me," Cash piped up. "It's legend, it really is."

Deciding to rescue the situation, Ness jumped to her feet. "Tea?" she enquired.

"Please," Ruby muttered, considering telling Theo and Cash to stop rabbiting on before swiftly deciding against it. They didn't need any further encouragement. "Overall, it's been another busy week but at least we've got some cases wrapped up. Two of them are ongoing, however. Ness and I had quite a time at Gilmore Street, the spirit there – that of a man, Benjamin Hamilton we think, who was the previous occupant – is very aggressive."

Theo turned serious. "Aggressive? And the rest! From what Ness said on the phone, he delivered quite a blow to your stomach."

"You didn't tell me that." Cash said accusingly.

"I… well, no I didn't. But that's correct, he did."

"Ruby!" Cash admonished.

Before she could reply, Ness started speaking. "His language is also foul, he swears – a lot. We get the impression – the distinct impression – he's something of a misogynist. A bit of a loner. Ben died at the house in his mid-eighties, in the living room. It was a week before his death was discovered."

Corinna raised an eyebrow. "A week?"

"Not as uncommon as you might think, sweetheart," commented Theo.

Ruby nodded in agreement. "Although Samantha Gordon and her family, which consists of her husband and two children, a girl aged ten and a boy aged thirteen, have experienced only standard phenomena, for us it was extreme. They've 'sensed' rather than seen anything and have suffered from mood swings too. Oh, and things keep going missing, she mentioned that yesterday: keys, the daughter's homework book, shoes, and make-up, that sort of thing. As we all know items going missing can be an early sign of a haunting. We've tried to find out about Ben, but there's very little on record. I've no picture of him to show you either, the article in the local rag that mentioned his death didn't carry one."

"He didn't even warrant that," Theo sighed.

"On the plus side, there's a resident in Gilmore Street, Delia, who knew something of him and was willing to speak to Ness and I. I've no picture but I can give you an idea of what he looked like at least." Ruby related all they'd been told, including Delia suspecting Ben of having Asperger's.

"Asperger's?" Theo queried. "That could account for his frustration."

"But of course he could just have been shy," countered Ness. "There's no proof."

"There never is," Ruby replied, expressing some of *her* frustration. "The strange thing is, although he was a loner, Delia considered him actually quite pleasant. At least he was never rude to her, not like he's been to us."

"That could be because he sees you as trespassers on his property," suggested Cash.

"And he knows what you're trying to do – move him on basically," Corinna added. "You know how resistant some spirits can be to that."

"Possibly," Ruby agreed, taking a sip of tea. "Delia thought he might have worked for the railways but obviously he'd been retired for a good number of years. I contacted Southern Rail yesterday to see if they had any record of a Benjamin Hamilton, but drew a blank, which is typical of any correspondence with Southern Rail really."

Everyone laughed, settling into the meeting. Ruby explained that they were all required on the Gilmore Street case and that a date was set for the following Monday. "But we need to go in prepared, turning up en masse might cause him to become even more aggressive. Hopefully, our combined effort might just be what's needed. We'll have to see."

"I take it the children will be at school?" asked Theo.

"Yes, and the husband will be at work. He's not so keen on us getting involved apparently, but I get the impression it's Samantha who wears the trousers in the Gordon household. What she says goes. Now, on to the second ongoing case, that of Ellie Grey." From fairly relaxed, all four faces suddenly looked engrossed. Even Jed bothered to prick up his ears. Ruby frowned. It was amazing the effect that girl had had, everyone responding to the fragility within her; responding to something anyway. "There've been two regressions this week, carried out by Ailsa Isaacs, both recalling the same past life. In it she's young, in her early twenties we presume; she's in a house; she's living with someone – again we have to presume here, but we think it's her husband, and she's terrified of him basically. He's a bad lot. That's about as far as we've got. About as far as we may ever get." Looking directly at Ness, she continued, "I know I've said this before, but I'm really not sure how much further we can take Ellie's case, if, in fact, it can be called that. As you all know, she thinks something terrible happened to her and her instinct is that the perpetrator was never brought to justice or might still be alive. Unlikely I know, but like I say, that's her instinct. What it has to do with Psychic Surveys I'm not really sure, but I'm willing to spend a couple more sessions on it."

Before Ness could protest, she added, "And I think we're better off moving the regression sessions to a more neutral location. Would Ailsa be willing to host them at either her place of work or where she lives?"

Despite Psychic Surveys being her business, Ruby couldn't help but feel uneasy waiting for Ness's reaction. It wasn't easy going up against such a 'giant' in the field.

After what seemed like ages, Ness replied.

"Ellie feels comfortable at mine. That's where the last two regressions have taken place and where for the sake of continuity – which is very important in a case like this – they should carry on. I really don't want the sessions relocated."

There was silence again, as though the room itself was holding its breath. All eyes were either on Ruby or Ness or looking carefully elsewhere – Jed in particular guilty of the latter.

"I don't think—"

"Ellie's a very fragile girl."

"I know that, Ness."

"You had to rush off after yesterday's session, so did Ailsa. But Ellie stayed behind. We talked."

"Oh?"

"You're dubious about taking on her case, trying to find answers, but answers is what she needs. The girl is adopted and she doesn't get on with her adoptive parents. They had two children after her, both naturally conceived, and she's always felt she was a bit of a 'rash decision' – her words not mine." All eyes were on Ness now as she continued. "She went off the rails when she was younger, had a bit of a breakdown I gather, and currently she's living in a hostel, trying to get her life back on track. What's happening to her – these flashbacks and dreams, these *feelings* – they're genuine—"

It was Theo who interrupted. "Not necessarily. People are more than capable of deceiving themselves – and by proxy *us* – by dredging up long forgotten images and impressions from the unconscious; scenes from a film perhaps, seen when young, or a story overheard. I'm not saying it's deliberate, not with Ellie, but often there's a more mundane explanation."

"Oh come on, Theo," Ness was clearly annoyed. "There are many extraordinary claims out there that can't be attributed to the mundane. What about children who can recognise relatives from an earlier life; who can identify long-dead family members from photographs they've never seen before? Yes, spirits go to the light but you know as well as I do that often they come back again, in another body, another country, in another era. Some cases aren't even linear and they're far from mundane."

"Yes, yes," muttered Theo, waving a hand in the air, "you're right I suppose, and, as for not every case being linear, don't get me started on quantum physics or we'll be here all day." Adopting a suitably sorrowful expression, she continued, "I have a sneaking suspicion about myself, you know; that I drowned in one of my previous incarnations. Reggie suggested a cruise once. I was horrified. I won't go anywhere near the sea if I can help it, I prefer a bit of terra firma. In relation to Ellie, all I'm saying is that perhaps something's been suggested to her and she's run with it."

"She can't even remember her name," Ruby pointed out. "That's convenient, isn't it?"

"What do you mean, 'convenient'?" Ness challenged.

"Well, I've been spending time researching this subject,"

answered Ruby. "Does anybody remember a film called *The Search for Bridey Murphy?*"

Only Theo said it 'rang a bell'.

"It's not surprising," Ruby continued, "it's an old film, from the 1950s but, and here's the point: it revolves around one of the best-known reincarnation stories out there apparently. In 1952, Ruth Simmons underwent a series of hypnosis sessions – regression in other words. She suddenly started to speak with a heavy Irish accent and remembered specific details from her life as Bridey Murphy, who had lived in Belfast during the nineteenth century. A lot of the things she said couldn't be verified, but she recalled two people from whom she used to buy her food, I forget their names, but anyway a search of the town directory for 1865 I think it was, listed them as grocers. Ruth was able to give details that could be corroborated. Ellie, so far, hasn't."

"She's only had two sessions," Ness defended.

"I know, but if she can remember certain things, why not names?"

Ness shrugged, looking genuinely perplexed. "I don't know, but Ellie's case *is* genuine. I'm trusting my instinct here."

"So Ellie stayed behind did she, and you talked to her?"

"I did."

"Okay," Ruby continued. "What I want to know, Ness, is this your case or Psychic Surveys? If it's the latter, shouldn't we have *both* talked to her?"

Again, the room held its breath.

"You rushed off—"

"Because the session had been declared over. Everyone was leaving. Or at least that was the impression I was given."

Their eyes locked.

"Decide, Ness, whether this is your case or a company case. I understand Ellie's fragile and I can see that you empathise with her, but if it's a company case, if it comes under the Psychic Surveys banner, then please, no more private interviews. Include me at every stage or take it off the books."

As Ness continued to stare at her, Ruby did her best not to look away.

Chapter Eleven

"THAT was a bit harsh, wasn't it?"

Later that morning, Ruby and Cash were in the car driving over to Hastings to join her mother and grandmother for lunch. Jed had decided to join them.

"Ruby, listen to me. What you said to Ness, was that really called for?"

Ruby was asking herself the same thing. Had she been too harsh? It didn't seem so at the time but in retrospect she wasn't so sure. All Ellie had done was stay behind for a little bit. All Ness had done was talk to her. Why had she got the needle about it? Was she feeling insecure? A little out of control even, her mojo still in temporary suspension? At least she hoped it was temporary.

"Ruby," Cash cajoled, "come on, talk to me."

She found herself gripping the steering wheel hard. "Look, Cash, I've got the afternoon off, let's not talk about work, about colleagues, let's just have a break. Ness and I... we're fine. I wanted to make it clear where I stood that's all. There's nothing wrong with that."

Her defensive response wasn't lost on Cash; his raised eyebrows were testament to that. Even so, she was glad he didn't persist.

The standoff with Ness had effectively ended the meeting. Everyone had started shuffling around in seats or fidgeting with mugs, pushing them back and forth, clearly embarrassed. Ness had been the first to stand up, her chair scraping against the floor.

"When would you like us to be at Gilmore Street on Monday?"

"Ten o' clock," Ruby suggested, keeping her voice steady.

"Ten o' clock it is. Have a good weekend."

Theo had stood next. "What are you up to this afternoon, Ruby? Not working I hope?" Not just a question there'd been a warning in there too.

"We're going over to Gran's. She's cooking for us."

"Good," Theo replied. "Perhaps leave the mobile at home, eh?"

With that she'd left the attic too. Only Corinna remained.

"Ruby, Presley and I are going to The Rights of Man for a drink later. Why don't you and Cash join us? If you're back in time from Hastings that is."

"Yeah, yeah, that'd be lovely. We'll see how it goes."

The way they were acting reminded her of how they had treated her last year, when she'd been affected so negatively by the entity. They'd tiptoed around her; been 'wary', before fully realising what the matter was, before *she'd* even realised. There was no need to be wary of her again, all she was doing was asserting her authority. Okay, she was young – young*er* than Ness – but there was no crime in that. Surely everyone could see her point?

For the rest of the journey she and Cash sat in silence, Cash turning up the CD player to listen to The Decemberists. He and Presley were in a band, Thousand Island Park, and the group currently playing was one of their biggest influences. Cash had replaced the drummer, Danny, who was a best friend of Presley's. He had committed suicide last year before Psychic Surveys could help him, convinced he was possessed by the devil – an entity similar to the one that had attacked Ruby. She wished they could have helped him. Cash might be the new drummer, but Danny wasn't forgotten.

Arriving in Hastings, Ruby drove towards the Old Town. The streets around her were busy, goods from shops spilling out onto the pavement, as eclectic a selection as was on offer in Lewes. Parking the car, she switched off the engine. As she did, Cash leant across and drew her to him.

"You work too hard, Ruby." His voice sounded muffled against her hair.

"Cash, I don't want to talk about work—"

"I know, I know, I'm just saying." He pulled away, held her gaze instead. "You never told me that Ben attacked you."

"It's nothing."

"It's hardly *nothing*, Ruby. I'll come with you all on Monday, shall I?"

She started laughing. "What you going to do? Square up to him for me?"

He tickled her ribcage, causing her to squeal out loud. "As a matter of fact, that's exactly what I'm going to do, square up to him if needs be. I've told you before, I ain't afraid of no ghost. Spirit or not, I'll sort him out."

"Sort him out? Cash! That's not the attitude." After a few moments her laughter died down, she started worrying again instead. "Talking of attitudes, mine's crap, isn't it? You're right, what I said to Ness wasn't called for."

Cash shook his head. Around his neck the obsidian

necklace she'd given him when they first met swayed slightly. "It was heavy handed, that's all."

"I *am* the boss!"

"And they're your friends, Ruby, not just your work colleagues. They've stood by you, through thick and thin."

She sighed, and had to look away. "Cheers, Cash, for making me feel bad."

"I'm not, I don't mean to." With one hand he turned her face towards him. "Take it easy, okay? Not just on everyone else but on yourself too."

"I just… I don't see where it's going with Ellie, that's all."

"Give it a chance and if Ness wants to take the lead, let her. This shouldn't be a matter of pride."

Pride – was that what she was guilty of, one of the seven deadly sins, feeding the 'bad wolf' within? Susan came to mind, someone else from last year, a grounded spirit that had been murdered by her so-called 'lover', her soul left to fester at the foot of a Victorian arched bridge on the Cuckoo Trail in East Sussex. A notorious site, it was known as 'Emily's Bridge', the legend of a local nineteenth century suicide attached to it. But if Emily *had* done the deed there, she'd moved on. It was Susan from a more recent era that haunted it; a young girl who was teased and tormented by local teens – teens who used the bridge as a gathering place and sensed a presence; were *excited* by it. In life, Susan had had Downs syndrome, a condition that was still presenting itself in death. Although she too had been aggressive at first, preparing to attack Ruby, they'd reached an understanding and finally, Susan had gone on her way. But she'd come back – albeit in an esoteric sense – to tell Ruby that she was good inside. Ruby could recite her words exactly: *Never forget how good you are, how bright you shine. Hold on to that.* Before she could ask her what she meant, *why* she had to remember, Susan had gone. That was the last she'd seen of her. Whatever the meaning, Ruby clung to those words – they seemed to be more pertinent now than ever.

* * *

"Ruby, Cash, come in!"

Sarah, her grandmother, held the door open for them, both Ruby and Cash kissing her on the cheek as they squeezed past, edging their way down the long and narrow hallway and into the kitchen beyond. In her late seventies, Gran was still a keen baker, often making her own bread and biscuits. Certainly she'd been busy today: the aroma was wonderful, and Cash was practically swooning at the prospect of sampling some homemade goodies. Her mother, Jessica, was already in the kitchen, stirring a pot of something. She beamed at her daughter as she entered, Ruby's breath catching slightly as she did so. This was the way she remembered her as a child – her mother beaming at her, laughing, always laughing; possessing such a zest for life. That had all stopped when Ruby turned seven. She felt a pang of sadness suddenly – for the years lost. Never to be regained. The waste.

Jessica too hurried over to give each of them a kiss and a hug, bending to give Jed, who was also sniffing the air, a 'pat' on the head. "Lunch is almost ready. I've made leek and potato soup and Gran's made bread."

"I can smell the bread," answered Ruby.

"Me too," Cash enthused. "I can't wait."

114

"Saul's going to join us, I hope that's all right?"

Jessica's one time partner-in-crime? Of course it was.

"Oh, there's the bell, I think that's him. I'll go and answer it."

As Jessica left, Cash turned to Ruby. "At least she didn't say '*talk of the devil*', that's something," he whispered.

Sarah, meanwhile, had entered the room. "I heard that, young man."

Cash looked horrified. "Oh, I'm sorry... I didn't mean..."

Ruby started giggling. "It's okay, Cash, Gran's not angry."

Humour – it was a weapon against the darkness – that was another thing Theo was always saying. And her gran would agree, wholeheartedly.

Ruby had first met Saul as a child, before the 'conjuring', and she'd been frightened by him, by the coldness of his ice-blue eyes and the hold he had on her mother. As young as she was, she could recognise how 'unhealthy' it was. The second time had been when they were gathering everyone together to stand against the entity – years and years later. His having been there when Jessica had raised it, it was only right he should be there when they tried to defeat it. Only slightly older than her mother, the experience had broken him too. Now in recovery, he'd put on weight and wasn't so stooped. He was more alive, his life force flowing within him instead of being leeched from him. Entering in tandem with Jessica – who was fussing round him – she directed him towards a chair and made him sit. As he did, he smiled wryly at Ruby, taking Jessica's 'fussing' in good heart.

At her grandmother's insistence, they all sat and lunch

was served, with soup ladled into large bowls and hunks of bread placed on a plate in the middle, which they grabbed at eagerly. As everyone talked in between mouthfuls, everyday chitchat, Ruby felt the earlier tension start to ebb.

After bowls had been cleared and all the bread eaten – Jed looking on forlornly, no doubt wishing he could indulge in a thickly-buttered slice too – the conversation turned to the business of Psychic Surveys, as she knew it would. Sarah and Jessica always wanted to hear the latest news, what cases she'd been working on, how busy she was. She didn't want to talk about work – she'd already told Cash that – but it seemed churlish not to give them at least a breakdown of the week's events. After that, maybe she'd broach the subject of holidays and tell them she was contemplating one.

She told them about the old woman in East Preston; the rabbit, about which even her grandmother had raised an amused eyebrow; Gilmore Street – leaving out the bit about the psychic attack; and, of course, about Ellie. It wasn't long before she regretted her honesty. Ellie's case was the one they were most interested in, Saul in particular.

"Reincarnation," he was saying, wiping at his mouth with a napkin, "it's a fascinating subject."

He'd found many subjects fascinating in his youth – she knew that from her mother – not least devil worship. And playing with fire, they'd both got burnt.

Warming to the theme, he leaned forward, Cash glancing at Ruby as he did – a message in his eyes. *You okay with this?* She was, or rather she might as well be. She could hardly tell Saul to shut up.

"It makes sense to me, reincarnation. It's logical. Of

course we come back, in various roles and guises, there's so much to absorb, not just about ourselves but about the world and what's in it, all the possibilities that exist."

Cash couldn't resist joining in. "But, Saul, what I don't understand is why come back here? Why not go somewhere else, another dimension? In a way, this world, it's like God's playground and we're his playthings."

"How do you know we don't go to another dimension?" Saul asked.

"I…" Cash shrugged. "Well, I don't. Although if you look at what's been documented so far, no one's ever recalled waking up on planet Zog."

"There's a theory," Sarah answered before Saul could, "that once a soul leaves the body it enters a state of unconditional love, one that is completely void of judgement concerning actions on Earth connected with the lessons it decided to experience in that life. In basic terms, there is nothing to be condemned or rewarded. It's… how can I put it, a *perfect* state. But how can we, as an assumed intelligence, appreciate perfection if we don't know imperfection? That's where this existence comes in. And yes, we may volunteer for various 'experiences' beforehand, some good, some bad—"

"And some downright horrendous," Jessica added quietly.

Sarah turned to her, "But we learn from them. Eventually. That's the point, darling, we *learn*."

"*Birth is not the beginning, death is not the end*," Saul said, "I forget who said that now, but I often think of this life as a dream, one we wake up from upon passing. We go home, to rest awhile and then we come back for more."

"We *choose* to come back for more," Jessica corrected. "I

don't think you can say that everyone does. I think some souls stay put." She turned towards Ruby, "Do you think she's genuine, this girl?"

At last – someone as cynical as her! Ruby was strangely grateful. "Ness thinks she is; in fact, Ness is driving our involvement with the case. I think it's outside our expertise. But I'm remaining open-minded at the moment."

"The best way to be," her grandmother concurred. "As I've taught you."

But the fact was she was still leaning towards *not* believing. Not in the concept of reincarnation – that made sense to her too. As Saul had said, there was so much to absorb, to experience, you'd need lifetimes to fit it all in. It was the girl herself she was having issues with, and the suspicion that her past life could be a world she'd created; a cry for attention, given her relationship – or rather *non*-relationship – with her adoptive parents.

"But we *do* create worlds, Ruby," Jessica said. "You know that. Nobody sees the same thing in the same way; we all have a different perception. It doesn't mean that Ellie's world is not real or that she doesn't deserve help."

Cash noticed their exchange. "It's incredible when you do that!" he said to Jessica.

"When she does what?" Saul asked puzzled.

"When she reads Ruby's mind. Theo and Ness can do it too. It's like some sort of superpower!"

"It's not a superpower," Sarah graced Cash with an indulgent smile as she stood to clear the dishes. "The brain is as complex as it is incredible. Perhaps what Jessica and those with her ability are doing is tapping into another part of it, that's all. A part we can all tap into, if, and pardon the pun here, we put our minds to it. Sadly, many refuse to even countenance such a notion."

"Because it frightens them," Cash suggested.

"That's right," Sarah agreed. "Fear is the greatest downfall of mankind. It takes us prisoner, stops us from feeling and experiencing fully. It seems a lot of people need several lifetimes just to understand that much. Now," she said, clearly deciding the subject had run its course, "who'd like a cup of tea?"

All four said they would. Ruby was rising to help Sarah when her mobile rang. Quickly she scrabbled in her jacket pocket to find it.

"Ruby," Cash admonished, "you should have left that thing behind, taken Theo's advice."

"I can't, Cash, I need to be on call."

"Says who?"

"Says me," she answered.

"If it's work…"

It was. Samantha Gordon's name flashed up.

"Hang on, I'll take this outside. I won't be long, I promise."

She returned less than five minutes later, her cheeks slightly flushed.

"Erm… sorry about this everyone, the visit's going to have to be cut short."

Jessica stood too. "Why, love, what's wrong?"

"The house on Gilmore Street, the one I was telling you about? Well, Samantha's going mad on the phone. Her daughter's just walked into the kitchen and, as she did, a mug came flying at her from the drainer and hit her on the head."

"Oh goodness," Sarah was all concern. "Is she all right?"

"Physically, yes, but mentally they're all shaken up. I'm going to have to go there straightaway and see what Ben's up to. Cash, are you coming?"

"Of course," he said, grabbing his jacket and following her and Jed out the door. "I wouldn't miss it for the world."

Chapter Twelve

"BLIMEY!" Samantha Gordon exclaimed on sighting them. "Talk about sending in the cavalry."

Ruby stepped forward and introduced the members of her team who Samantha hadn't met yet. Cash had called them on her behalf as they drove back to Brighton and, as usual, they'd dropped everything to help out.

"And you're all psychic, are you?" she asked.

Glancing at Cash, Ruby replied, "To varying degrees."

Clearly seeing no need to quiz them further, Samantha hurried them into the living room. Her husband – introduced as Jeff – was on the sofa, his arm around his daughter, comforting her. Their son, Leo, was clearly shaken too, cuddling into the side of his sister. Night had fallen and the drawn curtains gave the room a closed-in, claustrophobic feel.

"Oh," Samantha said, noticing what her son was doing, "so you're cuddling your sister now? That's a turn up for the books. You were bashing her on the arm with your book earlier." She shook her head in a show of despair. "My poor lamb, she's been getting it from all sides."

The daughter promptly burst into tears. "Mum, who threw that cup at me?"

"That's what these people are here to find out, Ruby," her father muttered, "*apparently*."

Ruby? So the girl had the same name as her. Although

she tried not to stare, Ruby did her best to get the measure of Jeff. He didn't appear to be a tall man; his legs, stretched out before him, looked on the short side. His belly bulged slightly under a light tee shirt and the hair on his head was thinning, despite his probably being no more than in his mid-thirties. It wasn't his physical appearance that concerned her, however, it was the distrust emanating from him. There were some people that didn't like 'her kind' and he was one of them. The fact that they'd even got through the door showed that Samantha Gordon really was in charge.

The sound of a door banging within the house – as though slammed in temper – made even the psychics amongst them jump. Samantha's hand flew to her mouth and her husband let rip an expletive. The young Ruby stopped crying and whimpered instead, her brother deciding to join her.

"What's happening?" Samantha gasped. "What the hell is going on? I didn't sign up for this when we bought the house."

"It's been worse since you called them in." Again, Jeff was muttering, not speaking to them, not even to Samantha; just throwing it out there.

Normally Theo would step forward at this moment and take charge. Her age lent her the authority necessary in such situations. But Ruby beat her to it.

"Right now, the assumption is that Benjamin Hamilton, the previous occupant, might still be in residence. Certain activity occurring in the house suggests that. Before I carry on, might it be a good idea to take the children to their rooms perhaps? I don't want to unsettle anyone."

"Unsettle anyone?" No longer passive-aggressive, Jeff

exploded, "I think you've done a good job of that already, haven't you? Look at my kids!"

Samantha was appalled. "Jeff! Please! We talked about this, we agreed this was the way forward, remember? The way to sort this problem out."

"I don't want my kids upset!" he retorted.

"The fact that they are is *not* Psychic Surveys' fault!"

Inwardly, Ruby groaned. They'd barely been here five minutes and already the situation was deteriorating – rapidly. There'd be a full-scale war amongst the living if she couldn't rescue the situation and quick. "Look, if you'd rather we left, Mr Gordon, I understand, but we're here now—"

There came a crash from the kitchen. The sound of a plate smashed against the floor perhaps? It certainly sounded like it. Their attention captured, all heads turned in the direction of the living room door, expecting the ghost of the tenant past to come hurtling through it and wrap his spectral arms around them in a far from welcoming manner. Trying to play it down, Ruby reminded herself what was really happening. Ben was feeding off the negative energy in the house – the fear – and growing angrier too. Considering he was already at fever pitch, this wasn't the best news.

Before she could say anything further, Ness came to stand by her side. "We can't deny that there's unusual activity in this house – activity of a paranormal nature. And, as you say, it's intensifying. We don't truly know the reason for that but, if you'll let us, we'll do our best to find out."

A part of Ruby was grateful for her colleague's firm, no-nonsense approach, but another part bristled. Pride – she must get it under wraps. And insecurity too, because that's what this was, she realised. She didn't quite feel the 'giant' that Ness was, or that Theo was. And she resented that.

Theo spoke loud and clear but her voice was soothing too. With children in the room, she was careful to tread softly. "Ness is right. We *can* sort this out, but only with your permission. And please, don't expect miracles straightaway, these things can take time. And effort. Rather a lot of effort, on everyone's part, including yours. It's essential to stay positive... optimistic. This is a beautiful house. I can see how much you love it. You've injected it with new life. You don't have to be at the mercy of what lingers here still. Not if you let us do our job. May we go into the kitchen?"

"Jeff?" There was a warning tone in Samantha's voice.

Whilst waiting to hear the verdict they all stood perfectly still, Cash's fingers only slightly brushing Ruby's in a show of support.

Jeff exhaled heavily. "Whilst you're busy, what the heck are *we* supposed to do?"

"Is there a friend you could—?"

"No! This is my house! Why should I leave it?"

"Fair enough," answered Theo, remaining determinedly unfazed by his attitude. "But leave the kitchen to us. Stay, here, in the living room."

He glared at Theo. "Why are there so many of you?"

"Jeff, stop asking questions. Let them get on with it!"

"All I bloody wanted to do was watch the telly tonight. Not much to ask for is it? A Saturday night in with my family and I mean *just* my family."

"Jeff!" Samantha said again, her face reddening – with anger or embarrassment it was hard to tell.

"Okay, okay, do what you have to bloody do," he relented.

"Thank you, Mr Gordon." As well as seize the moment, Ruby did her best to appease. "We'll, erm… we'll try not to be too long."

"Go through," Samantha nodded towards the kitchen, "and… good luck."

* * *

In the kitchen it was noticeably colder. Ben was here. No doubt about it. Although they still couldn't see him he was easy enough to sense. He was here and he was pissed off – beyond fever pitch. His anger was palpable.

Ness, ever practical, spied a broom in one corner, grabbed it, and brushed to one side the smashed plate. It had been thrown so hard it lay in smithereens. As much as they'd like to empty the kitchen of potential missiles, they didn't have time. But certainly what lay on the surface – more cups, a few plates, the bread board and a bottle of wine – they found room for in cupboards or the dishwasher. Ruby only thanked her lucky stars there was no knife block hanging around; she didn't fancy something sharp being thrown at her. She hadn't got her bag of paraphernalia but she could smell the scent of frankincense on at least two of her colleagues – an essential oil renowned for its protective qualities. They all had on their respective talismans as well, their tourmaline, their obsidian, pink quartz in Theo's case, and in Corinna's, a malachite necklace, a relatively new purchase, the green a wonderful contrast to her red hair.

There wasn't enough room to stand side-by-side, and so Ruby, Cash, and Corinna stood in front, Theo and Ness at the rear. Jed wasn't visible to her at the moment, but he was with her, she knew that. Lately he was *always* with her, or at least close by. Together, they sent a wall of light out to where Ben lurked, in the shadows, towards the back end of the kitchen.

Ruby drew her shoulders back and spoke out loud. "Ben, do you remember me? I'm Ruby. I came to see you before, a few days ago, along with my colleague, Ness. I know there are more of us this time but don't be alarmed. We're all here to help. We mean you no harm. I repeat, we mean you no harm and in turn we ask that you do not harm us. You've passed, Ben. I think that's something you're aware of. But your spirit remains grounded. We don't know why, not unless you communicate with us – peaceably," she reminded him. "Whatever reason it is, or *reasons*, we can help you. This must be a very confusing time for you, we understand that, but together we can make sense of it. We can walk with you to the light."

Although there was no reply, not even an expletive or two this time, the tension was building; each and every one of them could feel it.

"Ben, communicate with us. Tell us why you've chosen to stay."

The silence was stubborn.

"What you're doing," Ruby persevered, "staring at the new inhabitants of this house, hurling cups, hiding stuff, it's frightening them. And it's really not fair because they've done nothing wrong. Yes, they live here now, but they're looking after the house, they've redecorated, they can fill it with love if you let them. It's in good hands. You can leave knowing that."

A voice came from behind. "Ruby, I don't think this is

working—"

Maybe, but she wasn't ready to give up. "Ben, please, work with us, communicate, tell us what's wrong, we can help you. We *will* help you."

There were several spotlights in the ceiling above. The light from them had previously been glaring, but one by one they burst, plunging the kitchen into darkness. The suddenness with which it happened was startling. Around her, Ruby could feel her colleagues stiffen – everyone on guard. There was a creak and all heads turned towards it, anticipating. A cupboard door flew open and then shut again... open, shut, open, shut – it was relentless. Other cupboard doors too, as though joining in some kind of ghastly chorus, a cacophony of them. The noise was enough to cause Samantha to leave the safety of the living room and run into the kitchen, Jeff at her heels.

"What the hell—" she screeched before stopping dead. "Christ!"

Ruby was about to turn round, to try and reassure them in whatever way she could when she caught sight of a figure, crouching by the kitchen table, furtive yet menacing. A black figure, blacker than the darkness they'd been plunged into, the only thing truly discernible was his eyes. Her breath hitched. It was always the eyes – the window of the soul – *if* this thing had a soul.

"Of course he has a soul!" Ness whispered urgently. "Remember who we're dealing with, Ruby."

Ben – Benjamin Hamilton. That's whom they were dealing with, the past tenant of this house, once human and now adrift.

But his eyes, Ruby couldn't look away – it was as though they'd captured her. What was in them was not only horrifying but intriguing too. Such a vast range of emotions – and all of them so damned negative. The wall of light they'd sent out, it hadn't touched him. It hadn't even got close.

It was time to evacuate. What he was doing required a massive amount of energy, but she didn't think he was done yet. Knives came to mind again, there had to be knives in the drawers, sharp knives, maybe even a cleaver, something that could do serious damage. That could kill.

"Mum! Dad!"

It was the little girl.

Rapidly Ruby switched to thought, knowing Ben would be able to hear her well enough.

Ben, stop this! This is frightening the children and not helping you. Stop it at once. We're here to help you. Please, let us help you.

Fuck off, bitch! Or I'll skin you alive!

Skin her alive? What kind of threat was that?

Ben, why are you doing this? What's wrong?

"Ruby," it was Theo, "we've got to get out, it's dangerous to stay."

"Ruby, come on," Corinna echoed.

"Mum! What's happening? I don't like it!"

They were right. There was no reasoning with Ben. Not tonight.

Again, there was a child's cry. "Mum! I'm scared!"

"Darling, where are you going? Don't run off! Jeff, Jeff, go after her."

"Come on, Ruby, we've got to go. Now!" It was Cash, doing his utmost to cajole her. But Ben's eyes, the dark of them bored into the green of hers.

"RUBY!"

128

Was someone shouting at her or at the little girl?

"Ruby, we have to go."

"I can't…"

There was barking – furious barking – growling and a gnashing of teeth. She only barely registered Jed as hands grabbed her shoulders and dragged her backwards. The hands belonged to Ness. She'd been the one who'd shouted. There were more hands, Cash's this time, assisting Ness, getting her out of there, getting them *all* out of there as a mug flew out of the cupboard, smashed into the wall opposite, followed by another and another; a seemingly endless stream of them. From the wall a clock fell, a child's framed picture too. The kettle started to boil. What was it with the kettle? He seemed to have a thing about it. There were screams behind her; they hurt her ears, everyone was in retreat but still Ben's eyes held hers. Piercing orbs of wild fury and so, so defiant.

Someone was slamming doors again. Not Ben this time. It was Cash. Kicking the kitchen door shut, trying to contain what was inside. It broke the hold Ben had over her. The spell he'd cast. She blinked rapidly then looked around her. Everyone was tumbling down the hallway, spilling out into the street beyond as though the house was vomiting. The children were screaming. So loudly they screamed. She wished they'd stop. Jeff was shouting too. Samantha was crying. And people were materialising, real live people. It seemed like the entire population of Gilmore Street were forgoing their Saturday night viewing to see what the commotion was. They were making their way over to the frightened family wanting some kind of explanation; listening to the banging of cupboards inside – still opening, still shutting – a cheap psychic trick but oh so effective – and the smashing of crockery; pressing the Gordons for information and receiving only garbled replies; wanting to know who these people were that had tumbled out of the house with them – the *strangers*; looking at them in *that* way when Samantha did her best to tell them; staring, as Ben had stared. *Accusing*.

Chapter Thirteen

"SHIT! Shit! Shit!"

"Ruby, it's all right, calm down."

"No, Cash, it's not all right and I won't calm down. Did you see the way they looked at us, the other residents of Gilmore Street? Like we were the worst kind of people, like we were vermin. And that Ben, that bloody Ben. What the hell's wrong with him? Why's he doing this? What's his problem?"

"Have you got any whisky in the house, Cash, gin, anything?" Theo asked. "Get her a shot, a large one. She needs it."

"No, I don't—"

"Don't argue, Ruby. Just take the drink and get it down you."

They were back at Ruby's flat where they had taken refuge. Ruby sat on the sofa, too tired to argue, too distressed. It had been awful, truly awful. Not what had happened with Ben, they'd experienced worse, but the *aftermath* of Ben – the reactions from the living. She could hear them now – would hear them all night if the whisky didn't do its job and knock her out. 'They're what, Samantha? Psychics? There's a ghost in your house? Seriously? They're not having you on, tricking you? I'll bet they are tricking you; making it all up. People like that are experts in deceit. They take your money and run. Don't listen to them. Ghosts don't exist. It's the police you need.' On and on it had gone, the contempt and the vitriol. She'd wanted to yell at them, 'Listen to what's going on inside. You can hear it well enough. How can I make that up?' But by the time someone had gone in to investigate – and it was incredible how long it had taken that someone to pluck up the courage despite their cynicism – the banging and the shutting of cupboard doors had stopped. The carnage of Ben's psychic onslaught still remained however – but probably they would only see that as evidence of human behaviour gone mad, some sort of fracas or domestic that had spiralled out of control. Would any of them be able to accept a different explanation? Ever? Ah, the questions! So many questions!

Theo came over and took hold of her hands.

"I know. I know about the questions, they make your head hurt."

"It's not just that," Ruby tried to explain, feeling tears beginning to prick, "it was their expressions, their disbelief. And Jeff too, his attitude towards us."

"Ruby, this is an enlightened age, but we can't expect everyone to believe."

No, they certainly didn't. Not until they encountered a problem of the paranormal kind that is, and then belief was dredged up from somewhere. She knew that. She could handle that. Setting up Psychic Surveys on the high street was her way of saying to the world that she was here to help, that she was proud of her profession, that it was as valid as any other. So why had she felt so *ashamed* when they'd looked at her, at the rest of them, as though there were nothing more than cranks?

"Because you're tired, darling," Ruby could hear the exasperation in Theo's voice. "Because you need a holiday. How many times do I have to say it?"

"You need this as well." It was Cash, doing as instructed and handing her a generous tumbler of whisky, the pale amber of it glinting in the lamplight.

She took it from him and, as Theo advised, downed it in one.

The commotion had taken some time to peter out, and the children had grown hysterical at the prospect of re-entering the house. At least they – the inhabitants – had no doubts as to what was within. Not after what they'd just experienced. Even Jeff was ashen-faced; he kept casting furtive glances back towards dark windows, trying to come to terms with all that had taken place, to process it. Samantha was the brave one.

"Come on,' she'd put her arm round her husband, trying to coax him, "this is our house, you said it yourself. We won't be pushed out."

But it was clear they wouldn't be returning, not that night. Despite her neighbours' apparent concern, only Delia offered to give them shelter.

"I've got plenty of room, it'll be cosy." *And safe.* It would be that too.

It was Ruby and Cash who'd gone back in with Samantha to collect overnight stuff. Just before they re-entered number 44, a man asked if Samantha would like him to be the one to call the police, looking accusingly at Ruby and Cash as he said it. Tall and reedy, he didn't bother to hide the sneer on his pockmarked face.

"This is not a police matter," insisted Samantha. "These people will help us." Never had Ruby appreciated a vote of confidence so much.

Far from finished, the man reached out and laid a hand on Samantha's arm. "You've had a shock, love. We'll talk tomorrow. When you're making more sense."

Beside Ruby, Cash bristled – he was getting ready to give 'Mr Tall and Reedy' a rollicking or to deck him one – neither of which could be allowed to happen.

"Samantha, shall we…" Ruby said, trying to hurry her down the hallway.

Samantha nodded. "Yes, yes, of course, come on."

The tension in the house – although by no means gone – had dissipated. That was quite a display Ben had put on. It would have exhausted him. Even so, they didn't linger, Samantha didn't want to and neither did Ruby. She just wanted to get what was needed for the Gordon family, deliver them safely across the road and escape the 'rubberneckers' who were still crowded around outside. She was amazed the police *hadn't* been called; that someone other than 'Mr Tall and Reedy' hadn't taken it upon themselves to dial 999. And then she heard it – the police siren. Speeding closer.

Thank God for Ness and her police connections! Whilst the Gordon family, Cash and the Psychic Surveys team waited over at Delia's, the police searched number 44 Gilmore Street, locked it up on the family's behalf and then came over to interview everyone. Again and again, Samantha insisted the paranormal was responsible, not anyone living, and, because the police knew Ness, they were inclined to believe her – after a fashion. Still, Ruby detected a glint of disbelief in their eyes: a slight frown, a smile clamped down on. After the police had left, Jeff asked Psychic Surveys to leave too. Samantha didn't argue with him this time; she saw them out and at the door she whispered to Ruby that she'd be in touch. As they climbed back into their cars, curtains twitched and not so surreptitiously either, and Ruby almost prayed Samantha wouldn't ring, and that they'd never have to set foot in Gilmore Street again. Quickly she banished that thought – of course they'd have to, if Samantha wished it. That was their job. And Ben – the black crouching figure; his promise to skin her alive; the violence of the man; his eyes – if she never saw him again it would be too soon. But it *would* be soon: the Gordons couldn't stay at Delia's forever.

They'd driven back to Ruby's flat in De Montfort Road, coming together again under her roof and staying there for the next few hours, feeling the need for each other's company, those that were different to the norm, the outcasts. Briefly, she closed her eyes.

"What a mess," she lamented, despite the reassurances of her team. "What a bloody mess."

The police had got involved, plus the neighbours. Next it would be the press. *Any publicity is good publicity* was the saying, but not in this case. They hadn't been successful – far from it. That was the only thing the press would pick up on. All they'd be interested in, the *negativity* of it.

Asking for a second glass of whisky, she downed that quickly too.

Chapter Fourteen

"I can't believe you're doing this."

"It's my job, Cash!"

"It's Sunday, Ruby! If you won't take a holiday at least take a day off."

"But I can't, they need me—"

"They had no right calling you on a Sunday."

"Spirits don't realise it's Sunday for God's sake!"

"I know, but it's not the bloody spirit that called you!"

"Oh, Cash!" Despite herself, she had to smile. That's what he did for her: he lightened her, when she got too dark or too intense. Sometimes she wondered why he put up with her – the perfect boyfriend. She marvelled that such a thing even existed. But unless he was a master of illusion, it did.

When her mobile had rung this morning, dragging her from sleep, she was tempted to reach over, turn it off, and snuggle back into Cash. The warmth of his body was so inviting but whilst he slumbered on – it would take an earthquake to wake him sometimes, him and Jed – she'd reached over and checked the caller ID. She recognised the name as a client, one she'd spoken to earlier in the week regarding a 'haunting' in a house they'd just started to rent; a house with a history. A woman had lived there before, a quiet woman, well regarded by her neighbours. A woman, who'd shrugged on her coat one day, locked up the house behind her and made her way over to the village pond, whereupon she filled her coat pockets with rocks, as famous writer and perhaps the inspiration behind her actions, Virginia Woolf, had done, and drowned herself. After she had been reported missing, her body was found a few days later. The new occupant of the house – Lesley – who lived there with her partner, Steve, was convinced the woman had made her way back to the house, in ghostly form that is. Ruby had made an appointment to go and see them this coming week but obviously they couldn't wait – perhaps activity had ramped up in their house too. If so, she had no choice but to answer. Whispering 'Hello', she'd pushed back the covers and tiptoed from the room.

On the other end of the phone, Lesley whispered back, something that initially amused Ruby: there was something so infectious about whispering. But quickly she realised the woman was only doing so because she didn't want the 'ghostly' occupant of her house to hear her. Such a tactic wouldn't work; spirits tended to communicate in thought rather than words, but Ruby decided against telling her that, it would only add to her discomfort.

"I'm so sorry to disturb you," Lesley continued, "but the spirit… I don't know… she just seems so sad."

"If she committed suicide, sorrow would be her default emotion," Ruby explained.

"But it's been awful this weekend. I feel her everywhere I go in the house. And I can't stop crying. It's like I'm becoming her. I know it sounds silly—"

"No, it doesn't. Her mood is affecting you. That's what's happening." Or at least what Ruby guessed was happening.

"I don't think I can stand another day of it," Lesley had started to cry. "I'm sorry, I'm so sorry. I'm normally a happy person. That's *my* default emotion. But she's draining that happiness from me. Even my partner's noticed. He can't believe the change in me since we came here."

The despair in her voice moved Ruby, and worried her too. Despite knowing Cash would be cross, she offered to visit Lesley's house straightaway. As for the others in her team who also thought she needed a break, they didn't have to know, not until their catch-up meeting later in the week. She'd go there alone. She *wanted* to go alone; boost her self-confidence, which had been dented by yesterday's events. Waking Cash to tell him, he insisted on joining her too. He hated her going to client's houses alone, didn't think it was safe. It was part and parcel of her job, though, a fact she always retaliated with. On this occasion, however, she conceded, despite how cross he was that she was going at all.

Lesley and Steve's house was, in fact, a bungalow in the village of Lindfield, a forty-minute drive from Lewes. It was a beautiful village, with a rich architectural heritage. Many houses dated back to the fifteenth and sixteenth century, notably the Thatched House, which lay claim to having been a hunting lodge of King Henry VII. The Seears residence was not in the heart of the village, but on the outskirts and only dated back to the fifties.

The history of the unfortunate woman – Nancy Armitage – had been relayed to Ruby during her first phone call with Lesley. She'd been planning to carry out a bit more research about Nancy before she visited but caught on the hop like this there'd be no time. What she knew would have to suffice.

Lesley opened the door to Ruby and Cash, her tear-stained face breaking into a relieved smile. "I'm so glad to see you," she exclaimed. "Thank you for coming today. I really do appreciate it."

If Cash could catch thoughts she'd shoot him one along the lines of, 'See, sometimes you have to go the extra mile, people appreciate it.' It was good business practice and it might stand them in good stead if they were about to get a public lambasting, which she was convinced they were. Cash had argued otherwise, pointing out that she was worrying about something that hadn't even happened yet. She didn't court the press and amazingly none of her clients had spoken to reporters about them either, but she supposed she'd been living on borrowed time. Press attention – it was coming. Reminding herself to focus on the problem at hand, Ruby introduced herself and Cash to Lesley. Steve came forward too and shook their hands. His smile also held a tinge of sadness.

As Lesley rushed to make tea – something most clients did – Ruby tuned in. Nancy wasn't difficult to detect; she was standing in the kitchen, just behind Lesley as she found a teapot, started to warm it, and then searched for teabags. An outline at first, Nancy became more substantial as Ruby concentrated, grateful to Cash for keeping the Seears preoccupied with chitchat so that she had an opportunity to do that. Only once did Nancy glance towards Ruby, clearly becoming aware of her too. Her entire focus seemed to be on Lesley. It was as if she were *shadowing* her.

Moving to the conservatory to drink their tea – a selection of candle holders and framed photos dotted artfully around – Lesley and Steve embarked again on telling her what it was like living in the bungalow; how 'creepy' it got.

"It's like she's always with me, as though she follows me around," Lesley explained, pushing strands of reddish hair away from her face. She motioned to Steve. "He feels her presence too, I think anyone would, it's so strong but... I think it's me she wants, although I've no idea why."

Ruby didn't know 'why' either – not yet – but she did know that Lesley's instinct about Nancy's 'obsession' was right. She was standing behind Lesley again, staring down at her – a look of pure longing on her face.

What is it, Nancy? What do you want from her?

The woman's head turned at the mention of her name, confirming to Ruby her identity at least, but it was only for the briefest of moments.

Ruby would have preferred to be left alone with the spirit in order to connect further. Rather like Ellie's 'snapshots', Ruby sometimes experienced what she described as 'flashcards': a series of images flashing into her mind concerning the spirit she was focusing on, depicting their life and the events in it. It wasn't something that happened all the time, it was quite rare, and it wasn't happening with Nancy. The dead knew how to cloak themselves as much as the living. Maybe she'd be able to get further if the two of them were alone, but she guessed if Lesley left the room, Nancy would too.

She explained the situation to Steve and Lesley and they both decided to stay whilst Ruby did her best to reason with Nancy. During this conversation, Steve reached out his hand to cover Lesley's in a show of support that Ruby found touching.

Although able to communicate with the spirits in thought, Ruby decided she'd look odd remaining silent so decided to speak out loud.

"Nancy, I can see you, you know that, don't you?"

Nancy ignored her, so Ruby tried again, taking in her appearance, the plainness of her skirt and blouse, her flat shoes, her short, almost utilitarian haircut. Plain was how she'd felt in life and how she'd clothed herself in spirit. This was a woman who'd forgotten how to have fun a long, long time ago; who'd found life anything but. There'd been no light to balance the dark or the intensity; no Cash or Steve on hand to help.

"Nancy, what happened to make you so sad? You can tell us, we're listening. Nobody here means you any harm. We only want to help. All of us."

The spirit clenched her hands, a sign of distress.

"Nancy, please don't get angry." She really didn't think she could stand another spirit throwing a full-on tantrum so soon after Benjamin, but quickly she realised her worry was unfounded. There was no anger in Nancy, just a feeling of being thoroughly overwhelmed.

"What were you overwhelmed by, Nancy?"

Life.

At last she'd decided to communicate.

Lesley leaned towards Ruby slightly. "Is anything happening? Are you getting anywhere?"

Ruby nodded and smiled at Lesley, but quickly turned her attention back to Nancy, not wanting to interrupt the flow of communication.

"You keep looking at Lesley—"

"Oh my God, does she?"

"Lesley," Cash interjected, "it's fine. Ruby's got it under

control."

His soothing voice was so much like Theo's. Quickly, Lesley settled and then she started crying again, fat tears rolling down her face. "I'm so sorry," she apologised for the umpteenth time, "forgive me. This happens. The sadness, the grief... it comes in waves, huge waves that engulf me."

"Nancy's crying too," explained Ruby. "Looking at you both, I think you're around the same age, in your mid-fifties, is that correct?"

Lesley indicated it was. She actually looked much younger than her years, so did Steve, but Nancy knew better.

"What is it about Lesley that fascinates you, Nancy? We're curious."

Why not me?

Again, Nancy projected the thought but kept her gaze on Lesley steady.

"I don't understand, what do you mean 'why not me?'"

Lesley's eyes grew wide. "Is that what she said?"

"There's nothing to be worried about." It was Ruby who assured Lesley this time. At least she presumed there wasn't anything to be worried about. But she'd been wrong before. *Keep your nerve, Ruby, you can do this.*

She could, of course she could. But she had to admit, it would be so much easier to be left alone with Nancy but Nancy didn't want to play it that way. With the couple staring at her as intently as Nancy was staring at Lesley, she felt a bit like she had at Alicen and Andy's – like a performing monkey, even though they were perfectly nice people. Her paranoia was getting the better of her again. At any rate, what she was going to say next – and Nancy's reaction to it – would prove the turning point.

"Nancy, you've passed. You left your house one morning and made your way to the pond that lies just off the Lindfield High Street. Once there, you placed heavy stones in your pocket, walked into the water and drowned. You ended your own life. And yet you haven't moved on. Instead, you came home again, to dwell here in spirit. Nancy, do you understand what I'm saying?"

Tears continued to roll down Nancy and Lesley's cheeks.

"Nancy, why are you so fixated on Lesley? Your sadness is affecting her too. It's frightening for her. Nancy, are you lonely?"

Ruby could sense Nancy stiffen. A theory popped into her head concerning Nancy's return. If she was right, Lesley and Steve being here was even more of a problem. What should she do? Voice her theory or keep quiet? She took a deep breath and continued. This was her job and results were achieved in a variety of ways. She mustn't shy away from that.

"Nancy, you cannot take Lesley into spirit with you. I know you're lonely, I can sense that well enough. But you mustn't project your feelings and thoughts on to her any longer. You must leave. Your true home is in the light. You'll be happier there. And you won't be alone, not anymore."

Ruby held her breath – if Lesley didn't hit the roof, Steve probably would at what she was intimating: that Nancy wanted to *kill* Lesley, by manipulating her, by making her feel as she did, by driving her to suicide. She had a sudden vision of her career in tatters if she couldn't pull this off. After Gilmore Street, the last thing she should do is alienate more people.

Although Lesley and Steve looked shocked, as did Cash, they remained silent. Ruby felt like crying now, with relief. Even so, she started to apologise for her words but Lesley shook her head.

"It's okay. To be honest, I guessed that's what she was trying to do. I... well, I have been having thoughts lately."

"Sweetheart..."

Lesley graced Steve with a smile, "Don't worry, I wouldn't do anything, I wouldn't leave you, you know that. And I'm not angry at Nancy, not at all. I just feel so damned sorry for her. I've never suffered from depression, the black dog as they call it. I've never *understood* it. But I do now and it is... it's unbearable." Dabbing at her eyes, she asked Ruby if she might stand. "Tell me where she is, I want to talk to her myself."

Lesley's generosity was mind-blowing. Ruby recalled how long they'd been living here with Nancy, a good few months now, Lesley's mood deteriorating all the while. Yet she wasn't angry, not even at the threat of what Nancy ultimately wanted from her. In some people kindness reigned; anger didn't stand a chance. Ruby both admired and envied that. She informed Lesley that Nancy was right behind her and Lesley stood up.

"I've never done this before," she glanced only briefly at Ruby as she said it, her soft voice filling the otherwise silent room, "I've never spoken to her. Perhaps I should have done. It felt a bit, you know... strange."

"I do know," replied Ruby, "but if you could, I think it would help."

Lesley cleared her throat. "Okay, here goes. Nothing ventured, nothing gained." She couldn't know it but you'd be hard pushed to get a hand between Nancy and Lesley's faces. Their noses were almost touching. "Nancy, I'm so sorry for the misery you suffered in life. I'm so sorry that the happiness that I enjoy passed you by. That's what you meant, isn't it, when you said *why not me?* You want to know why you couldn't be happy too. But so many people aren't and it's not their fault. It's not your fault either. Depression is… a burden. I think that's the best way of describing it. And some people tire of carrying it. And do you know what? I don't blame them."

Whilst Lesley imparted her heartfelt words, Ruby looked at Cash. Her heart swelled at the sight of him. His eyes were shiny too, a reflection of her own no doubt, and Steve's. She wondered whether she should intercept, try and 'steer' Lesley, but decided against it. Nancy was listening too intently.

"Life *is* overwhelming, even I feel that at times. It's not for everyone. In fact, I sometimes think a lot of people are too good for this world. It can be harsh, completely crazy, and dangerous too. Even so, I want to carry on living in it for a while longer. And that's the difference between us, Nancy. I don't *want* to join you. I'm sorry you were lonely, I don't think you deserved to be, but people are strange sometimes; they don't reach out to others, even when perhaps they know that they should. Too busy I suppose, and… just too blinkered. So many people go through life unaware rather than uncaring, their sight turned inwards, their concern only for themselves. But I've learnt something by knowing you: to keep an eye out for others, to notice signs that might suggest all is not well and to help where I can. There's a woman who lives along the road, she's old, and she lives alone. Maybe I'll bake her a cake or something." Lesley laughed. "She'll probably think I'm mad, wonder what the heck I'm doing, but then again, she might not. She might invite me in for a slice and a cup of coffee. She might fancy a bit of a chat." She shrugged. "You never know unless you try." Growing serious, she gestured towards Ruby. "She said you've got a home to go to, a true home, not this one. I think she means somewhere like heaven, where you've people waiting for you. Why don't you go towards it, Nancy? You weren't happy here, so what's the point in hanging around and prolonging the agony? As I've told you, I'm not coming with you, not yet. Go, Nancy, but thank you because you've taught me to be a better person."

Ruby decided she had to say something and rose to her feet too.

"Nancy, suicide is not the ultimate sin some belief systems teach. There's no need to be afraid. You belong in the light and you always have done."

Nancy's eyes held Lesley's but slowly she turned her body towards Ruby, no longer ignoring her – or transfixed. Ruby seized her chance.

"Nancy, you've done *nothing* wrong. Go home and rest awhile. It's time."

It took a few more moments – moments in which everyone living could barely breathe, the anticipation was so intense – but slowly, slowly Nancy started to step back, away from Lesley, retreating farther into the kitchen, becoming less substantial, fading. But before she disappeared, Ruby saw that she looked younger, much younger, the pain that had aged her beginning to fade too. Any trace that remained would hopefully evaporate when the light overwhelmed her instead of life.

"The room feels lighter." Lesley looked around in awe. "It feels like... mine. Did we do it? Did we send her home?"

"*You* did it," Ruby said, also feeling bolstered.

"Me? Seriously?"

"Seriously, Lesley. You did a great job."

Chapter Fifteen

DETERMINED to make the most of the late afternoon and evening together, Ruby and Cash reclaimed Sunday. Before switching her phone off, she'd rung Corinna to see if she and Presley could make that drink they'd talked about the previous night. Corinna was delighted.

"But no work talk, Ruby. Promise?"

Ruby frowned. Was she really the workaholic they all insisted she was? She decided against querying it – she was in too good a mood.

The evening went well, the four of them bagging a table in the window of The Rights of Man pub and chatting amiably before heading further up the road to an Italian restaurant for a meal and even more wine. By the time Ruby and Cash were on their way home, Ruby's head was swimming, but it felt good, the amount she'd drunk giving her an excuse to act silly as she pulled an uncomplaining Cash through the front door and slammed it shut.

"Tell me, Cash," she said, draping herself over him, "are you really too good to be true?"

"You keep asking me this, babe," he replied, his eyes more serious than hers, "but no, I'm not."

"I don't keep asking!"

"You imply it."

"That's not the same."

"It's as good as."

She screwed up her nose. "Are you sure, though? You haven't got some deep, dark secret tucked away, something that will float to the top eventually and blow us out of the water? Ruin everything we have?"

"You're doing it again."

"Doing what?"

"Letting paranoia get the better of you."

She started to protest but he stopped her.

"Ruby, stop. We've had a great evening, let's just… continue to enjoy it."

She turned coquettish. "Oh, and what do you have in mind?"

Sweeping her off her feet, ignoring her protests, he carried her through to the bedroom and threw her on the bed. Stripping his tee shirt off, he stood before her, his caramel skin taut across his chest.

"Regarding what I have in mind, Ruby Davis, take a wild guess."

* * *

Cash had risen first the next morning, muttering as he got out of bed about the hell of early work appointments. Mondays were largely given over to admin for Ruby, there was nothing pressing, so she decided to sleep in for another hour or so and get to the office for ten. It'd been a heavy weekend in more ways than one, and her body was screaming for more duvet time.

Later on, after showering, dressing and with a piece of toast still in her hand, she let herself out of her flat. She had just put the toast in her mouth and the key in the lock when she heard a voice close behind her.

"Ruby, I hope you don't mind—"

"What?"

She spun round. It was Ellie, the morning sunlight bouncing off her hair, making it seem almost golden, and a tentative smile on her face. Ruby was stunned. She may have found out her mobile number from a business card but she sure as hell didn't have her home address on there! Hastily removing the toast from her mouth, she didn't bother to beat about the bush this time.

"How do you know where I live?"

"I… erm…"

"Well?"

"I'm staying not far from you, just round the corner, in Leicester Street. I've seen you coming and going. Lewes is a small place."

She was about to disagree, it wasn't that small, but then what Cash had said the previous night came to mind, about letting her paranoia get the better of her. Paranoia, pride, insecurity – all attributes she was allowing to dominate. She needed to watch that. It was perfectly feasible Ellie had seen her come and go several times. And she may well have seen Ellie, but not registered the fact. After all, there was nothing about Ellie that stood out. She wasn't being mean, just honest. Looking down at herself she wondered what it was about *her* that stood out – certainly not the clothes she liked to wear: jeans, boots, tee shirts and jumpers. She looked unremarkable and deliberately so. Being that way put her clients at ease.

"Well… erm… how can I help you, Ellie?" They had another regression session booked but not until Wednesday.

"I wondered if we could go for a coffee to talk about

another dream I've had."

"We can talk about that on Wednesday, perhaps meet a bit earlier. Right now, I've got to get to the office."

"Please, just a coffee, it won't take long."

And there it was, that thread of steel running through her, so at odds with her more vulnerable side. Ruby wondered what to do. She'd rather leave it until Wednesday but saying no to this girl was proving difficult. Again, she had that sense of unease. What was it about Ellie that set her teeth on edge? There was definitely some kind of threat but was it real or imagined? All the girl was suggesting was a quick coffee, would that be so bad?

"Okay," Ruby conceded. "We'll go to that café around the corner, but I'll have to be quick. I really do have a busy day ahead of me."

"I understand," Ellie replied. "Thank you."

Ruby started walking and Ellie fell into step beside her. The girl kept glancing at her and smiling, a 'grateful' sort of smile. Ruby felt uncomfortable because of it, disingenuous even. It was a good job Ellie couldn't read minds.

Thankfully, it was just five minutes to the café, enough time to comment on the weather – it was pleasantly mild, promising a good summer to come – and how busy the streets of Lewes were, with everyone getting into the stride of a new week. Ruby asked if Ellie had had a good weekend. She said it had been quiet. They were through the door before Ellie could ask about hers.

Selecting a table near the window, they ordered their drinks.

"Any food to go with that?" the waitress asked disinterestedly.

Ruby shook her head. *Let's keep this short and sweet.*

As the waitress retreated, Ruby noticed Ellie twisting a silver ring round and round the finger on her right hand – a nervous habit perhaps? At least she was leaving the sore patch on her arm alone.

"Ellie, your latest dream…" Ruby prompted.

Ellie straightened. "Oh yes, yes, of course. It's strange you know, but before I go to sleep at night, I just know I'm going back to my previous life. It's like it won't let me go. Not until I find out what happened to me, until I'm brave enough to remember it all. But slowly it's becoming clearer, bit by bit."

"Like a jigsaw, it's starting to fall into place."

"That's exactly what it's like. I knew you'd understand! There are still gaps in it. Big gaping holes, but I'm getting there. With your help."

"And Ness's," Ruby reminded. "Ailsa's too."

"Yeah, the three of you. Some feel their future is in good hands with certain people. Well, with you three, my past is." She paused for a second. "If I was dealing with this alone, I don't know, I'd be lost right now. I'd be so confused." The look on her face told Ruby she genuinely meant this.

The waitress returned and set their drinks in front of them, pointing to the sugar and sweeteners.

Lifting her cup and taking a sip, Ruby savoured the richness of it. The café might hire surly waitresses but the coffee they served was second to none.

Ellie too took a sip but then pushed her cup aside, still intent on trying to make sense of what was happening. "The dreams… the snapshots… it's like looking through a window. Sometimes there's frost on the window and everything's obscured, at other times it's crystal clear. This man I'm afraid of, there *were* happier times with him. In one of the snapshots, we were laughing, I mean *really* laughing. He'd said something funny, made a joke or something."

Remembering how controlling he'd been on their wedding day, Ruby asked, "Did he ever laugh at any of *your* jokes?"

"I… don't know. Why?"

"Because the way you've described the relationship so far, it seems to be a one-way street. It's his way or the highway."

"Yeah, it does, I agree."

"And we know it turned to shit the minute you stepped over the threshold into your marital home. Those were your words exactly. You've also seen scenes, or snapshots, with blood in them, your blood you think. We know it didn't just go wrong, Ellie. It went horribly wrong."

"It did. But what I'm trying to say is that there were good times also. They might have been on his terms, but from what I can see, what I can *remember*, I had feelings of love for him once."

"Love can be blind," Ruby replied, feeling the need to remain down to earth with Ellie. After all, the whole point of the exercise was to uncover an unsolved crime, not get caught up in the hearts and flowers of it all.

"It's still important," Ellie insisted. "It helps me to understand."

"Understand what?"

"The person behind the monster. It helps me not to be so scared. And if I'm not so scared perhaps I'll get a stronger vision of him – his name even. We'll be able to identify him."

"We'll need his forename *and* surname for that. And even then, it might not lead anywhere. You have to be prepared to accept that, Ellie. This could all be for nothing."

"I don't think so," she shook her head as she said it.

Ruby stood firm too. "We've said it before, both Ness and I, sometimes the past should remain where it is. Digging it all up again—"

"You said you'd help."

"I said I'd sit in for a couple more sessions and see where that gets us. After that, the case is up for review. Ellie, we haven't even got a location or a timeframe."

"We know it's a seaside town because of the gulls circling overhead. We know there's a pier, the one he wanted to find work on."

"Lots of seaside towns have piers, so it could be anywhere in the UK."

"Okay, but regarding timeframe, I think I've cracked it."

"Oh?"

"In last night's dream, I'm standing in front of a mirror, looking at myself. It's such a strange sensation, like I'm a passenger inside, hitching a lift, gazing outwards. I'm in a bedroom, a girl's bedroom and there are posters plastered all over the walls. I've got my radio on. It's my bedroom, I think, at my parents' house. I know what I'm doing; I'm going to meet him. I'm getting all dressed up." Ruby noticed Ellie's eyes growing misty as she recalled. "I'm so excited to see him again. Oh, that feeling! I've had boyfriends in this life, as Ellie, I mean. Well I've had a couple, but I've never felt the way I do in these dreams. It's like I'm on fire, Ruby, like I'm burning up! He's so handsome. I don't think he knows how much. It just doesn't register. He's got the sort of looks you dream about – *hero* looks. He's different, he's dark, he's mysterious, he's edgy, you know? Not like the boys on my wall."

Despite herself, Ruby was intrigued. "Who's on the posters?"

It was as though Ellie had gone into a trance, as if she were in the midst of regression. Ruby pushed her cup aside too, only half drunk.

"Ellie?"

"Clean-cut boys, four of them; there's wording just above them, the Fab Four. It's the Beatles, isn't it? That's what they used to call them."

"You mentioned a radio." Ruby felt like she'd stepped into Ailsa's shoes. "What's playing? The Beatles?"

"No, it's another song, but I don't recognise it or who's singing it."

"Never mind," Ruby said, "we can always come back to that another time. Tell me what you're wearing in this particular… dream."

"I've had my hair freshly done, it's bobbed and I'm pleased with how shiny it looks. I'm dressed in a pale blue jumper and darker trousers. They're navy, tapered. On my feet are slip-ons. I think I look nice, like I've just stepped out of a magazine. I hope he likes my new look. I hope he's proud of me. I'm so excited. I'm hugging myself. I can barely breathe."

"The Beatles on the wall, the way you're dressed, it sounds like the era you're in is the one we first thought of – the nineteen sixties."

"The swinging sixties! Oh, I think it is, definitely. And remember I said I loved Elvis, that I'm a real fan? It makes sense it's around then." She sighed, almost swooned. "It's such a wonderful time to be young, there's just so many more opportunities. For us too, for me and for him." Some of her enthusiasm starts to wane. "And then the dream changes. I can hear a voice. It's coming from below. Someone's calling me, my mum I think. Yes it's my mum; she's saying something about dinner. I shout back, tell her I'm not hungry and then I'm not quite so excited anymore. I stop hugging myself. Stand with my arms by my side instead. My eyes start to water."

"You're sad? Why?"

"Because I'm going to miss her and Dad. I'm going to miss my room too, the posters on the wall and the dressing table with my make-up on; the carpet, worn in patches where I lie on my tummy, my legs in the air, listening to music. I'm going to miss the world that I know, that I've loved."

"But you're only going out for the night."

"No, Ruby, I'm not. There's a small suitcase on the bed. I'm not just going out for the night. I'm doing a lot more than that."

"What is it, Ellie? What are you doing?"

"I'm running away."

* * *

It took a few moments but Ellie came to. She was wholly present now. Ruby sat back in her chair as Ellie did, the pair of them mirroring each other.

"Do you realise you went into a bit of a trance there, Ellie? Similar to how you are when you're under hypnosis, as if you've travelled back in time, or at least a part of you has."

"That's what it feels like all the time lately, as if I'm only half here. The other half is way back in the past. It's like quantum physics gone mad." Her stab at humour caused Ruby to smile.

"And this is ever since Katharine unleashed the beast, so to speak?"

Ellie smiled too. "The beast is about right."

"If we continue with your case, we may need to speak to Katharine. Would that be possible?"

"Probably. I can ask."

"Perhaps we ought to do that soon. Just to get a more rounded picture."

"I'm sorry it's all so bitty." Ellie seemed so downcast about it.

"Hey, that's okay. It's a process. You have to go through it." Ruby faltered. "Well, you're *choosing* to go through it. There's a bit of a difference."

"I… did Ness tell you about my background?"

Ruby was honest. "Yes, she did. That you're adopted, your relationship with your parents is troubled, that you live in a hostel at the moment."

Ellie nodded. "It's my Mum I have trouble with. She doesn't like me."

"I'm sure that's not true—"

"It is true. I've accepted it and so has she."

"Do you know your birth mother?"

"No, she left strict instructions for me not to find her. Even so, I've been tempted; it's not hard nowadays, is it? Not with the Internet and everything. But… I've resisted. I don't want to be disappointed again I think. At least in my past life I had a connection with my mother. I wouldn't have been so upset about leaving her if not. I was wanted back then."

Ruby frowned. "Is that what's at the root of all this?"

"It's just one part of it. I don't know who I am, *why* I am. But if I've lived before, even if that life ended badly, it means I'm someone."

"You're someone regardless."

"Perhaps. But there's a bigger picture, and that's kind of comforting."

"Even if you uncover a murder?"

"And a murder*er*," Ellie finished.

Cold comfort Ruby would have thought.

"Ness is a lost soul too, isn't she?"

"Ness?" queried Ruby. "Why'd you say that?"

"Because she doesn't belong anywhere either."

That was news to Ruby. "Did she tell you that?"

"No, but lost souls usually empathise with one another."

Ruby considered her words. She was right. That's what Ness had done, she had *empathised* with Ellie; taken her under her wing.

"So you don't know *why* Ness is a lost soul as you put it?" Ruby probed.

"No, I just know she is."

In a way Ruby was glad Ellie remained in ignorance too. If Ness had confided in her, someone she'd only just met as opposed to herself, whom she'd known for a number of years, she would have felt hurt. That Theo knew more about Ness was fine as they went way back, but Ellie was a newcomer.

Ruby! Are you adding jealousy to your list of sins?

No, she wasn't. She mustn't.

Ellie looked anxious all of a sudden. "You will help me,

won't you?"

"I've said we would—"

"It's just I really feel we're getting somewhere now. It won't be long until we've found out who I am and what he did to me. And that's all I want you to do. Help me find out. I promise I'll understand if you don't want to be involved after that, if for Psychic Surveys the case is closed. If there's anything to take further, it'll be my responsibility. But even if what I discover is horrible, it's something I have to do. If there's justice to be had, I'll work towards getting it. If not, I'll move on, leave behind that life, and what I've lived of this one too. But, I don't know, somehow I'll be whole. I'll be born again."

Born again? That was one way of looking at it.

Chapter Sixteen

HAVING said goodbye to Ellie, telling her she'd see her on Wednesday and hoping sincerely she didn't pop up out of nowhere any time before then, Ruby decided to walk the rest of the way to her office. There were no appointments in the book today. She needn't take her battered but reliable Ford, she'd leave it parked at home. She considered the meeting with Ellie to be a positive one. She felt better disposed towards her, especially as the girl had promised that after two more sessions it was over, for Psychic Surveys at least. Ellie wasn't so bad despite the unease she provoked, just different. And that whole issue the girl had around her identity, Ruby understood. Although she knew her parentage through the maternal line, Ruby had no idea who her own father was. All she knew – and this was information only recently extracted from her mother – was that he was a policeman, an ordinary man, not psychic at all. And married too. Jessica had been having an affair with him, that's why he'd walked away when he'd found out she was pregnant; he didn't want anything to do with her or the baby she was carrying and his 'real' life disrupted. Ruby hadn't asked Jessica for his name yet, but she would when life wasn't so hectic. She'd find out whether he was still alive for a start, and if so, whether he'd be agreeable to meeting her or not. One day, but not now; when she felt more able to deal with the 'or not' option perhaps, with the likelihood of rejection.

Reaching her front door, she dismissed such thoughts, focusing instead on the weekend just passed. Not a total disaster, it'd had its highlights: Nancy for example. Regarding Gilmore Street, she'd call Samantha and discuss how to take the case with Benjamin forward. Hopefully, the Gordons had calmed down, along with the fuss caused by what had happened. News tended to get old quickly. Current events took over. Thank God. Maybe Samantha had spoken to her neighbours and managed to fob them off. Hopefully she'd realised it probably wasn't best to keep going on about a 'ghost'. There were ways of announcing things to the world and the way she'd done it – hysterically – wasn't one of them. It'd be all right. It'd be fine. No need for the press to get involved at all.

Think positive, Ruby.

She would, and she'd stay that way. Attract the good things in life, not more trouble.

* * *

Climbing the stairs, step after narrow step, Ruby longed once more for an office on the ground floor. Not because she was unfit, but because it would lend her practice more respectability somehow. Attics and basements had a certain stigma attached to them; a somewhat 'hidden' quality. Even so, she was fond of her office in the sky. It was a home-from-home, although, as she opened the door and saw how cramped it was getting with furniture and books she decided it could do with a clear out – once and for all. No more threatening to do it, she'd schedule in a definite time. No sooner had she fired her laptop into life than the phone rang. Picking it up, she noticed the answer machine blinking furiously. No change there then.

"Hello, Psychic Surveys, how can I he—"

"Ruby, is that you?"

"Samantha, hi. Yes it's me. I was just going to call you."

"I'm so sorry," Samantha continued in a rush. "So, so sorry."

Alarm bells started ringing.

"Erm… I don't understand. What have you got to be sorry about?"

"The *South Coast Times* have been round. I tried to tell them what happened wasn't your fault, that you and your team were trying to get rid of the ghost. But I don't know, they just seemed hung up on Psychic Surveys more than anything. Kept calling you a ghostbuster."

Ruby swallowed. "A ghostbuster?"

"That's right. One of the reporters, only young he was, kept smirking. I hate that, don't you, when people smirk? Kept humming the words of that song, you know: 'something strange in the neighbourhood? Who you gonna call?'"

"Yeah, yeah, Ghostbusters. I get it."

Reaching one arm behind her, Ruby felt for the arm of her captain's chair and sank down onto it. Her worst fear had come true. The press had got hold of the story and they would vilify her. It might have been different if she'd succeeded, but she hadn't, Benjamin was still at large and the Gordons had had to move out. Remembering cases such as the Enfield Poltergeist, how decades later it was still talked about, Ruby shuddered. What had happened in Gilmore Street was prime tabloid fodder.

"Samantha, are you still at Delia's?"

"Yes, yes, my kids and Jeff, they won't go back."

"And who called the press?"

"Not me, Ruby, I swear! I wouldn't do such a thing. I believe in the paranormal, I've told you. It must have been one of the neighbours."

Of course it was, maybe the same one who'd called the police.

She glanced at her answerphone again, at the red light blinking, the digital display that told her eleven messages were waiting. How many of them were cases and how many of them reporters? She dreaded to think.

She let her head fall forward into one hand. She felt stupid for being optimistic earlier; for fooling herself it would be all right. She'd have to deal with the *South Coast Times*, hope that the reportage remained local and that it didn't spread further – although local was bad enough. Despite trying to cast their net wide, most of their cases *were* local – still. Only a few had come in from further afield, which they either travelled to or used freelance staff from a nationwide database they were developing of other willing psychics. There was no profit from those jobs, not yet, but hopefully there would be. You had to speculate to accumulate. She pulled herself up. There she went again – *hoping*. But that hope was dwindling. There was no doubt about it, if the article was negative, the impact could be huge. A witch hunt would result in her business being driven underground.

And stop, Ruby! Get a grip! You're getting carried away.

She also remembered Samantha was still on the phone – someone who needed her help. She wouldn't run and hide, even though she was sorely tempted. She'd face the storm head-on.

"Samantha, whatever happens with the press, I'll deal with it. Regarding Ben, do you want Psychic Surveys to take this case forward?"

"No question about it, I want you to come back."

"And your husband? It's important he's in agreement."

"Jeff will do what I tell him. Leave him to me."

"Samantha—"

"Honestly, he's fine, he wants it sorted, just like I do."

"Okay, let's focus on that then, sorting it."

"There's another problem, though."

"Another?" As if things weren't bad enough!

"The press, they haven't gone away, they're camped outside. I'm having a problem getting into my house so God knows how you're going to manage."

* * *

Ruby phoned Cash in tears. Next, when she'd managed to compose herself, she phoned the rest of the team, her voice a whole lot steadier. An emergency meeting was called – all of them emulating the solemnity of Ness, as they trooped into her office not even half an hour later. At her feet Jed was lounging, looking up every now and again to check on her. *I'm all right, Jed, honestly.* Or at least she felt better with her friends around her.

"It'll die down." Ness spoke first. "Press attention always does."

"But the people who read it, they don't forget," Ruby argued.

"Look," said Cash, "it's not Halloween. Minds are on where to go for the summer not spooks."

Corinna wasn't so sure. "Ghosts are a popular topic at any time of year, Cash. And it's the non-believers who usually shout the loudest."

Theo agreed. "The cynical are such a pain."

Using the example of the Enfield Poltergeist again, a case that had captured the attention of the country, so much so there'd been films made about it, Ruby pointed out that press attention doesn't always die down. Back in the 1970s, two sisters aged eleven and thirteen, who lived in a council house in the London Borough of Enfield, were targeted by a malevolent force. Ruby remembered being fascinated by the case as a child, studying several pictures in a magazine of the children levitating: suspended in mid-air by an invisible force before being hurled at the wall. The case held the nation spellbound for years, puzzling policemen, psychics, experts in the occult and hardened reporters alike, all of who spent time camping at the house to witness phenomena. As well as furniture being thrown, flying objects swirling towards witnesses, cold breezes and physical assaults, matches would spontaneously burst into flames – it really was quite a spectacle. Members of the Society for Psychical Research got involved, most notably Guy Lyon Playfair who wrote a book about it – a bestseller apparently – just one of many on the subject, some denouncing it as a hoax; others protesting stringently that it was genuine. As recently as a year or so ago there'd been a BBC drama about the event; a very good one, starring Timothy Spall as Maurice Grosse, the man who'd led the paranormal investigation. Ruby had enjoyed it, sitting on the sofa beside Cash, both of them enthralled. The family who'd endured such torture had long since left the house and another family lived there, one who didn't want to be identified. Whether it was the house or the family that was haunted, Ruby didn't know, but the fact they were still making programmes about the case, over forty years later, went to show the public had an appetite for this sort of thing – a *huge* appetite. It also showed there was currently a gap in the market and that a new 'Enfield' was needed.

The team listened to Ruby's concerns and then dismissed them.

"The important thing to do, Ruby, is not to 'big' it up in your mind like this. We'll go back to Gilmore Street, we'll send Benjamin on his way and we'll carry on with our daily business."

"But it's not that straightforward is it, Theo? Benjamin won't go!"

"He will... eventually."

"And meanwhile we're in a goldfish bowl with gleeful reporters looking on."

"Then we walk away," Ness suggested. "We refuse to get involved further."

"We can't do that," Ruby retorted.

"Why not?"

"Because the damage has been done! We're involved. If we walk away as soon as the heat is on, it would look... suspicious, it'd portray us in a bad light." Ruby exhaled heavily. "I'm only surprised the press aren't here already."

Ruby caught the look that Cash and Corinna exchanged.

"Cash, Corinna, what aren't you telling me?"

Corinna blushed, whilst Cash examined his shoes.

"Cash!" Ruby said again.

"Well, there were a couple hanging round actually, one from the *South Coast Times* and one from the *Sussex*

Express. I put them right, though, told them to scram."

Ruby closed her eyes. "So quick." It was all she could say.

"They're probably at a loose end," offered Cash. "I mean, it's not as if there's real news to report on, murders, rapes, wars, massive population displacement. Oh no, none of that grabs them. Get wind of a haunting, however…"

Ruby groaned as Theo glared at Cash. "There were only two of them, darling," the older woman emphasised. "Probably popped up in their tea-break."

"There'll be more." She knew it and they did too.

"So, we're the new Enfield," commented Corinna. "What happened with that particular spirit? Did they manage to shift it?"

"It's a long time since I looked at the case," responded Theo, "but from what I remember psychic activity diminished at the house but didn't die down entirely. Until the day they moved the family still felt as though they were being watched. The next tenants to move into the house also reported feeling uncomfortable. Their sons would wake in the night apparently, hearing disembodied voices. They moved out pretty swiftly too. The current family, as Ruby's just said, don't wish to be identified, so who knows what's going on."

"It could be that subsequent families were influenced by the power of suggestion," Ruby offered. "As with Ellie, it's imagination run riot."

"Ellie's case is genuine," Ness was quick to defend. "And it was never proved that the Enfield case wasn't genuine either. If someone like you is doubtful, Ruby, how can you blame others?"

Ruby bristled. She didn't need to be told off like a small

child. She wasn't doubtful; she was being realistic, or at least trying to be.

Cash broke a tense moment of silence. "So, we can't walk away, we've established that much. When are we going in again?"

"We?" Ruby queried.

"That's right, if this ship's going down, I'm sinking too."

"Cash, no, stay out of this—"

"I agree with Ruby," Theo voiced. "You don't need the hassle."

Cash shook his head; he could be as stubborn as the spirits at times. "I'm not psychic, I know that, but you're my friends." He turned to Ruby. "My *girlfriend*. I want to be there with you. And you know what else?"

"What?" said Ruby, feeling tears start to prick at her eyes again.

"That bag of yours, the one with the smudge sticks in, the crystals and all that jazz, it's getting bloody heavy lately. If I'm only there as your roadie, to fetch and to carry, to get you a sandwich or something in between Benjamin getting all princessy and hurling missiles at you, then that's my privilege."

Theo was misty-eyed too. "Do you know what you can bring to Gilmore Street that we're going to need a ton of, Cash?"

"What?" he asked.

"Your sense of humour. If I've said it once, I've said it a thousand times, we don't only go in with love and understanding even for the most pain-in-the-arse spirits; we go in with a lightness of heart. It's one of our most effective weapons. And we treat the press in that way too."

Both Ruby and Corinna screwed up their faces in puzzlement as she said this. "I don't mean belittle what we do," Theo explained, noticing, "I mean don't fight them. You can't. Not the media. Not only the newspapers, it'll be all over Facebook and Twitter soon enough too. Shrug your shoulders. Say 'yep, I'm a ghostbuster, it's a fair cop,' but say it with pride, not embarrassment. Ruby, it's a *bona fide* service we provide, as valid as any other on the high street. That's your business message, stick to it. There's *nothing* to be embarrassed about."

Ruby's heart sank even lower. "Facebook and Twitter? I didn't think about them."

"Yep," Cash agreed, "it'll spread faster than butter on toast."

"If we fail it *will* be an embarrassment," Ruby lamented.

"But we're not going to," Theo contested. "That's not something we do."

Ness smiled at the conviction in Theo's voice. Turning to Ruby, she asked the same question that Cash had earlier. "When are we going in again?"

"This afternoon. I agreed with Samantha we'd meet her there at three."

"And the press are camped outside?" asked Theo.

"Apparently."

Reaching down to retrieve her handbag, Theo started rummaging inside it.

"What are you doing?" Ruby asked, mystified.

"Checking I've got my lipstick," Theo replied, retrieving a burgundy tube with a gold rim. "If we're going to make headlines, I want to look my best. Anyone for a slick of *Parisian Passion*?"

Chapter Seventeen

THE more they knew about Benjamin Hamilton, the better. It might help them to find his weak spot. Before facing the world and those with flashing cameras who inhabited it, the team spent their time in Ruby's office trying to find out a few more details. Ruby and Cash searched online records; both Corinna and Theo spoke to different people at Southern Rail again, and Ness phoned her contact at Sussex Police who was going through police records for any mention of him. Jed was still present, but he was slumbering. She admired how unfazed he was, wished she could take a leaf out of his book. Despite realising the wisdom behind keeping a sense of humour, she found it difficult when all efforts proved fruitless.

"God!" she exclaimed when even Ness's contact drew a blank. "Why are some people so damned anonymous?"

Ness shrugged. "Because they are, Ruby. They *intend* to be."

"But he must have had family, been married or something."

"I've never married," Ness continued. "Never had children either. Some people don't."

"Are your parents still alive?"

Ness coloured as she answered. "No."

"Have you got brothers and sisters?" Ruby knew she was

probing but in the context of their conversation she thought it was okay to do so.

"I've got five."

"Five?" That astonished Ruby; she had expected the answer to that to be 'no' as well. "There you are then, you have family."

"But none that I keep in contact with."

None? Ruby was about to comment further but Theo broke in, effectively stopping the inquisition.

"Bloody Southern Rail! They're so unhelpful. People don't want to go the extra mile nowadays do they? Jobsworths, the damned lot of them."

"So nothing at all?" Ruby sighed as she said it.

"Nothing. I've no idea how long he worked for the railways; whether he was liked by his colleagues, or abhorred by them, I've got no insight at all."

"So, all we've got to go on is that Ben's a publicly pleasant albeit shy man, who's actually a writhing mass of hatred, anger and fear behind closed doors. We've no idea whether this was because he had Asperger's and was frustrated, or whether there's a much darker reason."

"Asperger's?" said Cash. "I reckon he's more likely to have Tourette's!"

"That too, probably," Theo replied. "No, we know very little about him, but sometimes that's just the way it is. *Oftentimes.* We mustn't let it get us down."

Cash nodded, deep in thought.

"What is it?" Ruby asked him.

"Have you considered that maybe it isn't Ben haunting Gilmore Street; perhaps it's someone else?'

"Who else?" Theo did the asking this time.

"I don't know, but if the cap doesn't fit and all that…"

"'If the cap fits, wear it', that's the expression," Ness pointed out.

"You know what I mean."

Ruby looked at Theo, at Ness. "But the cap *does* fit, in many ways."

"Even so…"

"Cash, with all due respect, we're the psychics. Trust us on this."

Theo took over. "Look, it's a male energy, and Ben, who died a very lonely death there, is the most likely candidate. We haven't got long before we have to be at Gilmore Street so let's not waste time complicating matters. We need to visualise white light and get our armour in place."

"And then what?" queried Cash.

"Then we do what the armoured do, dear chap, we go into battle."

* * *

The first people to do battle with were the reporters. As the team descended, there were more than two of them outside – there were four, and who knew how many there'd be in another hour or two.

It was a bright day but the camera flashes were brighter, blinding, in fact.

"The light, the light…" Cash whispered in Ruby's ear, causing her to smile instead of cry. What they'd done inside, spent time tuning into the light had bolstered her, made her feel strong again. The light did that. It lifted you when you could feel yourself sinking. Cash had the same effect.

"Miss, Miss, it's Ruby, isn't it? Ruby Davis? Can you tell us about the phenomena occurring at Gilmore Street? Is that where you're off to now? Is there really a ghost there? Do you think you'll be able to get rid of it? *How* will you get rid of it? Are you really psychic? Have you got rid of ghosts before?"

On and on the questions went.

"Just walk." Theo fell into step beside her. "Your head held high and a smile on your face. You've nothing to be embarrassed about."

Ruby shouldn't need her to keep reiterating that but somehow it helped. She *was* proud of what she did and some day soon she might have to speak to the papers too, but not now. They had more pressing matters to attend to.

Cash drove her Ford from Lewes to Brighton, insisting she focus solely on the task ahead, not expend her energy negotiating traffic. Corinna agreed, climbing in the back and sitting alongside Jed. Theo and Ness took Ness's car. They'd already agreed to park at Brighton Station.

"How are we going to approach the house?" Ruby had queried. "En masse or in two groups."

"Let's go together," Theo decided. "Bold is beautiful."

And now they were only metres away, Ruby making a conscious effort to keep her breathing steady. What kind of mood would Benjamin be in? Foul as usual or perhaps he was sorry for his antics, ready to leave everyone in peace. If they ever needed a miracle, today was that day.

Samantha hadn't exaggerated, as Ruby half-suspected, half-*hoped*. The press was out in force in Gilmore Street, attracting members of the public who were also standing and staring.

"Forge ahead. If we turn back now, they'll have a field day."

"They'll have a field day anyway, Theo," Corinna

commented.

"Whatever," Theo continued. "This is our job, what we're paid to do."

And how many of those who had parted with money for services rendered, wondered Ruby, would stick up for them if it came to it? Who would stand by their testimonials, given so freely when it's just a surname, a location, and a quote needed? Like Benjamin Hamilton, like Ness, she knew some people wanted to remain anonymous, but she hoped there would be enough of them to make a difference – to dispel the charlatan myth if it exploded. It wouldn't only be Psychic Surveys that suffered if they didn't; it would be the haunted and those that haunted them too. People would dismiss help instead of seeking it, and so many spirits would remain grounded.

As they pushed their way through the crowd, Samantha rushed forward.

"Oh Ruby, Ruby, you're here at last!"

The mention of her name was enough for the press to start jostling forward too, cameras clicking away again, questions fired. How big name celebrities put up with this kind of nonsense she didn't know. But then some people craved that sort of attention, encouraged it. She wasn't one of them.

"Excuse me, keep your distance please. Stop crowding us."

It was Cash, boyfriend, bag carrier, and now bodyguard.

"I said," he continued, trying to keep his temper, "keep back."

When still they ignored him, he threw his hands up in the air. "Bloody hell, what the fuck am I, invisible or something?"

Samantha took over.

"STOP IT!" she yelled, jostling her way through to stand in front of Ruby and blowing fury through her nostrils. A petite woman, not much taller than Theo, she suddenly had the same magnificent presence. Her voice, a little on the shrill side at times, Ruby had to admit, was loud and resonant. Certainly it stopped those holding cameras and digital recorders in their tracks. "I want you to remember that this is *my* house, my ghost and *my* life you're dealing with here. I don't know which one of my neighbours called you but when I find out, there'll be hell to pay. You're acting like vultures. Meanwhile, I have a problem, and it's these people I want to deal with it. Now get out of their way and let them go inside. If one of you dares set foot on my property I'll prosecute for trespassing, I swear."

Only a brief silence ensued before, yet again, a chorus of voices erupted. "But why don't you get the church to sort it? What's so special about these people? How do you know you can trust them? What are their credentials?"

"Come on," Cash said. "Let's just get inside."

Despite it being a tight squeeze, they managed to push their way into the house, Samantha closing the door firmly behind them. For a moment she leant against it, closing her eyes briefly as if relieved she'd got that far.

Ruby asked if she'd been back in the house since Saturday night.

"No, we've made do with what we've had and Delia's being so kind. To be honest, I think she loves having us there. The Scots are like that, aren't they? They're so hospitable. She's making such a fuss of the kids, baking cakes and biscuits for them, they can't believe their luck.

Jeff's a bit miserable, though. No change there then." Samantha laughed as she said it, but it was a nervous sound. She looked around. "Is Ben still here?"

He was, but the atmosphere wasn't as charged as it had been on Saturday night. Then again, the house had lain empty for a couple of days – he'd got his way, got them out. It might ramp up now that they were back.

"The mess in the kitchen…" Theo queried.

"It's still there I think," answered Samantha.

"Then we'll go and clear it up," replied Theo. "Samantha, you don't have to come with us."

"I want to, it's my house."

"Will Jeff be over any time soon?"

"He's staying with the kids, someone has to."

Not strictly true, Ruby thought. They had Delia to keep an eye on them. "Samantha—"

"Call me, Sam. All my friends do."

Ruby was touched that this woman was considering them friends, her faith in them untarnished. "Sam, if it starts to get a bit rough in here…"

"I'll get out, I promise. Leave the experts to it."

The experts? Ruby appreciated that sentiment too.

"To the kitchen," Theo instructed.

It was indeed a mess, Samantha mourning the loss of some of her prized china as she gazed around. "It's not expensive stuff but some of the mugs he's destroyed are my favourites. Tea just tastes better in them, you know?"

Everyone set about clearing up.

Wielding a broom, Ness said, "As the kitchen seems to be the centre of activity, why don't we move some of the stuff in here to the living room?"

"Anything sharp especially," suggested Ruby.

Theo agreed. "Knives can do a lot of damage."

"Anything can when hurled at high speed," Cash pointed out.

Samantha stopped what she was doing and straightened up. "It does feel a bit better in here, doesn't it? Maybe it's safe to come back?"

Ruby shook her head. "He's still here, I can feel him but at the moment it's in a remote sense. It could be that he's still recovering from the amount of energy Saturday night required. Or, that he's had time to think and is calmer. We won't know until we've emptied this room and tried to connect."

Samantha nodded towards Cash. "Good job we've got a strapping lad with us. Someone to help lug all this stuff."

"He has his uses," Ruby answered, smiling.

"Glad you think so," Cash batted back.

Ferrying stuff to the living room, they had to turn the light on. Not because it was a dull day, far from it, the sun was shining bright enough outside. It was because reporters were crowding round the windows, peering in, cameras held aloft and ready to catch the action – that goldfish bowl effect she'd worried about earlier. Doing their best to ignore them, they carried on with the job in hand, Ruby thankful that the kitchen was at the back of the house and therefore inaccessible to prying eyes – so many pairs of them.

An hour later, the team was satisfied that the kitchen was safe enough.

"Many hands…" commented Ness.

"I hope this works." Samantha sounded genuinely worried. "As lovely as Delia is, it's your own home you want."

"Of course it is," soothed Theo.

"Sam," Ruby continued, "I really think you ought to stay in the living room whilst we try and connect with Benjamin. Just in case."

Samantha held up her hands. "Your call. I don't want to be in the way."

As she turned to leave, Ruby turned also, back to the spot where she'd previously seen Benjamin crouching by the table. Pointing to it, she said, "That's where the spirit manifested, not fully, but an outline of him, although his eyes were clear enough."

"It's always the eyes," Cash said.

"It seems to be," agreed Ruby.

"I suppose an arm or a leg doesn't have quite the same effect," Theo commented. "It's nowhere near as scary."

"His backside might be, though," Cash countered.

Theo bellowed with laughter. "That's it, Cash," she said. "Anchor us with that humour of yours." Growing serious again, she asked Ruby if they should go ahead and communicate with Ben again.

"Yes, let's, but it's strange, the atmosphere does seem a bit lighter. Maybe he's not so angry."

"Let's just see, shall we?" It was Ness, obviously not convinced.

"Should we smudge first, get a bit of a cleansing underway?"

"Perhaps afterwards," Theo answered, "although we could do with opening a window, it smells so damp in here."

"I noticed that on my first visit here," Ruby replied. "It's kind of musty. Although Sam did say all damp problems have been treated."

"Old houses, as much as you try, you can't fix everything."

"But we can try and fix this," Ness muttered, referring to Ben.

"We can at that," Theo agreed.

After opening the window by the sink, pausing to fill her lungs with fresh air, Ruby started the address, reiterating that they were not there to harm Ben but to help. "You'll notice we've cleared the kitchen of potential missiles. I'd be grateful if you could refrain from attacking in any other way too. *Physical* attack I'm talking about: blows to the stomach. Benjamin, we're trying to understand you, why it is that you're grounded, that you're so full of hate and fear; fear being the dominant emotion, no matter how hard you try and disguise it. What happened to make you that way? In life, did you do something you're ashamed of? Is it retribution that concerns you? Talk to us. We'll listen."

All five stood perfectly still, Ruby feeling the power of love and light emanating from her colleagues. It was so strong, she felt *bathed* in it. Surely it was having an effect on Ben too, a positive effect that is.

Come on, Ben, where are you?

Was he hiding? Was that it? Despite his defiance the other day, had they cowed him? If so, he might be more amenable to moving on. And if he were, the show would be over. The fuss would die down. Unlike the Enfield case, which went on for months and months, this would be a paltry one-day affair as far as the public were concerned – nothing in comparison, disappointing; certainly not the stuff of books, films and drama. She found herself fervently hoping. *Please, please, let it be that easy.* What joy if it was!

She'd grab Cash, and Corinna too, maybe even cajole Theo and Ness into it, head to the pub and celebrate – buy the first round, the second, even the third. Damn it, she'd buy the entire pub a drink, she'd be that relieved.

"Ben," she called again. "You need to go to the light. Leave the Gordon family in peace and find peace yourself. And you *will* find it, because that's what there is on the other side. Peace. You're holding on to such negative emotions, but you don't have to, you can let them go. There's no judgement in the light either; you'll be welcomed, it's where you belong. Go, Ben, go now."

The atmosphere was as still as a millpond. No creaking of cupboards warning of an attack to come; no mugs hovering threateningly in mid-air; no kettle boiling. Ruby could feel hope radiate from her centre outwards.

"Has it worked?" Corinna whispered. "Has he gone?"

"I don't know, I can't sense him," replied Ruby. And she couldn't: it was as if the room was indeed empty. She dared to let hope envelop her.

"He has, he's gone—"

"Wait!" The command had come from Ness. "Something's wrong."

Ruby turned to look at her. "But the kitchen's empty."

"It's not the kitchen you're referring to, is it?" asked Theo.

From behind them they heard a scream.

"What the hell—" Ruby swung fully round.

It was Samantha.

Cash was already moving forward and the others followed at his heel. In the hallway, they found the door to the living room closed – had Samantha done that? Cash tried to open it but couldn't.

Another scream pierced the air. It wouldn't be only them who heard it; the reporters were sure to as well.

"Cash, open the damn door."

"Erm... hello, Ruby... that's what I'm trying to do here."

And he was, she couldn't deny it. He was throwing the full weight of his body against the painted wood and still it wouldn't budge.

"Is there a lock or something?" Ruby's eyes lowered towards the handle.

"It's Ben that's stopping us," Ness explained. "He can't keep it up, though, the door will weaken soon. Keep trying, Cash."

Cash did as he was told.

Bitch!

The word was whispered in Ruby's ear.

Fucking stupid bitch!

She whipped her head from side to side. "Where are you, Ben? Where the hell are you?"

"Right now, he's everywhere," Theo answered. "His presence is filling this house. Visualise white light and remember, Ruby, words can't hurt you."

No, but implements could and Samantha was in the living room with a ton of them, including the knives. There came a cry from within.

"Let me out, let me out. Please let me out!"

"We're coming, Sam, don't be frightened. We've just got to get the door open," Ruby yelled back.

"It's not locked!"

"It's, erm... it's stuck, Sam."

"Stuck? How come? I don't understand."

"Sam, hold on, we won't be long."

Samantha was getting very distressed. So was Ruby. Why, oh, why had they moved the knives into there? A loud thud from inside confirmed that Ben had resorted once again to throwing things. There was also the smash of glass. Poor Samantha – she was in the line of fire, at Ben's mercy. They had to get in there to get her out. She focused on the door, knowing that Theo, Ness, and Corinna were too. Ruby willed it to open as Cash started kicking it. A door did indeed fly open, but not the one they wanted. It was the front door, as suddenly and as violently as if a howling wind had got behind it.

Ruby's eyes widened in shock as reporters came pouring down the narrow hallway, a crowd of them, heading straight for Ruby and the team, desperate for a ringside seat. Jed also appeared, barking at them, trying to have a psychic impact, but they continued forwards, completely unaware of him.

"Cash!" she shouted.

"Just… one… more… kick." He sounded so out of breath. "One… more."

That had to be the case. It had to be! The damn door was fractured from the amount of abuse it'd taken. They'd be able to walk *through* it at this rate.

"There!"

The door gave way – finally.

There was no time to thank him as the reporters were upon them. They all started to surge forwards and then – as though they were one entity – they stopped. Samantha was at the far end of the room crouching as Ben had crouched – the only difference was that her hands were covering her face, hiding her eyes. Around her lay an array of broken goods, china primarily, the knives thankfully untouched. Even so, as Cash had pointed out, all implements thrown at high speed were dangerous. Had she been hit? Was she hurt? Before Ruby could find out, the kettle shot upwards as though it had rocket fuel beneath it. Ruby stared, they all did. Even Samantha couldn't deny her curiosity. She had splayed her fingers and was peeking through them. Who was he going to throw the object at? Samantha? One of the reporters? One of the Psychic Surveys team? Ruby herself? It wasn't a plastic kettle; it was aluminium, heavy enough, heavier still if it was full of water.

"Ben," Ruby called out, "this is getting you nowhere. Drop the kettle now."

She was getting tired of his games, tired of him. *Why are you doing this?*

Theo intercepted. "Ben, I know you're frightened, I understand that, but please, this has to stop. Listen to us. Communicate with us. Tell us what's wrong. We *can* help you."

Fuck off!

The words were spat at Theo as well as Ruby, although only the psychic could hear how caustic they were. Ruby glanced at Theo, seeing how worried her expression was, Ness's too. The reporters might not have been able to hear anything, but they could certainly see and Ben knew that. He was going to play right into their hands: a deliberate act of spite.

"Samantha!" screamed Ruby. "Grab a cushion and place it over your head." To the reporters, she yelled, "Duck!"

But the kettle wasn't hurled at them. With an almighty cry of rage, it was hurled at the window, smashing easily through the thin pane of glass to land at the feet of those who were still outside. As it did the sound of cameras flashing was worse than any insult Ben could conjure up.

Chapter Eighteen

THE next day Ruby didn't look at the papers, she didn't even leave her flat, but worked from home instead, hoping her office wasn't besieged. God knew what the solicitors below would think if it was. They were aware of what she did for a living, but as she was always very professional about it, so were they. She'd never invited press coverage before. And to be fair, she hadn't this time, but the press had found her – with a vengeance. She had several calls to make, clients who'd rung wanting an initial survey. But as she called them back, their responses were lukewarm.

"Do you know, I think I might have been imagining things," said one, a woman who had previously complained of footsteps on her landing in the night despite living alone. "You know how it is. You watch a few scary movies and tend to get carried away. I'll stick to rom-com from now on."

She was one of the more polite ones. "Thanks, but no thanks. I've changed my mind," was the only explanation offered by another.

So, you've seen the papers, she wanted to ask but didn't dare. She didn't want to know what was in them, even though Cash had been on the phone too, saying she needed to face up to it; hit back even.

"Bloody cheek," he fumed, "what they're calling you."

"Don't, Cash, just don't."

"I'll come round, work from yours."

"No, I've got Jed here, that's enough company for now."

"Charming."

"I didn't mean it like that, I… just… look, you said I needed a break, well today I'm going to rest up. It seems no one wants me anyway."

"Are people cancelling on you already?"

"You could say that."

"Has Theo or Ness been on the phone?"

"Yep, and Corinna. I've told them the same thing. I'm just going to take the day off. Tomorrow I'll form a plan of action with everyone."

"Tomorrow? Haven't you got the regression with Ellie tomorrow?"

"In the morning, but the afternoon's free. Well, it is now."

"And Samantha, have you spoken to her?"

"Not since yesterday. Theo helped her move over to Delia's and that's where she's going to stay. If this case can't be solved within a reasonable time, she's got a sister in Hove she can move in with. Either way, they're not going back to number 44, not until Benjamin's been dealt with."

"The poor Gordons," Cash sympathised.

"I know. I feel sorry for them too. She still wants our help, though. Those around us might be losing faith but she's flying the flag for Psychic Surveys."

The words were delivered wearily and Cash must have sensed this.

"You'll crack this case, Ruby, you always do."

Maybe, but what would it cost her? Her career or her

sanity? Right now it felt like they were both going down the pan. Saying goodbye to Cash, she finished up the round of phone calls, took the phone off the hook, lay back on the sofa, and watched telly instead, avoiding the local news too.

* * *

Wednesday dawned and Ruby forced herself to get out of bed. Business was business. She wouldn't be deterred. Perhaps she was overreacting anyway. Today's headlines might be about something else entirely. Even if they were, it didn't solve the problem of Benjamin. They needed to go back there, try again. Would there be a different outcome? Was it possible to simply wear him down? Samantha said they could return at any time. Well, she'd give it another day – perhaps two or three. By then the reporters would have got fed up of camping out, especially if it rained. Fervently, she hoped for a spot of inclement weather, a thunderstorm perhaps, lightning, a hurricane – anything to drive them away. She'd decide on a return date with the others this afternoon. But first there was Ellie to contend with.

Leaving her flat, she half expected to run the gamut of reporters there too – as Ellie had said regarding her birth mother, finding out where someone lived was hardly difficult nowadays. She was heartened to find the coast clear, perhaps interest really had moved on. Diving into her Ford, she deliberately took the road past her office. A car was parked outside, two men sitting in it, glancing at her building every now and then. Again she was heartened; there wasn't a pack of them, just a measly pair. Then again, as before, the emphasis would probably be on the house at

Gilmore Street. She'd have to phone Samantha and see. She still hadn't seen news coverage and nor did she want too. She sailed past her office, down the road to Ness's, keeping her eyes firmly on the road.

Ness answered the door promptly. "Good to see you, Ruby, come in."

Ushered through to the living room, she found Ailsa and Ellie sitting, glasses of water placed before them. "Would you like one too?" Ness asked.

"No thanks," Ruby replied. "Perhaps we should start soon. Our meeting this afternoon…"

"Yes, yes, of course."

Ailsa looked at Ruby. "Before we get cracking, I'd like to discuss with you what we have in mind today. I've discussed it with Ellie and she's in agreement." Ellie smiled in acquiescence as she said it.

Ness had already placed a chair by Ailsa, so Ruby went over and sat next to her, once again admiring her copious amounts of 'owl' jewellery. "Go ahead," she said, listening.

Ailsa cleared her throat. In her own way she was as theatrical as Theo. The pair of them would make a fascinating double act. "We're going back to the same life but we're going to be dipping in and out of it, exploring happier memories and some that are not so happy, leading us up to the point Ellie can't get beyond, neither during regressions, in dreams, or in visions. Today, our aim is to break that barrier." She focused on Ellie. "It's a bold move I know, but I feel the time has come. You said yourself your dreams are becoming more vivid, the flashbacks too. The last thing I want is for you to make that breakthrough when you're on your own. It could be too distressing. At least with us, it's in a controlled environment. Does that make sense?"

When she put it like that, Ruby thought it did.

"Ellie, did you tell Ailsa what you told me on Monday, concerning the timeframe?" Ruby asked.

"Yeah, I'm almost certain now it's sometime in the sixties. I've been doing what you suggested, looking at pictures of that period, and they do seem to click, the fashion, the décor, everything. Even though it's so long ago."

Ness pulled a face. "So long ago? Hardly."

"Fifty years have passed," Ailsa reminded her.

"Fifty years? Good grief! That much? How time flies."

Nobody could disagree with that.

"Right, let's get going shall we?" Ailsa suggested. "Ellie, are you ready?"

"I am," replied Ellie, kicking off her shoes and lying on the couch.

* * *

"I love it when he laughs, he doesn't look so moody then. It's his eyes that get me. I've never seen eyes like them before. They're... depthless."

"So you can see him, can you?"

"Just his eyes, but I know he's laughing, I can hear that well enough."

"Where are you?"

"We're in bed. It's our first time. Well, *my* first time. I was a virgin. All that talk of saving yourself for your husband, it's so old-fashioned, nobody does that nowadays. Mind you, a part of me wanted to do exactly that. But he thinks it's old-fashioned too. He gave me something to drink beforehand, said it would relax me. Told me if I let go, let him take over, I'd like it."

"And did you? Like it, I mean?"

"I… yes, of course. I like him. I more than like him. I'm falling in love."

"Regarding the sex, you don't sound so sure."

"It was a little rough, but just a little. He's a man, though, and that's what it's like with men. It hurt… you know, the actual act. But it does hurt. I've heard my friends talking about it. I expected it to hurt. He's laughing again. He's telling me about someone in his family, how he got one over on them. His brother, is it? I think so. His eldest brother. He's always felt in his shadow, looked down upon. But not anymore, he's stitched him up good and proper, that's what he said. I'm not sure how, he won't say exactly. But he's told the police something and his brother's in trouble. Might even go to prison. The thought seems to delight him. Says he'll get what's coming to him, what he deserves, that he should have been locked up sooner. He wishes he could shop the lot of them. Get them all locked up. His family are bad; he's trying to distance himself from them. I hate them because he does. I'm glad he's got away."

"Is there anything else you'd like to tell us about this memory? Where you are for example. Is it your house or his? Can you describe your surrounds?"

"It's not my house, and he doesn't have a house. At the moment he lives in a caravan. It's all a bit hazy, but I think that's where we are – his caravan. There are nets at the window, they're more grey than white. No curtains, though. And it's cold but I'm warm in his arms. That's where I want to stay. Why is it still so hazy?"

"Don't worry about that. That's normal."

"Is it? Because sometimes this doesn't feel normal, it feels wrong."

"Wrong? You've said that before. How does it feel wrong?"

"In a way I can't explain. I don't have the words for it."

"And yet you can explain other things. Your surroundings, for example."

"I know but then… words seem to fail me. Everything goes dark instead, and silent. *I'm* silent."

"Let's concentrate on memories. The more we can recall the more we'll understand. When did you decide to run away?"

"I… I don't know how that decision came about. I wasn't keen at first, I know that much. I love my parents. They've been good to me. I don't want to hurt them. But he says it's the only way if we want to be together, I have to go away with him. I do want to be with him, he knows that, but I'm still upset. Very upset. Every time I think about leaving my parents, I cry. And then he gets upset too. He gets angry. I can see it in his eyes. He's frustrated with me."

"If you love your parents, it's understandable you don't want to run away. But you did, we know that. How did he persuade you?"

"He said he'd marry me. He got down on one knee and said he'd make all my dreams come true. I couldn't believe it when he did. I was thrilled. There's still the problem of my parents, though. I want them to be at my wedding. But he says no, they don't like him, they'd never agree. But once we're married, they'll have to like him, won't they? He'll be my husband, their son-in-law."

"Can you remember an occasion when your parents met

him?"

"Oh, yes, I remember that all right. It was the first and last occasion. We're at my house, in the living room, all four of us. My mother's pouring tea. Her disapproval is so obvious. She's stuck-up sometimes is my mum. I love her but she can be a snob. My father's more lenient, but even he's not impressed and he seems to have no problem making it obvious too. My man, he's getting quieter by the minute, he's started mumbling in reply to the questions they're firing at him: what do you do for a living? What are your plans for the future? Where do you live? It's as if he's on trial. My parents seem oblivious, but his cup is trembling as he holds it. How dare they make him feel so small? It makes me more determined."

"To do what?"

"To love him and to be with him – no matter what the cost."

"I see. I want to take you forward now, to the days, the weeks, and the months after you were married? Is that okay? I want to take you to the first memory you ever recalled. When you were standing at the kitchen sink, when you were feeling so much despair. What went wrong with your marriage? It's clear you loved him, you've told us."

"I… I'm not sure I can do this."

"You can. We need to move forward remember, and break through the barrier – together. It might not be as traumatic as you fear."

"It is. It is as traumatic. It's worse. Far worse."

"Then that's even more reason you don't recall such a memory whilst alone. If I think you're too upset, that you can't cope, I will bring you back. You're safe. Keep that at the forefront of your mind. Come forward now – you're standing at the kitchen sink, there's a pile of dirty dishes in front of you, waiting to be washed. You're sad, you're angry, you feel like crying, but you daren't because he gets angry if you cry. He's coming. He's walking up the hallway. He's behind you. You turn around to look at him. What happens next?"

"It's what always happens next. He's going to hit me. His fists will come flying out and knock me to the ground. But first he takes my radio, my precious radio, and it seems to crumple in his hands. That's the reason for his anger this time – the radio. I'd been listening to it, humming along to a song, a song I loved but which made me feel sad, made me long for home. But I'd only been humming softly and the radio was low, so low. How did he hear it from the living room? Especially when he always has that telly blaring? How did he know? But that's the thing you see, he *always* seems to know when it comes to me. It's like his mind is linked with mine, as though he's wormed his way inside me and now he won't let go. I wish he'd let go!"

"Easy, take it easy. It's a memory we're recalling. Just a memory."

"He's so angry. But I don't know why. Was he always this way? Did I just not see it? Was I so in love with him I was blind to the truth? He's hitting me, over and over again. I'm used to being hit, to being abused and debased. That's what he does. He debases me. I'm not who I was, I'm a shell, a wreck. I don't even look like that girl who stood in front of the mirror, so excited, anymore. I'm someone else. Oh, I wish I was someone else. Not me, stuck here, imprisoned, being hurt, and knowing there's worse to come. I try to kick out, furiously I try to kick, but it's no use. And then he yanks my hair back, so viciously it feels like my neck is going to snap. He forces me to look at him, to stare into his eyes, into the bleakness of them. There's no vestige of humanity left, I'm certain of it. There was once, but it's gone. It's fled or been driven out. He's given into the dark side entirely. He's evil. And I'm evil too, by association. There's no goodness left in me anymore; no innocence, no love... just hatred. That's what's he done to me. Made me like him. The realisation, far from destroying me, bolsters me. Why should I be at his mercy any longer? Why don't I fight back? I never have before. I've always been too afraid. But the fear has gone. In an instant it's blown itself out.

There's a roar, a guttural sound, coming from deep inside me. I wonder who it is at first. Am *I* making that sound? Am I capable? It's so primal. The sound startles him and for a moment he loosens his grip. But it's just a moment I need. I can kick out now, my limbs seem freer, and I do. I watch in triumph as my aim hits home, as he falls to the ground, grabbing at his crotch. As bruised as I am, I jump up and grab at things, anything. The heaviest is a frying pan. I hit him with it, bringing it down with such force I wonder if I'm possessed, if something else is working through me. If so, I welcome it, beg it to lend me its demonic strength, I'd willingly trade my soul in return. It feels good, it feels wonderful, but it's not enough. He's screaming now. In between there are strange yelping noises, the kind a wounded dog might make. He's such an animal, such a damned animal! I want to hurt him so bad. I'm consumed by that desire. I want to kill him, but before that I want to torture him, threaten him as he used to threaten me. Carry them out one by one – slowly, leisurely.

But I have to be quick. I have to think fast. And I do. I do. I hurt him bad and his cries are like the sweetest song I've ever heard. I'm evil. I've crossed the line. And when he writhes and cries no more, I step backwards. Take another step, and another, out of the kitchen, down the narrow hallway. My eyes never leave his still and shapeless form. He's not handsome, not anymore; he's a slug of a man. I don't know if he's dead or alive and I don't care. Because either way this is where he'll stay. This is hell, the hell he created, the hell he deserves. I tell him this. I scream it at him. And I'll go to hell too, for what I've done. I accept that. But not yet I won't, not yet. Because I'm not dead, you see, I'm still alive.

Hell's still waiting for me."

Chapter Nineteen

AS Ellie sat bolt upright, her eyes still trancelike but wide open, Ailsa rapidly counted her down, brought her back to the present. At the same time, Ruby and Ness hurried forward, both as startled as she was. The last couple of sentences she'd uttered, what did she mean? How could you recall a past life if it wasn't exactly that? Just what was it Ellie was recalling... or playing at?

Ness caught her thought and looked sharply at her.

"Not now, Ruby!"

Ness was right. Now was not the time to entertain such doubts. Now was the time to focus on Ellie. The girl had sweat on her forehead and she was shaking like a pneumatic drill.

Ailsa soothed her, as did Ness whilst Ruby went to fetch her some fresh water. Returning to the room, she was surprised to see Ellie snuggled into the side of Ness, who had one arm around her, the other stroking her hair. She didn't have Ness down as a maternal type, not even remotely, but she was doing a good impression now. 'Lost souls,' Ellie had said, 'empathise with one another.' Whatever was happening, Ellie had brought out a much softer side in Ness. If the girl *was* playing at something, as she'd thought earlier, there'd be no convincing her colleague. Even so, as she handed over the glass, she asked

Ellie if she remembered what she'd said.

"I do, yes," the girl mumbled, trying to take a sip of water but shaking too violently to manage it.

"Here, let me," Ness said, taking the glass from her and putting it to her lips. "Sip slowly now, that's it, nice and slow."

Ruby sat next to Ailsa, who also looked troubled, and tried to wait as patiently as possible. It took a good few minutes but at last Ellie calmed.

"Only speak when you feel able to," Ness instructed.

"No, I do. I feel able to now."

"What did you mean when you said you were alive and that hell was still waiting for you?" Ruby cut straight to the chase. It had been a long session, a long morning and there was still the Gilmore case to sort out. "Ellie…"

"I don't know," Ellie said at last. "I don't get it."

That made four of them.

"But you killed a man, you remembered that?"

"Hang on, hang on, back up a minute." It was Ailsa, a rather shell-shocked Ailsa, holding up her hand. "We don't know for sure she killed anyone."

"It sounded like it, though," Ruby persisted. "After the fight you had, you mentioned his 'still and shapeless form'."

Ellie's sigh was ragged and she seemed to shrink inside herself. "I think… I think I *did* kill him, from the memory… from what I can remember. Oh God!" She let out a strangled cry. "I thought I was the one who was murdered, but it turns out I'm the murderer, the guilty one. This is awful!"

Ness's voice was firm. "From everything you've told us, the abuse you'd suffered, the humiliation you'd sustained, what happened finally between you was self-defence. He took you to the edge and he pushed you over."

"So this is a domestic abuse case," Ruby offered.

"This is a *cold* case," reminded Ness. And if it was Ellie who was the murderer, Ruby suspected that was just the way it would stay.

"I still don't know names or location," Ellie said, trying to stifle her sobs. "I'm useless!"

"Don't talk like that," Ness did her level best to soothe her.

"But you heard me, I wanted to hurt him, torture him—"

"You were at the point of desperation."

"It still makes it wrong!"

Ness sighed. "Murder *is* wrong. But sometimes it's... understandable."

Ellie did break down now, her whole body shuddering. "I'm so confused. This isn't what I expected. I've never hurt anyone, not in this life. Never."

Ness's arm was back round her shoulders. "We know you haven't."

"But like Ruby said, what did I mean – I'm still alive?'"

Ruby felt bound to offer some sort of explanation. "Perhaps... perhaps it means you expected to die during that encounter but you didn't; you turned the tables and survived. You went on to live, for a few more years at least."

Ellie shook her head. She really did look distraught. "What if it means something else?"

"Like what?"

"That my past self is still alive. That there are two of me!"

198

"That can't be." Ailsa looked completely perplexed. "Not in my experience anyway. A soul divided between two bodies? That's nonsense." She shared a look between Ness and Ruby, "Isn't it?"

"I would have thought so," answered Ness.

"Me too," agreed Ruby. "We don't know everything, I'll be the first to admit it, but I've never heard of anything like that before. Ever."

Ness reverted back to her more usual brisk self. "We have to assume that what Ruby said earlier is correct: you survived that encounter with your husband and went on to live for a few more years. Let's work it out. You're twenty-two, Ellie, which means you were born in 1993."

"That's right, November 18th."

"We don't know your exact age in your previous life, but if you don't mind me saying so, you sound starry-eyed, naïve, at least in the beginning – a young girl in love. For the sake of argument let's say you were twenty…"

"That feels about right," Ellie replied. "Sometimes, though, it's as if I'm much younger. But again, that can't be. I wish I could understand it all!"

"Don't fret. We'll get there. To inhabit your current body, you had to die before 1993 – we don't know when exactly, but presuming it was shortly before that date, you would have reached no more than your mid-forties. Regarding names and location, you really can't recall anything?"

"I can't, I'm so sorry." Again, Ellie dissolved in tears.

"Ellie," Ness continued, "we'll carry out as many regression sessions as you like until the mystery's solved."

Ellie lifted her head. "Really? All of you?" She looked at Ruby as she said it, the beseeching look on her face causing

199

Ruby to flinch slightly. One more session, that's all she'd promised. But how could she remind Ellie of that in the state she was in? Once again she felt a frisson of unease. What was it about Ellie that unnerved her? That gave her a sense of danger? Never one to ignore instincts, she was tempted to do so with this one. The girl was in turmoil. The mystery surrounding her had deepened. And she was involved. Had been from the beginning. How could she not see it through to the end?

"Ellie, when you first came to see us, to tell us about what was happening to you, you mentioned Katharine, the woman who started the ball rolling. She held onto your hands, caught images of the life you'd lived before but then seemed... unsettled by it. She told you to forget it, to focus on this life only, to be grateful that the past was behind you. Why do you think she said that?"

"I don't know. I told you, she's a friend of a friend. I don't know her that well."

"But you said we might be able to speak to her. Can you get in touch with her, sooner rather than later. Now, in fact."

"Now?" queried Ness.

"Why not?" shrugged Ruby. "We've got a bit of time to kill before the next meeting. If we can speak to her on the phone..."

"Well, yeah, if you think it will help. Let me text my friend, see if she'll pass on Katharine's number."

A few minutes later, Ruby was put through to Katharine.

"Hi," said Ruby, "thanks so much for agreeing to speak to me—" Before she could get any further, she was interrupted.

"You're Ruby Davis, from Psychic Surveys?"

"Yes, that's right."

"The one working on the Gilmore Street case?"

"That's right too." So Katharine had been reading the papers at least.

"I don't want anything to do with you."

Ruby was stunned. "Erm… listen, this is nothing to do with the Gilmore case. I want to ask you some questions about Elisha Grey; about the images you saw when you held onto her hands. She told us about your gift."

"My gift is genuine."

Again, Ruby was taken aback. "I realise that—"

"I should never have picked up this call, I was tempted not to when I saw that the number was unknown. I should have listened to myself."

"But I don't understand why."

"I'm not an attention seeker."

"And nor am I, Katharine."

The woman's laugh was scornful. "Not an attention seeker? Come off it! You've got a business on the high street. You charge money for what you do, you invited the press into Gilmore Street…"

"I didn't—"

"I'm warning you, don't you dare mention me with regards to this reincarnation case. I don't want my name dragged through the mud too."

Is that what they were doing, dragging her name through the mud? God, they didn't waste much time. She forced herself to stay calm.

"They don't know anything about the reincarnation case, Katharine."

"Make sure it stays that way."

"But Ellie's case…"

"Is something I don't want to get involved with either. Her past, it's dark, it's… complicated. Leave it alone. I don't understand it. Why do you people always insist on interfering? Why don't you know when to take a step back? I wish I'd never said anything now. Don't call me again and pass on the same message to Ellie. I don't want anything to do with either of you."

As the phone went dead, Ruby could only stare in disbelief.

Chapter Twenty

"SOME people don't help, Ruby, it's as simple as that," Ness said when Ruby relayed the gist of the conversation with the others in the room.

"That's right," agreed Ailsa, "all they're capable of doing is starting the ball rolling and then they step aside, leave it to others to deal with the fall out."

"Ruby, we don't need Katharine," Ness insisted. "We're making headway."

"Have you seen the papers, Ness?" Ruby asked, changing the subject.

"Don't worry about what's in the papers."

"You've seen them, though, haven't you?"

"Ruby—"

"Don't, Ness. Don't fob me off, tell me what they say!"

Ness took a deep breath and had to look away for a second. "They're saying what we feared they would. What we *knew* they would."

"That we're charlatans."

"Or words to that effect."

"But haven't they checked the website at least? The testimonials?"

"What do they care about testimonials?" replied Ness. "They want a story that will sell papers that's all, they don't want the truth."

"It's not fair, it's just not fair." It was Ellie, echoing Ruby's sentiments and sounding just as upset. "You're good people, you don't deserve this."

"They're having a field day with the fact that we charge for services," Ness continued. "Apparently we *swindle* people, fool them into believing ghosts exist and then take advantage of them – financially."

Ruby gasped. "But the Gilmore case, they saw with their own eyes the kettle hovering in mid-air and being hurled through the window. They saw the mess the living room was in."

"Staged apparently, though I'm not sure who they think was pulling the strings."

"Testimonials," Ruby reiterated. "We need people we've helped to come forward, to back us up."

"And I hope they will, Ruby, but don't bank on it. They haven't so far. The thing is, people don't want to get involved, especially if the spotlight turns towards them. The press can be merciless, most people are aware of that."

"But the Gordons…"

"The Gordons are lying low. I think after yesterday they're all in terrible shock, even Samantha." Ness corrected herself. "Samantha especially."

"But she wants us to carry on, she said so."

"I know she does, but let's leave it for a few days, okay? Let's wait for the worst of it to die down and for Samantha to recover."

Ruby would bet that was the general consensus amongst the others too – to let the heat evaporate.

Leaving Ellie in Ailsa's care and promising to be in touch soon, Ness and Ruby travelled back to Ruby's flat to meet the rest of her team – again giving the office a wide berth. Once they were all together Ness pressed her point home.

"If we leave the case for a week or two, the press will get bored, give up and go and do something else with their time. Regarding Ben, we know he's not going anywhere – more's the pity – and that he's more settled when we're not around, so we don't need to worry about him."

"We certainly don't," Theo agreed. "He's his own worst enemy."

"The press hate it because we charge." Ruby couldn't seem to shake that fact from her mind. "It's unethical apparently."

Theo's sigh was dramatic. "And what they're doing – fabricating stories on a daily basis – isn't, I suppose!"

"It's ridiculous," Corinna joined in. "We provide a much needed service. The amount of calls we get asking for help proves that, we're so busy!"

"Yeah, well, call me psychic, Corinna," Ruby replied despondently, "but I think we've got a bit of a dry spell on the horizon."

Before anyone could comment further, the doorbell rang.

Corinna jumped up. "I'll go. If it's a roving reporter I'll give him what for."

She returned to the room, with Cash in tow.

"No reporters," she said, looking much relieved.

Cash went straight over to Ruby. "Babe, sorry I'm late. You all right?"

"I'm better now that you're here." As he settled beside her, Ruby came to a decision. "Okay, I agree. We leave the Gilmore case for a week or two and let the fuss die down. Regarding Ellie, it's taken a bit of a strange turn. Ness and

I have spent all morning with her." As concisely as possible, she related what had happened. "It turns out there's a likelihood she was the murderer, not the victim."

"What?" Cash screwed up his face. "Ellie? But she looks so…"

"Innocuous?" finished Theo.

Cash nodded. "Yeah, I suppose."

"That's Ellie in this life. She was different back then."

"But, Theo," Ness argued, "she was still a young girl, still naïve, and vulnerable too."

"You're very fond of her, aren't you?" Theo smiled as she said it.

"I feel for her that's all. She's someone who wants to find herself."

"Find herself?" Cash repeated, smiling too. "You're not wrong there."

"I really don't know what to make of Ellie's case," Ruby said, sighing. "For a moment she thought her past self was still alive too, that her soul was divided, inhabiting two bodies."

"Nonsense!" Theo's view matched Ailsa's. "Souls are individual, they're unique. They don't *divide*."

"Then again," Ness countered, "if you can think it, it's possible."

Theo's shake of the head was vehement. "No, no, she survived the encounter that's all, a *dreadful* encounter. She walked away, much to her surprise."

"The murder," queried Corinna, "did she get away with it?"

"We don't know what happened next," Ness answered. "Whether there was even a murder, which is why more regression sessions are needed." Addressing Ruby, she added, "I know you've got a lot on your mind, but I don't think Ellie's case can wait. We need to keep up momentum."

Ruby decided to be honest. "I don't know if I believe her, Ness."

There was a moment of silence.

"It's just," continued Ruby, "it's all so odd with her, isn't it?"

"No, I don't think so," Ness responded at last.

"Well… one minute she can recall tiny details such as a water heater, the next she's saying that it's all wrong, that it even feels wrong to call her husband by that title and yet we know she's married to him. Her mind closes in on itself, it collapses. Those are her words by the way."

When Ness replied her voice was even. "It's ironic you don't believe her. It's a similar situation with the public regarding Psychic Surveys."

Ruby could see the parallel, knew what Ness was getting at, but even so, she wasn't *vilifying* Ellie and she said so.

"I know you're not. *I* believe her and her case is one we need to progress with, so we can reach a satisfactory conclusion."

"In case we don't succeed with Ben, you mean?"

"I hope we do succeed with Ben, but I'm a realist. Theo, you told me once there's no shame in walking away if a case is taking its toll on us. Maybe Gilmore Street is one such case."

"Ness!" Ruby continued to argue. "I've said this before, there *is* shame, *public* shame. If we don't solve the Gilmore case, people will lose faith in us. And if that happens, it's the beginning of the end for Psychic Surveys. Look, you carry on with Ellie if you want to, but I hope you'll carry on with Gilmore Street too. We might be having an enforced break, but our efforts should still be focused on getting to the root of what's grounding Ben. Whatever free time we have, we should spend digging and then digging some more. Everyone leaves a trail behind them, everyone. And we need to sniff it out." She took a deep breath. "I'm not going to be beaten. *We're* not. Not by a bunch of hacks intent on bringing us down for the sake of more sales. We're Psychic Surveys, we're good at what we do. The material world might forsake us but the spirit world has never needed us as much."

Again, that moment of silence and then Theo broke into a wide grin.

"Bravo!" she said, bringing her hands together and clapping. Corinna and Cash joined in. Even Ness looked impressed.

Cash rose and went over to Ruby's laptop.

"So, do you think you're ready to look at the papers now?"

"Bring it on," she replied.

Chapter Twenty-One

DESPITE her fears, there was very little national coverage of the Gilmore case. Fascination remained largely local, the *South Coast Times* in particular dining out on it. Only a couple of the red tops had run an article on it, using it as a 'filler' piece for inside pages. Other papers – more *prestigious* papers she supposed, the likes of *The Guardian*, *The Independent,* and *The Telegraph,* hadn't bothered with the story at all. Scanning the headlines, she saw that they were all lazy, lacking in imagination entirely, variations of 'who you gonna call…?' a hot favourite amongst them. How Ruby cursed that *Ghostbusters* film! Although Samantha assured them she hadn't mentioned that it was Benjamin Hamilton in the house, something Ruby had advised her about, the papers had done their homework, realised he'd died there and put two and two together, making much of his body having lain for a week before discovery. It was ironic, considering he'd barely got a mention at the time.

"What do you think of that, Ben?" Ruby muttered, continuing to read. "Fame at last." Her eyes on the next sentence, she groaned. "Oh no, look, they're saying the church should get involved, that it's a religious matter."

Theo snorted. "The church won't get involved, not for a long while anyway. There's too much red tape to wade through first." After a brief pause, she added, "You know this might be a good time to take that holiday we were talking about."

"Before it goes international you mean?"

"If you like." Theo was being as tongue-in-cheek as her.

Ruby shook her head. "I've told you I'm not running away. I'm staying put."

The next morning she got up early and made her way to the office. Yes, there were a couple of reporters outside, sitting in the same car she'd spied before, and yes they tried to talk to her as she approached, but she simply replied, 'No comment', unlocked the door and closed it firmly behind her. All the team were on the case regarding Ben, Theo and Corinna visiting the offices of Southern Rail in person this time: they must hold information of past employees on databanks somewhere. Maybe there was even someone in the offices who'd actually worked with him or could give them a lead to someone that had. 'Benjamin Hamilton,' she could imagine them saying, 'yeah, yeah, he worked here years ago, strange fellow he was, a bit shy.' It was a long shot, but any type of shot was welcome. Ness was trawling the roads close to Gilmore Street as well as businesses such as cafés and corner shops to see if anyone knew of him. 'And hang the consequences,' she'd said. 'They can't all be cynics, someone must be willing to give us an insight.' It was a difficult thing to do without a police badge: turning up at people's doors asking information about a certain someone, but the team figured that the recent publicity might have given them an edge. They were 'recognisable' to some now. There were even those who might be sympathetic to their cause, or at least aware of what they were doing and therefore less alarmed and more willing to help. 'God moves in a mysterious way,' quoted Theo, and maybe she was right. As for her, she was going through messages and emails, responding to those who were still calling in, despite the slur on their integrity.

Ruby had already spoken to Samantha and she was willing to wait regarding a return visit from the team, for all the fuss to die down and to see if they could find out anything more about Ben.

"He's a one, he's a bloody one!" Samantha had said. "He's got an unfair advantage being invisible. If I could see him I'd throw a teapot at him too."

Even though she was doing her best to sound valiant, Ruby could still detect shock and fear in the woman's voice. She hated to say it but felt she had to. "If at any time you want to pull us off the case, Sam, and hand it over to another psychic, I'd understand."

"No!" Samantha had insisted. "I like you, Ruby. I trust you. We'll get there."

Ruby could only hope so.

Knowing the Gilmore case was in good hands, she got on with everyday tasks, pressing 'play' on the answer machine. As disembodied voices filled the attic room, this time of an earthly variety, Ruby sat poised with her pen ready to take notes. Journalists – there were a few of them. 'It's a great story, Ruby. There's a lot of public interest. We'd love to hear your side of things. How do you cope with seeing ghosts? How many have you dealt with? Can you put us in touch with people you've been involved with? Would they be willing to speak to us? This could be great for business, Ruby, don't you think? You could go global, offices all over the planet. Just speak to us.'

She pressed her hand to her temple. Journalists were begging her to speak to them, she was begging Ben to speak to her – everyone was going round in circles and getting nowhere fast.

Continuing to sift through her voicemail, there were two that seemed to be connected, where the caller had obviously changed their mind about leaving a message and hung up. One after the other they occurred, and Ruby wondered who was trying to reach out to her and what the problem was. No matter. There was nothing she could do about it. If they wanted her, they'd call back.

The next message was entirely different.

"Ms Davis, are you there?" a female voice queried, a *distressed* female voice. "Please, please be there. My child is in danger. Someone wants her. And by someone you know what I mean. A ghost. Our house is haunted. We've just moved here. We're terrified. Please, you've got to help us."

Ruby's hand flew to the telephone. Most people weren't in danger when living alongside a spirit, but this person might be; she'd actually used that very word to describe their situation.

Her call was answered immediately.

"Thank you, thanks so much for getting back to me," the same woman said when Ruby introduced herself. After a few more brief exchanges, Ruby asked how old the child was.

"Five. This ghost, she appears most nights, tells her she wants her to come with her and that if she don't, she's going to hurt her, hurt us too. My daughter's terrified. *We're* terrified. She can barely sleep so we can't either. When we do manage to, she turns our dreams into nightmares."

The woman – Kaylee Grant – started sobbing, highlighting just how terrified she was.

"If you'd like to book an appointment—"

"I can't bear another night of this. I'll lose my rag if I do. Honestly, I'm telling you, it's doing my head in. Can you come now? I don't care what it costs. I want her gone."

"Ms Grant, about fees, we have a sliding scale—"

"Money's no problem, please come."

Deciding the woman was too het up to explain procedure further, Ruby took a note of her address and said she'd be there shortly. After terminating the call, she stood up, grabbed her jacket, and made for the door. No sooner had she reached it then Jed materialised, blocking her pathway.

"Move, Jed. I've got a job to go to."

Jed refused to budge, instead, his gaze intent, he lowered his head and shifted his feet to adopt a combative stance. Ruby laughed.

"What are you doing? Get out of the way."

When he still refused, she shook her head.

"You realise I can walk straight though you, don't you?"

She decided that's exactly what she'd do. The Grants needed her and there was no time to waste. She only hoped whoever was grounded at their household wouldn't prove as much a pain as Benjamin. Jed had to finally give way but he wasn't happy about it.

"I'll be okay," she called back over her shoulder. "Stop worrying."

Sulking, he slunk off in the opposite direction.

* * *

The Grants lived in Lewes on an estate just a few roads behind her flat. Located in a dip, there were several identical blocks. She had to go to number 84. Parking her car in the communal car park, she hoped the reporters camped outside her office hadn't followed her. She'd kept a careful check in the mirror and had driven a roundabout route to get here, dismayed she had to go to such trouble.

Before leaving her car she checked herself in the rear-view mirror, she looked presentable enough, minimal make-up, jeans, jumper and jacket; just like any other young professional. Thankfully it wasn't an effort to look 'normal'. She didn't have outlandish taste, not like Theo with her pink hair and selection of often clashing scarves, and she wasn't as sombre as Ness, who mainly dressed in black. She did her best to blend in. Any pictures of her that the press ran might well prove disappointing to the general public. Which was a good thing – the desired effect.

It took a moment to realise she was standing outside the right flat. It was one of many identical doors, standing like ducks in a row. It took another moment to realise the door was opening. A young girl appeared, Ruby would have said *too* young to be the mother of a five-year-old child. She was barely out of her teens. Nonetheless, Ruby smiled.

"Hi, I'm Ruby Davis, I'm looking for Kaylee Grant."

"That's me."

"Oh." So she *was* the mother. "Would you like me to come in? To discuss what we talked about on the phone."

"I'd love you to," Kaylee said and something in the way she said it put Ruby on alert. The girl was trying to stifle a smirk, a nasty one. *Turn and walk away,* her instincts cried. And she was on the verge of doing just that, when she heard a child start to cry, the sound emanating from within.

"Is that your child?" Ruby asked, just as Kaylee turned, clearly expecting her to follow. Staring at the girl's back, she noticed she was sporting tracksuit bottoms and a grubby cropped tee shirt which was more grey than white. Her feet were bare. Considering she knew Ruby was on her way, she hadn't made any effort with her appearance; even her long blonde hair was tangled. Ruby hoped the girl was more attentive to how her child looked at least.

Kaylee led her to the living room where a toddler, not a five year old, sat wailing, two rivers of mucus running from her nose to her mouth. Instead of going to the child and comforting her, Kaylee picked up a packet of cigarettes and lit one, inclining the packet towards Ruby as she did so.

"No thanks, I don't smoke."

"Suit yourself."

"Kaylee," Ruby ventured, "you sounded really upset on the phone."

Kaylee exhaled a long plume of smoke. "Can you feel her? The woman who haunts us?"

Instead of answering, Ruby nodded towards the child, who now had her fist stuffed in her mouth and was drooling all over it. "She looks younger than five. She looks pre-verbal." And therefore not able to tell her mother what she'd seen.

Kaylee just shrugged. "Can you feel the ghost? That's all I want to know."

Staring at the girl, Ruby was confused. She could feel something, but not an intelligent haunting as such, therefore not a soul grounded. What was here felt more residual than anything – like a bank of negativity; not even a bank, it was as much a part of the flat as the fixtures and fittings. It was a build-up, though, the Grants not solely responsible for it. This had never been a particularly happy place to live, Ruby guessed, right from the very first tenants; there'd been too much disappointment in life expressed within these walls, too much bitterness. No wonder the child was wailing so pitifully. Kids were nothing if not intuitive. Although she knew there was no point in carrying out a survey, Ruby explained that standard procedure was to do a walk around of each room in the flat, trying to tune into a presence.

"But the thing is," Ruby finished, "I honestly don't think there's anything here to worry about." Not of a spiritual nature anyway.

Immediately, Kaylee was on the defensive. "You calling me a liar?"

"A liar? No, no of course not."

"There *is* a ghost. Talk to it, that's what you're supposed to do, isn't it?"

"There isn't a ghost."

"There is."

The child continued sobbing.

Oh for Christ's sake, I could do without this!

Thank goodness Theo or Ness weren't here to catch her uncharitable thoughts. Perhaps she ought to show willing. Put on a show as it were – tune in for a few moments and then tell her again that there was nothing 'intelligent' to tune into. She pointed towards a chair. "Do you mind if I take a seat? I want to close my eyes and concentrate."

"What for?"

She explained.

"Be my guest," the girl answered. Considering this was what she wanted, she seemed begrudging all of a sudden.

The seat was as grubby as the flat's occupants, with dried-on jam stuck to one corner. Lowering herself, she carefully avoided that patch. How she wished Kaylee would pick the baby up, do something to distract her at least. But she didn't, she just stood there staring at Ruby. Doing her best under the circumstances, Ruby cleared her throat and closed her eyes. Rather than connect, she remembered Cash's constant worry about her carrying out initial surveys alone, and how often she argued with him about it. Right now, though, she felt he had a point: a good one. Jed barring the doorway also sprung to mind. He'd been trying to stop her she realised. Somehow he'd sensed there was trouble waiting. She had to get out of here.

Opening her eyes, she stood up.

"Kaylee, there is nothing here, no ghost, nothing to connect to, nada. And I think you know that. Whatever your purpose is in getting me here, I'm not interested. I'm leaving now. Please don't call the offices of Psychic Surveys again unless your problem is a genuine one."

The girl burst out laughing, but it wasn't a pleasant sound.

"Of course we're not haunted, no one is, you nutter. Karl, get out here."

The bedroom door burst open and a young man, also in tracksuit bottoms and a grubby tee shirt, appeared. "Kay, I said get her to talk about the 'ghost' so we could quote her. Why'd you have to go and balls it up?"

"Bitch is on to us, in't she? Just grab a few photos, that'll have to do. The papers will still pay for 'em."

The papers would pay for photos of her? So that's what this charade was all about? Like a geyser seeking release, anger

217

exploded.

"You bloody idiots! Are you seriously that desperate for money? If you are, here's a tip, try getting a job. It's the middle of the day, you should be working not lazing around here in this cesspit, ignoring that poor baby."

"That's it, photograph her, Karl. And press the record button on your phone too, we can say how she swore at us in front of Madison."

Ruby felt like flying at the girl, pulling her hair out, and kicking her to the ground. How much she wanted to do that surprised even her. She had to struggle to remain in control, to clamp down on more words that fought to surge upwards from deep within. Vile words. Profanities. She could almost feel sympathy for someone like Ben. But that's what this was all about – Ben and the Gilmore case. That's what had brought her to the attention of people such as these. She wished she'd never set foot in Gilmore Street as well as in this place. But she had. It was too late on both counts.

Pushing past Karl, hurtling down the hallway, her hair flying behind her, she knew in the next set of press photos she'd look anything but normal.

Chapter Twenty-Two

BACK at the office, Ruby was shaking so hard her teeth were chattering. Jed was looking up at her. The expression on his face wasn't smug – although he had every right to feel that way – it was decidedly sympathetic.

"I'm sorry," she told him, when she'd calmed down. "I'll listen to you next time. I promise." Blinking back tears, she added, "Thanks for trying to help."

Jed dropped to the floor and curled up.

Placing her elbows on the table, Ruby let her head fall forward into her hands. Caught swearing in front of a child – even if it had only been 'bloody' – would provide yet more ammunition against her. When *she* was a child and had told her best friend about her gift, despite her grandmother advising her not to, she'd been nicknamed *Spooky Ruby*. She'd managed to turn the tables, though, pointing out that it was Lisa who was the weird one for even suggesting such a thing. No longer best friends, she'd saved her own bacon at the expense of someone else's – an act of survival. Would she survive what was happening now? Perhaps. If she solved the Gilmore case.

Grabbing her phone, she was about to text Theo to ask if she'd found anything of use regarding Ben, when she heard her call up the stairs.

"Yoo-hoo, darling. Only me."

Ruby had never been so glad to hear her.

Theo bustled into the room, a big smile on her face. Hope dared to surge in Ruby. She wouldn't be smiling if her trip to Southern Rail's Brighton office had proved fruitless, would she?

"Theo—"

Before she could answer there was more movement on the landing outside and then Corinna appeared, followed by Ness. Both of them, Ruby was glad to note, also looking pleased. Putting the Grant episode behind her for now, she concentrated instead on what they had to say.

"Amazing really, what you can achieve in person as opposed to on the phone. I simply fixed that nice man in the rail office with my most charming of smiles and he crumpled, said he'd ask around immediately regarding Ben, and he did. Just like that," Theo clicked her fingers as she said it.

Ruby could well imagine what had really happened. Theo had squared her shoulders, thrown her head back, and stood there as though she owned the world, believing that she actually did, and convincing the man in front of her too.

"So," Ruby prompted, "he asked around and someone came forward?"

"Yep, they did," Corinna took up the story, settling herself into one of the chairs around the meeting table and swigging from a plastic bottle of cola. "Benjamin worked on the railways all his life; nothing high-powered, he was part of a maintenance team. He loved the trains apparently; they were his passion. The man who knew him thought they might be his only passion."

Ruby frowned. "Sorry? I don't understand."

"You guessed Ben might have Asperger's, well the man we talked to, Will, swore that was the case. Will's an old guy too, he's in his late sixties and fighting off retirement for as long as he can; said he's dreading it." Corinna paused to swig further. "Said he wants to work forever."

"How long did Will work with Ben?" Ruby asked.

"Just a few years," answered Theo, "but he didn't have a bad word to say about him. Said he was an amiable enough fellow, shy but good at what he did. Meticulous even. Kept himself to himself, as we know was his preference, but he wasn't bothersome in any way. Never upset anyone or got into trouble with the bosses, he was always punctual, that sort of thing. Never took a day off sick, despite the fact he was getting on. He was asked to work dos every now and then, but never went. Preferred to go home and watch the telly."

"So much so he died in front of it," remarked Ruby.

"If only we could say he died happy," Theo added.

There was a brief moment of silence in which Ruby considered telling them about what had just happened to her, but quickly, before her thoughts could be detected, changed her mind. Right now she wanted to focus on what was being said about Ben, to feel as if she was getting somewhere.

"Did Will mention anything else significant?"

"He did actually. It turns out Will has a nephew who's on the spectrum too and he made a very good point. People with Asperger's or any form of autism are no more likely to commit acts of violence than people who don't have the condition. Sure enough, there might be problems with anxiety and relationships, but that doesn't necessarily translate into violence, why should it? He says he's sick of the bad press autistic people get because they're different. Something we can understand."

Ness nodded in agreement with Theo. "I managed to speak to a few people who 'knew' Ben too, most notably the woman who runs the corner shop. She told me he was a frequent visitor; that he popped in almost every day to get his paper and a Mars bar. She said he never spoke to her, never even really looked her in the eye, but he always smiled as he handed over his money."

"Never looked her in the eye?" Ruby queried.

"That's right, but if he was on the spectrum, that's a common enough thing to do, or rather not do." Clearing her throat, she continued. "There was someone else too, a chap who lives in one of the streets nearby. I think perhaps their daily visits to the corner shop coincided, as he only ever bumped into Ben in the street. Apparently they'd nod at each other, exchange a 'how do you do?', that sort of thing. This chap, Duncan, was annoyed actually with the intimation that it's Ben dwelling in Gilmore Street still. 'He seemed like a decent sort,' he said. 'Not likely to cause any trouble, this side or the other.' Told me that Psychic Surveys was slandering his good name. Said Ben would be turning in his grave if he knew." Ness laughed, a sound Ruby wished she heard more often. "I was tempted to say 'that might well be the case, if he *was* in it. I refrained of course, pointed out that it wasn't strictly us doing the slandering, that it was the press."

"And what did he say to that?" enquired Ruby.

"That we were both as bad as each other."

Ruby sat back in her chair and sighed. "So, the general consensus is that Ben's a nice guy, harmless, no threat to anyone. Similar to what we know already, from what Delia told us."

"It does seem to concur," agreed Theo. "I know I'm repeating myself, but people wear masks. They rarely show the world their true colours."

Ness spoke again. "I'd be inclined to think the same, but for a third person I spoke to, the landlord of The Evening Star on Surrey Street, which is about a five minute walk from Gilmore Street. As well as chocolate, Ben also liked the occasional pint and it's there that he went to get it."

"So the landlord was singing his praises too?" Ruby couldn't help it, she was growing disheartened again.

"He was," answered Ness, "told me he sat at the end of the bar, never actively engaged in conversation but was pleasant enough when spoken too. He smiled a lot, even if it was into the distance. But something else happened, something far more interesting."

"What?" A little spark caught light inside Ruby.

"Well," Ness, normally so composed, looked excited too, her dark eyes lively, "it was a winter's evening and Ben had popped into the pub, the first time in a while apparently. He ordered his drink and sat in his usual spot. After he'd finished, he placed his pint down on the table and made his way home. The thing is, he'd left his scarf behind. The landlord, Rob, decided to go after him, as it was a quiet night and he wasn't the only member of staff on duty." Ness paused. "Rob seems kind, the sort that wouldn't want an old man to be without his scarf in cold weather. Ben was quite far ahead but Rob hurried along, catching up with him at the entrance to his house on Gilmore Street, just as he was opening the door and going inside. 'I've got your scarf,' he said, holding it up. Ben seemed frightened at first by his sudden appearance but then relaxed when he saw who it was. As Rob put it, he sort of barged his way into Ben's house, didn't really give him a chance to close the door on him. He wanted to check the old man was okay, you know? He worried about him."

Corinna's eyes widened. "Was it awful inside? A hovel?"

"I asked that. He said it was old-fashioned but it was homely enough."

"Samantha said the work they had to do to it after buying it at auction was extensive," Ruby highlighted.

"Yes, I'm sure it was," Ness replied, "but according to Rob the décor wasn't really a concern. The atmosphere, however, was."

"The atmosphere?" Theo raised an eyebrow.

"Yes, they went through to the kitchen and Ben took the scarf from him, still avoiding eye contact and placed it on the table, thanking him. Rob said he felt nervous, as if there was someone else in the house with them. He said he'd felt it in the hallway but in the kitchen it was intense. Again, worried for Ben, he asked him if he was all right, whether there was anything more he could do. Ben shook his head and said no. Rob was really reluctant to leave and Ben must have picked up on this. He told him to go, said he'd be all right, that he was perfectly safe. Thinking it was an odd word to use, Rob asked if he lived alone. Ben wouldn't answer, just repeated he was safe, getting a bit agitated while he did. Rob turned to leave but at the door he hesitated once more, reiterating that Ben was to let him know if he needed anything. Ben replied, 'It's fine, we don't.'"

"We?" queried Ruby.

"That's right, *we*," confirmed Ness. "Realising there was

no more he could do, Rob left. Ben never really came to the pub again, not whilst Rob was working a shift anyway, and it wasn't long after that that he died. Rob's been wondering about going to the *South Coast Times* with his story."

Ruby drew a breath inwards. "You advised him against that, didn't you?"

"I did and he agreed. He's no fan of the media either."

That was a relief. As Ruby mulled over Ness's words, something Delia said came to mind during their first meeting with her. She was telling them about Ben too, about her conversations with him, how she'd come right out and asked the old man if he was lonely. Leaning forward, she reminded Ness and enlightened the others about this particular snippet of conversation. "He said he wasn't lonely and he looked directly at her when he said it, which as we know, is something Ben didn't do very often, almost as if he wanted to press the point home." She sat back in her chair and agitated at her lip. Looking at Ness, at all of them, she said, "Damn it, you know what I think, don't you?"

Although all three nodded it was Ness who spoke.

"It's not *him*, is it? It's not Ben that's haunting Gilmore Street."

"Cash was right. We've been barking up the wrong tree all along. He said it might be someone else and I just brushed his suggestion aside." Ruby's groan was audible. "Christ, he's never going to let me live this down!"

Chapter Twenty-Three

THEO clapped her hands together.

"Regarding Cash, dear girl, bite the bullet and give credit where credit's due. As for you Ness, good work. Really good work."

"I thought so," Ness replied, pretending at smugness.

Corinna, on the other hand, looked decidedly perplexed. "But if it's not Ben, who is it? Who else died at the house?"

"That's what we have to find out." Turning to Ness, Theo asked if she could possibly bother her police contact again about the matter. East Sussex Record Office, The Keep, would be closed by now and, although it was open on Saturdays, they might be able to find out something that night. All of them felt impatient to do so.

"I can, he's erm… very approachable is Lee."

"Oh, is he now?" Theo shot back. "I take it you mean in all respects?"

Theo was well known for her gentle teasing of Ness – sometimes Ness took it in the vein it was meant – affectionately – at other times it irritated her. Thankfully, what she'd found out had put them all in a good mood, so she simply smiled in response before rising from her chair. "I'll go and call him."

Whilst she did, Ruby turned to her computer and typed in *44 Gilmore Street*, clicking on the 'Brighton History' site to find out when the street had been developed. Formerly known as Upper Trafalgar Street, it dated back to the mid 1850s, something she suspected if it was intended to house railway workers – Brighton Station had been built in 1840, a decade earlier.

"That's a lot of history," she muttered. *Unfortunately.*

Ness returned a few minutes later. "We'll have to wait a while but Lee's agreed to do his best. We have to remember, though, computerised police records only go back to the seventies and from the quick scan he managed to do whilst I was talking to him, there's no evidence of any 'foul play' having taken place at that address. In fact, there's nothing at that address at all."

"The seventies?" Ruby queried. "Ben's been there since the late sixties, so we need to go much further back than the seventies. I suspect trawling through the archives in the police vaults is too much of an ask, isn't it?"

Ness nodded. "Lee's a very busy man and well... that could take a lifetime."

"Yeah, yeah, I know it could."

"Let's sleep on it tonight," Theo advised. "Combine Lee's efforts with a trip to The Keep tomorrow. You never know we *might* find something of interest."

The emphasis Theo put on the word 'might' escaped no one.

* * *

London and Brighton Railway had built and owned the houses in Gilmore Street and thereabouts for railway workers up until nationalisation in the late 1940s. Records at The Keep were nothing if not expansive, including a general guide to tracing the history of a house, which they were all advised to read before making a start. The sentence

'Remember that if you live in a town it is more difficult to trace the history of your house' did nothing to inspire confidence. Even so, one of the assistants there, Sylvia, assured them they should be able to find names of families who'd lived there through the ages, even those who were tenants not owners, by cross-referencing a combination of trade directories, census returns and electoral registers. The task seemed a daunting one.

"Do you have access to the title deeds to this house you're wanting to know more about?" asked Sylvia.

"Erm… no," admitted Ruby. "We want to see what we can find out ourselves before bothering the client."

"Client?" Sylvia looked impressed. "Private Investigators are you?"

"Something like that," Ruby replied.

"Nice work if you can get it."

Not always, thought Ruby, as Sylvia retreated.

Shortly after the house was erected, the Harringtons had moved in, John and Elizabeth. How many children they'd had between them remained a mystery, but at least they had something to grasp onto now. They'd lived there for twenty-six years, then, in 1877, the Dochertys became tenants, George and Ann. Again, they'd been long-termers, living there well into the new millennium. In 1910, it had been Frank and Evelyn Turnbull; in the 1920s, Albert and Rose Fowler, and then in the late 1940s it had been sold to David and Betty Dolan. The next registered owner was Benjamin Hamilton.

Ruby tested the names on her tongue – John, George, Frank, Albert, and David – which one was their man?

Ness picked up on her thoughts. "Maybe none of them. Those couples would have had children and it could be one of them, all grown-up of course; something about the house and what happened in it, drawing them back."

Ness was right but they could only work with what they had. Trying to flesh out details as far as possible, the team endeavoured to track down the birth and death certificates of those they knew had lived there, but, of course, these didn't include actual details of *where* a person had died, just the city, which wasn't always Brighton.

As all four continued with their efforts – including scanning local papers as far back as possible for reportage of any other death at Gilmore Street, apart from Benjamin's, another arduous task – the hours raced by. The Keep closed at 4pm on Saturdays and it would soon be chucking-out time.

At quarter to four, Ruby sat back in her chair and rubbed at her eyes. "It's like looking for a needle in a haystack."

Ness agreed. "It is. And it's personal information that's the most useful to us. The kind you can't get by wading through acres of dusty tomes."

She was right. They still had so little to go on. Except…

"Hang on, Samantha was the one who brought the case to our attention. She said she felt like she was being watched, or rather *glared* at all the time."

"Uh huh," said Theo. "That's right."

"Well, later, she was attacked and prior to that, her daughter was attacked during the flying mug incident. Jeff, however, and his son were initially undisturbed by him; they only became frightened when they actually saw phenomena occurring rather than felt it." Ruby was warming to her theme. "And the way he treats us, the swearing, the blows, he's a misogynist."

"We already know that, Ruby. How's this helping?"

"It helps us, Theo, by building up a profile. The spirit at Gilmore Street is a complete mystery to us, his name, his reason for being there, his less than friendly attitude, everything. I don't get the feeling that he's someone from way back – his use of language is too modern for that."

"People swore back then," Ness insisted.

"Yeah, yeah, I know they did. It's just a hunch I've got that's all." Mulling it over a bit more, she came to a decision. "There's a way we can test it. Basically, the way it stands right now, every man who ever lived in that house is a suspect, with the possible exception of Ben. The kitchen is his preferred territory and he's filled with hate. And what are we always saying is at the root of hatred? Fear. He's frightened of a woman and what she did to him. So that means every female who ever lived there is a suspect too."

"Every female?" Ness queried.

"Yeah. The spirit refuses to tell us his name, to tell us anything, in fact, so we take another approach. We make a list of the women's names, we go back to Gilmore Street, and we shout them out, every last one of them."

"Until what?" Corinna asked.

"Until we get a reaction, that's what," Ruby replied, smiling.

* * *

Although the others were dubious, Ruby was pleased with her latest plan. Her good mood, however, didn't last long. Leaving The Keep she arrived back at her flat to a double whammy: her mother calling on the mobile and Cash arriving on the doorstep, one sounding pissed off, the other looking it.

"What the hell's this?" Cash said, brandishing a copy of the *South Coast Times* in front of her.

"Hang on, hang on," she replied, inserting her key in the lock and shushing him at the same time. "Mum's on the phone."

It was all Cash could do to contain himself. She didn't think she'd ever seen him look so furious.

"Have you seen the newspaper today?" her mother was saying.

"No," and despite Cash waving it in front of her nose, she didn't want to. Frustrating him further she kept her eyes averted. "Mum, it's best not to look."

"Ruby," Jessica's voice was much firmer now, "they are *crucifying* you. There's a picture of you running down a hallway, as if you're a criminal fleeing the scene. In the article it says you swore in front of their child, that you'd contacted them – the Grants – to say you'd found out that a woman had died a horrible death in their flat and that it needed to be cleansed. You basically barged your way in there, intent on creating work out of thin air."

"What?" Ruby had wandered through to the kitchen and had to sit as her mother continued relating the lies that had been printed. She turned to Cash, who was hovering over her.

"Here, give me that," she said, finally taking the paper from him. "Hang on, Mum, Cash is here, he's got a copy of the paper too. I'm just going to read what it says. I'll place you on loudspeaker, okay?"

Cash sat beside her as she did, pulling his chair close to offer what comfort he could. Which wasn't a lot under the circumstances. "Oh, Christ," she kept repeating. The pictures of herself were as bad as she feared they were going to be – she looked demented – but the lies the Grant family had told, the angle that they'd come up with to get themselves into the paper, the picture of them, Kaylee, her boyfriend or whoever he was, and the child, standing huddled together looking nothing less than terrified by her intrusion – absolutely *terrified* – was too much. Despite not wanting to read further, she couldn't resist. *'Come with me,' that's what Ruby said the ghost was saying, said she was standing in a corner with her eyes on my girl, but it's not true. Ghosts aren't real. We all know that. Even so, it freaked me out, I'm upset and because I am, so's my kid. We're hardly getting any sleep. She keeps crying, sometimes all night. That's what Ruby Davis has done to her, to us.'*

She could feel her body shaking as her eyes began to blur; could feel the surge of emotion rising; the tears that finally found release; could see all too clearly the ruin of everything she had worked hard for – so damned hard – as it lay in tatters around her. All because of Gilmore Street.

As she continued to sob, Cash grabbed her phone, said something to her mother about looking after her and that she wasn't to worry, then he turned off the phone and pulled her into his arms. She resisted at first; she just wanted to drown in sorrow on her own, pulling no one down with her. She wanted to sink to the depths, lie at the bottom of a cold, cold ocean, and sleep forevermore. She was exhausted and had been even before Gilmore Street, any last vestige of energy deserting her.

"Ruby, come on, you'll get through this, you know you will," Cash was murmuring. She slumped against him, buried her head in his chest. Was he right? Would she get through it? She wouldn't place a bet on it. "Ruby," he continued, doing his best to reach her, to bring her back.

"Let me help."

But how could he help? What could he do?

In the end what he did was perfect. He pulled her gently to her feet, led her into the bedroom and started kissing her, on her forehead, her cheeks, her neck, working his way downwards. As he did, he lifted up the light jumper she was wearing, pulled it over her head, and discarded it. Sweeping her off her feet, he laid her gently on the bed, removing the last of her clothing and his too before lying beside her. The warmth of him, the colour of his skin, the *smell* of him... she breathed it in, the wonderful familiarity. As though on a gentle decline, the despair she'd felt began to slide away. How could you feel despair when you had this in your life, a lover, a protector and an equal? Someone who, without a moment's hesitation, would follow you down to the depths, who'd stand beside you as you faced your greatest fear and who'd bring you back. Because that's what he was doing right now, not just touching her body, but her spirit too, *re-energising* her. He was the light to her dark, something she was truly starting to realise. As she started to respond, she decided she would lose herself, just for a while; focus only on him and the love he had for her, which she could at least return. As small cries began to escape her, she marvelled at how easy it was to leave behind the latest catastrophe. Right here, right now, it didn't seem to matter one bit. *This* was all that mattered: this flat, this room, this bed, and the two people on it. Yes, she'd have to return to the real world – of course she would. But, as his cries joined hers, she could stay lost just a little while longer.

* * *

Much later, giggling with Cash as they sat up in bed, actually *giggling*, Ruby felt a million miles removed from the earlier upset. Even so, she must phone her mum soon to make sure she wasn't worrying, although with Cash, Jessica knew she'd be in good hands – which made her giggle again.

Cash wrestled her back down. "What's so funny?" he asked, smothering her neck in kisses.

"Nothing, just a thought I had about being in good hands. A bit of a Freudian thought, considering what's just happened."

He pulled away, pretended at offence.

"Good hands. *Good*? That's as bad as saying 'nice'." He held one hand up in front of her. "These are magnificent hands, Ruby, nothing less."

"Then you'd better put them to use again, hadn't you? And afterwards I'll mark you out of ten."

"You'll mark me? I'll be off the scale."

As he buried his head between her breasts she felt like what she was – not *Spooky Ruby,* nor a charlatan, a swindler and a fake – but a young woman in love, and falling deeper by the day.

"Bugger!" The phone was ringing. "I thought you'd turned my mobile off."

"I did. That's your house phone, Ruby."

"Oh yeah," she laughed, "of course. The ringtone's virtually the same."

"Ignore it. It's not important."

She fully intended to, but it might be Samantha. Ruby had called her the previous night but there'd been no reply. Leaving a message, she hadn't said exactly what they'd found out, that it wasn't the spirit of Ben in her house, only that there'd been developments in the investigation, and asking whether they could arrange another time to go back to Gilmore Street, sooner rather than later. If it *was* Samantha, she really needed to answer. The fight in her was making a comeback.

Pushing Cash off, she rolled onto her side and grabbed at the phone beside the bed. "I won't be a minute, Cash. Meanwhile, keep those hands warm for me. I'll deduct points if you don't."

Cash merely snorted in reply as he rolled onto his back.

"Hi, Samantha, thanks for calling me back. We need to—"

"Ruby, it's Ellie. I hope you don't mind me calling."

"Oh, Ellie, hi, how are you?"

Beside her she heard Cash emit a deep sigh; he was clearly not impressed she'd answered the phone and now she was beginning to feel the same way.

Without waiting for her to answer, she added, "Look, Ellie, can this wait? Something's, erm... something's come up here at the moment."

Cash started laughing beside her, his irritation quashed, and she gestured for him to be silent.

"Oh, that's fine, of course, no worries," Ellie replied, sounding a little embarrassed. Had she heard Cash? Probably. He wasn't being very discreet. "I just wanted to say I felt really sorry for you the other day, how the press are treating you, how no one's come forward to stand up for what you do, so I thought *I* would. I spoke to a reporter this morning, Ruby, he's really nice, not like the others, he seems genuine, as if he cared about the case. I told him how much you're helping me, the progress we're making. He was really interested, impressed you know? It's going to be a good article I think."

As Ellie's words tumbled from her mouth, as Ruby's brain made sense of them, she almost dropped the phone. Cash tensed now, his laughter on hold.

"You've done what?" Ruby asked, aghast.

"I've gone to the press, about the reincarnation case." Ellie seemed to falter a bit, started stammering. "Th… that's okay, isn't it? I was only trying to help. I wanted to show that you take on unusual cases, cases you're not that comfortable with. If someone's in need, you don't turn them away."

Too incensed to speak, she could only manage, "Ellie… I've got to go," before ending the call, discarding the phone and lying back down on the bed. Raising her hands, she kneaded both temples with her fingertips.

Rising on one elbow, Cash loomed over her. "What is it? What's wrong?"

"Ellie's gone to the press and told them about her case, a case even I can't get my head around, let alone the public." Finally she stopped kneading and looked at him. "From the minute I met her, I knew I shouldn't get involved. There's something not quite right about her, Cash. The memories she recalls and how confused they are. She's trouble. For me she's trouble. That's my hunch and I was right. I was bloody right. She's just buried me deeper in it."

Chapter Twenty-Four

"THAT'S not the point, Ness, she shouldn't have gone to the press to talk about what we've been doing, not without asking me first!"

"She was acting from good intent."

"You keep saying that! But I don't believe it. I think the girl's deluded."

Although Ruby was speaking to Ness on the phone, she could well imagine the older woman's face hardening as she said that.

"Whatever we're going through, we, as Psychic Surveys, must still act in a professional manner. Calling one of our clients deluded is hardly a good example of that."

Ruby couldn't believe it. "What? Are you calling me unprofessional, Ness?"

Behind her Cash put a hand on her arm in an attempt to try and calm her but she was beyond that.

"As a matter of fact, I am."

"You've got a cheek! Regarding Ellie's case, *you've* been unprofessional all along. You forced me into it!"

"I didn't. You're your own person, Ruby, or at least you should try and be."

"I... I—"

Cash took the phone from her.

"Ness, look, it might be best to speak to Ruby another

time. She's already had a bit of a shock today with the latest news report; it's a bit of a crap one. Yeah, yeah, you've seen it? Kaylee Grant telling a pack of lies. She's still reeling from it to be honest, and then Ellie phones and drops the bomb. I'm sorry, you know how it is; it'll all seem better in the morning."

Cash ended the call and Ruby swiped at him, hard.

"Don't apologise on my behalf! I've got nothing to apologise for."

Throwing the phone on the bed, Cash grabbed Ruby by the shoulders. "For God's sake, ease up, will you? The way you're acting is making everything worse. Ness is your friend. She's not the enemy. She didn't know Ellie was going to talk to the press either."

"But if it wasn't for her I wouldn't still be involved with Ellie!"

"Either way, you are."

She pushed him off. "No, I'm not, not anymore. Ellie is *not* Psychic Surveys' responsibility."

Searching for her mobile phone, she picked it up and started tapping.

"Don't do anything you might regret, Ruby," Cash warned.

"I won't regret this, I'm handing the case over. Ness can carry on with it under her own steam. I'm done."

Sending the message she felt at least marginally better. She had wanted to pull the plug on that one for a while and now she'd done it. Ness would just have to understand. As for Ellie, she'd never have to speak to her again.

"I know we haven't got it in writing," she muttered, breathing fire, "but client confidentiality should work both ways."

Still angry, perhaps *because* she was angry, she decided to phone Samantha. If she was feeling more charitable – which she wasn't – she might be grateful to Ellie for forcing her hand. Anger was a lot more productive than despair. Before she called her, she quickly briefed Cash about their latest findings, and included an apology for dismissing so readily his suggestion that it might be someone other than Ben there. Giving credit where credit was due again, he didn't gloat, but encouraged her to phone Samantha too. 'Just don't let her know how angry you are,' he advised. His words and Ness's burned in her mind. *Whatever we're going through, we, as Psychic Surveys, must still act in a professional manner* and *You're your own person, Ruby, or at least you should try and be.* Slowing her breathing before she started dialling, she even forced herself to smile.

* * *

"Samantha, I think you're making a mistake."

"Ruby, that's the thing, I agree with you, but it's not me who's making the decision, it's Jeff. He's listened to me in the past. I have to listen to *him* now."

"But like I've told you, we've got further information – or at least we know that the grounded spirit is unlikely to be Benjamin Hamilton. We're making headway, if we can just go in again, we may get significantly further."

"I really would like you to continue, honestly I would," Samantha sounded genuine at least. "But Jeff's having a fit about what the local papers are saying. I mean, you have to admit, it hasn't exactly been in your favour, has it?

Especially that article today, it's erm…" Ruby didn't need her to say it. She looked a fool, rushing down that narrow hallway – *unprofessional.* Was there any point in telling her she was framed? Would it do any good to beg? No. Desperate was never a good look.

"Sam, tell me, what *have* you got in mind regarding Gilmore Street?"

"Well… quite a few psychics have contacted us." *Of course they have,* Ruby couldn't help the acidity of her thoughts. "And Jeff's busy lining up appointments with them, giving each of them a chance so to speak."

"And what if everyone draws a blank?" Ruby asked.

Samantha paused. "Oh, I'm sure they won't. I'm sure someone can move him on. He can't hang around forever, can he?"

To that end they'd have to wait and see.

* * *

Sure enough, the press did have a field day with Ellie's story, not even intimating, but coming right out and saying that there was nothing Psychic Surveys would stop at to fleece money off people, even taking advantage of young girls who believed their past lives were responsible for their current troubles. Yes, that 'nice reporter' Ellie had talked about had done his homework on her too. He had found out that she was adopted, had a troubled relationship with her adoptive parents, her mother in particular, and had lost her way – leaving school without qualifications, drifting aimlessly, dabbling with drugs, and was now in a hostel trying to get her life back on track. Ellie was painted as prey, and Psychic Surveys, Ruby in particular, as the vulture bearing down on her.

Add to the mix that Samantha had withdrawn Gilmore Street from them, and there seemed to be no hope of redemption. The papers had even started getting biblical about their prior involvement, one bright spark quoting Leviticus 19:31 – *Do not turn to mediums or necromancers; do not seek them out, and so make yourselves unclean by them: I am the Lord your God.*

"What the hell is a necromancer?" Cash has asked on reading it.

"It's the practice of communing with the dead to predict the future," Ruby informed him. "It's a term often used in black magic or witchcraft."

"Black magic? They're saying you're a witch?"

"It looks like it. I wonder if they'll say the same about the other psychics called in to deal with the case. Or if they'll be content with just targeting us."

"Depends if those other psychics fail or not," Cash replied, shrugging. "Failure equals death by exposure."

"Don't we know it," Ruby muttered darkly.

"Look on the bright side, though."

"You're telling me there is one?"

"Yeah, if whoever they get in fails spectacularly, it'll make you look good."

"Cash, *we* failed spectacularly."

"Oh yeah, there is that."

In the days that followed, Ruby spent time contacting those she'd helped in the past with domestic spiritual clearance, Alan Kierney in particular, who was also a high profile journalist. He owned Highdown Hall, the one-time home of 1950s film star, Cynthia Hart. Detecting her presence was still there he had been on the phone to them sharpish. Not the most pleasant of men at the time they were dealing with him, she wasn't surprised by his response. "No," he'd replied bluntly, "I don't get involved with the gutter press. If I see my name mentioned with regard to Psychic Surveys I'll sue." When she'd told Cash his reaction, he was only surprised that there was anything *but* a gutter press. Although several other clients she'd spoken to weren't as rude, the outcome was the same. They wanted to help, or at least they assured her they did, but they didn't want anything negative said about them either. They were living quiet lives now that the various spirits had gone and wanted it to stay that way. 'You know,' said one, 'Scarlett and Ellie are at school, if word got out, well... kids can be cruel.'

Ness was right about that spotlight: people didn't want to be in it. The only way Ruby could see round the problem was to speak to the press too. It was a gamble but it might pay off. The phone had stopped ringing so much, the number of new cases coming in much less. It was mainly Ellie who dominated the answer machine; she'd left several messages apologising profusely, one of them quite tearful. Ruby ignored them all. And of those from other people asking for help, Ruby was wary. Most seemed genuine but there were a couple of obvious pranksters, most notably the call from Helen Back. It had taken her a moment to 'get it' but she had – *hell and back* – very funny! Certainly Cash had thought so when she told him about it. It had kept him in stitches all evening. Yes, there were those that shunned the spotlight, but some, like the Grants, craved it – the wrong type unfortunately, the type who wanted to bury her further and for no other reason other than that they could. Boredom perhaps, maybe that's what lay at the root of their malice. Regarding her earlier idea of speaking to reporters, she'd go to Brighton, walk into the *South Coast Times* offices and demand to speak to someone. Meanwhile, she'd keep an eye on the papers as much as everyone else seemed to be doing – whatever failures and successes were due to take place in Gilmore Street – she wanted to know about them.

Chapter Twenty-Five

RUBY didn't go straight to the newspapers, barging in, all guns blazing like a warrior on the loose. Instead, Theo called and asked if she'd accompany her on a cleansing – 'under the Psychic Surveys banner of course' – to which Ruby had agreed. How could she refuse? It was her job, after all, *still* her job. Retirement was a way off yet.

"But are you sure it's genuine, Theo?" She was still so nervous about that.

"Dear girl, the woman we're going to visit is someone I know – not very well, admitted – but I can tell enough from her aura that she's a sincere person. There's no need for you to drive, we'll pick you up within the hour."

"Who's 'we'?"

"Ness and I."

Ruby gulped as she ended the call – this wasn't just a case of spirit rescue, this was friendship rescue too. Since their bust-up on the phone, Ruby hadn't seen Ness. Okay, it had only been a few days but normally they saw each other or at least talked on the phone or via text every day – so the 'separation' had been obvious – to everyone.

You don't have to go, ring back and say you can't.

She wouldn't describe herself as a sulker, but maybe she was deluded.

Of course you have to go, you have to remain professional, remember?

Well, she would. And it would be fine. As long as Ness didn't want to talk to her about Ellie, and inveigle her again.

Ness said nothing about Ellie. She hardly said anything at all, not to Ruby anyway. Clearly she was as upset as Ruby was. You could have cut the atmosphere in the car with a knife as they drove to Ringmer, on the outskirts of Lewes. *There you again with that knife business.*

'Knives' had been on her mind a lot lately, she'd felt a danger surrounding them, a danger surrounding Ellie too. Perhaps the danger was linked and actually a symbolic one. The girl was coming between Ruby and Ness, sticking the knife in deeper as far as the furore surrounding Psychic Surveys too. That's why she was bad news. To be fair to her, maybe she'd done both unwittingly but did that excuse it? Maybe, if Ruby had been in a better frame of mind, but she wasn't, she was feeling much the same as she'd done when gearing up to face her life-long demon. And now she was facing demons all over again, this time of a human variety. Would the battle never end?

If either of the women sitting up front had homed in on her thoughts during the journey, neither commented. And Ruby was grateful. She needed a break, needed to focus her mind on helping the woman who'd called them in.

Ness parked the car and turned off the engine. Meanwhile, Theo cleared her throat and started to speak. Normally so jovial, she was subdued today. What was happening, personally and professionally, was affecting them all.

"Before we go in, a bit of background. June is someone I know only barely. I go to a bridge class, so does June, and sometimes our visits coincide. We chat on occasion, over a cup of tea afterwards. She knows what I do and always appears interested."

"Well, if she didn't know then, she'd know now," Ruby muttered.

"Quite," agreed Theo, "but to be fair, *everyone* who knows me knows what I do. If they choose to de-friend me because of it, that's entirely up to them and their loss. Like others in the area, June's been reading about us in the papers lately and yesterday she contacted me. She was hesitant at first – so expect her to be nervous about our visit – but she feels there's a presence in her house, that of her sister, whom she lived with before her demise. She gets the impression her sister's not happy; that she's upset; that she wants her to go somewhere with her. In fact, the words that appear frequently in her head, especially in the dead of night, when, as humans, we're more receptive to what lies beyond, are 'come with me'."

Ruby couldn't believe her ears. *'Come with me?'* She'd been reading the papers all right! The Grant case in particular. "I don't believe it," she burst out, "this is another bloody hoax!"

In the passenger seat, Theo turned her whole body round to face Ruby, no mean feat considering the limited space in the car and the bulk of her. The expression on her face immediately quietened Ruby. She'd seen her angry before, but not *this* angry. "June is *not* a liar, and this is *not* a hoax! Ruby, you know about balance, about the yin and the yang. Nothing is ever all bad and nothing is ever all good, even when both situations appear that way. Look up from the bottom of that well you're languishing in at the moment and see the sunlight; it's there if you look hard enough. Reading about the Grants actually spurred June on to call me. It gave her the courage. This 'haunting' has been going on for a while. She's not frightened, not of her sister, but she's concerned. She's told no one about it so far – not even me, despite knowing something of my profession – for fear people would think early senility was setting in. To be honest, I think she thought it would resolve itself in time, but it hasn't. Now she realises it's typical of the cases we deal with. That debacle with the Grants highlighted that, and so she's come forward, at last. So choose to see the good in something every now and then. Choose to *believe*, Ruby, in others as well as yourself."

Before Ruby had a chance to retaliate, Theo turned to Ness. "And if you can't sort out what's happened between you, at least put it aside for now. I don't want any trace of bad feeling when we set foot in June's house."

As Theo wriggled her way out of the car, Ruby and Ness followed, not just Ruby feeling like an admonished child, it was clear that Ness did too.

* * *

As June led Ruby, Theo and Ness through to the living room, they were all smiles, Ruby in particular not daring to let hers slide for a minute, especially when Theo was looking. June was a small woman, her build as neat as the clothes she was wearing: slacks and a blouse. The fact she was nervous was betrayed only by the constant wringing of her hands.

"I loved my sister," she told them, "but I don't want to go anywhere, not just yet. I feel bad, though, you know…

we were very close."

"What's her name?" Theo balanced a cup of tea on her lap as she asked.

"Mary."

"And how did she die?"

There was the glisten of tears in June's eyes. "Cancer."

"I'm sorry."

June made an effort to brighten. "Thank you," she said. "It was certainly a very traumatic time. Mary wasn't granted a swift exit."

"Did she die at home?" Ruby asked.

"Yes, upstairs, in her bedroom."

"And is that where you sense her most?"

"Oh no. I sense her everywhere, even when I go out to the shops, she's always with me."

"And she speaks to you?" Ness said. "In your head you can hear her?"

June swallowed as she nodded. "Only the words 'come with me'."

Placing her cup on the table, Theo stood up. She'd already explained procedure to June, who gave them permission to carry out a survey. Upstairs, in Mary's former bedroom, the three of them stood side by side, trying to connect. Ness was the first to give up.

"There's no one here," she said.

"I realise that," Theo answered. "Ruby, do you agree?"

Ruby did. "We'd better break the news."

Back in the living room, Theo took the lead. "Apart from Mary 'speaking' to you, what else has been happening, particularly in the home?"

"What else? Erm… I'm not sure I know how to answer that."

"What evidence do you have to think that she's still here?"

June was aghast. "Aren't you the ones meant to find evidence, not me?"

Theo lowered her head slightly, not in dismay, it was more like a mark of respect. Then she raised it again, and looked June straight in the eye. "Why do you think you're being haunted?"

"My sister, I… I can smell her sometimes, the perfume she liked to wear, Eau Dynamisante, it's such a lovely smell, clean and fresh. When I'm sitting watching our favourite programmes, it's like she's sitting beside me. I can feel her, almost see her. It's so strange. Sometimes I think all I have to do is reach out and touch her – that'll she'll be there; that she'll smile at me like she used to, sometimes cheerfully, sometimes wryly, depending on what we were watching. Mary had a great sense of humour. I fancy I hear her laughing sometimes. It's a lovely sound, like tinkling bells I used to say."

All three of them listened as June spoke but it was Ness who questioned *why* she wanted them to investigate her presence. "Do you want us to move her on?"

June bit her lip, stared at her hands, which were clasped together. "Yes… No… I don't know. I don't want to think she's unhappy, that's the thing; that she's missing me."

Ness looked at Ruby; Theo did too. She might not be able to catch thoughts, but she knew what they were thinking clear enough; what they wanted her to point out. She swallowed, keeping her voice as soft as possible. "June, I think it's *you* who's missing Mary. She's not here, there's no spiritual presence in your home."

Instead of reacting, June just sat there. Ruby wondered

briefly if Theo or Ness would intervene, but they didn't; they were leaving it to her.

"I'm sorry Mary's not here," Ruby continued, "for your sake, I mean, but I'm not sorry for Mary – she's gone where she needs to go. She's on the next stage of her journey. It's better she doesn't remain grounded, that she felt able to leave." When June still didn't react, Ruby prompted her, "Don't you agree?"

At last June focused her gaze – she'd been staring into the distance before, the expression on her face nothing less than stricken. "You're wrong, she's still here with me."

"June, she's not."

June's eyes narrowed. "But what if you *are* wrong? Sometimes you must be, surely?"

Oh, yes, we're far from infallible, Ruby wanted to say but didn't. With June, she had to remain confident, sure of herself, *professional*. Only briefly did she glance at Theo, wondering if on some level this case had been deliberately manufactured, and if not by Theo, then by some higher power. Whichever way, her colleagues were not stepping in.

June was crying now – openly sobbing. Ruby stood up and went to kneel beside her chair, reaching out to take the old woman's hands. She was reluctant for Ruby to touch her at first, but then she clung to her.

"Do you think she's forgotten me?" she said, her voice frailer than before.

"Of course not. She'd never forget you; you're a part of each other. But it's better that we move on when we're done here, when it's our time to go. Psychic Surveys have dealt with so many who are grounded and it's fear, misery and longing that keeps them that way. You wouldn't want your sister to be experiencing those sorts of emotions would you?"

"No," June sniffed, "of course not."

"And you'll see her again, one day, when it's your turn to journey on. It's not over, it's never over." Words that she hoped would comfort June but which sent a slight shiver down her spine, a shiver she duly ignored.

June seemed to cave in even further on herself. "I miss her so much."

"I know, June. I know you do."

Disentangling her hands, Ruby reached up to hug the old woman. When she pulled away, Ness was beside her, holding out a box of tissues she'd picked up from the sideboard. Ruby took the box from her, making brief eye contact as she did, and then offered them to June, who took one and blew her nose. Quickly, she began apologising for 'wasting their time' but Ruby refused to hear it.

"It's been far from a waste of time, June." It had been humbling.

Ness made some fresh tea for them and they sat for a good long while listening to June as she spoke about her beloved elder sister and the lives they'd led largely together, each marrying and having children, but when respective husbands had died and their children had flown the nest, finding comfort in each other's company again. Ruby could easily understand how adrift June felt without her sister in her life; how she clung to more than just the memories, finding comfort in the 'ghost' of Mary – a conjuring that was certainly more benign than the one Ruby's mother was guilty of. Ruby was used to dealing with 'wannabes', but June she termed a 'wishful thinker', and therefore much more poignant to deal with. They also talked about more practical ways she could get out and meet people; perhaps more frequent visits to the bridge class that both she and Theo attended.

"Will you be going more often?" June asked Theo.

"I can do," Theo replied, "if you are." Smiling at the other woman, she added, "There's also a rumba class being held in Lewes on a Tuesday evening, I don't suppose you'd like to come along to that with me?"

"Rumba?" At first June was horrified and then a glint of mischief shone in her eyes, making her look young again. "Why not? What fun!"

Leaving Theo and June to discuss details, Ruby stood on the pavement outside with Ness, both of them taking a huge interest in anything but each other. When Theo bustled out, she suggested a trip to the pub for something to eat. Corinna was in the vicinity, so she joined them. Meeting her at The Green Man nearby, Ness and Corinna took their seats, whilst Ruby and Theo went to fetch drinks.

"I hope June's going to be all right," Ruby commented when they were at the bar.

"She will now we've got rumba to look forward to."

"You're really going to do that?"

"Of course. It might even help me to shift a few pounds."

Ruby laughed. "You're lovely just the way you are."

"And so are you, Ruby." Ruby was surprised to note that Theo had turned serious all of a sudden. "And, despite our differences, Ness is too." She paused, seemed to hesitate. "She's a very private person, as you are well aware, and that's annoying at times, I know, but she's private for a good many reasons. All I'm going to say is, she's been damaged."

"Damaged?" Ruby queried, taking two cokes from the cheerful barman and placing them down in front of her as she waited for two more to be served.

"That's correct," Theo replied, holding her gaze. "And Ellie's been damaged too, hence their connection, their bond if you like."

So they were back to Ellie again. Ruby sighed.

"Ellie keeps ringing me. Sometimes she leaves messages, other times the phone connects but she doesn't say anything. I know it's her, though."

"How do you know it's her?"

"Who else could it be?"

The final two cokes were placed in front of them. Theo took a sip from hers and then spoke again. "Regarding Ellie, do as you please. You don't have to continue with her case, not if you don't want to, but clearly the girl feels terrible she's upset you. Text her or something – firm but kind words. Look, Ruby, what I'm trying to say is make your peace with her. But most importantly make your peace with Ness. If this rift between you is allowed to continue, *that's* what'll harm the future of Psychic Surveys, not the press, not idiots like the Grants, not even Gilmore Street. We're a team, we're friends. We might not agree on everything, but we pull together. Either that or we fall apart."

Fall apart? Even more than they had already? That couldn't be allowed to happen. She *feared* that happening.

Ness was sitting a few feet away. She had to make a decision about what she was going to do.

"You take yours and Corinna's drinks," she finally

answered. "I'll take mine and Ness's."

Taking a deep breath she strode over to where the others were waiting.

Chapter Twenty-Six

AS Ruby handed over the 'peace offering' Ness smiled – understanding the intent behind it. They were back on track, or as near as damn it; making an effort at least. Ruby even asked about Ellie, whether any more sessions had taken place. Ness's face had darkened slightly but not because of Ruby's enquiry, rather it was because she was finding the whole case perplexing.

"Ailsa, Ellie and I have met again, on three occasions. Ailsa's plan is to take her forward, to beyond the terrible event that happened and I agree with her; there might be some key information there, something that might help us to solve who she is. But here's the strange thing. We can't get beyond her backing down the hallway. After that there's no memory whatsoever."

"Because of shock?" offered Theo. "Leading to denial."

"Or she could have reinvented herself," Ruby suggested. "Buried her identity along with the past."

Ness shrugged. "So deep that even hypnosis can't touch it? Possibly. It may also be because Ellie's distressed – she's had a lot to contend with recently."

Haven't we all?

The thought had formed in Ruby's mind before she could stop it. Ness looked at Ruby: had she detected it? Would relations between them break down again just when they'd been resurrected? She held her breath.

"Ruby, Ellie really is very sorry, you know. I've had a word with her too, about going to the papers. It's something she should have discussed with us; she realises that now. I think part of the problem she's having with recall at the moment is because she feels bad about what she's done. Maybe if you could—"

"Ness, I'll text her. Is that okay? I don't want to get involved again, I've made my mind up."

"That's fine," Ness said just as their food arrived.

* * *

Ruby didn't tell the others about her intention to talk to a reporter, she knew they'd try and talk her out of it if she did. But she was certain she had no other choice. After Ness dropped her back in Lewes, she walked to her car, climbed in, and drove to the *South Coast Times* offices in Brighton. She'd expected the building to be lively, tangible excitement in the atmosphere, and reporters rushing here and there, constantly on the chase for the next big story, but she was wrong. It was all rather soulless, as if everyone was bored instead. Having told the receptionist who she was and what she wanted, she took a seat and waited. Not for long as it turned out; a young man, good-looking, around the same age as her, in his mid-twenties, came hurrying down the corridor. *He* looked excited at least.

"Ruby Davis? Oh, brilliant! Thanks so much for coming in. I'm Robin King. I've left several messages with you. It's great you've decided to talk to us at last. It's a good idea; a smart move."

Ruby could only hope so.

Not wanting to venture further into the offices – the mouth of Hades as she likened it to – Ruby suggested they go and grab a coffee from the café outlet at Asda – that was about as neutral a ground as she could think of. Robin agreed, offering to buy not just the coffees but a blueberry muffin each too.

An affable chap, he started firing questions at her as soon as they were seated, reminding her of a puppy dog champing at his lead. Firmly, Ruby told him to let her tell her story the way she wanted to, or it was a no go.

"So far, the reportage is all about Gilmore Street being haunted; about how frightening that haunting is; how Psychic Surveys may or may not be genuine. You're looking for a new Enfield and you think you've found it."

Robin appeared almost nostalgic. "The Enfield case? I've been reading up about that lately. Wish I'd been around for it. Brilliant stuff."

"It wasn't brilliant for the family going through it."

"I suppose so." His concern was brief. "So come on, is Gilmore Street really haunted?"

"There is a spirit residing at Gilmore Street. The family testified to that and phenomena has been recorded."

"The flying kettle you mean?"

"That is what I mean."

"It's hardly spectacular though is it, a flying kettle?"

"What would you prefer, a body flying through the windows? That would sell more papers I suppose."

"God, wouldn't it just?"

Ruby sighed and bit into her muffin.

"So, it's Benjamin Hamilton, is it? We can't find any background on him."

"We don't know who it is," she answered, "it might not

be Ben at all. Don't drag his name through the mud along with mine."

"Who else could it be?"

She was growing tired of his inability to listen. "If we get the chance to, I'll find out, I'll make sure of it. But, Robin, seriously, this whole *Ghostbusters* angle it's… and pardon the pun here, it's been done to death. You want a new angle? I'll give it to you. As you know, I run Psychic Surveys, which is a high street business specialising in domestic spiritual clearance—"

"Domestic what?"

"It's spirit rescue, Robin, and it's really not that hard to understand. The dead interacting with the living is nothing new, it's always happened. There's a material world and there's a spiritual world and sometimes the veil between them is thin. It's not weird, it's not shocking, and it's not even remotely New Age. The methods we use, they're ancient not modern – and often, very often, it's not terrifying. It's mundane, in fact, and the job gets boring, just like any other job." She paused. "Although, to be fair, it does have its highlights. But, and this is my point, Robin, my main *point*; we help people, both the living and the dead, so that they can rest in peace, both in the true sense of the word and metaphorically. We provide a service, a much-needed service, as up until recently we've been rushed off our feet. And we do so in a low-key, practical, and professional manner. We inject the normal into paranormal if you like, which you can quote me on. And we *have* helped. If you look at our website, there are plenty of testimonials. I know you haven't heard them from the horse's mouth, but people who've been haunted tend not to like to draw attention to that fact, and I can't blame them. They've moved on, the spirit has moved on – it's over. That's the way they want it to stay."

"But you charge for what you do!"

It sounded like an accusation, causing Ruby's temper to flare.

"Yes, Robin, we do! We're human beings just like you, who have to eat, buy clothes and pay the rent. Why shouldn't we charge? We work hard enough. But we don't charge for all cases; we have a sliding scale and believe me, we don't earn much. Just enough to scrape by at times."

"I suppose—"

"There's no 'suppose' about it."

Robin didn't agree but he didn't disagree either. "So the spirit at Gilmore Street – you said it wasn't Benjamin Hamilton?"

"I said I don't know who it is. Not yet."

"But Ben died there."

"I know."

"Has anyone else died there?"

"Not to my knowledge."

"Then who is it? Who came back?"

Who came back? That's what they all wanted to know.

Rather than wait for an answer from her, Robin lifted a hand up in the air and waved it from left to right. "I can see it now," he said, "the headline: *'Who is the Ghost of Gilmore Street?'* Do you know what? It's actually much better that we don't know. People love nothing better than a mystery."

Getting carried away on flights of fancy, he wasn't listening to a word she was saying. Inwardly she sighed; she should have known. "Robin, I want this article to be about Psychic Surveys, about the work that we do."

Robin's sympathy seemed genuine. "Not very helpful, though, if we can't get some of those you've helped to come forward; to back you up."

"Because you'll twist everything they say. People aren't stupid, they know what the press is like."

Robin pulled a 'what me?' type of expression. He really did have that innocent look down pat. In a competition she'd give him ten out of ten.

"Don't take the piss, Robin. This is my business, my livelihood we're talking about. Present the facts as you've been told them for once."

Again, Robin held his hands up. "I will, I promise."

Folding the muffin wrapper into tiny squares, she asked very slowly and very deliberately, "But, Robin, does a reporter's promise mean anything?"

"Of course it does! Look, I get what you're doing, the point of it. And who knows, maybe *I'll* need your services one day."

Ruby looked at him, stared *intently.*

"What?" he seemed flustered. "What is it?"

"Where do you live?"

"Erm… in Hove, a flat just off Sackville Road."

"Sackville Road? It wouldn't happen to be Tennyson Court would it, the former site of Hove General Hospital?"

Robin's brown eyes grew even wider. "But… how did you know that?"

"Because I'm psychic, Robin, I'm the real deal. That building has quite a history; a lot of people have died there and often in very sad circumstances." She paused for effect. "Have you been experiencing anything strange lately?"

Robin had gone the colour of milk; she'd swear he'd

even started to tremble.

"No, well… not me. But my girlfriend lives in the block too. We've only recently started going out. She…" again he stumbled. "She hates living there to be honest, wants to move out and rent somewhere else. Says the atmosphere isn't quite right. Sometimes she can hear crying in the night. One time I heard it too. Right outside my bedroom door it was, but then I thought, no; sounds carry. It was probably one of the other residents."

Ruby stood up and made a show of smoothing her clothes. "It may well have been," she said, "but not necessarily a *living* resident. And hearing crying, well, that could just be the start of it."

"The start of it?"

"Oh yeah, things can get worse, much worse, and very quickly too. Especially if the spirit knows that you're aware of it, that you heard it crying. They latch on you see. They latch on and sometimes they don't let go."

As she walked off, Robin hurried after her. "If… if there is something, will you come round, take a look? Mates' rates and all that."

"Mates' rates?" she threw back over her shoulder. "So we're friends?"

Robin swallowed. "Well… we could be."

She stopped and turned round to face him. "Then do the right thing by me, Robin. I want a straightforward article, no sensationalism, nothing like that, and… regarding where you live, we'll see. There are a lot of charlatans out there, a lot of people who can't help. I can. Remember that when things get rough."

"I will. You can count on me."

As Ruby quickened her pace she offered up silent thanks

to the universe. So his address was Tennyson Court, was it? You couldn't beat a lucky guess.

Chapter Twenty-Seven

HER ruse had worked. Robin the eager beaver reporter remained true to his word. The article on Psychic Surveys was without sensation; it just reported the facts as she'd told them in a clear and precise manner. Any day now she'd get a phone call from Robin to come and carry out a survey on his and his girlfriend's flat, and of course she'd go; charge a nominal rate. He'd done her a favour, so she'd do him one. The article was picked up on by other journalists, however, and skewed slightly, the emphasis placed on one line he'd written in the article, '*Who is the Ghost of Gilmore Street?*' He might not have used it as a headline – he'd used *Psychic Surveys: Putting the 'Normal' into the Paranormal* – but others certainly had, and much speculation was taking place about the past residents of Gilmore Street. If any of their relatives that were still living saw the headlines, they might even come forward to shed more light on the mystery, either that or sue the media for defamation! As Theo said, you had to look for the good in everything. Another silver lining had come in the form of June. Completely off her own bat she'd rung the *South Coast Times* and told them how 'honest' Psychic Surveys were. At last someone had come forward.

"You never know," said Theo, "she might prompt the herd response."

"The herd response?" Corinna queried.

"That's right, one comes forward and suddenly they all do. It takes one person to lead the way."

To that end everyone kept everything crossed.

Meanwhile, in between working on the cases that came in, Ruby, much like the rest of the team and Cash too, kept abreast of the almost daily reportage. Psychics were coming and going to Gilmore Street, but none of them were getting anywhere. Ruby knew she shouldn't feel smug about that, but she did, whilst inwardly lamenting the fact that the sins of the 'bad wolf' were on the increase. The Gordons were reported as getting increasingly fed up with this lack of success, a picture of Samantha and Jeff standing together catching Ruby's eye. The expression on Samantha's face was nothing if not pissed-off. In contrast, Jeff looked incredibly sheepish. When she'd shown Cash the picture he'd laughed.

"Poor Jeff, I can imagine the ear-bashing he's getting behind closed doors. Who do you think they're going to call next, *Most Haunted*?"

"I'm only surprised Yvette and Karl aren't here already," Ruby replied.

Either way, the heat was off Psychic Surveys, it was on others instead, and just as harshly. But it wasn't the ridicule that Ruby was finding satisfactory, it was the fact that Psychic Surveys weren't the only ones claiming there was something untoward at Gilmore Street. There was now *proof* of paranormal activity, as person after person retreated from the house, declaring what remained inside a 'beast.'

Ruby had winced at that: connotations linked to the devil were never helpful. Corinna had walked past Gilmore

Street recently on her way to meet Presley at The Battle of Trafalgar, a nearby pub, and she told the rest of them that already a couple of houses had gone up for sale in the street. If other psychics started banging on about Lucifer, they'd *all* soon be on the market. Again, frustration surfaced: if only they could get into number 44. Would it be worth texting Samantha? If she could explain what they knew, she might be able to persuade her to give them another chance. Or get her to persuade Jeff at least. And there she stopped. *But what **do** you know exactly? You've no idea who the 'Ghost of Gilmore Street' is. Nobody does.* But someone, somewhere must know something. She'd go back to The Keep, dig deeper into the lives of past residents whose offspring might still be alive. Perhaps she could contact them. It shouldn't be too hard. Considering Ben's length of time in the house, there couldn't be many of them left.

There you go again, looking for that silver lining.

Well, she reasoned, it was a silver lining of sorts.

* * *

The day hadn't proved fruitful. Concentrating mainly on the offspring of the Fowlers and the Dolans, she'd cross-referenced various publications again to find out how many they'd had between them. The Fowlers had had six, all girls, and the Dolans a mere two by contrast, both boys. Utilising social media such as Facebook, Twitter, and LinkedIn, she couldn't find one person that fitted the stats she had – which were woefully sparse in the first place. The plan she'd come up with – using the women's names to provoke a response was still looking like the best option, if only she could press it into action. Growing tired, she'd left The Keep, returned to her flat, and curled up on the sofa for a power nap, Jed materialising out of nowhere to join her. The power nap turned into a good couple of hours – the rest deep and energising, exactly what she needed. When she woke, she checked her phone; she was due to meet Cash later in the pub. He'd texted to say he'd be in The Rights of Man at eight o' clock, Presley would be with him initially as they were coming straight from band practice, but then he was leaving to meet Corinna. As much as she liked Presley, Ruby was glad about that, at the prospect of having Cash all to herself. Pushing herself off the sofa, smiling at Jed who slumbered on, she made her way to the shower and stood for ages under the hot water, luxuriating. Afterwards, in the bedroom, she blow-dried her hair, pleased with the length of it. It was now a few inches past her shoulders and had a halo-like shine to it – a halo that at the moment felt rather misplaced. Normally, she wore barely any make-up, but this time she applied foundation, mascara, and lipstick – the works. She had a feeling about tonight – a frisson of excitement in her stomach – and wanted to make more of an effort than usual. After Presley left, perhaps she and Cash would go somewhere a little livelier than the Lewes high street; catch a train into Brighton, go to one of the restaurants there, or take advantage of the warmer weather and walk along the seafront, munching on fish and chips. The night was theirs to enjoy and enjoy it she would. Before leaving her flat, she texted Cash to say she was on her way but was popping into her office briefly to check messages. He'd texted back asking if it was really necessary to do that, but as it was only 7.20 and she didn't have to be at the pub until eight, she told him to stop moaning; she had time. His return message amused her: a ghost emoticon and a shrieking face emoticon side by side. In fact, it made her laugh out loud. Yes, it was going to be a good night with nothing on her mind but the two of them. After she'd checked the answer machine, that is.

As she locked her flat behind her, she shivered. It wasn't that warm actually; there was a distinct nip in the air. Shame, because it had been a sunny day. Wondering whether to go back in and grab a warmer jacket, she decided against it. Her denim one would have to do. Perhaps they'd stick to Lewes after all and leave the more lively locations for another time.

As she ventured up Irelands Lane and turned left onto the main drag, the excitement of earlier didn't die down; it was still there in the pit of her stomach – the fluttering of butterflies. Just why was she feeling this way? It wasn't as if it was the weekend. They could go to Brighton, but they couldn't exactly hop on a train to London, escape for a day or two, and languish in some top hotel somewhere, drinking champagne and making good use of the hot tub. Now *that* would be something to get excited about. Yet the feeling persisted that this night was going to be different in some way – significant – a night to remember. Just outside her office she stopped in her tracks. Oh God! Cash wasn't going to ask to move in with her, was he? Take their relationship to the next level? Not that she'd mind if he did, as it wouldn't be much different from the way things were now considering the amount of time he spent at hers. It's just that they hadn't discussed it formally. As she fished around in her pocket for the office key, she stopped again, distracted by yet another thought. Was he gearing up to ask her to marry him? Is that what she was sensing? No, no, he couldn't be! As much as she loved him, she wasn't ready for that, was she? She felt lightheaded at the prospect.

"Excuse me."

She was so lost in reverie, the voice from behind startled her.

"Sorry," she replied, moving out of the stranger's way – it was a man with his head down and clearly in a hurry.

Staring after him, she shook her head as if to disperse her runaway thoughts, and then a shiver coursed through her; a prickle at the back of her neck – a feeling that wasn't quite so exciting – a feeling of unease. *Familiar* unease. She swung round. Was there someone else behind her? She peered back up the street. There was no one and why should there be? Reporters at the moment were more interested in Gilmore Street. It was there they'd be camping out. Even the two parked outside her office had been gone for a while. Even so, her unease refused to dissipate. Again, she scrutinised the empty street before deciding to get a grip on her imagination: Cash going down on bended knee? What a notion!

Reaching the door to her office, she opened it and ran up the narrow stairs. It was bitter up in the 'gods', the ancient walls of the building retaining rather than combatting the evening chill. Instead of turning the main light on, she dashed over to her desk and switched on the copper angle-poise lamp – one of her recent bargain buys – and sat in her captain's chair as she pressed 'play'. There were only three messages, nothing too taxing, she hoped.

"Hi, my name's Ronnie. I've seen your website and I'm interested in the services you offer. My partner and I have just bought a house. I'm settled but he isn't; he thinks there's something 'wrong' with it. Greg's got an active imagination if you know what I mean, but I'd like to put his mind at rest. Can I book an appointment for an initial survey?"

Ruby took down his name and number – she'd call him back tomorrow – then pressed 'play' to continue. As she did, she heard a creak on the stairs. Her head turned towards it but she didn't pay it much heed. The building was old and it creaked all the time. The second message was another request for an initial survey. The day wasn't so fruitless after all. The third was something different, it was from an old school friend of Ruby's, mentioning that she'd read about her in the papers, thought that what she was doing was brilliant – 'really unusual' – and would love to get together for a chat sometime. 'The paranormal fascinates me,' her friend, Izzie, declared, 'I never knew you had a talent for it. You kept that hidden!' She certainly had. When she was a teenager she didn't want to stand out from the crowd. Besides, Izzie hadn't been a close friend; Ruby had sat next to her in English where they'd had a bit of a laugh, exchanged exercise books for doodling over, and had even been out at night together, but they belonged to different 'gangs' essentially. Still, it would be nice to see her again. She'd call her tomorrow as well, set a date, and catch up on what Izzie had been up to. Hopefully her reasons for getting in touch were genuine.

Glancing at her watch, she saw it was 7.50. She'd better get a move on or she'd be late. She could just imagine Cash making a fuss if she was. The scraping sound her chair made as she pushed backwards sounded ten times louder than it should have done. It was such a contrast to the silence. Dropping her pen on the table, she turned round and as she did, a shape loomed out of the darkness and lunged at her. She couldn't react, couldn't even scream. It wasn't so much the shock of seeing a stranger in front of her that had struck her mute, but the silver glint of what that person held in their hand – a knife. The gleam of it dazzled as it caught the moonlight.

Chapter Twenty-Eight

BEFORE the knife could make contact and slice through the thin fabric of her jacket, Ruby jumped aside. Both the stranger's cry of frustration and the weapon as it hit the hard wood of her desk chilled her. At last she found her voice and cried out.

"Ellie, is that you? What do you think you're doing?"

"You bitch!" the intruder spat. "You stupid bitch! How dare you?"

The stranger – definitely a woman – was blocking her path to the doorway. She had a long, dark coat on and a hat. A scarf was pulled across her nose and mouth. If it was Ellie, she was in disguise. The same height as Ruby and with a slim frame, she had brogues on – flat shoes, brown, sensible. All this Ruby took in in an instant as her brain scrambled to make sense of what was happening, grabbing on to every detail, *any* detail, that might reveal who stood before her. *Would Ellie wear shoes like that?* No. Also her voice was different – Ellie's was soft and lilting; this woman's had a rasping quality to it. Despite her suspicions about her ex-client, this wasn't her.

"Who are you? Why are you doing this?"

They were questions that wouldn't be met with answers, she knew that. She should save her breath, find a way past her. The woman's arm was raised again, the threat in her eyes all too clear.

"Don't," Ruby begged. What the heck was her problem?

As Ruby looked on in horror, the woman lunged once more. Was she seriously trying to stab her? There was no time to stand and wonder – she had to act. Get away before the knife plunged deep, connecting with something vulnerable, her chest maybe, beneath which her heart thumped.

Ruby met the woman head-on, not questioning the wisdom of it, the possibility of impaling herself on the knife. There was no piercing pain. Luck, if you could call it that, was on her side. Instead, as body crashed into body, the stranger fell back, as if she were made of nothing more substantial than feathers. Even in Ruby's shock and confusion, that fact registered. The woman might have a knife, but strength-wise, Ruby had the advantage.

The woman landed on her back as Ruby fell on to her knees. She needed to get up. Straightaway. Get out of the office and onto the street, where she could yell for help. No one would hear her if she cried out here. For the millionth time she cursed the office for being up on high. She also questioned how the woman had got in. Hadn't she locked the door behind her? Or had she just pulled it to? Although the door wasn't quite as ancient as the building, you did have to use force to close it behind you; force that she now regretted not administering.

Placing her palms on the floor, she pushed herself upwards, aware of a throbbing pain in both knees. Dismissing it, she set her sights once again on the door. It was close, so close. She could make it. It was just a few more steps. And then a hand darted out from below, grabbed tight around her ankle, and yanked. It took her by surprise and she felt herself topple again, her head hitting the floorboards this time, not her knees. Immediately, a dark cloud descended, warm and comforting – a sanctuary – but it was only temporary. The woman's voice dragged her back from the abyss.

"You couldn't let it be could you? For years I've been trying to escape and now you've brought it all back. You've brought *him* back. You fool!"

"Who have I brought back?" Ruby managed. "You're not making sense."

The woman's movements were awkward but she managed to rise, looming over her. Ruby continued to ask questions, not knowing what else to do.

"Why are you hiding your face?" She couldn't see the woman's expression but the hatred in her eyes was more than evident. It made her feel weak. "Whatever I've done, however I've upset you, I'm sorry. Stop what you're doing and let's talk. We can sort this out."

"You've interfered when you shouldn't have."

"Interfered in what?"

"You've resurrected him."

"Who?"

"HIM!" The woman's scream was shrill; as piercing as any blade. "And now the whole world will know. It's *you* who has to stop!"

Still Ruby was confused; her head hurt and the darkness threatened to encroach again. One half of her wanted so much to welcome it, but the other half knew she mustn't; that she had to stay alert. As the woman raised the knife, Ruby struggled to keep focused. She'd said the whole world would know: what did she mean by that? What had she done that she wanted to keep hidden? Raising an arm to protect her head at least, she tried to connect psychically with the woman, to see if she could extract from her an ounce of mercy. But those eyes – there was no mercy in them. They were black and so easy to drown in; to sink all the way to the bottom of that well she'd languished in before. And this time no sunlight would penetrate, not where she was heading.

As her whole body tensed, the woman's words raced through her mind again. *You've brought him back. And now the whole world will know... the whole world... he's back... he's back.*

"But he never went!" Ruby screamed the words as the knife hovered above her. It made sense suddenly. It all made sense. She was talking about Gilmore Street! The spirit that resided there – this woman knew him. *She* was who he feared – the woman that Ruby feared now too. She was at the root of it all. That frisson she'd felt earlier, that she'd mistaken for excitement, it had nothing to do with Cash at all. Somehow, she'd known this moment was coming.

"What the fuck?"

Had she heard right? Was that Cash's voice? Or was it just wishful thinking? How she longed for him, for escape. She wasn't ready to go, not yet... she couldn't go, she wouldn't.

"Ruby! Ruby! Get up. Are you okay? What a bloody stupid question: you're not okay, are you? What the hell's going on here?"

It *was* Cash, and Jed too, the dog coming over to Ruby and nudging at her, whining, willing her to be all right.

I am, I'm all right. Just.

As if through a haze she saw Cash turn to the woman,

the murder that had been in her eyes reflected in his. With one fell swoop he knocked the knife from her hand and sent her careering, straight into one of Ruby's precarious tower of books, to land heavily amongst them. Around her, the likes of Stephen King, James Herbert, and Phil Rickman lay scattered.

Her head pounding but her heart soaring, Ruby struggled to her feet as Cash let fly a long list of threats in the woman's direction, not least phoning the police and getting them to lock her up.

'Cash, don't, it's okay. Help me."

"Okay? Ruby, she was going to stab you!" As that fact sank in, panic replaced fury as he grabbed her arm and began to scan her. "She hasn't stabbed you, has she? I can't see any blood."

"No, no, Cash, I'm—"

"I've got to phone the emergency services. Where's my phone? Where is it? Shit! Did I leave it in the pub?"

"Cash!" She brought her free hand up to grab at him. "We've got a phone here remember? Look, I'm okay, I've banged my head on the floorboards, but I'm all right. Hold up on the police, the ambulance, or whatever. I want to speak to her first. This is to do with Gilmore Street."

The words were not delivered quite as coherently as she would have liked, they came out in a rush, but Cash got the gist. He directed her to her captain's chair and ordered her to sit. To the woman he growled a command not to move a muscle. Ruby braved looking over at her. She seemed as dazed as Ruby had felt earlier. She was going nowhere.

Before she started firing questions, Ruby looked at Cash – at the miracle of him standing before her.

"How did you know?"

"About you? Because of Jed."

Satisfied that she was okay, the dog was now sitting in front of the enemy – standing guard. As his words sunk in, she frowned.

"But you can't see Jed, so how…?"

"I can smell him, though, can't I? He was pulling that whole 'wet dog' stunt again. The smell was becoming more and more intense, unbearable even. I kept looking around me, thinking someone had brought a dog in with them and then I realised two things – first, it wasn't a 'live' dog responsible, and second, it wasn't raining outside. It was Jed. You were late. Something was wrong. So I got up and rushed here. To find this."

Even though it hurt to do it, she shook her head in amazement. Yet again Jed had come to her aid. Cash too – what would she do without them? Die probably. Certainly, that's what she thought was going to happen; that she was going to die. And she wasn't ready, she remembered thinking that: she couldn't go, she wouldn't. She'd stay…

The memory forced the air from her body.

"Ruby, what's happening? Are you okay?"

"Cash, it's fine, it's…" If she'd been killed, would she have done it? Remained here? Stayed grounded? No of course not, there was no way… was there?

"I'm calling an ambulance," Cash said when he got no further reply.

"No! Don't. I said I want to talk to her."

"Five minutes, Ruby, that's all you've got."

"That's all I need."

Ruby stared again into the eyes of her attacker. "Remove your scarf so I can see you."

She thought the woman was going to refuse, but boldly a hand shot up and, taking hold of the scarf, tore at it. Ruby gasped, as did Cash.

"But you're an old…"

She stopped herself just in time.

"An old woman? Is that what you were going to say? I'm sixty-eight. I've plenty of strength left, more's the pity."

Cash pulled up a chair to sit beside Ruby. "Cash, I think we'd better ask – sorry, what's your name?"

"Linda. My name is Linda."

"Cash, can you get Linda a seat too?"

"What?" Cash was incredulous. "You'll be offering her tea next."

"That's not such a bad idea—"

"I don't want tea," Linda spat, struggling to her feet.

"Cash, help her."

"I don't want to touch her."

"Cash!"

"All right, all right."

If he was ungracious about helping her, she was equally as ungracious about accepting. She was sixty-eight but in the artificial light of the room, her face looked older. The lines on it were deeply etched, around her eyes and mouth especially. Ruby knew without doubt hers had been a hard life. Even so, this wasn't the time for lenience. This was a time for answers.

"You're here about Gilmore Street, aren't you? About my involvement in it."

"Is it true? Is he there?"

"Is who there?"

"Just tell me!"

Ruby grew equally as angry. "Linda, that's just it: we

don't know who 'he' is! I presume you found out about Gilmore Street by reading the papers."

"Of course that's how!" Spittle flew from her mouth as she said it.

Cash leant into Ruby. "This is getting us nowhere. Let me call the police, and get her locked up. You've got to get to the hospital, check for concussion."

"This is more important than bloody concussion, Cash!"

"Which could of course be the concussion speaking."

"Please… just give me more time." She turned back to Linda. "Did you ever live at Gilmore Street? Who were you, a Fowler or a Dolan?"

When she remained mute, Ruby repeated the question. Still she refused to reply.

"Linda!" The desperation in her voice was not lost on any of them. Ruby made an effort to calm down and began to calculate instead. If she was sixty-eight, she'd have been born in the 1940s and was therefore more likely to be a Dolan. "You're Linda Dolan, aren't you?"

"I don't know what you're talking about. That's not my name."

"Then what is it? Help me!"

"I want to stop you, not help you!"

"Tell me who you are, who he is."

"The past should stay buried."

"But it's not, though, is it? It's coming full circle!"

For a moment Ruby thought Linda would leap out of her chair and attack her again, with bare hands this time, but thankfully she remained seated. Just as Ruby suspected they'd have to goad the spirit of Gilmore Street to get anywhere with information, she knew she'd have to do the same with Linda. But there was one thing she wanted

Linda to clarify first.

"Why did you decide to attack me in particular? I'm not the only psychic who's been called into Gilmore Street." There'd been a whole host of them after her. "If you haven't already killed the rest of them off, that is."

"You were the first, the one who got the ball rolling. And that article you were in recently, you sounded so smug."

"Smug? In what way?"

"You said it wasn't that man who'd lived there for so many years – what's his name? Benjamin. You said it was someone else; that you'd find out who he was come hell and high water; you'd expose him."

She was referring to Robin's report. Ruby had said words to that effect but not quite so dramatically; there'd certainly been no hell or high water involved. It was Linda who'd skewed facts this time and read into it what she wanted.

A thought occurred to her. "Did you ever try and contact me by phone?" She saw Linda's eyes flicker and move to the right slightly. "You did, didn't you? You called several times, but never spoke to me; you always put the phone down." A ruse she'd blamed Ellie for. Exhaling, she questioned her again. "Linda, are you afraid that if I expose him, I expose *you*?" Trying to quash her frustration at the woman's maintained silence, she added, "You did something to him, didn't you? You hurt him."

"The bastard deserved what he got!"

Glad of a reaction, Ruby seized the moment. "When did you live there? I don't recall there being a record of a Linda at Gilmore Street. In fact, I'm sure there wasn't." God, she wished her head wasn't pounding so much. She was beginning to feel sick too, and little wonder. But she needed to hang on, to remember a few more facts. "The house was owned by the Dolans from the late 1940s. Were they your parents or your aunt and uncle, something like that? They lived there until the late sixties when Benjamin Hamilton bought it. At first we thought Ben was the grounded spirit, but we don't think that now. But it's somebody with a strong connection; somebody to do with you."

Linda was breathing heavily now and kept swallowing.

"What did you do to him? Did you kill him? Did you dispose of the body?"

"No," the woman burst out, "I didn't kill him!" She then seemed to falter. "At least... I don't think I did. I don't know what happened to him." She shook her head as though a bolt of lightning had shot through it. "And there's no way I'd have been able to dispose of him as you put it. I wouldn't have been able to lift him, to drag him anywhere, how could I? He was a big man, a *slug* of a man."

Ruby's breath caught in her throat.

"Ruby!" Cash said, noticing. She couldn't put him off much longer. She had to hurry.

"What did you say, what did you just call him?"

Linda too was surprised by Ruby's reaction. "I called him a slug, because that's what he was – fat and lazy, sitting in front of the telly all the time. I hated him. I *still* hate him. If he's stuck in Gilmore Street, leave him to rot."

"Ruby, we have to get you to hospital. We've got to get you checked out."

"I know, Cash, I know we have. But we can't let her out of our sight."

"Ruby, you're delirious."

"No, I'm not. I'm honestly not."

A soul divided?

Ruby's mind began to work furiously. "We can't take her with us to the hospital, there'll be too many questions. I haven't got time for questions. Call Theo, Ness and Corinna, they'll have to drop what they're doing and come here, right now and take her back to my flat; stand guard." She'd never seen Cash look so bemused. Quickly she tried to explain. "Cash, I think I know what happened, the entire sequence of events. Linda *has* to come with us to Gilmore Street. His reaction to her will confirm his identity."

Before Cash could comment, Linda shot to her feet.

"No! I'm not going back. You can't make me."

Ruby sat up straight and fixed Linda with what she hoped was a steely glare. "I *can* make you. What you tried to do to me counts as attempted murder in the eyes of the law."

"Murder? I wasn't going to kill you. I just wanted to warn you off!"

"But it's your word against mine and believe me, I can fabricate the truth as much as anyone."

Cash stepped up to the mark. "She's also got me as a witness. I saw what you tried to do."

"No," Linda's voice was a whimper this time. "I can't do it, I can't."

Ruby remained resolute. "I'm sorry, but we all have to face our demons at some point."

Chapter Twenty-Nine

LUCKILY, it was as quiet at the hospital as it was on the streets of Lewes, so Ruby got seen to within the hour – another miracle. After a basic neurological exam to assess her hearing, speech, coordination, and balance, including the 'finger-nose-finger' test, Ruby was given the all clear but told to return if symptoms persist.

"Problems to look out for," the nurse told her, "include confusion, vomiting, seizures or fits of any kind and loss of memory. Basically, what you need now is rest. Avoid doing anything strenuous for the next twenty-four hours."

Chance would be a fine thing.

Before travelling to the hospital, she'd given Theo, Ness, and Corinna the key to her flat, and told them to take a now compliant Linda there and to keep an eye on her until she returned, when she'd explain all. And now she was back, with several pairs of expectant eyes trained on her, Linda's included.

Whilst Ness made tea, Ruby settled herself on the sofa. Everyone looked tired: she and Linda in particular no doubt. She'd have to explain her theory as succinctly as possible; no mean feat when she was still trying to piece it all together herself. But hopefully, as a team, they'd be able to make sense of it. Ness re-entered the room with a tray, which she set down before selecting a cup and offering it to their 'guest'. As it had been at her office, Linda's refusal was vehement.

"I don't touch tea."

"Oh, water then?"

"Nothing, I don't want nothing."

As Ness offered the cup to Corinna instead, Ruby decided to get cracking.

"Linda, we need to know the name of the man you lived with in Gilmore Street. And don't muck around with us, not at this stage. Just tell us straight. You know as well as we do that Gilmore Street isn't going to go away, and neither is he – yet. It seems Benjamin was able to put up with him and we have a theory as to why. In life the spirit was a misogynist; it's not men he attacks. Where the Gordons are concerned, it's Samantha and her daughter that have come under fire. Samantha's husband and son haven't suffered to the same extent. The reason why his spirit's grounded needs to come out into the open where it can be dealt with. If you know it, tell us. For both your sakes."

Glancing nervously at those who sat round her, Linda, to her credit, didn't hesitate. "His name was Quinn, Quinn O'Brien. And he was evil."

"Evil?" Theo queried. "That's a harsh word."

Linda was adamant. "It's the right word to describe him."

"Okay," Ruby seized back control, "so it's Quinn that haunts Gilmore Street, not Benjamin." His was a name she hadn't come across when researching the house. "Or at least it's very likely it's him. And this woman, Linda... O'Brien?"

"No! I ditched that name a long time ago. I'm a Banks."

"Banks," Ruby repeated. "Linda Banks was abused by him."

Linda's head snapped towards her. "How'd you know that?"

"Yes how, Ruby?" Ness looked surprised too.

"I have another theory and it's to do with Ellie."

"Ellie?" Ness questioned.

"I'm afraid so."

"Who's Ellie?" Linda was curious too. As for Theo, she wondered whether they'd better have a conversation in private before they continued.

"I understand your concern, Theo, but no," Ruby decided. "Linda's an integral part of this now. But before I go any further I want you to tell us, Linda, in your own words what happened to you both in Gilmore Street. After that I'll explain my theory and who Ellie is."

Linda was shaking visibly.

Ness noticed and sided with Theo. "Ruby, I'm not sure this is a good idea."

But it was Linda who answered her. "She's right. I need to tell you, I need to tell someone. Who knows, there might even be relief in it. I've lived in silence for such a long time, in hatred and in fear. I've lost myself. I don't know who I am anymore. As for what I've become, that attack on you…" She hung her head. "I did my best to run, to hide; I tried to forget. But every day's a nightmare because every day memories haunt me. I damned Quinn to hell, but I'm damned too."

Ness was visibly touched by her words. She leant towards Linda and placed a hand on her arm; a simple gesture – a kind gesture. One of solidarity.

Linda eyed Ness, her gaze hard at first but then it

softened. The gesture had had an effect. Ruby wondered if it was the first time anyone had touched the older woman in years, or had been allowed to. It was hard to believe, but she suspected it was true. Linda continued speaking.

"When I first saw Quinn, it was like I couldn't breathe. His eyes – gypsy eyes they were, so dark, the lashes around them so long – held me spellbound. He was staring at me too, just as intently. I fell in love with him the minute I saw him – the boy from the fair."

"The fair?" There was a frown on Ness's face as she said it.

"That's right, that's where I met him. He was Irish, came from somewhere near Dublin. He'd been in England for a few years, though. Came over at the start of the sixties, when he was fifteen. He wanted to escape his family, said they were no good. He hated to talk about them and grew anxious if I asked for details. I only ever did that in the early days, and I learnt quick enough not to press him. Even so, it made me wonder in what way he'd suffered at their hands."

"Whether he was also abused you mean?" Ruby posed the question.

"Abused? He must have been, tortured in fact, because Quinn knew how to dish it out. Whoever he'd learnt from, he'd learnt well. Sometimes I try and remember if there'd been early warning signs, but it doesn't matter how hard I rack my brain, I can't recall. I was too blinded by him."

"He was controlling, though, wasn't he?" Ruby replied, remembering what Ellie had said. "He asked you to run away with him. He knew your parents disapproved of your relationship; that they'd stop you from marrying him."

Linda was aghast. "That's right, that's right. But how'd

you know all that? Is it through Ellie? Who is this girl? How does she know about me? I… he was controlling, yes, but I mistook that for strength. I was young, I was naïve, not even twenty – what did I know of boys, of the world? But I was soon to learn. A baptism of fire. He wouldn't even let me tell my parents where we'd gone; he said it would spoil it, that *they'd* spoil it. All I left was a note telling them not to worry, that I'd be in touch. I don't know if they ever tried to find me. I don't think so. What I'd done, it must have been so disappointing for them. I was their only daughter and they wanted things for me, good things. I never saw them again. They're dead now."

"Never?" Corinna was shocked. "Not even after you'd left Quinn?"

"After I'd left Quinn? I couldn't! I was a monster by that time, the same as him. They wouldn't have recognised me. I didn't even recognise myself." One hand came up to rub at her temple. "The things I've done. Oh God, the things I've done."

"If this is too distressing for you, Linda," Theo interrupted, "we can always stop, get some rest and carry on tomorrow."

Linda refused. "No, if I don't say this now, I never will. I hate him! But then I hate myself. I don't know which one of us I hate the most. He turned; the minute we set foot in Gilmore Street he turned. He said he'd got us a palace, that I'd love it. Wouldn't let me see it before I'd said 'I do'. What a joke! It was no palace. It was empty, it was dirty, it hadn't seen a lick of paint in years. When I saw it I couldn't hide how disgusted I was. As soon as he closed the door of that hovel, he started. 'You're never satisfied, are you?' he said. 'Always disappointed – in the wedding, in the house, in me, and everything I've done for you. You think you're better than me, don't you, with your posh parents, the house that you grew up in, your education? You think I'm scum; Irish scum.'"

"The man had an inferiority complex," remarked Theo.

Linda didn't disagree. "And then he hit me – that's right, on our wedding day, not even an hour after we'd exchanged vows; he hit me, cut my lip and blacked my eye. And I knew... I knew that was the start of it; that there was worse to come, much worse. Why I didn't leave then and return to my parents, I don't know. I was just so embarrassed, I think and... scared. I was scared. He imprisoned me, in that house that was so old fashioned and so different to the house I'd grown up in. It was drab and it was dreary. There were things that crawled in the night; that covered the walls. I tried to clean it. I did my best. But it was like him – rotten to the core. I got resentful. How dare he bring me here? How dare he hit me? I missed my parents!"

Listening to her, Ruby was puzzled. "I don't understand, when were you at Gilmore Street? There's no record of you being tenants."

"A friend of a friend owned the house, that's what Quinn told me; another Irishman."

"Yes, yes," concurred Theo, "Dolan is an Irish name."

"I don't know what the deal was, Quinn took care of all that. All I know is that the owners had left and this friend of his was starting a job elsewhere. They were selling the house but meanwhile they wanted rent for it, a peppercorn rent Quinn said, and little wonder the state it was in. We were there for several months, the best part of a year I suppose, although it seemed like so much longer. During that time Quinn grew fat. He'd left his job when we came down from the midlands; told me he'd easily pick up another. But he didn't, just a bit of casual every now and then. We survived on cheap food – bread, potatoes and tinned stuff; it was all so bland. He'd hit me for that too, as though it were my fault. I could have got a job, supported us, but I wasn't allowed to go anywhere by myself. I could only go out with him, and even that was rarely, but when we did, I used to think maybe I could make a break for it when he wasn't looking – take off, escape. But he was always looking, that's the trouble. And my hand… he used to hold it so tight I thought my bones would break."

"What about the other residents in the street?" Cash asked. "Weren't they curious about you at all? Didn't they come knocking?"

Linda cocked her head to one side. "I used to wonder about that too. Didn't our neighbours want to know about the newcomers? About me in particular? I must have looked a fright, I was so shocked and bewildered. And I was so *thin*. Hardly a picture of marital bliss. But people only see what they want to see, don't they, and nobody saw me. I'd become invisible."

"Blasted Brits!" Theo sniffed as she said it. "In other countries neighbours make an effort to get to know each other; there's a sense of community, but not here, oh no. Here we keep ourselves to ourselves, we look the other way."

"Which is why Benjamin wasn't found for a week," mused Corinna.

"Ha!" Theo replied. "He was lucky. Some are left for much longer than that. What about that poor girl who wasn't discovered for three years? That's right, three years! She lived in a block of flats in central London; she had a job, friends, and family, but you're right, Linda, somehow she was invisible. How could that happen?" She apologised. "I'm sorry. Listen to me ranting. Please, carry on."

There was a brief moment whilst everyone did indeed consider Theo's words – the case she was talking about had made headline news in 2011. The woman, only in her late thirties, had concerned Ruby greatly. She'd wanted to go to her flat and make sure her spirit had moved on; wasn't anchored – like so many were – by loneliness. But she couldn't just turn up – that wasn't the Psychic Surveys' way. If new tenants encountered a problem, she could only hope they'd call, or that someone else, someone genuine, would deal with it. Before the moment could stretch into several, Ruby prompted Linda, who duly carried on.

"Quinn chained me to that kitchen sink, or as good as. I was his slave, making him endless cups of tea whilst he watched the telly. He demanded cup after cup of the stuff." She looked at Ness, who'd remained largely quiet throughout, absorbing every word. "That's why I don't drink it," she explained, "won't go near it, in fact. Even the smell of it is enough to make me sick."

Immediately, Ruby covered the top of her mug with her hand.

"It's fine, it's okay, I… I'm not worried about tea right now. That's the least of my problems." Linda took a deep breath. "I was at his mercy, in the kitchen and in the bedroom." She leaned forward conspiratorially. "He had a problem in that respect. He had difficulty, you know… getting it up. Never before we were married, mind, only afterwards. You'd think I'd be grateful that was the case, wouldn't you? But I wasn't. It didn't stop the violation."

Ruby too felt sick, but at the way in which Linda had suffered. Not wanting tea either, she asked Cash if he wouldn't mind taking the mugs from the room and depositing them in the kitchen. He did, hurrying back afterwards.

"That was life week after week, month after month for me – nothing less than a nightmare. Can you blame me for breaking? For fighting back? I didn't know I was going to do it, honestly I didn't. I didn't know I had the strength, but I did; it came from somewhere deep inside; it rose up and possessed me. I was in the kitchen, standing at the sink, staring out into a dull day. I'd never felt so hopeless, or so angry. The emotions in me were simmering, like stew in a cauldron. He wanted tea." Linda's laugh was bitter. "No surprises there. I took him a fresh cup and came back with the half finished one. He was watching the telly, laughing at something, I don't know what. I was so homesick, not just for my parents, but for my old bedroom too, my sanctuary. I loved music back then, like all the kids did; I was mad for it. I'd had a record player at home, plenty of records too. I was spoilt, I suppose. I only had a radio at Gilmore Street. That tinny little thing was my one luxury. It's amazing I was even allowed *that*. Whilst he continued to watch his programme, I wanted to listen to music. Back in the kitchen, I turned it on. A song was playing; I remember it so well. It was by Tom Jones: I was keen on him too. It was one of his latest hits. The words were so poignant, as if Tom knew about my situation and had written it just for me."

"Tom Jones?" Ruby sat up straight, remembering what

Ellie had said. "What's that song of his?" She looked at Theo. "*The Green* something?"

"*Green, Green Grass of Home*?"

"That's it, that's the one!" Ruby almost yelled back.

Linda was nodding too. "Yes, that was it. But how—"

"Ruby!" At last Ness spoke up. "What's going on here?"

"Ness, I think you know what's going on, but let Linda finish her story."

Although she was impatient – they *all* were – Ness complied.

"It was *Green, Green Grass of Home* – I haven't listened to it since. Can't bear to. Quinn came up behind me, startled me. He said I was playing the radio too loud, that it was disturbing him. It wasn't. No way. How he heard it over the noise of the TV I shall never know. He picked it up. I knew what he was going to do. I darted forward and tried to take it from him. The radio was my only link to the outside world. It kept me sane. He sent me flying as we wrestled, straight into the kitchen table. As he began to twist and turn the radio in his hands – to destroy it – my sanity fled. I couldn't survive without it. I honestly felt that way. He threw it to the floor, smashing it to pieces, then turned back towards me, as I knew he would, his fists bunched. Have you ever been hit by someone you loved, any of you? It hurts. Not just on the outside. It hurts so much."

Ness was close to tears herself. "I... I know what it's like," she answered. Ruby looked at her, stunned by the revelation. Ness had been a victim of domestic abuse too? When? But it wasn't Ness telling the story.

"It's his eyes I remember the most – looking into them and seeing the evil that lay at the heart of him – actually *seeing* it. And somehow that evil found *me*. It reached out and wormed its way into my heart too, like a disease; it was infectious. His mug that I'd fetched earlier from the living room was on the table. I grabbed it; swung it at him; smashed it against his skull. He staggered. I rose. I continued hitting him, I was so angry. He fell. The dishes in the sink – the dirty, greasy dishes – I grabbed them next, smashed them over his head one by one. I loved seeing him cower like I'd cowered. And then a frying pan, still thick with lard and bacon rind, I brought it down over and over again. He was groaning, pleading, crying. I couldn't believe my ears and eyes. He was *crying*! But he hadn't shown me any mercy when I'd pleaded and cried. I…"

When she faltered, Ness gently encouraged her onwards.

"The kettle had only recently boiled. I set it to boil again, willing it to hurry. Lifting it up, I brought it over to him. He looked up, just terror in his eyes now, sheer terror, and I poured. Over his face, his arms, his chest and his fat gut. I poured until it was empty, watching as his skin began to burn and blister. And then, and then…." Her words ended on a sob.

"Linda." As Ness had done, Theo reached across to her. "It's okay. You can stop there. We understand. Corinna, get her some water. She needs something to drink."

A few minutes later, Corinna came back with the glass, handed it over and then pulled her chair to sit closer to Linda, placing one arm around her shoulder. Linda considered herself evil for what she'd done, but everyone in the room was reserving judgement on that right now. As Ruby sat staring at her, stunned to hear all she had from the horse's mouth rather than via Ellie, she tried again to make sense of it. *A soul divided?*

Theo and Ness both looked at her but it was Theo who spoke. "In the kitchen, Ruby. Now."

Chapter Thirty

"A soul divided? You really think that Linda is in part Ellie?"

"How else do you explain it, Ness?" replied Ruby. "Their stories are virtually identical."

"But… it's so unlikely."

Ruby disagreed. "You said it yourself. If you can think it, it's possible."

"I know, but even so, it's a little too far-fetched, even for me." Ness shook her head. "No, I'm inclined to agree with Theo on this one. Souls are individual. They're unique."

"You agree with me?" Theo raised an eyebrow. "Makes a nice change."

Ignoring her, Ness continued. "If what you're saying is true, Ellie thinks she killed Quinn. Does Linda corroborate that?"

"Linda doesn't know if she did or not. He was an inert mess on the floor when she left, and what happened to him afterwards she hasn't a clue."

"If she'd left him for dead, he would have been found," Theo pointed out. "And, as we know from your special friend in the police force, Ness, there's no record of another death at Gilmore Street. Certainly not a murder."

Despite the mention of her 'special friend', Ness didn't rise to it. "The strange thing is, as I've already told you, we can't get Ellie past the point when she fought back."

"That's right," replied Ruby, "you said it's as though her memories have fallen off a cliff from that point onwards. They just don't exist."

"But obviously Linda's do. We need to quiz her further."

"Tonight?" Theo looked at her watch. "Give the poor woman a break, she's had enough for one day, I should think." Turning towards Ruby, she said, "And so have you. You need some sleep."

Ruby couldn't argue with that. She was so tired from earlier events, she felt like someone had pulled the plug on her. "But we can't let Linda disappear."

"We can't hold her prisoner either," Theo protested.

"No, I realise that but I get the impression she wants resolution just as much as we do. She needs to come back to Gilmore Street with us."

Theo was horrified by Ruby's suggestion. "If it is Quinn, we know he can get physical, and seeing Linda might tip him over the edge. Remember Highdown Hall and Cynthia's reaction when we brought her old flame Rawlings into the room? Poor Corinna, she really copped it."

"Theo's right," Ness looked pained to admit that yet again. "Quinn's violent enough as it is."

Ruby only agreed in part. "But don't you see? If Linda's there it forces the issue, which could mean fast results."

"Ruby," Theo admonished, "this isn't about fast results. This is about spirit rescue. Or have you forgotten?"

"No, I haven't forgotten but I'm also aware that we're in the public eye. Like I said, we need a resolution."

"A resolution that's in the interests of both parties."

"But Linda's plagued by him, Theo, and, in turn, she plagues him. Shouldn't they face up to each other? Lay their demons to rest."

"All this talk of demons," Theo said, "I don't like it."

Ruby forced a smile. "At least it's only in a metaphorical sense this time."

"I don't know; Quinn seems pretty demonic to me."

"He had an inferiority complex," Ness reminded Theo. "Which you yourself pointed out. Leaving home at fifteen and travelling to another country to get away from his family – I think we can assume his childhood wasn't idyllic."

"Safely assume," Theo elaborated.

"Ness…" Ruby didn't know if now was the right time to say what was on her mind, but she decided to go ahead anyway. "I didn't know you'd been a victim of domestic abuse too."

Ness's brush-off was immediate. "This isn't about me. Let's focus shall we?"

She should have gone with her earlier instinct and kept quiet.

Theo exhaled in exasperation. "There's another problem with your plan, Ruby. Aside from the possibility of Linda's sudden appearance riling Quinn so much that the damn house falls down around our ears – which might be a bit of a bonus come to think of it – Samantha's husband doesn't want us back there. He's intent on exhausting every other avenue instead."

"Once I've told Samantha the latest development, she'll deal with Jeff." Ruby was quite sure about it. "Her ultimate aim is to get her house back, so if she thinks we can achieve that, we'll be in. No, getting into Gilmore

Street isn't the problem. The problem we have is deciding whether to take Linda there and… Ellie too."

Ness shook her head as vehemently as Linda had done when offered tea. "I definitely don't want Ellie involved, not at this stage. Not whilst we're still trying to work it out. Ellie's a fragile girl, she's been through a lot. There is simply no way I'm taking her into Gilmore Street, and you won't be able to persuade me otherwise. And, frankly, I'd rather Linda didn't come with us either. It should just be us going in there, armed with this new information."

Ruby held up her hands in submission. "All right, okay, we do it your way."

"Good," Theo said, although she still didn't look satisfied. "Ruby, you call Samantha in the morning and see what you can sort out. Meanwhile, talking of Linda, where's she staying tonight? A hotel?"

"I don't think coming down here was that premeditated, she's got nowhere booked. It doesn't matter, though, I'll offer her the sofa-bed." Noticing a frown on Theo's face, she added, "Don't worry, Cash is staying and Jed too."

"You'll be fine then, but, to be on the safe side, hide your knife block." After a little more thought, Theo added, "And the kettle."

* * *

Ruby phoned Samantha as soon as it was decent the next morning, with the news that they had discovered the spirit's identity.

"Quinn O'Brien? How'd you find out?"

Ruby told her, a potted version anyway.

"Wow! His wife's still alive? And she's sure it's him? *You're* sure?"

"As sure as we can be. Do you want your house back, Sam?"

"You know I do. We're at my sister's now and it's driving me mad. What with her family and my family, there's not enough room to swing a cat." She paused. "Or a kettle for that matter."

It was good to see Samantha retaining a sense of humour.

"Then we need to go back to Gilmore Street. But there's one thing stopping us. Your husband."

"Jeff? Okay, okay, look, don't worry – he needn't know a thing. I'll say I'm out with the girls and then meet you with the key. I want you to go back, especially after what you've just told me. How soon can you meet me?"

"Tonight, let's do it tonight."

"Under cover of the darkness?"

"Exactly." Leaving it until late there was a chance any lingering reporters would be gone, tempted by the warm lights of a pub interior instead, or a meal on the table at home waiting for them. She asked Samantha not to tell anyone about what they'd planned, not even her children, and Samantha agreed.

"Good luck, Ruby, I'm counting on you."

"No pressure then," Ruby laughed, feeling exactly that – under pressure.

* * *

Later that morning, Theo and Ness arrived on Ruby's doorstep. Clearly relieved to see that Linda hadn't done a bunk in the night, they sat down with her to answer her questions but also to ask a few more. Allowing them to take the lead, Ruby listened as Ness quizzed Linda about life after Gilmore Street. There'd not been much of one, it seemed. Unsure if she'd killed Quinn or not, she'd taken flight and disappeared entirely. Moving from place to place, as far afield as the Highlands, she'd lived like a nomad, renting various flats, working in bars or on farms for cash-in-hand, and regularly changing her hair colour, her hairstyle, even her name on occasions. She'd given her former home, the Midlands, a wide berth.

"Did you ever check the newspapers to see if there'd been a murder reported at Gilmore Street?" Ness asked her. "For curiosity's sake, I mean?"

"I checked nothing, not for years. I didn't want to know. And I'm not sure if that's because I'd have been frightened by the truth or disappointed by it. Disappointed I think. I *wanted* him dead you see; he deserved to die."

"Judging by everything we know, you didn't kill him," Theo decided. "Rather like the Brighton Trunk Murders, his battered, bloodied and abandoned body would have caused national speculation. At the very least there'd be some sort of record of it and we know there isn't. Not unless someone else discovered him and hid his body, but now we really are clutching at straws. No, the likelihood is he survived; took himself off somewhere, perhaps even back to Ireland, to lick his wounds. It'll be interesting to see exactly when he died, though, and the cause of death. To which end Corinna's at The Keep trying to find out. Because, you see, at that juncture, Quinn *did* return, the spirit of Quinn that is. You condemned him to hell, Linda, and that's what Gilmore Street represents to him – hell."

"For me as well," Linda pointed out.

"It's hell for both of you."

Linda compressed her lips and looked away.

"Linda," Theo continued, glancing at Ruby as she spoke, "I know Ruby wanted you to come to Gilmore Street when we go back to confront Quinn, but Ness and I have advised against it."

"I don't have to go back?" Linda asked the question of Ruby, not Theo.

Ruby endeavoured to explain. "We're worried about your safety. He's as violent in death as he was in life, and seeing you might antagonise him."

"But I want to go back!" Linda flashed before making an effort to calm again. "I know I said I didn't want to. But I've since thought about it. I want to face him. I *need* to. Me and Quinn, we've got unfinished business."

"Unfinished business?" Ruby queried.

"Look," Linda said, looking really quite distressed, "I know you wouldn't lie to me, I do. I think you people are genuine, but I want to make sure you really do move Quinn on. That he's gone. That this world isn't home to him anymore." A plea in her eyes, she added, "That's the only way I can go on."

"Linda…" Ness started to try and dissuade her but Ruby interrupted. Linda's words had been heartfelt. They'd also struck a note of concern deep within her – '*That's the only way I can go on'* This was a woman still on the edge. At no point had she managed to pull significantly back from the precipice. The effect of reading about her past in the newspapers, travelling down to seek Ruby out to vent her anguish on her, proved that. Despite what Theo had said, a fast result, *any* result, was needed, lest there be another tragedy.

"Ness, Theo, we can always remove Linda if it gets too much."

"But what about our safety?" Theo argued. "That matters too, Ruby."

"Please," Linda implored. "You said we need to face our demons at some point. He's mine."

Ruby knew from past experience that these were not empty words. When she'd first said them to Linda, she'd meant it. Sometimes, no matter what the danger, it was the only way. She caught Theo looking at her, *listening* to her thoughts, knew what she was doing – weighing up the situation, the pros and the cons. Linda's words earlier – the veiled intimation – had struck her too.

"Linda," when Theo spoke it was in a careful and precise manner, "if you do come with us to Gilmore Street, it's important that you realise it's for the sake of resolution, not vengeance. I know this is hard, but I'm asking you to take pity on Quinn for the tortured soul that he still is."

"Pity?" Linda almost choked on the word.

"Yes, pity," Theo was undeterred. "If a person is happy they don't inflict damage on others. Quinn was clearly *very* unhappy."

"He stole *my* happiness. My innocence too."

"I know he did, but do you want to continue the battle or end it?"

"I… I want to end it."

"Then – and I know this may sound intolerable considering your history – you fight him with love, because that's the only thing that'll work. If you go into Gilmore Street with hate in your heart, we'll lose."

"I can't love him!"

"You loved him once. Hold on to that."

Instead of baulking, as Theo clearly expected, Linda asked another question. "If I didn't kill him, does anyone

301

need to know, about me, I mean?"

"The police?"

"The press too. The thought of our names entwined forever…"

Cash came into the room. "Like Bonnie and Clyde, you mean?"

"Cash!" Theo admonished. Sometimes humour was not appropriate.

Wincing, Cash did an about turn and left the room again.

"I can't promise anything regarding the press," Theo answered, "but if you didn't kill him, there's nothing to fear from the police. Not anymore."

Linda swallowed. "You keep mentioning Ellie, this girl who seems to know all about me. Who is she?"

"She's a client," Ruby didn't dare look at Ness as she said that. "We don't quite know how she's been able to see things through your eyes, but we'll discuss that after our visit to Gilmore Street."

The doorbell ringing interrupted them.

"That must be Corinna," Ruby said, rising.

It was. The youngest member of Psychic Surveys entered the room in a flurry. "Linda, you didn't kill Quinn O'Brien!"

Linda closed her eyes. Despite what she'd said earlier, the expression on her face was one of relief rather than disappointment.

Corinna plonked herself down on a chair and continued to enlighten them. "Your marriage is listed under England & Wales marriages, in Brighton."

"That's right," Linda confirmed, "the Brighton registry office. It was just us, well… us and two strangers who'd agreed to act as witnesses, Quinn literally just plucked them off the street." She shook her head. "Hardly the big day every girl dreams of. The date was March 15. It was raining."

"We know it was raining," Ruby and Ness said together.

"Sorry," Ruby continued. "It's because of Ellie we know that; that was one of her memories. She couldn't recall location, but she said it was a seaside town, with a pier. In those days, Brighton had two, and Quinn wanted to find work on one of them."

"He did, on the Palace Pier, but just for a day here and a day there."

"Anyway," Corinna was obviously eager to press on; to reveal the 'main' news, "it took a bit of digging – and Sylvia was a godsend – she helped me out loads, but from the details we had we managed to find out he was born in Ballinagar, which is south of Dublin when I looked it up on the map, in January 1945. He died in 1989. The cause of death was prostate cancer."

"Cancer?" Linda queried. "He would have been forty-four."

"Forty-four?" said Ness. "So he was twenty-two when you married him?"

Linda nodded. "And I was nineteen."

They were both so young – one naïve, the other damaged. The information also validated what Benjamin had said to Delia – that he wasn't alone *anymore*. When he had first moved into Gilmore Street, there would have been an atmosphere from what had happened previously, but it would have been residual; extreme emotions printed like a stamp on the atmosphere. Later, when Quinn returned, the haunting would have become 'intelligent' with the spirit *in situ,* and Benjamin would have felt it so much more. Even so, at no point had anyone who knew Ben mentioned that he seemed distressed or scared. On the contrary, he just seemed to mosey along in his own world, something that suited Quinn who was locked in his own world too.

Reining in her thoughts, Ruby asked Linda if knowing for certain she hadn't killed Quinn, helped.

"I can't tell you how I feel," answered Linda, a tear betraying her. "I honestly don't know." Looking at Corinna, she asked where he'd died.

"Brighton. He never moved away."

There was a definite crack in Linda's voice. "All those years," she whispered. "All those years he was alive and so was I."

"Were you ever worried he might come looking for you?" Corinna quizzed.

"I knew he wouldn't."

"How?"

"I just did," was her enigmatic reply.

"You thought he was dead for a start," Ruby reminded.

"I *hoped* he was dead. There's a difference."

"Linda," Theo warned. "Don't sink into hatred again."

She looked Theo in the eye. "I'm trying not to."

Chapter Thirty-One

DIVIDED equally between two cars, the six of them travelled to Gilmore Street, having arranged to meet Samantha at eight o' clock.

"What if reporters are still there?" Corinna quizzed from the back of Ruby's Ford.

"Then let them take pictures," answered Ruby, "do what they have to do. It is what it is now."

Gilmore Street, however, was surprisingly quiet as they drove past it to find a parking space. Her hunch had been right: the reporters, fed up with camping outside, had gone in search of a pint or a hot meal. Perhaps they'd be back later, perhaps not. Oh the irony if they managed to move the spirit on and their moment of glory went un-captured! So be it. The Gordons moving back into their house would be testament enough that they'd succeeded.

Waiting on the pavement for the others, Ruby wondered how Linda had been in Ness's car. Had she been nervous on the journey over? Changed her mind again? It couldn't be easy to return to hell.

To her surprise Linda approached with nothing less than a look of stoic determination on her face. Ruby hurried over to her.

"Are you sure you want to go in?"

"It's now or never."

"Then let it be now," Theo said, coming up to stand beside them. "Any sign of Samantha?"

"There she is." Ruby pointed to Delia's house.

Samantha emerged and quickly crossed the road. Dressed in a long white shirt and denim leggings, she shivered slightly from the cold. "A girls' night out, eh? Or as good as!"

"Don't mind me, I'm proud to be one of the 'girls'," Cash replied, grinning.

Ruby checked again with Samantha that Jeff had no idea where she was.

"No. Believes every word I tell him, that one. It comes in handy on occasions, I can tell you." Growing serious, she turned to Linda. "I don't think we've met before? Are you going in too?"

"Sam, this is Linda, the woman I was telling you about."

"Quinn's wife?"

"His *ex*-wife," Linda corrected.

Samantha shook her head. "Blimey, and I thought mine was a miserable bugger. You had your work cut out with him, I'm guessing."

"You guess right," Linda replied, before averting her gaze.

"Sam," Ruby interrupted, "can we go in, get off the street?"

"Yes, yes, of course. Don't want to alert our nosy neighbours, do we?" Considering the way she raised her voice when she said 'nosy', it seemed that's *exactly* what she intended to do.

"Sam," Ruby reminded her, "we don't want the press here if we can help it,"

"Oh, they'll be here at some point, don't you worry,

doing their usual round of drive-bys. Incredible they are, like a swarm of locusts. They won't give up."

"Sam…" Ruby all but pleaded.

"Come on then. You'll find it quite different inside. The people that have come here before you they've removed virtually everything. Quinn…" she seemed to test the name on her lips, "loves to get heavy with his hands."

"Believe me, I know," Linda muttered.

As she led the way, Samantha continued chatting. "I don't mind coming in with you. It's strange but with you lot I feel safe enough to do that. Even after what happened to me in the living room. The people we've had here since – honestly, what a motley crew. Some were very serious, very studious, whereas others were a right bunch of hippies; reeking of incense and dressed in tie-dye, the men with long goatee beards, the women all airy-fairy." She stopped at the door. "At least you lot look normal." Her gaze rested on Theo's pink hair. "Sort of."

As she inserted the key into the lock, Ruby could feel Linda go rigid beside her. "Are you sure you're okay?" she whispered.

Linda merely nodded.

"If at any time you feel you can't cope, we'll get you out."

"Get *him* out. As much as I'm tempted to leave him."

"We can't, the Gordons…"

"I know we can't. I realise that now. Let's get this over and done with."

"Linda, when I said I'd press charges, I didn't mean it."

"A jail cell doesn't worry me, not after living here."

"You're not afraid?"

Linda dragged her gaze from the door to look at Ruby.

"Afraid? You didn't see him, like I saw him, at the end, *our* end, I mean. He was pathetic. He soiled himself you know? I left him a wreck."

Ruby didn't doubt it. But before she'd done that, he'd wrecked her.

"Come on," she said, moving forwards.

* * *

The house *was* empty. Samantha hadn't exaggerated: every conceivable weapon had been removed – including the kettle, *particularly* the kettle – and put into storage. Ruby was glad. It was just Quinn versus them – and there were more of them. All that filled the house was hatred; it seemed to have soaked like blood into every wall, every floorboard, and saturated them.

Protection procedures had been put in place. Earlier, Theo and Ness had spent quite some time visualising white light, wrapping it around Linda as well. They had then equipped her with tourmaline – the queen of the protection stones – and asked her to visualise white light too. It would not only protect her, Theo said, it would aid in the healing process. They were armed and ready for combat, all of them steeling themselves as they ventured towards the kitchen, the hub of activity. Ruby noted the almost awestruck look on Linda's face as she took in her surroundings, all bright and white, so different to how she remembered them, and how Ellie had described them. The only thing similar perhaps, was the slight smell of damp in the air.

"Linda, are you okay?" she checked again.

It took a few moments for Linda to reply; she was still

looking around her. "It's funny, this was the way I imagined our house was going to look, before I first set foot in here – all clean and modern. More fool me."

"Linda—"

Before Ruby could say anymore, he erupted. Not swearing this time, but screaming – one word surging upwards from the depths: "*Noooooooo!*" On and on it went, like a roll of thunder. Even the non-psychic could sense the anguish in the atmosphere. It *was* Quinn then and he'd seen her: Linda.

"Sam," Ruby said, the din in her head causing her to shout. "I think you'd better leave."

"It's my house."

Fair point. They couldn't make her, only advise.

"Hold onto Corinna's hand then, to Cash's; stand between them. They'll keep you safe. Linda, you stand between Theo and Ness. I'll stand in front."

As everyone shuffled into position, Ruby started speaking.

"We know who you are; we've been calling you Benjamin Hamilton, but we were wrong and we apologise for that. Our mistake must have been frustrating for you. Your name was Quinn O'Brien. We also know what happened here, specifically what took place in this kitchen. And yes, we've brought Linda back, whom, in life, you were married to."

The fucking slut!

"Quinn, stop it. We're here to help."

Get her out!

"No, Quinn, we're here to get *you* out; to send you to the light. We know you were unhappy, and that you made Linda unhappy. You used physical force against her. In the end she snapped; she turned on you. But, Linda is learning to forgive, to let go, and you need to as well. You're in hell, Quinn, but only because you choose to be. You don't have to remain. There's peace waiting in the light, for you and for everyone. Go towards it."

GET HER OUT!

Behind her Theo was growing worried.

"Ruby, perhaps Linda should leave, until we've made some headway—"

Samantha also took the opportunity to speak. "What's happening? What's going on? It's getting so cold in here. It's bloody freezing."

Quinn was materialising – his eyes again very clear, although the rest of him was still merely an outline, and trained solely on Linda.

BITCH!

Ruby turned to Linda. "I know it's galling, I understand that, but will you take the lead, Linda? Will you tell him you're sorry for what happened at the end?" Seeing the horrified look on her face, she added, "It's the only way."

"Is he sorry for what he did to *me*, for how he destroyed my life? Is he?"

"Linda!" Theo was calm now but how much longer she'd remain that way was anyone's guess. "We've talked about this, we've been clear. You are *not* here to exact vengeance. The only way to fight hatred and anger is with love, which is an infinitely more powerful and constructive emotion."

"He destroyed me!"

"No, he didn't." It was Ness, her voice urgent. "He *tried* to destroy you, but you didn't let him. You got your vengeance when he was alive."

"It's not enough." Tears were springing from Linda's eyes. "Where is he? Where's the bastard? I want to see him."

"You don't, Linda, believe me you don't," replied Ruby.

Ignoring Ruby, Linda pushed past her.

Ruby shuddered. "If you must know, he's standing in front of you."

And he was – right in front of her – staring at the woman who'd condemned him to hell all those years ago. Ruby made to step forward, but Theo reached out a hand and stayed her. Her expression said it all – they knew this line of action would provoke the spirit. But sometimes extreme measures had to be taken and this was one of them. Would their gamble pay off?

Even though she could only sense him, Linda addressed Quinn.

"I used to be a nice person. I liked myself. I had a future and prospects... good prospects. I was going to secretarial college, but then I had the misfortune to stumble across you. I fell for your charm and believed your lies. And what did you do? You *contaminated* me with your filth. Why'd you do it, Quinn? Why? What happened to make you that way?"

Quinn continued to stare at her, the look in his eyes blood-curdling.

"Linda..." Ruby chanced, but there was no stopping her now.

"Wrap her in white light," Ness advised. "Wrap them both in it." – an attempt to help them climb out of the swamp they'd fallen into.

"I was reminded by this woman," with her thumb Linda made stabbing gestures towards Theo, "that I loved you once. I'd forgotten that, do you realise? I'd actually forgotten. How's that possible? I've no love for you now, though. I'm trying to find forgiveness instead. For your sake as well as mine. But do you know what? I can't find that either. You *deserved* what I did. I wish it was me that killed you, not the cancer. I hate you, Quinn, for what you did. For what you turned me into."

"Linda, this isn't helping," Ruby stepped forward. "In fact, it's downright dangerous. You'll both remain in torment at this rate."

Linda ignored her. "I hurt you, Quinn, I hurt you so bad you messed your pants. I frightened you, didn't I, which is why you never came after me. I frightened you much more than you ever frightened me. What I did – the *last* thing I did – was evil, pure evil. Even you couldn't compete."

Ruby glanced at Theo, at Ness. What was she talking about – the *last thing* she did? Was she referring to the burning or something else? Praying Linda would listen to her this time, she demanded to know, "Linda, what haven't you told us? Linda, come on, we need to know!"

Theo had had enough. "Get her out of here. Cash…"

Before Cash had a chance to comply, the tension in the room exploded. Again, there was a roar in Ruby's head and she screwed up her eyes against it. As she did, she felt a blow to her stomach, followed by another, and yet another – Quinn's fists striking her over and over: a psychic attack but no less painful for it. Instead of going to evict Linda as Theo had instructed, Cash went to Ruby instead as she doubled up. Jed too was hurling himself at Quinn, snarling, snapping, and baring his teeth, but to no avail. He was viciously kicked aside.

"What's happening?" shouted Cash, bewildered.

"Quinn's attacking Ruby," Theo quickly answered. "He's punching her in the stomach. We all have to get out of here."

As everyone except Linda turned, the kitchen door slammed shut. Why hadn't the 'experts' removed it when they were preparing the house for exorcism? "Shoddy work," Ruby heard Theo mutter. Doors were a well-known hazard – a tool used by wound-up spirits to form a physical barrier. Quinn had employed that 'tool' before and now he was doing it again.

Conversely, elsewhere in the house, doors began to open and shut, the racket deafening.

"What's he doing? What's he bleeding doing?" yelled Samantha.

At this rate the neighbours would flood back, and the reporters – everyone.

When Quinn finally let them go – *if* he did – they'd be spat back out, ejected again, their moment far from glorious.

"Quinn," Ness shouted, "you're not welcome in this house! You must go. It's in your interests to go! Why do you want to remain in hell?"

Ness rushed to join Cash, together with Theo and Corinna, but Linda stood firm.

"He's saying something, isn't he? I can't hear him, but I know he is."

Theo turned to Linda just as the spotlights overhead burst. "Yes, he is saying something. He's calling you a murderer. But you didn't murder him. We know that. So what's he talking about?"

Not waiting to hear her reply, Ruby dropped to the

floor and curled up in a ball, Cash lying over her for protection. Quinn was spinning furiously, deciding which one of them to attack next. His eyes rested on Corinna.

"Corinna!" Theo warned. "Watch it, he's coming for you."

As quickly as Quinn moved, so did Ness, shielding Corinna as Ruby was being shielded. As Ruby looked up from her position on the floor, she saw Ness wince as she received blow after blow into her side. Meanwhile, Samantha had edged her way to the door, her lips moving furiously.

"Even if you do get rid of him, I'm not staying. He's ruined this house for me now. It'll never be the same. Never." Her words ended on a sob.

Theo, do something!

Ruby hated to shift the onus onto Theo but she didn't know what else to do. She sent the thought out clear and direct, knowing that she'd catch it.

"Linda," Theo's voice was urgent, "he's attacked Ruby, right now he's attacking Ness, and all the while he's yelling 'murderer'. You mentioned 'unfinished business'. Please, if there's something you're not telling us, tell us now, because believe me, this situation can get worse."

Rather than reply, Linda just stood there, staring straight ahead. Ruby found herself mentally pleading with her too.

Linda, please help us.

How much more could Ness take, could any of them take?

Linda!

At last Linda started speaking, her voice at first a whisper in the darkness but growing stronger.

"He's right, I *am* a murderer."

Cash moved slightly, allowing Ruby to sit more upright. She was safe for the moment; Quinn had swung round and was looking at Linda. All of them were. Waiting for what was coming.

"I thought I'd murdered Quinn, but I was wrong. I know that now. But the baby," she paused. "Well… the baby didn't get away so lightly."

"The baby?" Ruby gasped.

Linda continued staring. "That's right, I told you I was evil and I meant it. Don't go to the light, Quinn, burn in hell. As for me, I'll burn right alongside you."

Chapter Thirty-Two

THE sound that emanated from Quinn now was not one of anger it was one of agony – terror and grief mixed up in it. Ruby too felt alarmed. With Cash's help, she struggled to her feet; the pain from Quinn's blows causing her to take a sharp intake of breath.

"Linda," she implored again, "we need to know what you're talking about."

But still Linda refused to say. Instead she remained trance-like.

Theo crossed over to Ruby. "We *do* need to know, but not now. We have to get out." To Cash she said, "I'll look after Ruby, just get the door open."

With no hesitation, Cash hurried over to the door, to where Samantha stood with her back against it. "Help me," he said, "let's get out of here."

Together they started yanking on the handle.

Meanwhile, Theo and Ness – the 'giants' as Ruby thought of them – drew closer to Quinn, whose eyes were still trained on Linda and his fists clenched by his side, ready to strike. Ruby felt pride but this time in a positive sense – if her colleagues were nervous of him, they showed no outward sign.

"Quinn," Ness said, doing her utmost to reason with him, "I know in life your actions were questionable. It's never right to use physical violence against a person or to try and control them. But I also know that at the root of such actions lies fear." Would Quinn appreciate Ness's insight or would it elicit more violence? At the door, Cash and Samantha were still tugging at the handle, a few expletives escaping from both of them at various points. "I'm guessing your childhood wasn't an exemplary one. There was damage done to you. Quinn, were you beaten?"

Ignoring her, Quinn began to raise one hand as if to deliver a blow. When he did, would Linda feel it? Ruby guessed she would. His energy was at peak level; a psychic attack would cross the line; become a *real* attack.

"Quinn," Ness continued, her voice not unlike Ailsa's – smooth, monotonal, hypnotic even. "Although you're not answering me, I think you were beaten. A lovely little boy, you were born into the wrong hands, *brutal* hands." Ruby sensed the atmosphere shift slightly, a swing from anguish towards something else – self-pity? If it was, it could be just as dangerous. Still Ness persisted. "But here's the thing, Quinn, the glorious thing. When a soul is born into this world, it's pure. We come from the light, and we go back to it. During our stay on this plane our experiences bend and shape us, sometimes in a positive way, sometimes not. If we are struck, we may choose to strike out too; it's the only way to dull the pain inside, at least temporarily. But then the pain builds up, becomes worse than ever. And we explode with it, we do; I understand that. You're not the first to be affected and you won't be the last. I was beaten too, as a child. The choice I made as an adult was never to do the same thing. You still have choices, Quinn, even now. *Particularly* now. We know that evil was committed here," Ness looked at both Quinn and Linda as she said it, "but it's the act that's evil, not the soul behind it. There will be atonement on the other side, I won't lie but not hell. *This* hell is of your own devising. It's a world you created and you can let it go. Let *us* go."

Was he listening to Ness? Were her words making sense to him? Ruby couldn't call it either way. She caught Cash looking at her, a question in his eyes – should he and Samantha carry on trying to open the door? She nodded in reply. Most definitely: the attacks could start again at any minute. No sooner had she thought it than it happened. Quinn lunged at Linda and she stumbled backwards as he closed his hands around her neck.

"Wha… what's he doing?" There was genuine terror on her face. Somehow Linda hadn't expected him to do that; she still thought she had the upper hand. She was wrong. He had pushed her too far and now she'd done the same to him. Linda started clawing at her neck, trying to throw the attacker off but it was impossible to get a grip on spectral hands.

"Cash!" Ruby screamed. "Get the door open!"

They had to get Linda away from Quinn. They had to know the full story.

"Cash!" she screamed again.

"I'm trying! The bloody thing won't budge."

Meanwhile Theo and Ness were still trying to reason with Quinn but he was beyond listening – his only intention was to break the woman who had broken him. And he could do it, Ruby had no doubt. His hands were tightening around Linda's throat and her face was turning crimson as she struggled to breathe, her legs beginning to buckle beneath her. They had no other option but to open the kitchen door, drag her away from him and get out of

Gilmore Street. Nothing else mattered, not the press waiting – *if* they were waiting – the neighbours, nothing. It had come down to basics, to survival.

Joining Corinna, Ruby rushed towards Cash and Samantha: perhaps with all four of them tugging or pushing the door would cave in, one way or another. Linda had fallen to the floor now, the dark shape of Quinn on top of her, his grip relentless. He would either succeed in strangling her or her heart would give out in shock. Every second counted. Theo and Ness were sending as much light and love as they could muster to combat the darkness in him, to try and dissolve it, but he was blacker than pitch. If he won this battle, if Linda died… It didn't bear thinking about.

She and Corinna did their best to help Cash and Samantha, but it was a case of too many people making matters worse.

"Just let me focus," Cash instructed, waving the three women away. Not a split second later he hurled himself at the door with all the desperation of something rabid. Jed, meanwhile, had run through the door and was barking at them from the other side, urging them to hurry.

We're coming, Jed! We're coming.

Silently she willed Cash on.

Believe he can do it. Believe!

She daren't look at what was happening behind her.

He can do it, he can!

Sweat was pouring off Cash's face.

Cash, please!

Suddenly Cash was through the door, flying into the hallway and smashing into the bannisters opposite. He'd done it! A small triumph that seemed huge. He must have hurt himself on impact, certainly the whoosh of air that left his body suggested it, but he was needed still.

"Cash, help me get Linda out of here! Corinna, Samantha, stay by the door, put your full weight against it, make sure it doesn't shut again.

Doubling back, Cash and Ruby reached Linda. Theo and Ness had already started to tug at her but Quinn was proving too strong. His energy was bound to wane at some point, but when?

"We need to lift her," Ruby said to Cash.

Bending, he placed his arms under Linda and wrapped them round her torso. Ness and Ruby grabbed a leg each and Theo continued to send white light towards Quinn, her face almost fierce with concentration.

"Go, go, go!" Ruby said, indicating to Cash to get moving.

Immediately, he obeyed. "It's like she's made of stone!" he complained.

Ruby didn't have time to explain that Quinn was weighing her down.

"Just get her through the door!"

"Quinn," Theo entreated him, "if you kill Linda, the chances are she'll remain grounded too, right here, with you. Is that what you want? Either of you? To be stuck here again, side by side?"

The slug that Linda described him as, continued with his aim – to destroy.

"QUINN, STOP!"

Ruby interrupted Theo. "We need to get Linda out of the kitchen, down the hallway and out of the house; Quinn won't leave Gilmore Street, he won't leave hell." She felt Linda's body go limp. "Time's running out,

Theo."

Theo transferred her attention to Linda, "Okay, okay. Hang on, Linda, do you hear? Hang on."

Jed was beside Ruby, nudging her urgently and whining.

With Corinna and Samantha ensuring that the kitchen door remained open, Cash, Ruby, and Ness pulled Linda through it, Cash at the helm. In the hallway, Quinn looked up as though surprised to find himself there, but quickly he collected himself, snapped his head one way and then the other – searching for a way to stop them leaving, the only way he knew how – by means of violence. Not Cash, he wouldn't attack Cash; he preferred to pick on the more vulnerable of the species. Releasing Linda completely – a mercy of sorts – he spun around to face Ruby and Ness.

Ruby tensed, knew Ness was bracing herself too. A few more yards, that's all there was to go. How was Cash going to open the front door? He had his hands full. She damned the narrowness of the hallway: they were filling the width of it, but Corinna or Samantha had to find a way to squeeze past, drop to the floor, crawl under their feet – anything.

Freedom... never had it seemed so tantalising.

Deciding on his target, cold, hard hands started squeezing Ruby's neck, the strength in them belying his ethereal state. They were like steel.

Ruby sent love towards him and understanding, wave after wave, but it was no good – he wasn't in a receptive mood. Hell was all he remembered, perhaps since the day he'd entered the world.

"Ruby, can you cope?" Ness asked, knowing full well what was going on.

Unable to speak, she sent a thought instead.

Get us out. He won't leave Gilmore Street.

She was beginning to gurgle, her eyesight swimming in and out of focus. Her tourmaline necklace formed something of a barrier between them but even so, there was no denying it, what he was doing, it hurt. How she longed for fresh air, to breathe freely.

You bastard, Quinn!

She couldn't help thinking it.

You deserve to rot in hell!

"Ruby, stop that. You cannot fight hate with hate."

Was that Ness admonishing her or Theo? She couldn't tell.

"Ruby, we're almost there."

'Almost' was too far away.

She could stand no longer, so fell to her knees. As his hands grew tighter still, hatred seemed to pour from him and into her, the coldest of liquids. If she were Linda, she would have done the same thing when the chance presented itself. She would have turned on him, maimed, tortured and beaten him. She would have taken it further, made sure she killed him. Revelled in the culling. It would give her such strange comfort to watch his life force drain from him. He'd ruined Linda's life and now he was trying to ruin hers – destroying all she'd worked so hard to achieve: her reputation, her livelihood. He was trying to take her from the man she loved too, and from her friends, Theo, Ness, and Corinna. How she'd miss them if he succeeded.

Was it Linda who'd said evil was infectious, or Ellie? Perhaps they'd both said it. A soul divided: one and the same.

There was no air left in her lungs now. This was it – she'd cross and she'd get her revenge. Like Linda, that's all she wanted – to make him pay. And she would. He'd never have witnessed evil like it. She'd welcome the bad wolf to the surface, let it devour the good wolf; she'd be everything its darker shadow was. And he would suffer. Oh, how she'd make him suffer!

"Ruby! Ruby! Breathe, in and out. Come on. Breathe!"

Ruby's eyes snapped open. What was happening? Where was she? Shouldn't she be dead? A bright light caused her to squint. There was a street lamp directly above her. Shifting her eyes from it, she looked into the eyes of Cash instead. They were so different to Quinn's; so full of warmth – the light to her dark. This wasn't hell. This wasn't the other side. She'd been dragged back, the tide of hatred within her beginning to recede.

"Cash!" She reached up to throw her arms around him and then drew away, looking frantically around her. "Where is she, Cash?"

"Linda? She's fine; she's conscious. Theo and Ness are seeing to her."

"Who opened the door?"

"Corinna did, she had a job getting between everyone's legs I can tell you, but she did it. Samantha's just slammed it shut, locked Quinn back in."

"We need to know the full story."

Cash shook his head vehemently. "Ruby, you need to rest."

She pushed him away entirely now and with something akin to relief, noticed only a few neighbours had gathered, their faces stunned, not knowing what to make of the latest events. "Are there any reporters?" she asked Cash.

"There's no one with a camera, no."

That wouldn't last long.

"Where can we go? We have to get off the street."

"Delia's." Samantha was standing nearby and it was she who answered. "Come on, she's waving us in."

Ruby didn't need asking twice.

Chapter Thirty-Three

HALF walking, half stumbling, the team made their way over to Delia's living room, the 'normality' of her chintz decor like the most refreshing of breezes. Linda had been helped to the sofa and was currently lying on it, her face pale, and her breathing shallow but regular. Theo had asked Delia for a cold facecloth and pressed it to the prone woman's forehead.

Ruby crossed over to her. "Linda, do you want us to call an ambulance?"

She raised a hand. "I'll be okay, just... get me a glass of water, would you?"

"Water?" Delia queried. "It's a reviving cup of tea you'll be wanting."

Ruby stopped her. "No, she prefers water. I'll go and get it."

Linda might refuse tea but the others were gasping for a cup, so Delia joined Ruby in the kitchen to explain she'd make a pot anyway.

As she bustled around Ruby, she sighed. "It's a right old to-do over there, a real debacle. The rumour is it's the devil himself in residence. No wonder people want to move. The thing is, who's going to buy the house now?"

"Quinn's not the devil," Ruby countered, "as much as he thinks he is."

Remembering the hatred she'd felt towards him, how much she'd wanted to hurt him, she'd need to keep that in mind about herself too.

"Quinn you say?" Delia continued. "Is that his name?"

"It is, Quinn O'Brien. He lived there briefly before Ben moved in. Linda, who's on the sofa, was married to him."

"She's his wife?" Delia was aghast.

"Ex-wife," Ruby replied.

Delia leaned forward – her eyes alight. "Tell me all."

"I would, Delia, but I don't know the full story myself. That's what I'm going to find out now."

"Och, I'll hurry with the tea then," Delia declared. "I don't want to miss a word."

* * *

Ruby waited until Linda had drained half her glass before she started her interrogation, glad to see colour returning to the older woman's cheeks.

Drawing a breath, noting how sore her throat was, the windpipe severely bruised, she was about to speak when Linda stopped her.

"I know what you want," she said, "and I'll tell you. Why not? I'm damned anyway, despite what you say."

"Linda—" Theo began but Ruby interrupted.

"Let's just listen." There was no way she wanted Linda distracted.

"Help me to sit up."

Ruby did as Linda asked, puffing up a cushion behind her, before taking her seat again.

"The reason I was crying at the kitchen sink was because I'd realised I was pregnant. Not far gone, but I was so thin

I was beginning to show already. I couldn't hide from the truth much longer. On one of the few times he could manage it, Quinn's seed had taken root, his *demon* seed."

Ruby noticed Corinna's eyes widen at Linda's graphic choice of words. Delia, who had re-entered the room, issued a breathy 'oh my!'

Linda leaned forward and clutched Ruby's arm. From the look in her eyes, Ruby could see that she was back in hell again, fully immersed.

"I had wanted a child so much, but not now, not *his* child. Can you understand that? I wanted nothing that was a part of him."

Ruby nodded. "I *can* understand. Back there, in the hallway, he had his hands around my throat. I wanted to retaliate, to do what you did, to hurt him. He brought out the worst in me. I wanted to kill him too. And I would have. I would have."

It was Linda who seemed shocked now. She stared at Ruby and, as she did, an understanding passed between them.

"I believe you," the older woman said at last.

"Whatever you've done, we won't judge you," Ruby assured her. After the feelings that had enveloped her, she was in no position to.

Linda swallowed. "Oh, I think you will."

"Just tell us," Ruby pleaded.

"I intend to," Linda replied, taking a few moments to compose herself. As she spoke, she kept her voice controlled, initially at least.

"As I began to gain an advantage over Quinn, a plan formed in my mind. Not only would I show him no mercy, I wouldn't show any to the child inside of me either. How could I love something that was a part of him? Impossible! I don't think I could ever love again. That emotion – that capability – was dead. And soon his child would be too. And I'd make him watch me kill it.

It would hurt Quinn. I knew it would because there was a time he said he wanted children. Not before we were married, surprisingly, it was afterwards. We were upstairs in bed. He'd tried to foist himself on me but failed. Usually he flew into a rage about this; he'd kick and punch me; he'd tell me how ugly I was; that his failure was my fault. How could anyone want to make love to someone so weak and pathetic? But this time was different. He rolled onto his back and looked up at the ceiling. I thought he was working up to a rage, or that he was making me wait – sometimes the anticipation of his fists was much worse than the actual act. He was shaking, the bed was too; in anger I wondered? I waited, trembling just as violently as him. When he spoke again, his voice was thick. I realised then that the bed was shaking because he was crying, his chest rising and falling with each sob! I could hardly believe it, that this monster was capable of tears. Wondered if I was dreaming. Should I reach out and comfort him? I couldn't! I couldn't! I waited for him to speak instead.

'It'll be different if we had a child,' he said. "*I'll* be different.'

I didn't reply.

'We can learn how to love it and it will love us back. Imagine that?'

I had – once. There was a time when I had wanted a boy so bad; a tiny version of the man I loved. Now that thought filled me with horror. Absolute horror. He would be someone Quinn would teach the vilest of lessons to, just

328

as he'd been taught, passing down from generation to generation nothing but a thirst for violence and subjugation. It might be that I'd fear my own child too in time; that he'd turn on me, his own mother. I'd have two of them to contend with then. No, Quinn was talking nonsense. There was no way he could love it back. He had no love inside to give, no beating heart, just a cold, hard lump of coal, which had been fed nothing but darkness. I didn't give him any comfort, I turned on my side, away from him, expecting that to ignite his fury at least, but he left me alone that night. He let me lose myself in sleep.

But I knew then how much it meant to him to have a baby. And although I still didn't want to get pregnant, at least I had a weapon. Standing in front of him I realised that what I was about to do would hurt him more than a beating and boiling water ever could. Oh God!"

"Linda…" Ruby urged, "don't stop. Tell us what you did." For a moment she doubted that Linda was going to continue, that she wouldn't be able to find the words but she did… eventually.

"He didn't know I was pregnant. But I made sure to tell him as he lay on the floor, blood pooling around him. I said that a child was growing within me, *his* child. I saw him look up, a glimmer of hope amongst despair. He tried to lift a hand, to reach out. And then, as I used my fists to beat my own stomach, I saw that hope shrivel up and die. I was not going to have his child and he knew it. He couldn't control me any longer, only watch as I beat myself, as I pummelled and pummelled. Despite the plea in his eyes, I walked away, started backing down the hallway, reaching the front door, still pummelling, one fist after the other, waiting for the flow of blood, which I knew would follow: a sign that what'd he'd planted in me, like him, was destroyed."

Like a drowning woman that had suddenly broken the surface, Linda gasped, her body shooting forwards before slumping. Everyone else remained still, trying to digest the latest revelation.

Fighting to control her breathing, Linda managed to speak.

"You see what I mean? I'm worse than Quinn, much worse. I killed my own baby."

Hardly able to conceal her shock, Ruby asked when she'd miscarried.

"Not long afterwards, just a matter of hours. I left the house, went to the station, and caught a train to London; somewhere I'd be even more anonymous. I found a public toilet, locked myself in, and waited. The gush of blood was horrendous, the pain. I…" She sobbed again and brought one hand up to cover her face. "That poor baby, that poor, poor baby."

Only Ness remained dry-eyed. "Your baby…" she repeated but then her words trailed away.

Linda didn't seem to hear her. "You talk of the light, but I'll never find it. Not after that."

Ness turned to look at Ruby, stared at her for a few seconds, then turned to Theo. Ruby could almost see the mechanics of her mind working furiously.

"Ness…" Ruby enquired and then stopped. *'Your baby.'* – She had said it as if she was searching for another meaning.

Your baby… your baby…

What could that meaning be?

Your baby…

330

The realisation when it came, was electric.

"Your baby was Ellie!" Ruby eyes trained solely on Ness, she continued, "I'm right, aren't I? That's what you're thinking?"

Ness nodded slowly as though coming to terms with it herself.

A soul divided? No. They'd been two separate souls in one body.

It took Ruby a moment to realise Linda was speaking. "Ellie? The girl you keep talking about? The girl with my memories?"

Theo had slumped too, but not in shock or despair; in amazement. "Of course!" she exclaimed. "That makes much more sense."

Corinna looked at Cash – twin expressions of bemusement on their faces. "Could someone help us make sense of it too?"

"And me," Delia piped up from her corner. "I'm completely baffled."

Samantha could only shake her head. Words had failed her.

"Ruby," Ness said, still ashen. "Would you like to explain or should I?"

Ruby hesitated, wondered where she should start. "I'll… erm… I can try."

"Would you like more tea, dear?" Delia asked gently.

"Please. That'd be great."

"It's on its way."

A few minutes later, with a warm cup clutched between her hands, Ruby had sorted it enough in her head to tell Linda what she thought. No, not what she thought, what she *knew*. Her theory – as she'd called it before – could only be the truth. Extracts of what Ellie had said during her regression sessions came to mind. She didn't have her notepad with her to cross reference facts, but she could recall several of them well enough. How Ellie had said she didn't know who she was; that she wasn't herself anymore; also how trapped she'd felt when Quinn had begun attacking her in the kitchen – *entombed*. At one point she'd likened herself to a passenger, hitching a lift in someone else and gazing outwards. Little wonder. And tea, she never drank tea; didn't like it, Linda had passed on that aversion too.

She had to check one more thing.

"You never gave your baby a name, did you, Linda?"

"No. The last thing I wanted to do was make it more real, not when I wanted to get rid of it."

Which is why Ellie had never been able to recall it. Clearing her throat, she started from the beginning.

"Ellie came to us because she started having dreams of another woman; dreams that turned into visions – snapshots she called them. They occurred in the daytime as well as at night and they were really vivid. She told me she was being haunted – by herself. A friend of a friend called Katharine had set off the visions, someone who has a unique psychic ability. She claims she can see who a person was in their past life. She held on to Ellie's hands and… well… she saw a woman, standing at the kitchen sink and fighting back tears. She felt her despair, her fear – emotions in turmoil, emotions that were crushing her, that's how Katharine described it. Katharine then let go of Ellie's hands as if she'd been burnt; what she had seen seemed to unsettle her and she refused to continue. She told Ellie to leave the past alone, to keep it buried; that it was complicated." Ruby looked hard at Linda. "But as we both know, sometimes the past won't leave *us* alone."

"Ruby," it was Theo, knowing what she was referring to: her own demon, "drink some tea."

Ruby did, grateful for the warmth of the fluid as it eased her throat.

"These visions frightened Ellie; they were increasing in frequency as well as intensity. She said she felt threatened still, as if the danger wasn't over. As if it had been left unfinished. We took Ellie's case on. I was reluctant to I must admit but Ness persuaded me to give it a shot; to try and understand what was happening to her. She thought it would be good for Psychic Surveys; that it would build on our expertise. We offered her several regression sessions, undertaken by Ailsa Isaacs, who specialises in that field. Ness and I sat in on them. The life Ellie recalled, Linda, was *your* life, told to us by her just as you've told us since, sometimes word for word. You know you called Quinn a 'slug of a man'? Ellie used those words too. Thinking about it now, I would say Ellie also recalled her own life in the womb, but somehow her memories merged with yours. Often she couldn't 'see' properly or recall her name, that sort of thing. There were also times she felt it was wrong calling Quinn her husband, yet at other times she was fine with it – a result of the confusion, I guess." As her words were coming out in something of a rush, Ruby stopped and took a deep breath before continuing. "Your memories, your feelings, your experiences, they manifested in her mind, became a part of her psyche and subsequently her soul."

All the while Ruby was speaking, Ness was shaking her head, not in disagreement, in awe. "Anything is possible," she muttered.

"Yes," Ruby concurred, "*anything*." She felt awed too. "At first, when I discovered how similar your stories were, I thought you and Ellie might be the same soul divided. But you're not, you were two souls under the same roof so to speak; the bond between you so strong that Ellie shared everything with you, even memories of events that happened before she was in your womb."

"*Before*?" Linda quizzed.

Ruby nodded. "These memories may well have been flitting through your mind after she'd been conceived, maybe as an attempt by you to make sense of all that was happening. What we do know is that they were all significant events – the first time you met Quinn; the first time you were intimate; when he met your parents; your wedding day. Events that are a part of your history and therefore a part of you." Glancing at Theo, she added, "I suppose we nourish the child inside us in more ways than one."

"That's right," Theo said, smiling at Ruby. "But before we go any further, I think we have to point out that a case such as this is… unique. Certainly I've never come across one like it during my lifetime. And regarding babies picking up on their mothers' emotions, there's enough proof out there to show that stressed mothers are at a higher risk of miscarriage and stillbirths." She looked directly at Linda. "You were under an enormous amount of stress. You were so young, so bewildered by what had happened to you; you were just so damned *shocked*. There's every possibility you were going to miscarry anyway and that what you did, your actions, had no bearing."

"I'm not looking to be absolved."

"I realise that—"

"And it doesn't matter," Linda insisted. "The *intention* was there."

Theo couldn't argue with that.

Linda started speaking again, clearly doing her utmost to take it all in – they all were. "I understand a foetus can feel the mother's emotion, I get that; but to *see* through her eyes, to be able to access her memories…"

"Is incredible," Ruby answered when Linda hesitated, "but we have to remember the foetus is a vehicle for the soul and as young as the physical body might be, the spirit is ageless. What it catalogues from the moment of conception, what it *stores*, is quite clearly everything that impacts on it."

"There's also such a thing as soul groups, Ruby," Theo added, "and before Cash can beat me to it with one of his prized quips, I'm not talking Marvin Gaye or The Drifters here; I mean in a spiritual sense. You see, we don't just break away from the mass individually; we break away as a group – a group we return with again and again, often in different guises. A father may be a son in the next life, for example; a wife might be a daughter; which could account for why, when we meet someone, we seem to *know* them, because deep down we *do*. In simplest terms, your soul group consists of people you have *chosen* to experience certain human experiences with in order to understand them; the good, the bad, and the downright ugly, with a view to working your way through issues and finding a resolution. According to this belief, Linda, Ellie and possibly Quinn, might be part of the same soul group." Theo paused and looked round at her friends, a smile on her face. "As for us, I like to think you're all part of my soul group, and yes, Ness, that does include you, very much so." Before Ness could comment, she added, "But, Ness, I also think you're part of *their* soul group, Ellie's, Linda's and Quinn's."

Ness frowned, and was about to comment, but Theo was keen to get her point across. "We all know how fond you are of Ellie, how much you identify with her. I know you empathise with Linda too, and with Quinn, because of what you've gone through in the past, with your own family."

"I don't want to talk—"

"I know you don't and this will be my only mention of it, but Ellie got to you more than she should, and perhaps there's a reason for that. You knew deep down you had to help her. And in doing so, help yourself."

"But she came to me first, not Ness," Ruby pointed out.

"She came to you because of Psychic Surveys," Theo replied. "Because you're out there – you're on the high street, a company with a good reputation, despite what the press are trying to do to you. And through you she met Ness. The thing is, Ruby, once you open doors, people will walk through them, and I'm not just talking about the doors in your mind. And what's happened, how the two cases are connected, it's no coincidence either. I agree with Einstein about that. It's the Higher Power working in mysterious ways again, the reasons for which I'm sure will become blindingly obvious to us when we're on the other side. But for now, whilst we're here, let's do what we have to do – what the universe wants. This matter needs wrapping up: it's getting old, it's getting tired, and it's dragging on. Everyone who's involved needs to move on, not just Quinn. Agreed?"

"Agreed," both Ruby and Ness said.

Linda, who was listening as intently as the rest of them, still wasn't convinced. "All this talk, you make it sound as if something miraculous has happened when all I feel is cursed."

Ness refused to indulge her. "But it *is* a miracle, Linda. It's good trying to emerge from bad."

Briefly Linda closed her eyes. Ruby felt for her; there was a lot to take in; a lot that the limited human mind had trouble comprehending, even a psychic's mind.

Opening her eyes, Linda's thoughts returned to the baby. "If it was a boy, though—" But there she stopped, finally willing to believe the evidence so far. "But of course it wasn't. It was Ellie. It was a girl, *my* girl." She seemed to fold in on herself. "If I'd known there might have been a chance for us, I would have left her in me; taken her away from Quinn, far away. I'd have moved to another country, brought her up by myself. I don't know... was I too damaged by then? A lost cause? I must have been, to do what I did."

As Ruby tried to comfort her, Cash moved over to the living room window to take a look outside. "There are reporters out there now, Ruby. I reckon one of the neighbours has been on the phone."

"Bloody neighbours!" Samantha found her voice at last. "Always interfering."

Ruby couldn't think about neighbours and reporters now. What was happening outside the house seemed a million miles away, except number 44 Gilmore Street, which was always on the radar. Delia had gone to fetch a box of tissues and Ruby handed one to Linda. After Linda had blown her nose, Ruby forced her to make eye contact again in an attempt to press her next words home. "Linda, what you did was *not* evil, not under the circumstances. You weren't thinking straight."

"I'd gone insane you mean."

"But you're not insane now. I said before I wouldn't judge you and I don't. I don't condemn you either. I don't think there's a single person in this room who would, not now they know the full story, how much you've suffered, how much you *all* suffered."

Everyone voiced their agreement, strongly so. Linda's tears halted: she looked around her, hardly able to believe it. Theo nodded for Ruby to continue.

"After you left Gilmore Street there are no more memories from Ellie. She did die at the house I think, miscarried, as you say, a few hours later, in London. In some ways, perhaps that was a miracle too. You're right, Quinn was damaged, and he'd damaged you. Perhaps her life would have been as miserable as yours. And perhaps that's what motivated you: the child's wellbeing – be it a girl or a boy. A mother's love in other words."

"A mother's love?"

"Yes, something you're still capable of, even after everything."

"How do you know that?" Linda's voice had a plea in it.

"Because you're mourning her loss, still, after all this time."

"Mourning?" Linda repeated. "A mother's love?" Her next words were so low Ruby could barely hear them. "I've never thought of it that way before."

"Perhaps think of it that way from now on. That's the choice you have."

Linda looked up. "But just now, in Gilmore Street, I

wanted to hurt him so bad; have one last attempt at it. Once again I used our child as a weapon."

"And you succeeded. But you see, that's a good thing too because it's shown us something. If he's capable of being hurt, he's not evil either. And if he's not evil, we can reach him."

Ruby noticed a proud smile on Theo's face and smiled too.

"Ruby," Cash's anxiety was growing, "there's a heck of a lot of them out there. More than I've seen before. What are we going to do?"

That was the million-dollar question.

"Ness…" Ruby didn't have to say anymore, Ness knew what she was thinking. The smile on her face was not just an acceptance of Ruby's silent apology regarding their head-to-head over Ellie it was also a go-ahead. "Linda," she continued, "I don't want you going back into Gilmore Street. Whether you're part of his soul group or not, I don't think it's constructive. You and Quinn have come to the end of the road – in this life anyway. But, if she's willing," and Ruby had an inkling she might be, "I'm going to ask Ellie if she would."

"Ellie?" Linda gasped. "He'll… he'll hurt her."

"Perhaps he won't," Ruby replied. "But, don't worry, I'll go in with her. She won't be alone." To Samantha, Ruby said, "Is that all right?"

Samantha nodded. "I trust you, Ruby. More than I trusted any of that other shower."

"Thanks," Ruby murmured, humbled that she did.

Linda was clutching at her arm again. "I'll get to meet my… I don't know what to call her… Ellie. I'll get to meet Ellie?"

"You will and she, erm… from what I know of her, needs a mother figure."

"She doesn't have one?" Linda was surprised.

"It's a long story but let's just say you could be a godsend."

Chapter Thirty-Four

THANKFULLY, Ellie was only too willing. In fact, despite the magnitude of what Ruby asked her to do, explaining as concisely as possible the events of the last twenty-four hours, the girl was at pains to apologise to her.

"I'm sorry about what I did, I was only trying to help."

"Ellie, no pun intended, but that's old news," Ruby had replied, "and it's not you who should be apologising, it's me. *I'm* sorry I was so reluctant to help you. I could give you a thousand excuses why: my workload was too much at the time, I was tired, I didn't want to diversify, I didn't *believe* you, I felt threatened by you even." Now she realised the threat she'd sensed was actually around Linda – her subconscious trying to warn her. "We can discuss all that at a later date. Right now we need your help."

"There's no question, I am going to help." Before Ruby could respond, Ellie continued. "But I can't believe it. No, that's not true; I *can* believe it. I don't know... it's so unreal, but at the same time it feels so real. I'm sorry. I'm gabbing on again, aren't I? But it just... it makes sense now, all of it."

"That jigsaw we talked about, it's a puzzle no longer."

"Exactly. Thanks so much for finding all this out."

"It was a team effort."

"Yeah, you, Ailsa and the rest of Psychic Surveys, you

smashed it."

Despite her enthusiasm, Ruby felt she had to warn her again, press the point home. "Ellie, Quinn is very angry, he's violent too. There's danger—"

"I know there's danger, but he's my dad – or rather he *was*. I have to try. Besides which, you'll be with me and I trust you, Ruby, I always have."

Ellie's faith in her, Samantha's faith in her, spurred her on. *Trust in yourself now, Ruby. You can do this – you can move Quinn on.*

For the first time she believed it. They had Linda's 'weapon' on their side.

* * *

Linda had been nervous about meeting Ellie, and had started shaking at the thought of it.

"I *killed* her, Ruby, she'll never forgive me."

"I think you'll find Ellie's the forgiving kind. Besides which, she *understands,* remember?" Something else occurred to Ruby. "Linda, would you mind showing me the inside of your arms?"

"My arms?" Linda didn't appear keen at all.

"Humour me," responded Ruby.

As she tentatively lifted up her sleeves, Ruby's hunch proved correct. There were silver and white lines on both arms, but particularly on the arm where Ellie scratched at her eczema – another manifestation of their bond.

"I self-harm." The shame in Linda was awful to see.

"I guessed," Ruby replied.

"She's the best of us, isn't she? Ellie."

"She is."

Leaving Ness with Linda – it was imperative Ellie met

Quinn before her former 'mother' – Ruby had managed to get Theo on her own. "I still can't believe we've had the answer all along."

"That's the advantage of being loud and proud," Theo answered. "As I said, Ellie might never have come to you if the service you provide wasn't a public one. And Linda, she would never have known what was happening in Gilmore Street if the national press hadn't picked up on the story."

"You're making the press seem like our friend rather than the enemy."

Theo burst out laughing, one of her infamous bellows that had you quickly reaching to cover your ears. "Perhaps that is a step too far." Serious again, she expressed concern about Ruby and Ellie going into Gilmore Street on their own. "We should all be there, there's safety in numbers."

"But you'll be just outside, within shouting distance." Ruby paused. "You could chat to our old friends, the reporters, whilst you're waiting. Get Delia to make them a cup of tea. The thing is, Theo, I don't want to overwhelm Quinn, not like we did before. Despite everything… he's a sensitive soul."

"Chat to the reporters?" Theo's face was comical.

"That's right! According to you, they're in this just as much as we are."

* * *

"All you need is a red carpet," Cash muttered. "It's a bit remiss of them not to provide one, I think."

He was right, Ruby felt like the world's biggest celebrity as she walked from one side of Gilmore Street to the other, amid the cameras clicking. Making the most of the moment rather than shying away from it, she threw her shoulders back, held her head high, and took confident strides. Beside her, Ellie did the same. In the crowd, she saw Robin giving her the thumbs-up.

"We're rooting for you, Ruby," he yelled. "Good luck!"

Before Ruby and Ellie entered the house, Cash reiterated that the rest of them would be just outside. "We'll break the door down if necessary." Referring to the fact that he'd already done that twice in Gilmore Street, he added, "It is, after all, a speciality of mine."

Ruby laughed, feeling comforted. There was still a chance after all that this wouldn't work, and that breaking down the door for a third time might actually be necessary. If that was the case, they'd have done all they could; she was out of ideas. They might even have to walk away. She'd tell Quinn that; make sure he knew it was his prerogative to stay in hell if he wanted to.

She told Jed to stay put as well, but he didn't seem to need reminding. As he stood beside Cash, the dog dipped his head as if giving her the go ahead. Tending to use him as a barometer, she took that as a positive sign.

Turning to Ellie, she said, "Are you ready?"

"I'm ready," replied Ellie, a smile brightening her face.

Opening the door to 44 Gilmore Street, the pair of them stepped into the hallway, Ruby shutting the door behind them – shutting them in. Even though she had Ellie with her, she couldn't help but feel a frisson of fear and had to remind herself to breathe evenly; not only that, but to keep what was bad inside caged; to *understand* evil but not emulate it. There was no evil in Ellie, which was important to remember too; nothing for Quinn to latch onto.

It's only you where that applies.

Ruby shook the thought from her head, refused to even entertain it.

As Linda had done, Ellie looked around her in wonder. "It's not the way I saw it through Linda's eyes, but this is it. This is the house. I can't believe I'm here."

"It must feel strange."

"It feels a whole mixture of things."

Giving her a moment to come to terms with it, Ruby suggested they walk towards the kitchen.

"That's where I died, isn't it?"

"Linda miscarried in London," Ruby reminded her. "But yes, it's likely the kitchen is where you passed."

"We'll never really know, will we?"

"No," Ruby admitted. "Not for sure."

This time Ellie's smile held nothing other than sadness.

Walking further into the house, Ruby wondered if the dark figure of Quinn would come rushing down the hallway at her, or worse, at Ellie. She forced herself to keep moving, one foot in front of the other. It was time to step up; to be a 'giant' alongside Theo and Ness.

Despite her fanciful notions, there was no sign of him. Could his early spectacular display of energy have exhausted him?

At the door to the kitchen, Ellie fastened her pace and took the lead, surprising Ruby. She was about to stop her, when Ellie started speaking.

"Dad?" she breathed into the darkness of the room. "Dad, are you there?"

Ruby swallowed. What would Quinn's reaction be to the word 'dad'?

Switching on a torch she'd borrowed from Delia, she

followed her in too. "Ellie," she said, "let me explain to Quinn first…"

But Ellie wasn't listening. She turned to Ruby, her eyes wide. "He was my dad, Ruby! I know it was in a former life, but even so. And Linda was my mum. Do you know how incredible that feels – to know you've got history?"

What could Ruby tell her? That she only half knew? This wasn't the time.

"Ellie, I appreciate what you're saying, but let me speak to him first."

Although reluctant, Ellie backed down, nodding for her to go ahead.

Shining the light into the corner where Quinn had first materialised, Ruby addressed him yet again.

"Quinn, it's me, it's Ruby. And this time I haven't got Linda with me; I've got Ellie. Ellie is… was your daughter, the baby that Linda beat out of her."

She paused – waited for her words to sink in.

Was that a figure unfolding? It was. It was Quinn, definitely depleted, but gaining in strength, becoming more substantial. She had to hurry, to explain.

"Your baby did die, but she came back again, and somehow she's found you, and Linda too. It's her soul but in a different body. In this life, she's known as Ellie. She's young, strong, and beautiful. She's the best of both of you. You wanted a child, I know you did; Linda told me. And she's here, she's found you. She wants to let you know that there's something good within you and from it, she emerged. You're not evil, Quinn; you're not damned and you shouldn't be in hell. If you go to the other side you can begin to work things through, *all* of your issues. And you'll be given help to do that. But right now, look at your daughter; at the beautiful something that's a part of you."

The torch dropped from Ruby's hand as she was thrown backwards, crashing into the wall behind her.

"Ruby!" Ellie screamed. "Dad!"

Once again Ruby hadn't seen Quinn coming: one minute he was crouching by the kitchen table, struggling to materialise; the next he was on her, his hands tearing the tourmaline necklace from her neck before closing round it. Without her great-grandmothers' heirloom, she felt naked, vulnerable – far from the giant she wanted to be. Beforehand, the necklace had provided some protection, a shield; now there was no barrier between them. She had to be quick, *Ellie* had to be quick. Soon, with the pressure at her throat mounting, she wouldn't be able to say anything at all.

"Ellie, don't call the others, not yet. Talk to Quinn; talk to your dad; you're the only one who stands a chance of getting through to him."

Ellie hesitated, her eyes darting between the door and Ruby.

"Ellie, please… there's not much time. Talk to him!"

"I can't see him!"

"It doesn't matter. Talk to him. He can hear you."

That was it, she could say no more. It was up to Ellie now. Her life depended on what the terrified girl would do next.

"There's knocking at the door, I think they might have heard me scream."

Please, Ellie.

Ellie darted to the hallway and shouted, "It's all right, we're okay in here."

The knocking died down.

Good girl, Ellie, good girl.

The fact that Jed had stayed put and hadn't run through the front door, as he was able to do so easily, strengthened Ruby's belief that the key players were *in situ* – no one else was needed.

Re-entering the kitchen, Ellie walked boldly over to where Ruby's body was pinned. That streak of steel in her, Ruby was grateful for it.

"Dad, stop it. Stop what you're doing."

Quinn didn't even turn to look at her.

"Dad, please, I'm begging you."

Her words were falling on deaf ears.

"DAD!"

Even though she tried to suppress it, panic started to flare in Ruby. That confidence she had tried so hard to summon was beginning to wane. She tried to imagine it as something physical, did her best to keep hold of it, but her grip was nowhere near as impressive as Quinn's.

Why wasn't he listening? Didn't he believe them? That must be it. He didn't believe them! How could they make him? What else could they do? She could feel her eyes bulging, her sight dimming. He didn't believe them and now she would pay the price. It had been a mistake to bring Ellie here – *another* mistake – one of a series – a whole catalogue of them. But it had also been the only option left to them. Miserably, she realised Quinn was going nowhere. Hell was all he knew. The last thing he wanted was resolution. If she tried she could fight back, but she was tired, too tired. But more than that she didn't want to fight like with like, not in Quinn's case, not anymore. It got you nowhere. Just plunged you into hell alongside him – an intolerable concept. Even so, the temptation, oh, the temptation… Ruby only hoped that the others would burst in before she could give in to it, and before he turned his attention towards Ellie; that the girl would be saved at least and not meet her death again in this house. Surely they would come? Jed would have sensed how wrong it had gone. He'd be here any minute. Wouldn't he? The seconds were ticking by. There was no longer a clock on the wall but she imagined the one that Ellie had described during one of her regression sessions; the lonely sound of it as eternity stretched out before her – an endless road, disappearing into the distance. Where was he, her protector? A closed door was no barrier to him. Not even to Cash. Why weren't they running down the hall, miraculously appearing as they did when Linda was attacking her in her office? She needed them – again. Her eyes were fluttering, beginning to close.

What was that in the distance? *Who* was that? Not someone from this lifetime. It was someone she'd never met, but someone she recognised all the same from photographs she'd pored over in the past. It was an older woman, distinguished, *discerning*. It was Rosamund, her great-grandmother. What did she want? Although so far away, Ruby could see there was a smile on the other woman's face. Was she going to beckon her? Tell her to come forward, not her body but her spirit; cross the great divide. But Rosamund stopped smiling, nodded instead, and started to recede.

You can do this, Ruby.

Rosamund's parting words formed in her head.

You can do this.

She wouldn't have left her if she didn't think so – not Rosamund. From what Gran had told her, she had been strong, down-to-earth, and fearless; someone Ruby aspired to be like. It took a supreme amount of effort, but she forced her eyes open, focusing on Ellie. The girl had started to sob.

"Oh God, Ruby, what he did to my mum!"

She was looking towards the kitchen window, at something other than the cold ceramic of the sink. "I can see it all so clearly, every cell in my body can feel it. He terrorised her." And then she stopped, faltered slightly before carrying on. "I… I can see something else. More memories. But they're not Mum's. They're *yours*, aren't they, Dad? They're your memories. I can see them too! Even though I never inhabited your body, I can see them." She gasped again. "Your family, they were…" Ellie seemed to struggle to find the right word. "Feral."

Was Quinn's grip around her neck lessening or was she imagining it? No, there was definitely less pressure. She was rising to the surface, able to tune more clearly into what Ellie was saying.

Ellie's breathing had quickened, similar to the way it did when you were watching a particularly scary film on TV. Suddenly, Ruby understood. What she was seeing *was* horrifying.

"You were so young. How could they do that to a child? You never knew love, did you, Dad? You were beaten; *starved* of all that's good in life, by your father, your brothers, all of them. But most of all by your mother – she stood by and did nothing. She looked the other way. It's her you blame the most, isn't it? For letting it happen, for letting you down. What made them like that? How far back does this go? How many generations? Who's at the beginning of it all?" She shook her head violently.

"Whoever it was, what a weight of responsibility to carry. What a legacy to leave."

Quinn turned from Ruby to Ellie, releasing her entirely – almost as sudden a gesture as it had been when he'd attacked her. She fell back against the wall and slid down, one hand reaching out for her great-grandmother's necklace, needing it more than ever; the *comfort* of it. After a few moments scrabbling blindly about, her fingertips brushed against the cold hard stones – thankfully still intact – and closed around them as eagerly as Quinn had closed his hands around her neck. She snatched them up towards her chest. They felt wonderful, as good as being able to breathe.

"Ruby," Ellie's concern was clear. "Are you okay?"

"Carry on, Ellie," Ruby croaked. "I'll… I'll call for the others if needs be."

Ellie started speaking again. "Dad, I can see something good now. Oh, this is better, much better. It's you and your first sight of Mum. You're at the fair, working one of the stalls and she's suddenly there in front of you. You're finding it hard to believe your eyes – she's petite, she's pretty – she's the most beautiful girl you've ever seen. Because you, even you, can recognise beauty when you see it." Ellie shook her head. "The trouble is, you don't know what to do about it, do you? How to treat this precious gift that's come into your life, and who incredibly thinks that you're beautiful too. You want to love her, but where do you start? Thoughts crowd your mind – dark thoughts that drag you back to the life you tried to escape, and you let them in, you give them access. *She's too good for me. She won't stay with me; her parents won't let her. I'm a traveller. I'm a waster. I'm nobody.* But you can't let her go. You'd rather kill yourself… or her. She comes away with you; she agrees; but the disappointment in her face when she sees this house, you can't bear it. She was disappointed by the wedding too, wanted a big do, with her parents there at least. She misses her parents; yearns for them more than she yearns for you. It's the start of so many disappointments and so you do the only thing you know how to – you lash out. She'll stay with you; you'll make her stay, and she won't show any more disappointment. She'll keep her mouth shut; do your bidding, whatever you want. She's yours; the only good thing you ever had."

"Except you," Ruby reminded Ellie, never taking her eyes off Quinn, assessing his demeanour all the while. "He had you."

"Yes! Yes, that's right. I was your second chance, wasn't I? Your chance to get it right. Except you never knew about me until it was too late; until she was beating me out of her. She didn't give you that second chance."

Quinn's body was shaking. Ruby didn't know if it was from anger or grief, as it was impossible to tell from her position. But she didn't dare move; didn't dare interrupt. This was family business.

"I'm sorry I never knew you, Dad, despite everything, and what you did to Mum. Maybe we'll meet on the other side, or even in another lifetime, in better circumstances. Maybe you'll be my dad again. Maybe we'll be friends. Who knows what's in store for us. But I've got a feeling, Dad, a strong feeling. I think we will meet again and it'll be a good life. We've paid our dues. We've suffered enough. We *deserve* a good life. But right now, this life is over. Your *hell* is over. Go to the light that Ruby talks about; you have to, because I'm not staying, there's no point. You're dead. I'm not threatening you, Dad, but once I leave this house I won't come back. Mum's alive and I'm seizing my chance to get to know her. That's *our* second chance and I won't ruin it. But I won't think of you as a monster and hopefully Mum won't in time. Not… not when I tell her what I saw."

Quinn's hand was rising; slowly, slowly, it was rising.

"Ellie, start to back out. Listen to me, get away from here."

Ellie stood her ground.

"Ellie, he's preparing to strike again, call the others!"

Ellie ignored her. Ruby tried to call instead but her throat was too sore. All that emerged was a pathetic croak. "Ellie!"

Finally Ellie glanced at Ruby. "Stop panicking. He won't hit me. And you never would have, would you, Dad, had I lived? I have every faith in that. And do you know why? I'll tell you why. It's because I *trust* you."

There she went again, using the very same word she had used to Ruby – such a *healing* word.

Miraculously, Quinn's hand started to lower. Ruby could barely believe the evidence of her eyes.

"Go now, Dad. You got your second chance after all. Don't ruin it. Don't let it always be the past that defines you. Triumph over it instead. If you can do that, if you can dig deep into the chambers of your soul, I promise that I'll remember you. And I will *only* remember you with kindness."

Ruby dared to straighten up. Quinn was backing away, towards the corner of the kitchen he had first appeared in, where the table used to be – the one he had crashed into; the one he had sent Linda crashing into so many times.

Was he going? Was he doing as Ellie had asked, taking his second chance? Had she cracked it – cracked him – but this time in the best of ways?

"Goodbye," Ellie whispered and Ruby sensed rather than saw the glint of tears on her cheek.

Chapter Thirty-Five

DESPITE what she had said, Samantha had decided she and her family would stay at Gilmore Street. Jeff wasn't so sure. He still didn't believe their problems were over, but one look at Samantha and he knew not to go against her again. Thank God for strong women, Ruby thought. She was glad she had so many of them in her life.

Although he hadn't materialised, she heard Jed bark.

"Yeah, yeah, okay, and strong dogs too."

Cash walked into the living room where she was resting on the sofa.

"And strong men as well, *good* men. I'd never forget to count you, Cash."

"What?" Cash clearly didn't have a clue what she was talking about. He shook his head in a perplexed manner and continued with what was on his mind. "I've just popped into your office, Ruby, like you asked me, to check the messages. Bloody hell, it's gone wild. All that positive press attention – your business is going to explode, in the best possible way of course." He broke into a grin. "I think you might need to set up a separate concern, though."

"A separate concern?" Ruby was curious. "Why's that?"

"One specifically for animal spirit rescue."

Now she was the one baffled. "What do you mean?"

He had one hand behind his back and now he brought

it forward, waved a newspaper in front of her. "Look," he said, opening it and pointing to an article inside. "The Haires went to the paper too; told them about the rabbit!"

Ruby groaned. "Oh no, not the rabbit!" The fact they'd moved a rabbit on, it just gave the press more ammunition to have a dig at them.

"Ruby, don't look like that; it's a great article. That friend of yours, Robin, he's the one who wrote it, I think it's going to get you a lot of fans. Spiritual rescue of a human kind is one thing but everyone wants their cat or dog to make it all the way to the Rainbow Bridge, where the animal spirits play. I tell you, it's going to get a lot of people rooting for you."

Ruby had to laugh. "Well, perhaps you're right, or at least I'll choose to think you are. Maybe there's an animal rescue type out there with psychic abilities; perhaps we can tempt them with a bit of freelance."

"You never know your luck. Here budge up and let me sit down."

He didn't just sit; he lay, wrapping his arms around her. At her feet, Jed materialised in his usual curled position. The dog loved it when it was the three of them snuggling up – a family of sorts.

"How are you feeling?" Cash murmured into the thickness of her hair.

"I'm all right, just tired. My throat's better. It's not so sore."

"Rest. That's what you need to do. Rest."

"I will." *For now.*

She closed her eyes but it was actually Cash who fell asleep first. Again, Ruby couldn't help but laugh – he was as bad as Jed in that department! She tried to drift but it was hard to shut down; there was still so much racing through her mind, although it wasn't all bad, not by a long shot.

Ellie and Linda had finally met, their reaction upon seeing each other incredible to witness. It was truly as if each had found someone they'd been looking for all their lives. There were no recriminations, Ellie certainly didn't think Linda 'evil' for what she'd done; she had sympathy for her instead – sympathy and love. As for Linda, she only had love for the girl standing in front of her – it seemed to burst from every pore. She was seizing her second chance too.

When it had just been the Psychic Surveys team alone again, Corinna had wondered how Linda and Ellie's relationship would develop.

"In the way it was always meant to," Ness had replied.

Corinna was still curious. "Ruby, did Ellie tell you exactly what she saw regarding Quinn? How much he suffered growing up?"

She hadn't told her and nor would Ruby quiz her about it. In some instances, ignorance was bliss. She knew all she had to know.

But Corinna wasn't satisfied. "As Ellie said though, who first kicked off the cycle of abuse in that family and why? How far back does it go? Just how many lives were affected and what if other members of his family are grounded for the very same reasons as Quinn? How will we ever find out?"

Theo had put her arm around Corinna then. "We all have questions about this case, sweetheart; I've dozens too. But we also have to remember that there aren't answers to everything. There are mysteries in life and mysteries they'll remain, no matter how much we dig. We can only do so much about helping others too. Certainly I can't afford a tour round Southern Ireland searching for grounded members of the O'Brien clan just yet, but maybe one day. What's the town you said that Quinn grew up in?"

"Ballinagar," answered Corinna.

"Perhaps we'll organise a jolly over there."

"A jolly?" questioned Ness, looking aghast at her choice of word.

"Yes, Ness, a jolly. Got to have some fun in between the hard work."

Although they had all laughed as heartily as Theo at that, Ruby was still agitated. Whilst Cash had been at her office this morning, Theo had popped round and she couldn't resist mentioning to her about the bad wolf; how ever since facing her own demon it rose so readily to the surface.

Theo listened and then asked her what she was worried about exactly.

"That it hasn't gone. That it's still inside of me, a part of me."

There was relief in voicing it.

Theo had looked at her before replying, obviously taking a few moments to consider her reply. "Ruby, I know you think of me and Ness as 'giants' in the psychic field, but you're a 'giant' too. A giant who defeated what plagued you for so long; what plagued your mother too, and to a certain extent your grandmother. All three of you were affected. But it's important to remember that that particular evil was external, not internal. It's *not* a part of you."

"Then why does the dark take me over so completely

sometimes?"

"But it doesn't, that's just it. You fight back, all the time." Theo had shifted on her seat, her not inconsiderable bulk making the chair creak slightly beneath her. "Ruby, the darkness within us is nothing to do with our souls. It's human. We have a predisposition towards it. That's the human psyche for you. But even then there's balance. No human is wholly evil; no one is wholly good. Why do you think you have to be the exception?"

Ruby had hung her head. "I... I don't know."

"You're being hard on yourself, Ruby. Come to think of it, that's something that *is* unbalanced about you – you give yourself a hard time when you really don't have to. And – I've said this before as well, countless times, especially lately – you work too hard. That's bad for your health as well as your soul. It's bad for your relationship too. Cash loves you. But everyone has a breaking point, which this last case highlighted. Learn from it. Evolve."

Having delivered such wise words, Theo had wandered off, leaving Ruby to ponder. She bit her lip; sleep didn't seem so important anymore. Instead, she elbowed Cash in the side.

"What is it? What's happened?" he cried.

"Nothing, nothing's happened!"

He turned to her. "What is it then? Why'd you wake me up?"

"Because I want to go on holiday."

"On holiday? What, now?"

"No, not now!" Again, she elbowed him, unable to keep a lid on her laughter. "But soon, very soon, maybe in a couple of weeks or so. Can you take time off work for a short while?"

"My work? Yeah, yeah, of course I can." His familiar grin was back. "There's got to be some perks to being your own boss."

Something she was about to find out.

"Okay, let's do it," she decided.

"Yes!" Cash punched the air. "Where shall we go, Mauritius, Barbados, Jamaica…"

"Hang on, Cash, calm down a bit! I don't think finances are going to stretch that far. Besides," she joked, "I'm not sure if a dog can accompany us abroad. They have rules about that sort of thing, don't they?" She shook her head. "No, I was thinking somewhere more local, Lyme Regis perhaps, the Jurassic coast; we can go fossil hunting; sit on the beach; gorge on fish and chips; find a cosy pub and just chill together. I even know a place we could stay."

"Do you, how come?"

"Contacts," Ruby replied. It wasn't so far from the truth.

Slowly Cash nodded. "Lyme Regis you say? Okay, you've sold it to me! Dinoland it is." He followed the direction of her gaze to where Jed was now sitting up, his wagging tail showing he was also excited at the prospect of a holiday. "So, Jed's coming too?" he asked, smiling.

"Damn right he is. This family sticks together."

"That's right, Ruby, we do."

As Cash pushed her back down on the sofa again, his intention was clear. Happily she succumbed, pleased to be welcoming back the light.

THE END

A note from the author

As much as I love writing, building a relationship with readers is even more exciting! I occasionally send newsletters with details on new releases, special offers and other bits of news relating to the Psychic Surveys series as well as all my other books. If you'd like to subscribe, sign up here!

www.shanistruthers.com

Printed in Great Britain
by Amazon

46088617R00205